WAIL OF THE BANSHEES

ROBERT POULIN

WAIL OF THE BANSHEES
Robert Poulin

Printed in the United States of America.

Ghost Watch Publishing
Plattsburgh, New York 12901

For more information about this book visit: www.ghostwatchpublishing.com

Edition ISBNs
Trade Paperback 978-0-9894469-0-7
E-book 978-0-9894469-1-4

Cover art and design by Hannah Carr
Book design by Christopher Fisher

PUBLISHER'S NOTE: This is a work of fiction. Names, characters, places, and events herein are either the product of the author's imagination or are used fictitiously. Any resemblance to actual persons, living or dead, is entirely coincidental.

To my mom, who taught me that even though I'd never be able to drive a car due to my blindness, I could still be President of the United States if I wanted to. Lofty dreams and hard work are the key ingredients in overcoming limitations.

Thanks mom, you will always be my number one hero.

Acknowledgements

A project like this has many important contributors. Hopefully I won't forget to mention anyone, but I beg forgiveness if I do. Thanks first and foremost to my Fiancée, Tina Cook, for her support and for putting up with me while the computer took up most of my free time. I want to thank my wonderful editor, Jaimee Finnegan, for her hard work; she put the soul into this novel. Thanks to Hannah Carr, the cover artist for this book, she did an amazing job. Thanks to the team at The Editorial Department who did the interior layout, formatting, and conversions for the eBook as well as the print version. A very special shout of thanks to Beatrice Beguin and her colleagues at the New York State Commission for the Blind and Visually Handicapped (CBVH). Without them Ghost Watch Publishing wouldn't have been possible. Finally, I want to thank my beta readers, Debra Piper, Karen Figary, Jessica Middlemiss, Justin Sharp, Don Sharp, Christy Hoke, and the readers at Authonmy. com. I also want to put a good word in for the Writing Excuses Podcast and Publetariat.com, I learned a lot about writing from these websites and continue to use them.

WAIL OF THE BANSHEES

1

GETTING YOUR THROAT SLIT in a dark alley really sucks.

Even worse than that is having to watch your blood spill onto the garbage strewn pavement of that dark alley and being powerless to do anything about it.

I stood above my crumpled form watching in sick fascination as a dark pool of blood gathered around me. It really is amazing how much blood there is in a human body; you really can't imagine it until you've seen it.

I was rooted to this spot from the first instant following the brutal attack. I was forced to watch as I died at my own feet. I wanted to cry out for help but my throat refused to produce any sound, and I couldn't seem to move my new spirit body. It was after three in the morning and the shadowed streets of West Philadelphia were quiet; no one came to help as I watched myself gasp for the last time.

I waited for the white light, for my spirit to rise up into the celestial city of the Almighty. When this didn't happen, I braced myself for the impending descent into the fiery pits of hell. Still nothing happened.

A half hour passed before I saw the flashing lights of a slowly moving patrol car. An officer was moving along the sidewalk peering into the dark alleyways of the street while his partner trailed in their squad car. After a few more minutes of searching, a beam of light swept over my still body. The young cop let out a cry of discovery and ran forward drawing his pistol while calling out to his partner. Philadelphia's finest had found me; unfortunately they were too late.

My name is Veronika Kane and I guess I'm a ghost now.

Today, or I should say yesterday, was my twenty first birthday. I'd gone out with some of my friends from the University of Pennsylvania to celebrate my now legal drinking age. We'd partied late into the night, getting smashed and having fun doing it. As the night wore on, friends left and new ones arrived, but in the end I was the last to say goodnight to my favorite club: The Electric Factory in Center City. I rode the bus back to West City where my apartment was located, but rather than transfer to a second bus I decided to walk the remaining seven or eight blocks to my home. The fall evening was comfortably cool and I wanted to sober up a little before bed. This was only my second time getting drunk, and I wasn't used to the dizzying feeling that came with it. My ears were buzzing like the crackling speakers before Motley Crew took the stage, and the earth wouldn't stop moving even when I paused to catch my breath.

The attack came suddenly, without warning. I was grabbed from behind by powerful arms. One quickly wrapped around my neck while the other pinned my arms to my sides. The man was tall. I'm five-nine but he towered at least six to eight inches over me. He picked me up off the ground and whispered in my ear.

"Shhhh ... be a good girl and be still," his voice was gruff and he stank of onions and rotten meat.

Fear washed over me like a bucket of cold water being dumped over my head. My stomach lurched and sudden nausea threatened to make me puke. I tried to struggle, but the intense fear that wracked my gut and the sickening vertigo that was overwhelming my senses conspired to make the attempt at resistance futile. I fought against the rising panic that threatened to engulf me and tried to calm myself through meditation exercises. It was the most difficult thing I'd ever done, but the years of grueling training in my dad's dojo kicked in and I was able to calm myself enough to think past the terror that made it near impossible for me to breath without hyperventilating.

The man slung me over his shoulder and I promptly barfed all over his back. He growled in anger and disgust but didn't flinch or put me down to clean himself off. He just started walking. He carried me several blocks until he turned into the dank alley that I now found myself in. Throwing up had made me feel a little better. The world wasn't spinning anymore, but I still felt weak and sick. Once we reached the back of the narrow alley, he swung me back around to his front but didn't put me down. Instead he maintained a tight hold on me with one powerful arm. I heard him fumbling around for something in his coat, and I instinctively knew that I had to get away now. This was probably the only chance I'd get; I slumped against him as if I'd fainted. Fear and hope warred over me and threatened to make me puke again as the man loosened his grip on me and began lowering me to the ground. As soon as my feet hit the dirt and garbage strewn pavement I shot my right elbow back and connected with his ribs. He let go of me in surprise, and I launched myself forward, running for the street. But I was still intoxicated, and he was quicker than me. He cried out in rage and caught me from behind before I could escape. I whirled around and tried to push him back with a front kick but he sidestepped my clumsy move, and I stumbled past him and fell into a pile of garbage. Desperation overwhelmed the hope that had filled me just a few moments ago. I scrambled ungracefully back to my feet and started running. Laughter chased me and all hope died when I realized I was going the wrong way. The back of the alley was blocked off.

My attacker didn't bother trying to catch me this time though. He simply came up behind me as I desperately searched for another escape route: perhaps a basement window that I could crawl into. He reached around me and slit my throat with the long knife that he'd drawn from a concealed sheath. I watched, stunned, as my body fell forward. My spirit though remained erect, rooted to the spot.

I got my first glimpse of my attacker's features as he stared down at me with wide and unblinking eyes. He was a giant of a man, standing almost six foot five and muscled like a body-builder. He was quite handsome with long, chestnut brown hair that was bound in a ponytail. His nose was long and narrow, while his cheeks were dimpled. He had a sharp chin and full lips; straight white teeth gleamed in the darkness as he smiled down at my crumpled form. His eyes were midnight black and seemed to hold a madness that was all consuming. He licked the blood coated knife that he'd slit my throat with and shook his head at me.

"That's what you get bitch," he said. "I could have taught you so much. You would have screamed so prettily, and you would have learned so much. But you had to ruin it all by trying to escape. I couldn't let that happen. There's still too much work to do, so many pretty things to teach how to scream. I can't serve the Dark Master if I get caught. It's such a waste, I know, but I just couldn't take the risk with you."

He removed a thin brush from an inner pocket of the jeans jacket he wore and dipped it in the expanding pool of blood at his feet. He then used the brush to write words upon the wall of a nearby building. I stared at the writing in surprise; it appeared to be in Akkadian, one of the later cuneiforms. Ancient languages were a particular interest of mine: Akkadian culture had figured prominently in several of my projects at Penn. I didn't know what the words said though. I wouldn't be able to decipher them without a few books that were in my apartment. As you might imagine, dead languages take a very long time to master. I couldn't begin to imagine how this guy could write this language, let alone understand it.

Satisfied with his handiwork, the killer surprised me once more by looking directly at me: the ghost me, as if he could see me. He grinned and then walked out of the alley leaving me alone to die.

2

THE YOUNG OFFICER BENT OVER my still body reaching for my wrist to check my pulse. After a moment he rose, shaking his head at his partner who had parked the police cruiser facing into the alley so that its headlights could offer more light. The second officer used his hand radio to call for the forensics team and a homicide detective. The two men then set about making sure that the area was secure. I watched numbly, still unable to move or make a sound. Within minutes of the call-in, distant sirens could be heard; they grew louder as the emergency crews approached the crime scene.

The ambulance crew was the first to arrive on the scene; jumping out of their vehicle they rushed forward, medical kits in hand. The officers tried to wave them off but one of the EMTs, a young lady about my age, ignored them and continued to move towards me while her companion, an older male, changed directions and ambled over to talk to the officers. The female medic froze when she saw the pool of blood around me, and I saw the light of hope die in her eyes. She came forward anyway and checked my pulse before withdrawing and beginning the long wait for the forensics team to start their work. Once all the evidence was gathered from the crime scene, the EMTs would transport my body to the city morgue. Two more sector cars arrived on the scene next, followed by a homicide detective in an unmarked vehicle, and finally the forensics team was last on the scene. A crowd of onlookers had begun to form on the opposite side of the street. They were kept at bay by a uniformed officer.

The homicide detective, wearing a cheap dark suit, entered the alley as soon as he arrived. He inspected the scene without touching anything. He was of average height with piercing blue eyes, curly dark hair and a neatly trimmed mustache. He stayed near me until the forensics crew arrived. He had a sad but determined look about him; his presence somehow comforted me. The forensics team did their work quickly but carefully, taking photographs of the scene and then collecting various samples. The city medical examiner took charge of my body: he was a pudgy balding man with glasses. He examined my body thoroughly and spoke quietly into a mini-recorder. The detective had moved off to consult with the original officers on the scene and he was joined by a second detective. She was a tired looking woman in her middle to late thirties. As soon as the forensics team was done with the preliminary cataloging of the scene, the detectives joining the medical examiner and began to search through my pockets and hand bag.

"Hey Bob," said the male detective. "How's it fucking hanging?"

"Still got that potty mouth I see," Bob, the Medical Examiner, retorted. "I would have thought you'd have cured him of that by now Wendi."

The female detective, Wendi, shook her head with a sigh of the long suffering.

"Not fucking likely," the male detective replied. "You find anything unusual?"

"Not really," Bob answered with a shake of his head. "It's

what it looks like: her jugular was slashed with a very big knife. She bled out. The attacker was strong and big and knew how to use a knife; the cut was clean and very precise. There's bruising consistent with large hands on her arms and shoulders. She was killed here in the alley but was probably grabbed elsewhere. There are also signs that she vomited recently."

"Veronika Kane, age 21," said the male detective as he read my license. "God damn it. It was her fucking birthday."

"Hold it together, Frank," said Wendi. "At least this one didn't have to go through what the other ones did. I wonder why he killed this one so quickly."

The male detective, Frank I guess, didn't say anything for a moment. As he continued to search through my purse, Wendi searched my body; both wore latex gloves.

"I'll leave the rest of this in your capable hands," Bob said standing up and heading off towards his car. "Come by tomorrow for the autopsy report. Maybe preliminaries will be ready from toxicology."

Wendi waved goodbye to the departing medical examiner, but Frank didn't seem to notice his departure.

"I'm guessing she put up more of a fight than our guy is fucking used to," Frank finally said in reply to Wendi's question. He'd retrieved another card from my wallet. "She's a fucking jiu-jitsu master with credentials from the University City Dojo according to this."

All those years working out, learning to defend myself, the competitions, the grueling hard work, the broken bones, all of it had been a waste. Why was God punishing me? Why had He let me be killed in such a brutal way without even a chance to fight back? Why was I being forced to stand here, unable to move or speak? Why was I being forced to watch this horrific scene out of a Law & Order episode? I suddenly recalled what a born-again friend had once told me, "Hell isn't a fiery pit. It's existence without God, all alone for eternity." Was I in Hell? Had I truly been so bad that I deserved this end?

I had worked hard my entire life, earning A's and always coming near the top of the class in school. I was athletic. I had played several sports but favored the martial arts, both hand-to-hand and sword forms. My parents were immigrants from Russia; they had fled the Iron Curtain of the early sixties to find a new life in America. My father opened the University City Dojo and my mother worked for a telecom company. I was a lone child. Now my parents would have nothing. I never did drugs, and last night had only been the second time I'd ever gotten drunk. I had overcome the teenage peer pressure to have sex, saving myself for someone I truly loved. Was it because I went to church infrequently, didn't confess my sins every day, wasn't born again, wasn't a Jehovah's Witness or a Mormon? Somehow, I'd always believed that being a good person was good enough, that God as a loving father would accept me for who I am. Apparently I was wrong.

"It's really a shame," said Wendi. "She might have been able to kick his ass or at least get away if she hadn't been drunk."

"How do you know she was fucking drunk?" Frank asked.

"A little deductive reasoning," Wendi answered. She raised my limp hand and turned it over so that the purple entrance tattoo that had been stamped there was visible to Frank. "She spent some time at the Electric Factory. The stamp is dated. We can start tracking her movements from there. I'll bet you twenty bucks that when toxicology comes back it will show that she was drunk. It was her twenty first birthday after all, and Bob said she'd vomited recently."

Frank shook his head, a sad expression on his face.

So, a short life's hard work came down to one mistake. One failure. Some people spend a whole lifetime avoiding consequences; apparently I wasn't so lucky. The truth of what Wendi said hit me hard. Though my attacker had been much bigger and stronger than me, I knew that things would have been different if I hadn't been smashed. The chances of my having been able to escape were very high; I had managed to free myself of his grasp twice. With my full faculties I was sure that I could have eluded him. I wanted to cry, to scream, but neither tears nor sound would come. I just stood there frozen, surrounded by lights and people, but I was dead and alone now. I would never see my parents again, never hold my mom or laugh with my dad. A whole life of promise and hope was lost to me. I'd never marry or have kids of my own.

"Hopefully the fucking forensics team will turn something up," said Frank. "If Veronika's death gets us the fucking clue we need to nail this asshole, her death won't be completely meaningless, though I fucking doubt that that will be much of a consolation to her parents."

Frank stood and moved to the nearby wall where my assailant had written on it with my blood. He withdrew a sheaf of paper from his pocket and compared the notes on it to the writing on the wall.

"It's fucking exact," he said. "The wails of the spirits shall herald the Dark Master's victory over death."

"I still think there's something wrong with that translation," said Wendi. "It just doesn't sound right."

"Look Wendi, we've fucking been through this before," exclaimed Frank in exasperation. "If you want another fucking translation bring it up to Templetown. Just because Penn is preeminent in archaeology doesn't mean they fucking know everything. Since there might be a fucking religious context involved in this case maybe your old man will be able to help."

Wendi grimaced in frustration but finally nodded. She was a pretty woman in that girl next door sort of way and unlike her partner, she was dressed elegantly in a grey Theory suit with red silk blouse and stylish but utilitarian shoes that matched the suit. Her eyes were brown as was her curly, shoulder length hair.

"Alright," she replied dejectedly. "I'll take it over in the morning. I think we're done here."

"Rest in peace Veronika Kane," said Frank as he looked over

my fallen body one last time before he and Wendi withdrew from the alley and headed for their respective cars.

The paramedics were finally allowed to come forward. I watched with a sense of finality as they lifted my body onto a gurney, wheeled it to the ambulance, and a few moments later quietly drove away. The forensics team returned to bag all of the trash and debris they could lay their hands on. When they'd taken everything that wasn't nailed down, a clean-up crew was called in to get as much of the blood off the ground as they could. The result was that this alleyway was now the cleanest in the city, though it was now haunted by a ghost and marked with a water proof chalk outline of a body. The writing on the wall was also cleaned away, it had been extensively photographed, and the ubiquitous yellow police crime scene tape remained as evidence that a crime had taken place here recently. Once the clean-up was completed, I was again left alone, still unable to move or call for help.

3

I WAITED FOR HOURS, alone with my thoughts. I feared that I would be stuck to this place for eternity. As the hours passed and dawn approached, a mist began to fill the alley. Within minutes the street was obscured and the buildings around me were barely visible; their looming shadows seeming to brood over the landscape. I shivered as a sense of dread washed over me.

Another hour passed. Dawn bloomed over the city, but the mist did not die out. The city was strangely quiet; no traffic seemed to move on the street beyond the alley. Suddenly two large shapes appeared at the mouth of the alley. They looked vaguely human but something was weird about their forms. They were dark and massive, probably around seven feet tall, and their shape reminded me of the Thing from The Fantastic Four comic books. I wanted to run, to scream for help, but I was still stuck in place, unable to do either. I closed my eyes tightly, praying that I would wake up from this obvious nightmare.

"Here it is," one of the monstrous creatures said in a deep guttural voice. "It be another shade."

"This be the last one to harvest," said the other creature, this one's voice was grating, like fingernails on a chalkboard. "This one not banshee like supposed to be. Great Master will be angry."

"Yup," echoed the first black monster. "We hurry now; tell Great Master what we find."

I opened my eyes futilely hoping that I would be back in my apartment. The things were standing just a few feet from me now; one of them reached an enormous clawed arm towards me. The creatures were black as night with glowing red eyes, no noses that I could see, and red gaping mouths with unnaturally white, jagged teeth that a great white shark would be jealous of.

I was still clearly in the nightmare.

I tried to shy away from the things touch but was still unable to move. I convulsed in agony as the creature's claws tore into me; they sank deep into my ghostly body. I was finally able to scream; all of my fear, anger, frustration, and pain bubbled up in a long wail that seemed to shake the buildings around us.

The demonic apparition that held me paused to peer more closely at me.

"This one scream like banshee," it said.

"It be a shade," said its companion. "See it? It not a pretty banshee; it all foggy like a shade. Now we go."

I looked down at myself, noticing for the first time that my body was different. In life I'd been beautiful: long straight black hair and piercing blue eyes had framed a delicate face. My lips had been full, my nose perfectly shaped. I had an athlete's body with long, perfectly toned legs, small hips, a flat stomach, and boobs that guys couldn't take their eyes off of. Now, my body was wreathed in a grey, misty fog. My features weren't visible beneath the thick cloak of fog that wreathed my form. The brute that held me had buried its claws deep into me; there was no blood, but it still hurt like hell.

The ghostly thug pulled on me. There was resistance for an agonizing moment and then a tearing feeling. Once more I screamed, more in hopelessness than pain. As the creatures carried me to god knows where, I wept, the tears finally flowing. I also found that I was able to move, for all the good that did me now. I knew instinctively that the tearing that I'd felt a moment ago was my last connection to the living world. I was in hell or something near enough to it. My life was over; there was no going back now.

4

THE CITY OF PHILADELPHIA is one of the oldest and largest cities in the United States. It was the nation's first capital and the city where the Declaration of Independence and the Constitution were written. Men of power and renown have walked its streets: men such as Benjamin Franklin, Thomas Jefferson, and George Washington. It is a city where the tale of bygone years can still be viewed in the majestic structures that dot the modern cityscape. It is a city of vibrancy and a teaming population that is always on the move.

I was born and raised in Philly; it's a city that I love. It's in my blood. The city that the black creatures carried me through now was not the Philadelphia that I'd grown up knowing. The mist continued to shroud the landscape though full light had come. I saw no people, no traffic, and the buildings we passed seemed empty and foreboding. As we moved towards Center City I could easily recognize many landmarks of my beloved city, but there were many structures that I didn't recognize. Everything was older, as if the entire city had been pushed back into the mid nineteenth Century. I saw only a few buildings that bore the hallmarks of modern architecture.

"Where are we going?" I asked, finally getting the nerve up to speak.

The monster that held me shook me violently. I gasped in surprise but managed to suppress the wail of anger and frustration that I so badly wanted to unleash upon it.

"Puny shades don't talk to specters; only talk to other shades. Must listen to specters like me," growled the demonic creature that was carrying me. Its companion laughed at me. The sound reminded me of the cackle of a jackal.

The sinking feeling in the pit of my stomach got even worse, if that can be believed. I assumed that in referring to me as a shade, the demonic thug, apparently called a specter, was classifying me as a lesser being. I was quickly beginning to think that my earlier fears of being left alone for eternity would have been preferable to being a bitch toy for the amusement of these black hearted specter bullies. It hardly seemed fair that I should be a lowly shade. After all, I'm the one with a black belt. Why couldn't I have entered the afterlife as one of the big goons? I mean, surely the afterlife doesn't discriminate against you based on gender, right? After some thought though, it occurred to me that the job of "ghost bully" must be reserved for assholes. I settled down into sullen silence brooding upon the unfairness of life.

The specter who carried me suddenly lurched to a stop. I looked around in puzzlement. The area was surrounded by what looked like mid-rise tenements and I finally saw some activity. Shades like myself were congregating in a square in front of what looked like an eighteenth century inn. I studied the shades to see if I could discern any differences between them and myself, but I saw none. They were featureless, misty grey people. Unlike me, however, they all wore red metallic collars that looked more solid and real than anything else in this ghostly world. As I studied the strange scene, the purpose of the collars was horrifically revealed.

A group of five hulking specters exited the inn and strode into the midst of the milling shades. The shades leapt out of the specters way clearing a path for them, but the thuggish monsters couldn't resist their baser instincts. Two specters each grabbed a random shade and tore into them with their vicious claws. The unfortunate beings cried out piteously, but this only produced hoots of laughter from the other on looking specters. Three shades from the crowd suddenly fell to the ground, thrashing, kicking wildly, and raising such a din that I was sure they must be heard as far as City Hall in Center City. I noticed that the shades were clawing at their necks. Their collars were glowing, bathing a ten foot area around them in a hellish red light. The crowd of shades shied away in horror from their unfortunate companions, while the specters clapped and cheered like spectators at a football game.

"Stop it!" I shouted, anger overcoming my fear. It was all to much. I was raised to be a fighter not a victim. My dad had come from a land of tyranny and he'd instilled in me a special hatred of tyrants and bullies.

Without thinking about what I was doing, I elbowed the specter who was still holding me and was surprised to hear a grunt of surprise or hopefully pain come from it. The specter dropped me, and for a moment I was free. I took two steps towards the thrashing shades but my two captors were on me before I got any further. I'm not sure what I would have done if I'd made it into that mass of shades, but without understanding the rules of this ghost realm, I was just outclassed and out of my element. The two brutes began to give me the worst beating that I'd ever suffered up till that point.

I thought for sure that the specters were going to kill me if that was possible here. I have never felt such pain. It was like having every inch of your skin ripped in long strips by razor blades, and just when you thought that there was nothing left for them to tear into, it started over again. It seemed to go on for hours. I don't know if I blacked out. I'm not even sure whether or not I screamed or cried; there was just agony, no room for anything else.

"Enough!" A new monster said in a voice that was both commanding and chilling. Through the haze of my pain, I saw something tall and emaciated standing over me; it was wearing a hooded robe. Within the shadows of that dark cowl I saw a skeletal face with glowing red eyes.

"This shade hit me," one of the specters whined. I wondered if this gaunt creature was their Great Master.

"You have punished it sufficiently for now," said the skeletal figure, turning back towards the inn. "It must not be damaged until tested, now go finish your task before you are punished."

My captors didn't need any more encouraging. Without further delay I was picked up and slung over a thickly muscled black shoulder as if I were a sack of potatoes. I looked about in dazed confusion and noticed that the square was now empty save for the robed skeletal creature who was headed towards the inn. In the distance I saw the shades being herded by specters toward what looked like a railroad station.

I was carried a short distance until we once again came to a stop. The road ahead came to an abrupt end at a massive, gaping chasm. It stretched north and south as far as I could see in the misty cityscape. There was no bottom to it, as far as I could tell. Although the mists were thick on the banks of the chasm, they didn't extend over or into its depths. After a moment of studying our surroundings, I realized that the chasm must correspond to the location of the Schuylkill River in the living world. I wondered if all waterways were bottomless pits in this shadow world of ghosts.

After some moments of impatient waiting, I became aware of what looked like a ferry barge gliding towards us. It was made of some shiny blue metal that gleamed pristinely in the morning mist. Like the red collars that the shades wore, the blue metal of the barge seemed more real, as if it didn't share the ghostly properties of everything else in the shadow world.

It moved quickly and quietly. Neither sails nor oars were visible. I couldn't even hear a motor running. It just seemed to be flying on the air currents. There was no cabin on the deck. There was simply a large, mostly empty flat space that could probably hold hundreds of people. There was, in fact, a small group of passengers on its deck. Most were shades with their usual escort of specters. There was also a group of ghosts that I hadn't seen before. These new beings looked like normal people, except their bodies were surrounded by a black nimbus. It was as if God had reached down and traced an outline around them with a black magic marker. I desperately wanted to ask my captors what kind of ghosts these things were, but after my earlier experience I decided not to push my luck.

The ferry pulled up to the bank and its passengers immediately began to disembark. I noticed with interest that the ghosts with the black nimbus around them wore no collars, and the specters seemed to show them deference. All the shades that were disembarking wore the red collars, though I noticed that there were noticeable differences among this group of shades. There were a small number of them who seemed to be in the process of shedding the mists that shrouded them. Parts of their bodies were becoming visible and black outlines were becoming evident. The specters treated these ghosts like children rather than slaves, and some of them even went about unescorted. The majority of the shades remained obscured by their mist cloaks and they seemed apprehensive around their changing brethren.

Once the barge was unloaded, my escort carried me onto the deck. I noticed that they shied away from the blue steel deck, preferring to stay on the red metal path that crisscrossed the deck. In the center, a large red metal disk was the focal point of the red paths. Upon that hub stood another of the tall robed beings that I'd seen in front of the inn. As soon as we reached the center area, the skeletal monster gestured towards a blue steeled wheel that protruded from the boat's hull.

The ferry lurched and pulled away from the bank and glided

swiftly towards the Center City side. At first I thought the wheel was spinning of its own volition or by the will of the reaper like creature, but then with horror I noticed that a ghost was lashed to it with fine cords of the same red metal that the collars were made of. This ghost was different from all the others I'd seen. Its features were clear and beautiful. It was awash in a white glow. I thought for sure that I must be gazing at an angel. Its eyes were crystal blue, and in their depths I could see agony and sorrow but no despair. It saw me gazing upon it and made to turn away as if in shame, but it seemed to read something in my own eyes. Unspoken words passed between us. It was like a kind of telepathy, but instead of words spoken into my mind, it projected emotions. It seemed to tell me that there was hope; that I must not give into the despair that our tormentors would inflict upon me. I took heart in that moment. There was good-ness and perhaps hope in this realm after all.

Our commiseration was broken by a howl of rage and a blur-ring red iron scythe took that beautiful face off in a single stroke. The angelic being was left with no eyes: just a gaping dark hole where its mouth and nose had been. It cried out in anguish, and I turned away in horror. Skeletal hands jerked my head around forcing me to look at the horrific sight.

"There is no hope for you," said the hateful being in the same chilling voice that its predecessor at the inn had used. "God has abandoned you to eternal punishment. You are ours. Learn to serve the Great Master and you will be blessed with transforma-tion and made into a new creature in his image: a darkling."

The monsters grip grew tighter with each word it spoke until I thought my head would be crushed like a melon. My stomach actually hurt as a result of the near constant fear that gnawed at me, but then I noticed that the angelic ghost's face was slowly growing back. I suddenly realized that as long as I didn't allow them to break my spirit the damage they could do to me was limited. Hope is what would enable me and others like this holy ghost to fight back. Pushing my fear deep into me, I resolved to act as meekly as possible. I would bide my time and learn all that I could so that when the opportunity presented itself I could act as decisively as possible

"I understand," I said in as contrite a voice as I could muster. The pain in my voice helped convince it that I was being sincere. It released me, and I quickly averted my eyes, keeping my head down and my shoulders hunched and doing my best to look like a frightened mouse which was pretty easy to pull off since I was scared out of my mind anyways.

Another few minutes passed before the barge bumped the eastern shore of the chasm. I let out a silent breath of relief as my specter escort carried me off the ferry. I felt the reaper like being's eyes on me the whole time; its malevolent gaze weighing me. The shore was packed with more waiting ghosts. Most of them were shades accompanied by their ever present specter guards.

The specter that carried me wasted no time deliberately making its way downtown at a hurried pace. I watched the city pass by eerily silent and absent of any traffic save the occasional ghosts. It mostly resembled the city I was familiar with, but in places there were buildings that only existed in pictures in the modern world. The skyline was dominated by One Liberty Place and City Hall. It seemed mostly naked though without the dozens of other skyscrapers that made up the cityscape in the present. Besides these differences, the ubiquitous fog clung to the world lending the city that I had grown up in and loved dearly a truly alien feel.

We finally reached our apparent destination: Washington Square. The ghost version of this historic public park and neighborhood was alive with activity that I hadn't seen since arriving. Ghosts were all over the place, going hither and thither on errands, conducting business, and socializing at what appeared to be cafes. There was a bazaar where vendors sold various objects made of the red or blue metal that I'd seen upon my journey here. There was also a platform where shades were apparently

being sold into servitude. There was even a rock band perform-
ing on a stage; their guitars were made of red metal with blue
filament strings. It suddenly struck me that all of the solid looking objects were made of one of the two metals. There were all
kinds of ghosts of many shapes, sizes, and hues. The one thing
that all of the free ghosts had in common was a shadowy aura
surrounding their forms while the collared slaves were all misty
grey shades.

My escort headed towards a massive stone structure in the
northeast corner of the square. I recognized it from descrip-
tions I'd read when studying the history of Philadelphia: the
infamous Walnut Street Prison. The place had been the first in
a new system of reform prisons: a penitentiary where prisoners
were kept in solitary confinement so that they could contemplate their actions and repent. The place had been notorious
for its debtor's prison. Both the British and the American's had
used it to warehouse prisoners of war during the Revolutionary
War. Though the building had been a historic site, it had been
demolished because of the horrible atrocities and deaths that
forever stained its memory.

I saw as we approached the edifice that the entire building was
enmeshed in blue metal filaments covering the stone wall like
a net. I guessed that the metal was what prevented the ghostly
prisoners within from escaping by simply passing through the
walls. Of course the guards at the gates were all specters. They
sported red metal chain vests, helmets, and swords.

"We bring harvest," intoned my escort as we reached the gate.

"What we do with harvest?" asked one of the guards.

"Keep harvest safe for testing. Great Master orders this."

"Harvesters do good work," praised the guard.

"Keepers work good too," my escort returned the compliment
to the guard.

The apparent ritual completed, the gates of the Walnut Street
Prison opened and one of the guards gestured to my escort to
put me down.

"Put shade down. Make it walk," said the guard. "Me not like touching dirty shades."

The harvester specter put me down with a snort of derision.

"This one cause trouble," he said pushing me towards the keeper.

The keeper grabbed me, its sharp claws digging deeply into me. The other guard got behind me, and before I knew what was happening, it reached around and placed a red iron collar around my neck.

"No trouble now," laughed the guard as it released me from its clawed grip.

I was pulled forward into the darkness of the prison and the gates behind me clanged shut with a note of finality. It wasn't completely dark in the prison; there was a hellish red glow to see by. A chill settled over me as I was guided through the labyrinthine halls of the prison. The sounds of weeping, an occasional wail of agony, and the heavy breathing of desperate prisoners were all part of the ambiance of my new home. It made me long for the mist like world that a few moments ago I'd believed was hell.

5

I was led deep into the prison through a labyrinth of corridors and finally was pushed into my own six by six cell which had blue steel mesh covering its walls and bars. The cell was completely empty: no bed, no toilet, no wash basin, nothing at all. I sighed. What did I need that stuff for anyway? After all I'm a ghost. Those objects would have helped my mental state at least a little though. The lack of them just made me feel all the more lonely and helpless. That was the point I guessed.

Rather than dwell on my isolation and sense of loss, I decided to study the blue steel mesh. During my trip through the ghost city, I'd seen both the red and blue metals used in a variety of ways. I'd quickly made up my mind that the red iron of my collar was something to fear and loath; it was a devil's iron. The blue steel, however, interested me because it seemed to make the darker creatures of this place uncomfortable. The blue steel seemed more abundant and appeared most often to be manufactured into tools and useful objects such as tables, containers, mining implements, and all manner of other objects including the ferry. The red devil's iron, that name seemed appropriate to me, seemed to be far less common and was primarily used in the collars and weaponry carried by specters and the reaper like beings. I wondered if the disparity in the apparent availability of the metals was due to the rarity of the devil's iron compared to the blue steel. Perhaps it was due to it being hoarded for military purposes. It did seem that the specter guards of this prison had no lack of the red metal being equipped with both weapons and armor made out of the vile stuff. Also, the slave population seemed like it could be huge. The collars probably drained the overall availability of the iron.

I reached out a tentative hand and brushed my index finger against a filament of the blue steel that lay like a web across the stone wall of my cell. There was a light shock as of static electricity, but it wasn't painful. It was as if a switch had been turned on inside my ghostly body as a strange energy coursed through me. I concentrated on the feeling, searching for understanding. It was as if I'd somehow bonded with the mysterious substance. Like my very being was somehow connected to it. Touching it made me feel alive. Some of the fatigue and pain from the day's experiences seemed to recede.

"I wouldn't play around with that stuff too much if I were you," said a female with a melodic voice. I whirled around to confront the speaker. "Celestial steel is poisonous to ghosts if exposed to it for too long. That's why most tools have a devil's iron handle."

"Who are you?" I asked.

"I'm here to prepare you for the testing," said the new ghost. "You can call me Delilah."

The cell door slid open and a beautiful young woman dressed in a white and red colonial era dress stepped into my cell. The door closed behind her. Delilah looked like a living person except for the black nimbus that surrounded her. She was young, in her late teens or early twenties, with blue eyes and aquiline features framed by long lustrous black hair.

I moved as far back from her as I could manage in the tight confines of the cell. The black nimbus that surrounded Delilah gave me the creeps. I don't know why, but my instincts were screaming at me not to trust anyone who was touched by the dark halo. My gut told me that Delilah wasn't here to help me; she wanted to use me for her own nefarious purposes. Intuition aside, I had to pretend that I wasn't repulsed by her though; she might be my only chance to get the cursed collar off of my neck. Fortunately, Delilah expected me to be terrified of her and didn't seem to mind my reaction to her presence.

"What test?" I asked.

"The test is what will determine your place in our society," Delilah said. "It will tell us what kind of ghost you are which in turn will establish what kind of job you will have."

"Isn't it obvious what kind of ghost I am?" I asked letting a little bitterness creep into my voice. "I'm a shade aren't I?"

"You are indeed a shade, but that doesn't tell us what your capabilities are. Shades are the weakest and therefore the lowliest among us, but there are different power grades among them as well. The weakest shades are nothing more than slaves while the strongest of them can fill important roles in society and even eventually transform into darklings. I, myself, was once a shade."

I stared at Delilah in surprise. This dark being had once been a shade? How had she become so dark?

"What must one do to become a darkling?" I asked.

"That is a lesson for another time and only if you are lucky enough to be more than just a slave or laborer. First, there are basic things that you must know. Are you ready to learn?"

I nodded.

"The first thing you must know may seem self evident, but you would be surprised at how many newly harvested souls delude themselves."

Delilah paused dramatically before continuing.

"You are truly dead. You are a ghost in a place we call Limbo. Limbo is a shadow reality which lies closest to the physical world. It is a reflection of the living world. Beyond Limbo is Pandemonium and Tartarus; beyond them are the Lake of Fire and the Celestial Gates."

I chewed on this information for a moment while Delilah paused to study my reaction.

"You are a shade: a lesser ghost who has been relegated to servitude because you failed to choose a side. You straddled the fence being both good and bad. In the end, your lack of commitment made you weak and God has rejected you. The lords of Limbo have not rejected you, however, and you now have the opportunity to serve and perhaps join the team that you should have joined in life."

My mind raced. Was this creature telling me that all of that stuff I'd learned in church was true? Was there really a war being waged between God and the devil? Was Delilah an agent of the devil and was she trying to recruit me?

"I and all of the other free ghosts in Limbo are called darklings. We are ghosts that have shown our worthiness to the Master of Philadelphia. We have been tasked with sowing the seeds and reaping the harvests that bring strength and balance to all creation."

"And what of the angelic ghost that I saw on the ferry?" I blurted.

Delilah's eyes suddenly blazed crimson, and the collar around my neck responded, pouring wave after wave of agony through my whole being. I staggered, reaching a hand out to steady myself. The pain suddenly lessoned as my fingers brushed the blue steel mesh on the wall. I dropped to the ground and thrashed about, but I made damned sure some part of me stayed in contact with the blue steel. The collar still caused incredible amounts of pain, but it was much more tolerable than it would have been otherwise.

After a few minutes of this torture, resulting with me lying on the ground weeping and begging for mercy, Delilah finally turned away and the pain subsided.

"You do not speak unless given permission, and you may never speak of the luminaries," she said in a gentle voice. "They are prisoners of war and only specters, reapers, and properly authorized darklings may have any dealings with them or even speak of them. Is that understood?"

I nodded, and with great effort I forced my aching body to move, slowly getting back to my feet. It's strange to have an aching body. I'm a ghost. Shouldn't I be immune to such things? Was it merely my imagination?

"There is little time before the testing, so we'll have to speed this up," Delilah continued. "Every ghost is classified by its ability to interact with the living world."

"Those unfortunate souls that can't interact with the material plane in any way are called anisi: the lost. Their lot is to work the mines and man the front ranks of the armies of night; even darkling anisi are relegated to menial tasks."

It struck me that the masters of Limbo must really be afraid of the luminaries given how violently their minions reacted whenever I showed any curiosity about them. My mind drifted thinking of the possibilities while trying to glean what truths I could from the propaganda Delilah was feeding me.

"The next ghost type are called apparitions. They can manifest themselves in the living world and their form can be made visible to mortals, but that is the extent of their useful abilities. They also are typically used for mining although some do serve in other specialized roles. These are the most common ghosts in Limbo."

This caught my attention a little as I recalled all the claims about ghost sightings. Philadelphia was a veritable hotbed of ghost activity if the paranormalists could be believed. I hadn't ever put much stock in such things, but I guess they had been right after all.

"Next are the Phantoms. These ghosts can manifest in the living world taking whatever form they wish. They also have the added ability to create real sound in the living world. Phantoms are counted as valuable tools in the sowing teams."

"What are sowing teams?" I asked.

Delilah glared at me, anger and some other emotion warring with each other across her beautiful features. I realized that I'd spoken without being given permission. I braced myself for what was inevitably coming but I also raised my chin and glared at Delilah defiantly; my stomach was doing fearful flips.

"You remind me of myself child," she said finally with a sigh of disapproval. "It took me a hundred years to become a darkling because I was so damned stubborn. You can't beat the system. Give in to it and you will find it can be quite rewarding. You don't have to go through years of endless suffering like I did."

I bowed my head to her in apparent submission, but on the inside I remained defiant. I promised myself that I would never become like Delilah. I needed to be smart though; open defiance would only lead to punishment. Rather than making them break my spirit, I needed them to believe that I was ready to serve. That I was ready to do anything that would help me avoid punishment. It dawned on me that if a shade could become a darkling, then why not it's opposite? A luminary perhaps? Maybe the luminaries weren't abandoned troops in God's army or prisoners of war. Perhaps the luminaries of Limbo were shades who refused to give into the system and had given themselves over to God's grace. Clearly though, if this were the case, things hadn't worked out so well for the fellow on the boat. I didn't want to become a darkling, but neither did I want to become a luminary if it meant I'd have to spend eternity as a slave. It seemed like I was in a catch twenty-two situation. My stomach began to hurt once more as my anxiety levels rose.

"Very well child. I will reward your stubbornness this one time, but do not expect it again. Sowing teams are specialized ghost units that go into the living world to prepare souls for the afterlife. Limbo only accepts the souls of those who have died as a result of intentional violence, therefore the sowing teams work hard to bring about such horrible occurrences. The teams sow madness and paranoia; they manipulate the weak minded and push them over the edge until they've created monsters. The best sowers are artists; their works always make the front pages of newspapers. If you're lucky and you prove powerful enough for the privilege, perhaps you'll be a sower some day."

I stared at Delilah in horror. She was telling me that ghosts were interfering in the lives of living people causing chaos in their lives. If Delilah was to be believed then ghosts were at least partially responsible for the madness that the living world had descended into over the last century. Ghosts were driving people insane in order to cause death and mayhem: it was truly diabolical. My mind grew numb as I considered the implications. It seemed to me like Hell was cheating; it was using the ghost realm to increase its chances of winning whatever war was being waged. Why would God allow such a ploy to continue? All the chaos in the world suddenly made much more sense, and all those ghost stories seemed all too real.

"In any case we must continue," said Delilah. "The poltergeist is the most valuable of ghosts having the ability to manifest in the living world and to manipulate physical objects there. Like the phantom, they can project sound, but unlike them they can also control electricity. There's at least one poltergeist on each sowing team. I myself am a poltergeist."

"There are just a few more ghost types to cover. The Banshee is a crazed female ghost who has the same abilities as the poltergeist but also has the capability of destroying things with her screams. The Banshee's ability to cause destruction is the same in the living world as it is in Limbo. Unfortunately, the banshee's tortured death leave them quite mad and difficult to control. They are just as likely to destroy your own forces as they are the enemies. We have seen a surge of them being reaped in Philadelphia lately."

A chill went down my spine as I listened to Delilah and recalled the words the detectives had read written in my blood on the alley wall where I'd been killed. "The wails of the spirits shall herald the Dark Master's victory over death," it had read.

The female detective had believed there was a problem with the translation, could the word that was translated as spirits actually be banshees I wondered. The specters had come looking for me in that forsaken alley as if they'd known I'd be there. Another thought struck me: did the creepy way that my killer had looked directly at my spirit and spoken to me as if he knew I was there indicate that he was knowingly working with the spirit world? Whatever the serial killer's foreknowledge of the spirit world might be, it did seem like he was, at the very least, a pawn of a sowing team. I had to fight back against a sudden wave of tears that threatened to spill out of me. I wasn't just the victim of a crazed man, I was the victim of something far more sinister and evil, and now they wanted me to join their team. Rage blazed up deep within me squelching the urge to cry that had threatened to break like a dam just a few moments ago. Was no one going to stand up to these people?

"The reapers are the captains of Limbo," Delilah droned on seemingly unaware of the emotions she'd unleashed within me. "They are in charge of the day to day administration of the Master's affairs. They are very powerful and can wield death in the living world."

I was going to have to even the score, figure out a way to help the cops, and put an end to the serial killer's reign of terror. The first thing I needed to do was to pass this test. I really needed a job on one of those sowing teams. Instead of planting poison, however, I planned to sow some whoop ass on a killer and maybe some ghosts too. Yup, I'm not too full of myself: locked in a cage, controlled by a medieval torture collar, not knowing a thing about my abilities or even if I had any, and here I was planning to save the world from psychos and evil ghosts. My father always did tell me I could succeed at anything I put my mind too. Of course the trouble is that it's always much easier to succeed at things in your own mind than it is in the real world. Oh well, who am I to doubt? I'm a ghost. Reality just doesn't seem so limiting anymore.

"Wraiths are the rulers of Limbo's cities. They are the most powerful of ghosts and the rarest. They …"

A skull rattling roar shook the building for a moment, interrupting Delilah's instruction. She sighed and waved a hand at the cell doors which opened at her silent command.

"It's time for the testing, follow me."

6

DELILAH LED ME THROUGH the dark corridors of the Walnut Street Prison and finally out into the mist shrouded courtyard that lay at its center. There were a dozen shades lined up near the doors from which we emerged; a half dozen specters prowled the grounds, their malevolent red eyes burning with hunger. Dominating the center of the courtyard sprawled a squat, single story building. The cries of several desperate women could be heard coming from that forlorn structure.

Delilah nodded towards the line of shades and I obediently moved to take up a spot among them. We waited for several more minutes; the eerie cries of the tortured women weighed heavily on me and the other shades, while the Specters seemed to delight in them as if the cries were music to their ears. Finally, a tall, gaunt shape emerged from the opposite end of the courtyard and strode towards us, robes flapping ominously in the still air of the ghost world.

"Begin," The reaper ordered as it came to a stop several yards away from our line.

One of the Specters stepped behind the first shade in the line while Delilah moved to stand in front of it. The specter suddenly lunged forward and buried both of its clawed fists deep into each side of the shade's body. The pitiful ghost let out a shriek and tried to pull away from the Specter, but it was too deeply impaled on the specter's monstrous claws.

"Calm yourself," Delilah ordered. "No further harm will be done to you as long as you obey. The test to discover your place in the Armies of Night has begun. Pain, anger, vengeance, and hatred will make you strong. Focus on these and the Lady of Nightmares will bless you with the strength to be of use in the Armies of Night."

The shade visibly calmed; Delilah's melodic voice added potency to the rituals words.

"Now, close your eyes and picture the living world as you remember it. Push the fog away with your mind."

It took several minutes of coaxing from Delilah but eventually the ubiquitous mists drew away from the shade leaving it in a bubble of clear space. Delilah ordered the shade to continue thinking about the living world. About what the people there might be doing. About friends and family. After another minute or so, sounds of wind and traffic emerged from the bubble; the wailing from the central building suddenly stopped. Seconds later we could see that the shade was now standing on a busy street corner; people passed by and through it, while cars moved on the nearby road. I recognized the area around Walnut and Sixth Street on Washington Square; my heart leapt in my throat as I experienced a deep sense of longing for home.

"Very good," purred Delilah. "You have already shown us you have some power. Now concentrate on your body. Visualize yourself as you were when alive; make those people see you."

As the shade began to concentrate on its body I became aware of some strange things that I hadn't noticed before. The specter tasked with holding the shade seemed to be intensely uncomfortable and I saw that its arms vanished at the point at which contact was made with the living world. As I continue to study this phenomenon, I noticed that the specter seemed to be straining as if invisible bonds held it. I suddenly realized that the specter was unable to move: it was somehow paralyzed.

After what seemed like a great deal of time, but was actually only about ten minutes, people on the street began to react to an apparent apparition. Instead of walking through the ghost, they gave it a wide birth, and after a few moments a crowd began to gather nearby; cameras flashed and people pointed at the ghost excitedly.

"Step back into the mists," Delilah ordered, her voice dripping with disdain.

The shade reluctantly stepped back into the mists which were apparently still visible to it. The bubble of home vanished and we were all left with the cold mists of Limbo. The wailing of the tortured souls in the central structure resumed and the paralyzed specter was once again able to move.

"Apparition," declared the reaper. "The Fixer is looking for some new slaves. Send it to One Liberty Place."

The shade wailed as it was marched away.

The testing continued for more than two hours until it finally reached me at the end of the line. There'd been eight apparitions and three anisi; a harvest that none of my captors seemed pleased with.

A specter took its place behind me and I braced myself for the attack that I knew would come. Delilah confronted me, a gleam of expectation in her eyes. Though the specter's claws sent rivers of molten agony through my ghostly veins, I refused to cry out or cringe. I stared defiantly into Delilah's eyes and she nodded with satisfaction.

"Clear your mind. No further harm will be done to you as long as you obey. The test to discover your role in the Armies of Night has begun. Pain, anger, vengeance, and hatred will make you strong. Focus on these and the Lady of Nightmares will bless you with the strength to be of use in the Armies of Night."

I ignored her words and with eyes still open I pictured the corner of Walnut and Sixth and pushed back the mists with my will. There was a grunt of surprise from the specter as the mists parted and I found myself standing on the now haunted street corner. I could still feel the specters claws within me, holding me to Limbo like a tether, but I could sense its vulnerability here. I pushed at the mist harder and they rolled further away from me. The specter gave a sudden howl of fear as I felt its very being begin to unravel.

"Stop that immediately," Delilah shouted angrily. "Pull the mists back closer to you, or I promise that you will wish that you had never been born."

Delilah didn't scare me much, at least not if I hadn't been wearing this stupid collar, but the reaper that watched the proceedings had a creep factor that made my teeth chatter with terror. I still didn't know enough about this new world let alone my own capabilities. Now wasn't the time to give away my rebellious intentions.

"Sorry," I said in as contrite a voice as I could muster. "I didn't know that I could do that. None of the others did it."

I drew the mist back closer until I felt the specter solidify. I sensed that the thing was now terrified of me though which was just fine by me.

Before Delilah could give me any instructions, I pictured myself as I'd been in real life and willed myself to take tangible form. I suddenly felt heavier, and more solid. Real. I looked down at myself and saw the attractive twenty one year old that I'd been in life. I was wearing the same clothes as I'd worn the night of my death. I concentrated hard and was rewarded with a new look. I now wore a black mini skirt, a red tank top, and three inch red pumps. A look around showed me that I was quite visible to the world around me. Men were openly gawking at me and a sudden screech of tires informed me that my presence had nearly caused an accident. The haunted corner was suddenly not haunted anymore.

"Impressive," said Delilah. "Now, see if you can recreate the sound of those screeching tires. Concentrate and place the sound behind some of those pedestrians; let's see if you can give them a good scare."

I picked out a handsome middle-aged man, probably in his late thirties. He was dressed in a black suit. I pegged him as a lawyer or corporate officer type. I waved to him and he immediately changed his course to join me at a nearby bench. He smiled at me as he approached.

"May I help you with something?"

"Well," I said with a blush. "I'm looking for Cheerleader's Gentlemen's Club. I have an interview there at two o'clock."

"Ah," he said looking at his watch. "You don't have much time; that's in Penn's Landing not too far away from here. I wish I had time to give you a ride, but I'm already late for an appointment myself."

"Not a problem," I said smiling at him. "Just give me directions. I'm sure I can find it. Being a little late won't really matter; all these places care about is whether you have a nice set of boobs. I should be fine."

"Umm …" he tried to speak but was apparently having difficulty forming the words. I smiled even more widely at him and made sure to bend over just enough so he could get a good look at my cleavage.

"It's ok. Maybe we can go for drinks later?"

"Uh … yeah!" he said fumbling in his coat pocket and withdrawing a card. "That would be great."

"Great, my name is Veronika," I concentrated as hard as I could as I extended my hand out to take the card from him. My fingers wrapped around the small piece of paper and I pulled it to me with relative ease.

"Uh …" he said again looking down at my half exposed chest. "I've gotta go. I'll see you later."

He hurried off without giving me directions to Cheerleaders. I looked at the card and saw that his name was Sam Burton; an associate attorney at Carlyle, Higgs, & Foster.

"That isn't what I told you to do," came Delilah's half excited half angry voice. "I guess that will have to do for now. I want you to release your physical form. There's one more test for you."

I reluctantly released the image I'd formed of my body and felt myself grow lighter once more. I filed the image away into the archives of my mind. I had returned to my shade form, hovering over the sidewalk of Washington Square; people once again avoiding the haunted corner where hot ladies suddenly vanished into thin air. The business card lay several feet away: a simple piece of reality that was beyond my grasp now.

"Now go over to that parked car and start it up."

I felt the specter tense up inside me as I moved away from the mists of Limbo to reach the nearby car. I paused a moment once I reached the navy blue Pontiac Grand Am contemplating my next move. I thought about manifesting myself physically again, but my gut told me that this part of the test required me to try something else. I tentatively reached my hand towards the car. It passed through and I slowly moved forward pushing my whole body into it until I stood in the driver seat, my upper body sticking up through the roof. I sat down, concentrating on giving myself just enough substance to feel the car around me but not enough to become visible to the world. The maneuver seemed to work, allowing me to sit in the driver's seat without passing through it.

I put my hands on the steering wheel and foot on the gas pedal and concentrated, willing the car to start. I sat there for almost five minutes growing more and more frustrated as nothing happened. I was about to give up when memories of old TV shows gave me an idea. I reached a finger towards the ignition and willed an electrical spark to flow from me. I almost sank through the car seat in sheer surprise when a current of electricity shot out of my finger and into the ignition. The car shuddered and came to life. I wanted to let out a shout of triumph but instead put a little pressure on the gas moving the car forward a few feet. I silently thanked my dad for the times we'd watched all those dumb cop and robber shows, especially the ones involving the thieves hot wiring the cars they were steeling.

"That's enough, return now," Delilah ordered.

I instinctively willed some of the mists of Limbo to flow into the car so that the electricity coursing through it could be smothered, the fog obeyed and the car stalled and died. No sense in wasting gas and polluting the environment. I was elated. Not only had I proven myself to be powerful, I'd also proven how resourceful I could be. Mom always said I was too smart for my own good. I silently prayed that this demonstration would get me a better position than being someone's bitch slave. I reluctantly left the car and Washington Square behind, walking into the mists and the Limbo that was now my world.

"Poltergeist," declared the reaper as I stepped back into the forlorn courtyard.

The terrible creature took two long steps towards me and leaned forward till its red, glowing eyes were even with mine.

"This one is insubordinate. It tries to do good. It smells wrong to me …"

The reaper cocked its head and it sniffed at me. It stared at me for another moment then straightened, looming over me.

"It is strong, potentially one of the most powerful tools we've harvested for our Master in many years. It will join your sowing team, Delilah. It is your task to teach it, to corrupt it, and make it into a tool that I can present to our Lord."

"I'm honored to serve you, Warden. I will make her the most fearsome poltergeist in all of Limbo," replied Delilah.

7

I STOOD IN CENTER CITY gazing at the gleaming tower that is City Hall. The building with its massive statue of William Penn at its apex has always fascinated me. Delilah was standing at my shoulder, also looking at the tower, but her stare conveyed discomfort rather than interest.

"There are places of power in the world that are dangerous to our kind," she said, continuing her instruction. "It doesn't matter whether you are in the living world or in Limbo; they should be avoided at all times."

"And City Hall is one of these places," I guessed. "What makes it so special?"

"Wizards built it and placed powerful wards around it," Delilah answered.

I turned to stare at her.

"Wizards? You mean like Gandalf from The Lord of the Rings?"

"I do not know anything about this Gandalf, but if he is anything like Merlin, then the answer is yes."

"Seriously?" I said with incredulity. "You're saying magic is real?"

"Of course magic is real," Delilah answered with the patience of a mother instructing her child. "Why should that be hard to believe? Isn't your continued existence something like magic?"

I considered this for a moment. Why should the existence of magic surprise me in light of all that I'd learned since my murder? It seemed that everything that I'd considered to be mere fairy tales was potentially real.

"What about vampires, werewolves, and faeries? Are they real too?"

"Of course," Delilah answered in an exasperated tone. "You modern people with all of your science have become blind to the reality that is all around you. Up until a century ago, people took it as a matter of fact that the supernatural world was as real as God is. The modern age's blindness to half of reality has made it vulnerable to the schemes of the shadow world. It makes our job easier."

My mind reeled with new understanding and possibilities. The world was a far more dangerous place than anyone realized.

"So what purpose do wizards fulfill?"

"Most wizards fancy themselves as the protectors of man-kind," Delilah said with a sneer. "They are among the few people in the world who have full knowledge of the supernatural, and they do what they can to thwart the machinations of the various players. Fortunately, they are few in number. They are typically the ones responsible for building places of power in order to provide safe havens for mankind. There are, of course, some few wizards who are motivated largely by the need for more power. Though this motivation is one that we share and understand, we still avoid them because their power is too unpredictable, and an unwary ghost can quickly become enslaved to their will."

"Do we have any relationships with any of the other super-natural creatures?" I asked curiously.

"In general we only have contact with normal people. Sowing

teams are to avoid contact with other supernatural beings. Only the Masters of Limbo may deal with other supernatural beings. That is why I am showing you the places and people to avoid."

For the next two days, Delilah took me on a tour of supernatural Philadelphia teaching me about the places to avoid and how to recognize unnatural beings. The majority of this tour was conducted in the living world at night when the preternatural beings were most active. There are a surprising number of places in the city that are frequented by other worldly beings. Pretty much most of the big attractions such as Independence Hall, Congress Hall, and the Franklin Institute are protected by magical wards that will warn a local wizard of a supernatural intrusion. Most surprising to me was the number of nightlife hotspots that are actually owned by monsters. My favorite club, the Electric Factory, is owned by vampires! Glam and Brownie's Pub are but two establishments of no less than eight that are owned and operated by faeries. All throughout the city there are bars, stores, subway stations, skyscrapers, tourist attractions, museums, and churches that I was warned about. Added to this list was Eastern State Penitentiary which was, according to Delilah, Limbo's most powerful haunt and home to my new master.

Recognizing and avoiding other beings of shadow is as simple as reading their auras. An aura is a shimmering halo of colorful energy that envelops most beings. It takes a little concentration to see an aura and if you have the proper training you can figure out what a creature really is by reading its aura. Most humans can't see auras but a few special ones like wizards and mediums can. Wizards tend to have a blue or blackish aura depending on the level of corruption their soul has endured. I didn't actually get to see a wizard, however, as Delilah said that if we got close enough to see one chances were better than good that it had already spotted us. She said that there was only one wizard in Philadelphia that she was aware of: a man named Nathaniel Carter; she wouldn't tell me anything else about him.

Vampires have a red aura while were-creatures have green

auras, and faeries have a rainbow of dancing colors that herald their nature. These we saw in spades as there is a sizeable community of all of them in Philadelphia. Delilah explained that while all of the supernatural creatures we were watching were capable of observing us if they so chose, most of them were oblivious to our existence and probably wouldn't care much about us even if they did see us. We were beneath their notice and the ghost community liked it that way.

8

I WOKE FROM MY FEW HOURS of sleep as my cell door slid open. Ok, I wasn't really sleeping, but I call it that because it helps me feel more normal. While I don't need to sleep anymore, I do need to recharge every so often. The more time I spend in the living world, and the more power that I expend, the weaker I grow until I am no longer able to use my powers or materialize in the living world. At that point it becomes necessary to fall into a deep meditation in order to feed off of the energies of Limbo. As I understand it, most ghosts need to spend quite a few hours in this state each day. I, however, have found that I only need four to six hours at the most. I think the celestial steel bond that I've developed has something to do with this.

I continued to experiment with the celestial steel during the nights when I was brought back to my cell to rest after a day's training. The training really wasn't difficult and didn't tax much of my reserves, though it did appear to do so to the other students in my group. The training was in basic living world operations and included various manifestation techniques and how to deal with the laws of physics which still affected us in the living world and, to a lesser degree, in Limbo. I made sure to look every bit as exhausted as the rest of the students and, as a result, found myself with a lot of unobserved free time. I spent most of that free time touching the blue celestial steel mesh in my cell, and enjoying the strength and peace that it seemed to imbue me with.

It was while holding the metal one night that I accidentally discovered the full extent of my affinity for it. I was wishing that I had a bed made of the stuff to lay on when all of the blue metal in the room began to flow and then formed itself into a bed. I was shocked by this but even more terrified about what would happen if Delilah should walk in and find that my bars had become a bed. I frantically tried to figure out how to get the metal to return to its original shape. I found that with a little effort of will, I could command the celestial steel to form into any object that I desired, from weapons to works of art. It was amazing how the metal would move like liquid, form into an object, and be strong enough to pierce stone walls. The effect was like the new breed of Terminator's in the second Terminator movie. Very cool.

The Walnut Street Prison was to remain my home until I had proven myself a trusted member of Delilah's sowing team, after which time I would be allowed to choose my very own haunt in the city. In the meantime, I spent my days training in the use of poltergeist powers: learning how to affect the minds of mortals, how to create illusions, and how to move things with my mind. In the evenings, I spent time with Delilah herself who taught me how to survive on the streets of Philadelphia, both the living and shadow versions. Finally, at night, I slept and secretly trained myself in the use of celestial steel. There was no way that I was gonna let Delilah turn me into another monster to prey on humanity. I needed to be ready to fight back, so I listened, watched, learned, and waited.

It was fitting that the banshees, with a new addition added to their ranks last night, chose the moment that my cell door slid open to begin their long day of wailing. A smiling Delilah stood in the doorway beckoning me to follow her. Today was the first day of my field training as a member of her sowing team.

I followed her through the dark prison and into the misty streets of Philadelphia. Butterflies danced nervously in the pit of my stomach. Two other ghosts made up the sowing team. Both of them were phantoms that went by the names Freak and Monster. I doubted that these had been their real names in life, but they both seemed to be into the whole Goth thing. Both ghosts were veteran members of Delilah's team and had regarded me with suspicion and hostility when she'd first introduced me to them a few weeks ago. It's good to know that my charming personality doesn't impress monsters.

We headed west towards Gray's Ferry, no one spoke though it was clear that Delilah was in a good mood. Word of the new banshee had spread like wild fire the night before, and all of the city's important ghosts seemed extraordinarily pleased with this bit of news. Freak and Monster glared at me the whole way; they still didn't like me even after a few weeks of training together. It must be jealousy because I'd proven to have more power than both of them put together. Neither of them could stay in the living world for more than a few hours, and that's why we were crossing the length of the city on this side before translating to do whatever we were going to do. As we boarded the ferry that would take us to West Philly, I recalled Delilah's warning given to me last evening as she concluded the day's lesson.

"Do not forget yourself Veronika. As long as you wear the collar, we can find you anywhere in either world. There's no place to hide that we can't find you. We will hunt you down and punish you. You will scream for a full decade before we give you a chance to redeem yourself. And do not imagine that you can remove the collar. Only a reaper can do so once you have earned our trust."

"From here on in," she'd continued. "You must obey. The work we do is important to our Master's plans. They have been in the works for years, even decades in some cases. We will not allow a willful child to disrupt our plans. I am taking a great deal of risk in entrusting you on a field assignment before you have proven yourself. Do not disappoint me."

Delilah's words filled me with as much dread now as they had when she'd spoken them. Why was she taking me on a field mission when at best my behavior to date was 'willful', or some might even say rebellious? What game was she playing at to take such a risk? The dread that filled me wasn't largely based on Delilah's threats but primarily due to the wicked gleam in her eyes while she spoke them. I feared that whatever the sowing team was up to this day, it was going to be something that would horrify and probably scar me if I participated in it. Delilah planned to corrupt me by making me do evil, and even if I refused to participate, just standing by and doing nothing could be just as damaging to my psyche. The devil's iron collar burned at my neck and felt heavier than usual. It trapped me.

A sudden movement from the center of the ferry caught my eye. At first I thought it had been a trick of my imagination, but then I noticed that the luminary bound at the center of the vessel was gazing directly at me. Its head was twisted at an odd angle. I was shocked to see that its face had grown back completely, leaving no visible scars. Our eyes met and it spoke to me in my mind.

"Trust yourself. You are stronger than you know, stronger than they can guess. Remember that spirit is stronger than iron."

The communication was cut off by Delilah, who stepped between us, blocking my view of the luminary. She looked at it with distaste, and then turned a smiling gaze back to me.

"Come, it is nearly time to disembark. It won't be long till we enter the living world. Won't that be nice?"

I nodded noncommittally, moving to follow her. A moment later the vessel struck the western bank and we disembarked. The shades waiting to cross to the other side parted before us as we strode forward. I saw many of them staring at me with envy in their eyes. The pitiful creatures actually wished they could be in my shoes. I suppose I couldn't blame them. At least I had a fighting chance to take my own unlife into my hands; they were fated to be slaves for eternity. At that moment, I realized that it wasn't enough to just free myself. I had to help these poor souls as well. Their hopelessness gave me strength and hope to move forward. The luminary's words gave me a germ of a plan.

9

THE MISTS OF LIMBO PARTED before my will and I quickly stepped into the living world in an area that I recognized as "The Meadows". In the old days, this had been a rural part of the city; small farms had dominated the landscape here in those days. The area eventually grew into a bustling community that supported the Philadelphia International Airport which had been built nearby on the dredged site of the former Hog's Island. The neighborhood fell on hard times in the 1970's and went through a phase of urban renewal that largely failed; much of the neighborhood's housing was abandoned. The 1990's saw the urban blight give way to industry: oil storage facilities, warehouses, factories, oil refineries, a sewage treatment plant, and an occasional housing development took root in the revitalized neighborhood.

I looked around and saw Freak and Monster materialize behind me. I was gratified to see that both of them seemed to be working at making the translation. Delilah had arrived first and nodded in satisfaction at me. Apparently she'd noticed how easily I'd crossed the barrier between Limbo and the living world. It seemed to come naturally to me, barely requiring any effort or concentration on my part; it was as if I belonged here. A pang of loneliness and sorrow tore at my gut for a moment, but I pushed it aside viciously. My father had always taught me to be practical. He said that I didn't need to like or be happy about any given situation I found myself in; I just needed to find contentment in it, to find a way to make the best of the situation. He taught me that things could always be worse and I'd always found this to be true. Even in a position as sucky as the one I found myself in, I was better off than those poor shade slaves, and the luminary lashed to the wheel of the ferry. I didn't have time to feel sorry for myself; there was work to be done, and ghosts to help.

I looked at my surroundings and noted that it was early nightfall. The city was alive with lights and traffic was steady. Airplanes arrived every few minutes, and the passengers headed into Center City via the nearby I-95 access ramp. We stood on the side of the road beside an old, abandoned looking warehouse which stood forlornly on a barren lot. Across the street from us rose a massive oil storage tank. The lot was fenced off and trucks occasionally came in and out of the stony driveway.

After making sure that we were all with her, Delilah marched straight towards the old warehouse. As we approached the three story brick building, I noticed that there were lights shining through windows in the southeastern end of it. Delilah didn't bother heading for the entrance but instead made for the nearest wall and simply walked straight through it. I followed without thinking twice, I'd done this in training; my vision went black for a moment as I passed through the brick wall. Freak and Monster were right behind me. On the other side, we found ourselves in a dark hallway. Though there wasn't much light, our ghostly senses allowed us to see as if we were wearing night vision goggles, although the world was bathed in a blue glow rather than green.

Delilah was already moving down the hall towards the South, and I quickly followed. There were several doors on the right side of the hall, but Delilah passed them without slowing down. I gave the rooms a quick glance as I passed but found little of note: a few offices and an old break room. The corridor came to an end at a set of closed double doors. Once again, Delilah passed through the doors without pausing. I followed and emerged into a large chamber. It was some kind of receiving room by the look of it. I glanced behind me and watched as Freak and the Monster both emerged from the double doors. I noticed that both seemed to have lost some cohesion. Moving through physical objects forced a ghost to expend higher levels of power than normal. My training had taught me that ghosts are still subject to the laws that govern reality; when we bend them we pay for it in some way. The more powerful the ghost, the more able they are at overcoming the barriers of physical law; weaker ghosts, on the other hand, are far more limited when operating in the living world. Freak and Monster were clearly weaker ghosts than me. They were tiring already and we'd just got here. Delilah had told me that most ghosts can only operate for a few hours in the living world before they'd need to return to Limbo to recharge. We'd found during my training that I could remain for days before needing to recharge.

Light was streaming into the large room from an open doorway in the southeast corner. Delilah was already moving in that direction. I trailed her, my senses straining to catch the barest hint of whatever might be of such importance to have brought her to this place. We reached the open door and found ourselves looking into a well lit conference room. The room was occupied by five men. Two of the men were sitting at a table in the center of the room. One was reading a magazine while the other fiddled with a cell phone. A third man rummaged through a crate in a corner of the room. The last two men were working with an array of weapons which littered a table against the southern wall. I stared, stunned at the assortment of weapons.

There were at least a half dozen AK-47 machineguns and just as many submachine guns and pistols of various types as well as two gym bags full of ammunition. Even more frightening were the explosives segregated from the firearms at the other end of the table. The men were all dressed in black fatigues with black tee-shirts and jackets.

The walls of the room were plastered with photos, newspaper clippings, maps, and other materials. I moved into the room and, when Delilah didn't object, I took a closer look. A sudden chill went down my spine when I realized that all the materials referenced various buildings on the Penn University campus. It quickly became evident that Irvine Auditorium was a key target of these men. I turned a wary eye toward Delilah waiting to see what was going on.

The man who'd been rummaging in the crate rose having gathered various electronic parts. He moved over to the explosives and began to assemble them with a practiced ease.

"Ok Freak, it's time to get started," Delilah said.

The men were oblivious to our presence, of course, and the room had remained silent except for the noise of weapons being loaded and bombs being assembled. Freak stepped up close to the man with the cell phone and reached a misshapen finger towards the device. The quiet of the warehouse was suddenly disrupted by the cell's loud ringtone blaring Van Halen's "Jump". The five men suddenly became alert, stopping their activity to look at the one with the phone.

"Here it is boys. Stay cool," said the one reading the magazine.

"Ed here," answered the one with the phone.

There wasn't an immediate reply, but when it came I knew right away that Freak was doing the talking.

"Are you ready," Freak asked, his deep voice projecting through the cell.

"Soon," Ed replied.

"Good. You are satisfied with the materials?"

"Top notch shit, man … the homos and their friends are

gonna get a blast," Ed said. His companions chuckled in appreciation of the apparent joke.

"Good. Best get moving; the rally will begin in two hours."

"Don't worry. The fireworks tonight won't be in celebration of gay pride. Tonight, we'll send a message loud and clear. A line in the sand will be drawn and war declared on the fags and their socialist friends. We ain't gonna let them destroy America."

Delilah made a cutting gesture and Freak withdrew his finger from the phone. There was a click and the connection went dead. The men moved with purpose as they finished their preparations, finally putting everything into big hockey gym bags emblazoned with the shield of the University of Pennsylvania Quakers. Delilah watched the activity with a satisfied smile on her face.

I looked around, desperately trying to understand what was going on. I found the answer tacked on the wall overlooking the weapons table: a front page headline clipped from the Philadelphia Inquirer read "Mayor to Rally Support for Gay Marriage Law". I recalled that recognizing the rights of gays to marry had become a big and very controversial topic in the city. It seemed like things were coming to a head, and Limbo was poised to reap the rewards of the ensuing chaos. If these men succeeded in their plans, Limbo would reap a great harvest this night. I couldn't allow this to happen.

I pushed my anger and disgust aside for a moment and turned to face Delilah. I needed to stall for a moment in order to come up with a plan.

"How are you controlling them?" I asked, nodding towards the bustling men around us.

"Controlling them?" Delilah asked, a puzzled look creasing her features.

"How are you making them do this?" I asked in exasperation.

"Ah, you think we are forcing these men to commit an act of mass destruction," she said with a smile. "That is not the case. Only the Masters, full wraiths, can possess living beings and force them to do things against their will. We have simply encouraged these men to do what is already in their hearts. We helped these men come together with likeminded men who had both the desire and skills to commit such a grand crime as these men will commit tonight. We aren't forcing anyone to do anything they don't already want to do. We just help them make their fondest wishes come true."

My anger flared up again as I looked at these five men. They had no excuse for the evil that they were planning. Delilah might be providing the motivation and the tools to carry out the mass destruction that they were about to undertake, but it was the evil in their own hearts that had brought them to this point. I had no time to spare for them. Whatever happened to them due to my actions in the next few moments, it was upon their own heads, not mine. I would spare no thought to their safety. Ultimately, I had to stop Limbo from reaping its planned harvest.

"Alright," said Delilah. "It is time to get moving. Freak, you and Monster stay with these men. Make sure they don't get weak kneed. Don't interfere with them unless they need a little encouragement. Don't over play their emotions either. We are close to completing this project; no mistakes now. Veronika and I will go ahead to the auditorium to make sure everything is ready."

"Ok," said Freak. He looked excited at the idea of being put in charge.

Delilah turned and headed out of the room giving me a curt gesture to follow. I tensed and moved forward as if to obey her but at the last moment I veered off and lunged for the bag of explosives.

"Stop her!" I heard Delilah scream, but all my concentration was on the explosives and the energy I was calling up from deep within me. As soon as my hands touched the bag of explosives, I released a massive charge of electricity similar to what I'd used to start up the car during my testing, but in a far larger and less controlled burst. The bolt that shot out of me was so intense that it instantly fried the bomber who was still loading the bag. The guys playing with the machine guns barely had a chance to register surprise before the explosives went super nova.

I was momentarily blinded by the flash of brilliant light produced by the massive explosion. The delay between light and sound was barely perceptible so close to the epicenter of the blast, but it was just enough time for me to push myself through the veil that separates the living world from Limbo thereby avoiding being deafened. My last view of the scene was of the blast radiating outwards, tearing though everything in the room. I saw Freak standing stunned, gaping at the oncoming destruction, while Monster was rushing towards me, passing into Limbo after me. I could see nothing of Delilah before the mists of Limbo swallowed up my view of the destruction I'd wrought in the living world.

10

MONSTER WAS INDEED WELL NAMED. As he passed through the veil separating the worlds, he transformed, growing double his original size, face contorting and stretching into an apelike visage with shark like fangs. His arms grew long and muscular; the massive hands were tipped with razor-edged talons. He towered over me, growling menacingly.

The smart thing for me to do would have been to run, but I didn't want this thing on my heels. Besides, I wasn't sure if I could outrun him anyways. I was relatively certain that Monster had used up a great deal of his power already while I'd barely scratched the surface of my own power reserves. He had far more experience as a ghost however, which canceled out my power advantage. What really scared me right now was not knowing where Delilah was or what she was doing. I had to get away and get this damned collar off me as quick as possible or she'd make me regret the day I was born.

Monster was clearly enjoying himself as he fueled his re-maining power into intimidating me. The look of surprise on his face was priceless when I darted towards him, ducking beneath his raised arms and placed both of my hands on his muscled stomach. Instead of releasing power into him, as I'd done with the explosives in the warehouse, I opened myself up like a drain in a fountain and with force of will pulled at Monster's power: his very essence. He screamed in terror as my attack had an immediate impact. His power flowed into me like a flood. He tried to pull away, but I moved with him, and he was already too weak to push me away. His monstrous form shrank to half its size within a few seconds of my attack. At about the minute mark, his entire body imploded and became a vortex of energy which continued to pour into me.

The speed at which I'd completely consumed an experienced ghost of Limbo was stunning. I felt energized, and more powerful than ever before. I'm not sure what inspired me to do what I did, but it gave me a fighting chance to get away. Wasting no more time, I turned and fled from the Meadows neighborhood.

I moved swiftly, avoiding the areas that I knew were frequented by the city's ghostly population. Thanks to Delilah's street survival lessons, I had a pretty good idea of what streets and neighborhoods to avoid. I used back streets and alleyways, heading North until I reached the Wynnefield Heights neighborhood at Ford Road just South of the black pit that was the Belmont Reservoir in the living world. I passed the Woodside Amusement Park, which is only a memory in modern Philly. I tried not to think about what might be watching me from the old wooden roller coaster or the dilapidated Ferris wheel whose upper carriages vanished into the mists far above.

I turned East and continued until I finally reached the bottomless chasm that is the Schuylkill River in shadow Philly. I looked across the chasm into the shrouded Fairmont Park. The hundreds of feet between me and the other side may as well have been a hundred miles. I couldn't get across using the ferry and there were no unguarded bridges that I knew about. I was either going to have to fly across or find another way, but if I wanted to stay free, I was gonna have to get across as quickly as possible.

Flying across isn't as crazy as it sounds. I'd seen some ghosts flying during my training excursions with Delilah. When I'd asked about it, Delilah had informed me that only the most powerful and oldest of ghosts had the strength to sustain flight for any meaningful period of time. I had no idea how to do it or if I even had the strength to accomplish it, but my plan required that I get across to Center City quickly. I couldn't afford wasting time trying to find an alternative route that might not exist. Every moment that I wore the collar was ultimate peril for me. If Delilah got her hands on me after what I'd done to ruin her scheme she would make me pay.

I made up my mind to give it a try. After all, falling into a bottomless pit was likely preferable to falling into Delilah's hands. Quite frankly, I had little idea how I did any of the things I'd done. The lightning bolt that had blown up the warehouse and Delilah's plans was sheer luck as far as I was concerned. I'd had no idea if what I was trying to do would work. And swallowing up Monster? I had no idea where that action had come from either. I was acting on pure instinct. The luminary had told me to trust myself; I couldn't see any reason to not take its advice.

I went to the western side of the wide avenue that bordered the Schuylkill, took a deep breath, and without further thought sprinted towards the chasm. As I neared the dark pit, I heard a screeching sound behind me.

"There she is! We have her cornered."

I spared a quick glance behind me and saw Freak, along with three specters, emerge from a nearby alley. They were much closer on my heels than I'd guessed. I smiled at Freak and leaped as my last step took me to the edge of the bottomless river. As I soared through the air, I concentrated my will and envisioned myself flying upon a current of wind. A sudden blast of air blew my hair back from my face, and I was lifted higher into the misty sky. I willed the wind to carry me forward at a greater velocity, and I instantly shot forward. The far bank was speeding towards me. I experimented, willing the wind to turn me and I suddenly found myself speeding back the way I'd come. For the second time today, I saw Freak standing and gaping at me. I laughed with pure joy as I whipped myself back around and headed towards Fairmount Park.

A couple hundred yards into the shrouded park, I urged the wind to a calm and, with far more effort than I expected, I was able to land safely. Though flying would have gotten me to my destination far quicker than going by foot, I felt the energy that was required was too costly. I couldn't afford to weaken myself any further. I still felt quite strong, but I had no idea how much of it I'd need before I was able to rest again. Prudence seemed the wiser course at this point.

Fairmount Park is the incorporated park system of Philadelphia and refers to many different park areas throughout the city. The section that I found myself in was part of the athletic fields division. In living Philadelphia, dozens of well maintained multi-use fields lay scattered over the landscape. In Limbo, the area was heavily forested and blanketed by the ubiquitous mist.

I immediately moved South, passing another large pit of nothingness that was the East Park Reservoir in the living city, until I came to historic Kelly Drive. Kelly Drive parallels the Schuylkill River and is a popular destination for those who enjoy water recreation of all types. I stayed on the eastern side of the street, moving through the shadows cast by nearby buildings and trees. I had just passed the historic Boat Row when the eerie silence of the shadow city was shattered by a shrieking horn blast that sent shivers down my ghostly spine.

The alarm had finally been sounded. Now the city itself would be after me. I smiled grimly and kept moving South, although I did slow my pace a bit and watched my surroundings even more carefully. I was gambling that the powers that be in the city would expect me to flee North. They wouldn't dream that I was foolish enough to head South into the most heavily haunted parts of the city. It seemed likely to me that a reaper would be taking charge of the search which meant things were bound to get complicated.

A half hours careful progress Southward had brought me to the Fairmount Water Works region where I almost walked into a gang of specters. I was moving alongside a Greek Revival building, which housed the now unused water works system of an earlier age, when five specters rounded the corner of the building moving in the direction in which I was heading. Their red eyes shone brightly in the dark mists and they moved with purpose. They were alert with an air of coiled violence about them. I froze and did my best to melt into the shadows of the nearest pillar, but I knew that would only delay the only possible outcome. I was going to have to run for it. Desperately, I reached for the wind that would carry me into the sky and away from the creatures, but at the last moment I changed my focus to the mists around me. Instinctively, I called the mist to me and laid it about me in a thick cloak. My heart pounded in my ears as the glowing eyes of the specters drew closer.

They passed me by without a glance and I waited a full three minutes before I dared move. When I did, I kept the mist wrapped around me until I was a full mile from the water works. When I reached Eakins Oval on the tail end of the Benjamin Franklin Parkway, I reluctantly released the mist cloak. The cloak was fairly easy to manage, but it did drain power. It wasn't very much, but I didn't want to risk using any more than I needed to. Besides, the ghost community generally avoided the museum district: especially the Parkway. Delilah had told me that Franklin had been a powerful wizard who'd placed powerful wards throughout the city. His landmarks were feared. I frankly couldn't bring myself to fear Franklin. He was a personal favorite of mine. Whether he'd been a wizard or not I couldn't say, but I had faith that whatever magic he'd hedged the city in wouldn't hurt me unless I meant it ill.

I continued my trek South following the Benjamin Franklin

Parkway, passing the Rodin Museum and the Majestic Central Free Public Library. As I approached the Vine Street Expressway, however, I began to regret having dropped the mist cloak. The expressway was one of several major arteries used by the ghosts of Limbo to travel to the Western part of the city. Unlike in the living world where the expressway runs at street level some of the time and at lower depressed levels at others, in Limbo it runs above the city like you'd expect from a normal highway. This means that it offered a splendid view of the surrounding cityscape to anyone traveling upon it. I quickened my pace until I'd passed beneath it. Continuing on, I reached Logan Square with its central fountain and ring of historic edifices like the Cathedral Basilica of Sts. Peter and Paul. I crossed the square to the Franklin Institute and circled the massive structure until I reached 21st Street which I turned onto and once more headed South.

I soon entered the affluent neighborhood of Fitler Square with its Victorian age townhouses framed by manicured European style gardens. Ancient oaks towered above the streets and houses of the neighborhood creating an effective screen from the rest of the city. The mists of Limbo seemed less thick here as though the living world was closer somehow. I turned West onto Pine Street, heading back towards the Schuylkill. I passed the square for which the neighborhood is named. The square is famed for its Victorian fountain and sculptures of various animals such as turtles, a grizzly bear, and a ram. In Limbo these sculptures frightened me; they gave off an aura of watchfulness and baleful menace. I hurried on, looking over my shoulders for any signs that the things were alive in some way. I didn't relax until I reached 26th street some few blocks away.

I paused long enough to draw the mist cloak about me once again as I approached the East bank of the Schuylkill. My destination had once been an important area for the unloading of coal from upriver and had featured a shipyard at one point. The United States Navy had even had a substantial base nearby. In Limbo these facilities still existed, and a portion of the city's shades worked on the construction of ferries and trains here. This meant that a substantial portion of the devil's iron and celestial steel were stored here as both were required in the manufacturing process. Celestial steel was what I was after at the moment.

As I had expected, there was little activity going on in the yard. Neither shades nor specters were out and about. I carefully circled the large complex of buildings and finally found a single specter standing guard at the door of a squat three story building. I guessed that this structure was used as a barracks for the slave shades. Everything was apparently under lockdown until they could capture me. So much fuss for little ole' me? It seemed silly. Confident in my mist cloak's ability to hide me from casual observation, I moved into the center of the depot heading towards the warehouse that I knew housed the celestial steel that I needed. I silently thanked Delilah once more for her street survival lessons. She had given me much valuable information that I intended to make the most of. She'd shown me how the city works; how traffic moves, how things are made, where ghosts live. I'd used those lessons to learn where important resources were stored, what streets and buildings weren't used, and how the city was patrolled.

The warehouse was unguarded; the doors were barred with a devil's iron chain and lock. I didn't bother with the door though. Instead I passed my hand through the wall until I encountered something solid. As expected, the inner walls were covered in celestial steel mesh: a standard security procedure in Limbo. As usual, the touch of the steel brought a sense of well being to me. I smiled and gently willed the mesh to part for me. I followed my hand through the wall and emerged into a large, unfurnished chamber. The room was bathed in a soft blue light which emanated from the tons of raw celestial steel stored in piles throughout the room.

I moved deeper into the room picking out a pile of the raw ore. Touching the mound, I willed the ore to form into a knife. The steel moved as if it were living liquid and coalesced into a five inch razor sharp blade with a hilt that fit perfectly in my hand. It looked and felt exactly the way I pictured it in my mind. I lifted the knife to the collar around my neck and, sliding the blade carefully underneath it, I slowly brought force to bear against the devil's iron collar. There was a hiss, a slight resistance, and then the delicate collar was tumbling away as if trying to escape the touch of the blue steel blade. I gingerly caught the collar before it could clatter onto the ground. Though the thing made me uncomfortable, I couldn't leave it behind as a clue. I would have to find a better place to dispose of it.

Having freed myself of the collar, I turned to arming myself. I created a steel mesh suit of armor complete with a belt and sheaths for the knife and sword that I was going to make next. The sword was a thing of beauty: a katana that the master crafters of ancient Japan would have been proud of. Once knife and sword were sheathed, I made a fine necklace with a cross. Star of David dangly earrings followed. Lastly, I shaped a mirror and got a real good look at myself for the first time since dying.

I stared at my reflection in dumbfounded surprise. I had expected to see a vaguely human shape shrouded in mist: a shade. Instead I stared back at myself; the self that I remembered as a living person. I was lovely. My hair was jet black and long, reaching to mid back. I had blue eyes, an aquiline nose, high cheek bones, pouty lips, and a strong chin. I was wearing a form fitting suit of glowing blue chain mail that showed off my generous curves. I concentrated for a moment and the mail was replaced by a black Theory suit that continued to show off my womanly body but somehow managed to convey elegance rather than coquettishness. Though the mirror showed me what I wanted to see, I could still feel the armor and weapons that I was still in fact wearing. I looked down at myself to dispel the mirrors phantom image but found that I was indeed wearing the clothes from the mirror and that my body was no longer shrouded as it had been since arriving in Limbo. I played around with my looks for a few more minutes, the little girl in me laughing with joy at getting to play Barbie again. I found that I could change my hair style and color with a though; I could change my features and body shape. In short I could look like anyone I wanted to look like. In the end, I settled for the real me, wearing the form fitting chain mail. That was totally me.

I looked back into the mirror and noticed some subtle changes in me. My eyes no longer had the look of mischief. Gone was the childlike smile. My jaw was set with determination, my eyes fierce and calculating; they danced about looking for signs of danger. My bearing had been open, inviting, and friendly in life. Now I was more like a cat: cautious and ready to pounce or flee at a moment's notice. Death had changed me.

As I stared at myself, my brows suddenly knitted in worry. I was wasting time. All of shadow Philly's most evil ghosts were hunting for me and I was standing around looking at myself. Gosh, had dying also turned me into a narcissist?

I put the mirror back onto the pile of ore and willed it to return to its original form. I then returned to the wall that I'd passed through. I concealed myself in the mist cloak once more and passed through the girl shaped hole that I'd made in the steel mesh upon entering. Before leaving the warehouse behind, I reached back into the building and touching the steel I willed the mesh to close back up, thereby leaving no trace of my ever having been here. I proceeded to the nearby bank of the Schuylkill chasm and gleefully hurled the devil's iron collar into its bottomless depths.

Now I was going to need a place that I could call home for a time. Every ghost needs a haunt: a place to rest and hide. I might look mostly like my old self, but I was still a ghost and subject to the basic rules of that state of being. Home would also be the headquarters from which I hunted my killer in the living world and hatched plans to free Limbo's slaves and end evil's hold on the world of the dead.

I had the perfect place in mind, but it lay at the heart of the city right in the middle of evil's domain. A smart girl would have tried to get out of town or at the very least found a hole on the edge of town to burry herself in. Not me. I headed back towards Pine Street and the heart of the city. What can I say? Smart isn't my strong suit I guess. If you're going to be a ghost, why not live dangerously? It's not like you're going to die or anything.

11

I was passing Fitler Square once more when the sense of being watched suddenly became overwhelming. I glanced towards the park and froze when I saw the sculpture of the grizzly bear staring right at me; its eyes glowed red giving it a menacing aura far beyond what such a creature could have induced in the wild. The grizzly sculpture moved languidly, stretching its taut muscles and licking its lips hungrily. I'm not sure if I imagined it, but I could swear it grinned at me. I noticed more movement out of the corner of my eye; a quick glance around the park showed me that the rest of the sculptures had also awakened.

I'd been moving down the center of Pine Street comfortably wrapped in the mist cloak when I'd reached the square. I'd once more picked up my pace as the park gave me the creeps. Now I knew why this was; the place had its own haunts. The animated sculptures could be an illusion. Many ghosts are capable of such feats, but this felt real. My senses screamed at me that these things were far more dangerous to me than any phantom could ever be. This could still be an illusion though; a clever distraction to keep my attention from the real threat that was sneaking up on me. A chill went down my spine at the thought. Could a reaper be stalking me?

I desperately wanted to look around. The space between my shoulder blades was itching badly, but my training in dad's dojo had taught me to never take my eyes off of a certain threat. In a situation that included potentially hidden foes, it was best to keep moving thereby making yourself a more difficult target to hit or to sneak up on. I moved while I focused my will and tried to 'feel' around me using my mind instead of my eyes. I know that sounds corny, I'm not a Jedi after all, but my ghostly powers were shaping up to be very similar. What could it hurt to try? The only entities that my mind touched were the creatures in front of me. The waves of pure evil that radiated from the sculptures made my ghostly skin crawl. They were creatures of hatred, and I, unfortunately, was the focus of that hate. I wanted to run, but I knew that running from these monsters was futile. They would chase me down, tear me apart, and then leave me for the reapers to find. I could try to fly away, but doing so this close to Center City would dramatically increase the chance that I'd be discovered. My only option was to stand against them and hope they would decide that I wasn't worth the trouble. Yeah, I know, fat chance I'd have that kind of luck.

I slowly maneuvered my hands to the hilt of my sword and knife as the bear growled at me and took a deliberate step towards me. The moment my hands made contact with the celestial steel hilts of my weapons, the fear that had torn at my ghostly innards from the moment I'd laid eyes on the awakened sculptures was banished. The grizzly roared suddenly, and it charged me. The thing moved with far more speed than I would have guessed. My blades barely cleared their sheaths before it struck me like a freight train.

The sudden impact was unexpected, and I found myself flying through the air with a massive grizzly bear riding me. Its claws tore at my throat and face. The good thing about being a ghost is that I don't have any breath to lose, so I was able to avoid being stunned by the impact. What sucks though is that I can still feel pain, and boy did those claws bring me agony.

We sailed into a nearby carriage house, and as we fell to ground, I concentrated, willing my body to become more substantial. The move cost me some extra pain as the physical alteration made me more vulnerable to common damage such as that suffered by a fall, but what I got in return was well worth it. Hitting the ground I rolled with the impact and passed right through the surprised and less substantial bear. In Limbo things behave the way our minds expect them too; we can't pass through other ghosts or objects without an effort of will to do so. The issue is further complicated when dealing with beings who have their own will; I can't pass through another ghost if she uses her will to deny me that ability. The maneuver I used on the bear was one I'd learned from Delilah. It was called tethering and was generally used in the living world to overcome certain physical laws. In this case, I was able to negate the bear's will by becoming more substantial than it and therefore automatically forcing it to pass through me.

In one fluid motion, I used the momentum of the roll to summersault to my feet, and simultaneously swung my katana in a precise arc towards the just emerging head of the ram sculpture that'd followed in our wake. The creature was caught completely by surprise as it was momentarily blinded by its passage through the carriage house wall. The celestial steel blade struck its neck and cleaved right through. The body continued charging forward and crashed into the rising bear. The head rolled away; the red flames of its eyes going dark.

Knowing that the bear would recover quickly and not knowing where the three turtles were or what they were doing, I decided that taking to the air was my best option for gaining any kind of advantage. I called the wind and leapt into the air and allowed my body to return to its normal state before hurriedly passing through the ceiling. I darted towards a nearby tree in order to gain some cover. I brought myself to a hover among the tall oak's foliage and desperately scanned the street and park below searching for the turtles. I found them right away and relaxed a bit. They at least moved at a speed equivalent to their living brothers beyond the veil, and hadn't even reached the street yet.

The moment of relaxed guard almost cost me my freedom as a sudden roar startled me into action. I didn't even think. I just acted, releasing the wind that kept me aloft. I dropped towards the ground, my ghostly body subject to Limbo's pull as it would be in the living world. The now winged bear sailed over my falling body. It growled in frustration as it attempted a tight turn and instead got tangled in the oak's branches. I called the wind back to me, and I sped back upward, blades held overhead. I rammed into the bear from below driving both katana and knife up to the hilt in its hide.

The bear roared in agony, its thrashing body sent me careening through the air and ripped the katana from my grasp. I did manage to retain control of the knife though. I regained control of myself quickly, shooting upward to evade any attack directed at me while I spun out of control. No attack came, and I circled around to get a better view of the bear. It was still thrashing about in the tree's branches. A blue fire was pouring out of the gaping wound in its underside. I watched in fascination as the celestial steel katana burned and consumed the creature. The glow in its eyes went out before it fell to earth. I swooped down and yanked the sword free from the now crumbled bear sculpture.

Instinct warned me of another danger, and I whipped around in time to see the nearest turtle staring at me from fifty feet away. It opened its mouth and a jet of liquid flame shot towards me. I flew backward avoiding the flames. Instead of dying out though, they coalesced into a fiery being wielding its own flame blade. A look at the turtle it had come from revealed that its eyes had gone dark and it stood motionless: a statue once more. Fear gripped my soul as the flaming being rushed towards me. Was this a demon?

I met the demon's charge, parrying its deadly thrust with practiced ease. The celestial steel blade blazed with blue flame when it met the demon's sword. We traded blows, testing each other's skill. I rode the wind as if I'd done it my entire life. I became an extension of my sword, moving with speed and grace. The demon proved to be a competent warrior, meeting my attacks and feints with skill. Though I held a masters rank in Kendo, I knew that we were evenly matched.

"Surrender now ghostling," the demon said, sending an overhead blow towards my head. I barely parried the attack as at the last second the blow was turned into a thrust that would have skewered my face. "My brethren will be joining us soon. You cannot stand against the might of the Dark Master. Surrender now and perhaps we will protect you from the reapers."

I delivered a series of swift strikes and then leapt away speeding towards the roof of a nearby townhouse. I took a moment to get a look around for the other two turtles and saw them continuing to inch towards us. I knew that I was doomed if I didn't end this fight soon. I dove suddenly and screamed in agony as the demon's flame blade raked across my right leg. Gritting my teeth, I shot straight back up and slammed into the surprised demon. I dropped my knife, pulled myself along the demon's form, and wrapped my free arm around its upper sword arm. Its body seared my ghostly form, but I ignored the pain. The demon was momentarily confused by this new tactic, making it slow to react to such an insane maneuver. The hesitation cost it its existence.

I wrapped my legs around the demon's waist and used my freed hands to remove the celestial steel necklace from around my neck. I placed it around the demon's. It stared down in shock as the blue cross settled upon its flaming chest. It tried to reach its hand up to rip the artifact away, but it was too late. I released it and sped away as the blue flames erupted through its body.

I didn't wait to watch it die. Time was not on my side. I was tired and hurt pretty badly. Both celestial steel and devil's iron can cause real wounds to ghosts, wounds that bleed our power out, and only rest can heal them. Delilah had told me that there were other things that could harm ghosts but hadn't elaborated. Apparently demon fire was one of those things, big surprise there. I wouldn't be able to handle another one of the demons, let alone two. On the other hand, I couldn't run. Leaving them to hunt me would be too dangerous. I needed to deal with them now. I focused my will and pushed at the mists of Limbo.

The translation into the living world was harder than it had ever been. I was weakening rapidly. I found myself on Pine Street near Fitler Square. I hurriedly landed as flying in the living world would use up far more juice than in Limbo. I made my way into the park. As I'd hoped, I found that several of the park's sculptures had been vandalized. The ram's head had been severed while the bear had been pounded into slag. One of the turtles lay on its side, head smashed to powder. Katana still drawn, I moved to the final two turtles and with swift strokes took off their heads. I was glad to see that celestial steel worked as well in the living world as it did in Limbo. Delilah had said it couldn't be brought across the veil which proved that she was either a liar or simply not all-knowing; probably both in her case.

I returned to Limbo and sighed with relief when I found that my gambit had paid off. The final two turtles stood headless and unmoving. There were no demons around. A quick search of the area turned up the celestial steel cross I'd used on the demon lying in a heap of ash. It was undamaged. I retrieved it along with my discarded knife.

Tired and very sore, I set off for the center of the city. I gathered the mist cloak around me and worked my way cautiously down Pine Street once more until I reached Fourteenth Street. I then turned north until I came to Walnut Street. It proved nerve racking to cross as it was a key artery into Washington Square: ghost central in shadow Philly. I continued Northward to Chestnut Street which was also a potentially active street since it was so close to the heart of things on this side of the veil, but once again I saw no ghosts and was able to reach my destination unmolested. Orianna Street is narrow here between Chestnut and Market streets. It could easily be mistaken for an alley. I crept along it, going North towards Market Street and smiled with satisfaction when I spotted a large three story brick house on the east side of the street.

In the living world the house no longer stands. Instead, a steel frame marks its former location. Franklin Court is a tourist attraction complete with a museum that lies underground within the old house's basement. Its purpose is to provide a window into the life of Benjamin Franklin. In Limbo, Ben Franklin's house still stands and the evil inhabitants of the city steer clear of it fearing Franklin as a powerful wizard who warded his favorite places in the city. His house was a perfect haunt for me.

12

I DON'T KNOW EXACTLY HOW LONG I slept. I've never seen a working clock in Limbo, but I was certain that it had been for much longer than usual for me. Gazing out the window of the second floor room that I'd chosen as my resting place, I could see that it was day time, but the mists prevented me from ascertaining much more of use. Not surprising. Ghosts don't care too much about the specifics of time. We've got all the time in the world after all. Time is for those with a limited amount of it or for those who've got work to do. Since my killer was continuing his reign of terror in the living world, I had to be concerned about time. Some girl out there was running out of it. I had to help her before she became another banshee. Delilah had let slip during one of our training sessions that the continued creation of banshees was a majorly important thing to the Master's plans. Screwing up the Master's plans and getting revenge on my killer simultaneously was too good an opportunity to pass up.

I took stock of myself and found that I was completely healed from the past days wounds. I was also fully rested. My power was fully restored. In fact, I felt much stronger than I'd ever felt. It was possible that absorbing Monster was responsible for this phenomenon. Using my powers as much as I did yesterday probably had something to do with it as well. I figure that it is kind of like going to the gym and working out my ghostly muscles. Whatever the explanation, I was glad for it. I was going to have to face a reaper sooner or later.

I pondered what I should do to help capture my killer. How could I assist the PPD? I mean Philadelphia is huge with over a million citizens; I couldn't go house to house looking for him. Well, I actually I could, but there was no guarantee I'd find him that way particularly if he moved around a lot. Besides, it would take far too long. What could I bring to the investigation that the police didn't already have?

I smiled. The police didn't have a ghost. They were bound by the laws of the country and state that protected people's civil rights. Unfortunately, legal procedures often get in the way of catching the bad guys. I was betting that there were places that hadn't been searched yet because of the lack of probable cause. They couldn't just barge into people's houses without a warrant, but I could. The cops couldn't pass through walls either and didn't have my supernatural senses; I could be their spiritual guide to help them see through any fogs put up by Limbo. So clearly what I needed to do was join the investigation. The irony was that Delilah had spent weeks teaching me how to interact with the living world. I was going to use all of the tricks of manipulation that I'd been trained in to help the PPD catch my killer.

So, my first order of business was to find detectives Frank Cooper and the female investigator Wendi. They had been at my crime scene and had talked like they were involved in the investigation of my killer. There was something about Frank in particular that I trusted, no point in ignoring my instincts at this juncture. Not really knowing much more about the two detectives nor about how the PPD operates, I decided that starting out at headquarters made the most sense.

Before leaving, I decided to walk through the spacious house getting a good look into each room. I had searched the house last night before falling asleep, but I'd been exhausted and heavily injured making it quite possible that I'd missed something. There was an energy that pulsed throughout the structure. It made me feel as though there was something important to find. It didn't feel threatening, just important. I found what I'd missed: the way into the basement. What really surprised me was that the door leading down below had a one inch thick plate of celestial steel covering it on the inside. Excitement filled me at the prospect of having discovered some kind of secret vault.

I pushed my way through the door, willing the celestial steel to part for me. As usual, the steel opened before me, and I descended the stairs until I reached a large room below. Like the warehouse I'd raided the day before, the room here was bathed in a soft blue glow, and I found myself staring at several piles of raw celestial steel ore. I stood dumbfounded for a moment. Who had brought all this steel down here? How had they done it? The stockpile was impressive; there wasn't as much as there'd been in the warehouse, but there was enough ore that I could use to make weapons and armor to equip a small army.

I searched the rest of the basement and found more piles of ore, but the most intriguing find came in the final room. There were no ore piles in this chamber. Instead, celestial steel had been used to write a message on one of its walls. The flowing script read;

"Young lady, my eyes have grown dim and my body frail, but I have done what I can for you. I hope you have already discovered how to shape the metal so you will know what to do with it. The road ahead is a difficult one for you, but you must tread it if the apocalypse is to be averted. My house is warded and keyed to you. You are safe here. You may also visit other places in the city where I have placed more wards. I have left you other messages that may prove useful in the

future, but for now you must stop the Tormentor and bring sanity to the banshees. Trust yourself, and the providence that has guided you to this place. Remember this: in your most desperate hour, raise your eyes to the sky to shatter Penn's curse and awaken the Guardians."

At the bottom, the message was singed "Ben".

I stared incredulously at the wall. Could this message truly come from Benjamin Franklin himself? Was this intended for me?

I shook my head trying to clear that dazed feeling you get sometimes when you hear news that is too hard to believe. Since this was Franklin's basement, it seemed plausible that he was responsible for leaving the stores and message behind. A few months ago, I would have said that this was an insane conclusion, indeed impossible, but since becoming a ghost I've seen things that make receiving a personal message from a long dead historical figure seem perfectly normal. The ghosts of Limbo were apparently correct to fear Franklin. He was, indeed, a wizard. But how had he left these things behind here in Limbo? Had he become a ghost as well after his death? Where was he now? Maybe wizards were able to use magic that allowed them to cross into Limbo, granting them the ability to interact with thing on this side. More mysterious to me was the question of how he'd known that a young lady with the celestial steel shaping ability would find his vault. It didn't seem likely that I'd get answers to these puzzling questions any time soon, if at all, so the only thing a practical ghost girl can do is to have faith that she perhaps has friends in high places and to muddle about as best she can.

There was much to ponder in this message. According to Franklin, an apocalypse was coming in the living world and I had to help stop it. This definitely sounded crazy and scared the crap out of me. I'm not freaking Buffy the Vampire Slayer. I'm just a dead girl. How the hell could I save the world? And what the hell was this Tormentor the message said I had to stop?

Whatever it was, it really sounded like something I should stay away from. I know I've now faced demons and all but it's not an experience I want to repeat. I'm a well trained martial artist with a lot of unarmed and blade skills but I'd never intended or wanted to use them to fight supernatural monsters. And that bit about Penn's Curse sounded particularly ominous. I had no idea how to do any of this stuff and more importantly I had no clue about where to begin. For my own sanity, I would stick to my plan of putting an end to my killer's reign of terror and maybe additional information would crop up in the interim.

I stepped up to the wall, and, with my right hand stretched forward, I willed the writing on the wall to reshape itself into a handful of claw like nails. I concentrated on each claw, willing them to slide beneath my own ghostly nails where they could lie in concealment. I expected the process to be uncomfortable, but it wasn't. I know that it was a weird thing to do, but you never know when you might need to have concealed weapons, and Wolverine is so freaking cool. Before leaving the basement, I fashioned a pair of rings and a bracelet which I put on.

I exited my haunt and turned Northward heading for Race Street where the Philadelphia Police Department headquarters was located. I briefly considered translating over to the living world right here at Franklin Court but decided that I wanted to see if the city was still in lock down and what forces had been brought to bear now that they'd had the time for a full mobilization. Whatever I did in the living world, I was always going to have to come back here. Like it or not, Limbo was my home now. I would rather find out on my own terms what the security situation was rather than be surprised later when I was running from trouble.

Buoyed by the knowledge that one of America's founding fathers had prepared the way for me, and not without a little trepidation, I pulled the familiar mist cloak around me and set off to catch my killer.

13

THE CITY HAD INDEED been mobilized. Just a few paces up from Franklin Court, the alley-like Orianna Street crossed Market Street on its northward journey. Market Street is a major thoroughfare in both the living world and in Limbo. A glance both ways down the wide street showed me several patrols of specters moving along the road in both directions East and West. There were specters on guard duty at many of the intersections along Market. Fortunately, I didn't see any reapers, and, with a little care, I was able to get around the patrols and guards who couldn't see through my mist cloak.

I was on Market Street for only a few moments: first crossing it and then moving West along it until I reached 5th Street. I snuck past another guard unit and headed north towards Race Street. The next major intersection that I came to was at Arch Street where I found the situation to be much the same as on Market, though here I did spot a reaper. It was several blocks away from me, moving Westward accompanied by three specters and a darkling. I let them move down several more blocks till the mists hid them from my view; then I hurried across the street. It felt like I was a turtle crossing a highway: I was tense with fear. At any moment the reaper could appear and squash me. I was able to make it across without incident. Moving North once more I passed the US Mint on my right before finally reaching Race Street.

Race Street proved to be quiet. No patrols or guard posts were visible, at least not this close to Franklin Square. The park dominated the blighted neighborhood. A sense of creepy watchfulness permeated the region. I reminded myself that Ben Franklin hadn't actually had anything to do with the park which bore his name. It was renamed in his honor many years after his passing. The Vine Street Expressway loomed in the background, its baleful presence hanging over the neighborhood like a watchful predator.

I decided that I'd seen enough of what was happening in shadow Philly. They were looking for me in force. I suspected that there were many things that I hadn't seen or guessed at, but I didn't need to worry about those now. It was enough that I knew that Limbo was far from a safe place for me. It was going to be hard to move around in the ghost world for a long time to come for me. I reminded myself that I was going to have to pay particular attention to the sky and the rooftops. Though flyers weren't common they did exist. The thought sent a shiver down my ghostly spine, and without further delay I pushed the veil between the living and the dead worlds aside creating a doorway which I quickly passed through. I pulled the misty door closed behind me letting the tension I'd been carrying with me since leaving my haunt out in a great big sigh of relief.

The world beyond was alive with activity and bright with light and life. It was early morning and traffic, both vehicular and pedestrian, was heavy. It felt so good to be home again. It was like a weight was lifted off of my shoulders. I was relatively safe here. Delilah had confirmed my suspicions during my training informing me that Limbo's specters couldn't pass into the living world because of some unknown defect in them. Furthermore, only a small number of darklings were trusted enough to be allowed to make the translation. Avoiding such a relatively small number of ghosts should be easy if I was careful, and even if I was spotted, I had a better than good chance of escaping or fighting them off on this side. I had to be cautious though. Every bit of power that I expended here would force me to return to Limbo that much sooner. I had to conserve my strength so that I could remain on this side until my killer was caught.

I stepped onto Race Street and started heading west toward 8th street where the Roundhouse, Philadelphia's police head-quarters, was located. I walked along Franklin Square pausing long enough to look at a newspaper that was being read by a man waiting at a bus station. The headline on the front page read "Terrorists Blow Themselves Up While Preparing To Attack Undisclosed Targets In City". The picture showed the wreckage of a massive old brick warehouse. I only got to read a few lines before the gentleman turned the page on me, but the basic gist was that things were still under investigation and that the country had dodged a real threat since Homeland Security seemed to have no information on an imminent attack. I briefly considered causing the wind to blow the paper back to the first page despite what the man wanted to read, but I decided that this would be a waste of power especially since I already knew the details better than the journalist did. As I prepared to move on, a picture of a decapitated turtle sculpture caught my atten-tion. The headline read "Fitler Square Sculptures Suffer Horrific Vandalism". The bus arrived as I began to read the article and the man folded up his paper and clambered onto the waiting vehicle, leaving me standing alone on the side walk.

I continued on until I reached 8th Street and the unique building that is the police headquarters in the city. The Roundhouse is by no means old in comparison to many of the city's other landmark buildings but time hasn't been kind to it either. Maintaining the department's facilities is a low priority when compared to the importance of fully funding street operations. Philadelphia is a pretty dangerous city, at least in certain parts. It ranks fifth in the nation in violent crime with over three hundred murders in an average year. Statistics like this forced the mayor to allocate most of the PPD budget into crime prevention and fighting leaving only chump change to spend on capital improvements.

The building got its name from its circular shape and the fact that it looks like a set of handcuffs from an aerial view. Beyond the Roundhouse stretched Chinatown: one of my favorite places in the city. The smells that wafted over me from the nearby neighborhood made me sad. I would never again be able to enjoy pork fried rice, egg rolls, Pork Lo Mein, or any of the other myriad of yummy items on a Chinese menu. Shaking my head sadly, I strode up the front steps of the Roundhouse and passed through the glass doors.

The reception area was large and crowded with people. Three officers manned the glass windows which dominated the far wall. Next to them was a door with a black name plate reading "Employee's Only". I ignored the tumult of this room and went straight for the employee door, phasing through it and finding myself in a short hallway. The floors were carpeted in an industrial grey while the walls and ceiling were painted off-white. There was an open door on my right. The front desk officers were working inside. Straight ahead the hall emptied into a larger room.

I stepped into the reception office and began to search the desks and the nearby walls for a listing of department locations. I found one and noted that homicide was on the second floor. I was about to leave the room when the words "Task Force Banshee" caught my eye. A memo stapled to the wall between two work windows read; "refer all Task Force Banshee calls to the Commissioner's office. This includes all calls directed to task force personnel. All tips are also to be routed to the Commissioner." A list of task force personnel followed. The names Frank Cooper and Wendi Kapudo were among them. I had a sinking feeling in the pit of my stomach as I departed the reception office.

The large room at the end of the hall was, in fact, an atrium bustling with uniformed officers and plain clothed detectives. Small groups of cops congregated here and there or moved with purpose towards one of the many hallways that adjoined the atrium. The room was circular, laden with furniture and snack machines. I considered simply flying up to the second floor but discarded this idea as being too much of an energy drain when other means were available. I went straight for the bank of double elevators that dominated one side of the chamber, joining a group of cops as they stepped into one of the opened elevators. I was momentarily worried that I would be forced to ride the thing up and down until someone picked the second floor, but I need not have worried as several of the officers were heading to the same floor that I was heading to.

As the elevator began its ascent, I began to sink through the floor. I had to concentrate, tethering myself to the elevator in order to rise with it. Ghosts are also subject to some of the laws of natural science. Gravity is one of those forces that we are subject to in both the living world and Limbo. Since I didn't have a physical form and the elevator was defying gravity itself, my natural inclination was to sink through the elevator's floor until I reached the solid earth below. I had to alter my body enough so that it actually gained a physical presence. Delilah called this process "tethering". The physical alteration required for tethering is miniscule: no more than the mass of a grain of sand. I had enough physicality to ride the elevator without passing through it, but it was small enough that I still remained invisible to the passengers.

I got off on the second floor and began to search for the homicide department. It didn't take much time for me to find the unit, but I couldn't find any sign of the two detectives that I was looking for nor was Task Force Banshee to be found. I decided to head up to the third floor. The Commissioner's office was up there. Maybe Task Force Banshee had been assigned to that office.

The administrative floor of the Roundhouse was plush compared to the rest of the building. There were colors, fine furnishings, and the atmosphere felt unhurried. I found the Commissioner's wing easily enough and went straight for his executive assistant's desk. The woman was in her mid to late thirties and very attractive. She was speaking on the phone when I entered her domain; she was apparently discussing a scheduling issue. Her computer screen showed a display of the Commissioner's schedule, and I noticed that a one hour block of time was reserved for "Task Force Banshee Briefing" in the three to four o'clock slot. The time on the computer showed nine-forty-three, so I still had a lot of time to look around. Finding the offices of the task force took more effort, but I finally found myself heading back down to the first floor. I felt relatively confident that I was finally making progress.

Task Force Banshee occupied a block of offices off of the main atrium. It included a half dozen offices surrounding an open area filled with cubicles. There were only two detectives in the vicinity at the moment. I was relieved to see Frank Cooper and Wendi Kapudo sitting at their desks which faced each other. They were speaking softly.

"This is bullshit," Frank cursed angrily waving a hand towards the ceiling. "We were the leads on this case till they got involved, and now we're fucking stuck with nothing but paper work while the trail gets fucking colder and colder. These dumb asses are looking in the wrong fucking direction. Why can't anyone fucking see that?"

"Calm down, someone will hear you," said Wendi looking over her shoulder nervously. Assuring herself that no one was lurking, she went on in a near whisper. "It's that so called outside expert profiler that's mucking everything up. Why they suddenly decided to disregard Geisel's report is beyond me."

"They're all fuckin' idiots if you ask me," Frank snorted with derision. "I've never seen such a piss poor investigation in my fucking life. This case has been fucked from the start."

"Yeah," Wendi agreed pursing her lips pensively. "I thought we had a break with the Kane girl. There were some promising leads, and at least it felt like we were heading in the right direction. Then there was that avalanche of tips and interference from the politicians. It's all a mess now for sure."

"That's a fucking understatement," Frank said "These assholes are looking for a foreign terrorist now. What fucking lunacy. I say we start working on our fucking own. Maybe get Geisel in with us."

"Shhhh …" Wendi waved a hand at Frank. "Do you want to get us fired? Let's go talk over some coffee."

"I don't fuckin' care. As long as this maniac is caught," Frank snarled. "But let's go for a coffee. This fucking place makes me sick."

I watched the two detectives head out. I thought about following them but decided that I would learn little more from them. A foreign terrorist? This sounded very much like Limbo's dark hand manipulating the politicians. It now seemed very likely that Limbo had an agent in this very building. I needed to be extra careful.

A bulletin board filled with newspaper clippings caught my eye. It looked like a good place to start. The articles were arranged in chronological order giving a bird's eye view of the history of the case. It started with the very first murder nearly six months ago. There had been a total of ten murders, including myself. The papers became increasingly critical of the police's inability to catch the killer or prevent girls from being taken. The FBI had joined the case, and the political heat had led to the Commissioner taking a personal role in the investigation. Strangely, a CIA profiler had been brought onto the case according to a recent article.

The most recent article sent a chill down my incorporeal

spine. The headline declared "The Tormentor Strikes Again!" A quick read revealed that the Inquirer had learned details about the way the girls were being murdered from an inside source close to the investigation. According to the source, the girls were tortured in the most brutal of ways. The expertise displayed by the killer and his ability to keep his victims alive for days under the most painful of circumstances had led the editors to give the killer the nickname "The Tormentor". The article went on to reveal that the torture was so severe that most of the girls had permanently damaged their vocal chords as a result of hours of screaming.

By the time that I finished reading the article, I was shaking. This was the fate that that bastard had intended for me. He'd wanted me to scream. This was how the banshee's were being made. The method of my murder had been a mercy. The fact that the papers were calling this mad man the Tormentor could not be a coincidence, especially considering the message left behind in Franklin Court. I had to stop this guy before he made anyone else suffer.

I moved to a second bulletin board that contained photos and profiles of each of the victims. It was surreal to see myself on that board. I studied each photo, memorizing the faces and profiles of each victim. I felt a kinship to these young women. We were sisters now whether we wanted it or not. A great sadness filled me; it was hard to contemplate the lives that had been shattered by our killer. He'd not only caused us pain but he'd caused suffering for all of our families and friends. I felt a sudden burden: a need to help them. I was fortunate enough to have avoided the suffering that they'd endured. I needed to help them somehow. After all, like me they weren't truly dead, at least not their spirits. The screams of the suffering banshees that had been part of the daily life of my recent stay at the Walnut Street Prison now intruded on my thoughts, and I felt guilty that they should remain imprisoned and suffering while I was free. The Tormentor must be stopped before he could add to their number, then I'd find a way to free them along with the shades and together we'd make the evil beings of Limbo pay.

I found the majority of the evidence locked in one of the offices. A thick file for each of the victims was stacked on a table. I spent energy to give my hands a physical presence and began flipping through each file. It was a nightmare. Words cannot accurately describe the horrors perpetrated on the Tormentor's victims, and I guessed that the photos only did a somewhat better job. Each picture was a fresh horror that my mind refused to accept as reality. How could anyone be so evil as to do these things to another person? My killer had broken these women; he'd deconstructed them, destroying their bodies and minds alike. I wept silently and tearlessly as my heart broke for each of the victims. The urge to vomit plagued me as I forced myself to look at each graphic picture. I owed it to my sisters to fully understand the depths to which they'd suffered. A white hot rage began to burn in the pit of my being as time wore on. I couldn't let fear or doubt in myself stop me from fighting against such evil. I spent hours poring through those files before I finally moved on to the other evidence.

I searched through a pile of suspect files hurriedly scanning photos in the hopes of seeing the face that I would never forget. I didn't find him; my killer wasn't among the suspects. The trail was cold and the evidence was practically non-existent. I perused other files finding the profiler reports and read each of them.

Geisel Adams was the profiler traditionally used by the PPD. Her profile had been provided early in the investigation. She predicted that the killer was male, more than six feet tall, and stronger than the average person. She postulated that he would have served in the military and had advanced medical training including surgery and trauma care. The report concluded that the killer wouldn't have a police record, was probably an Ivy League college graduate, was certainly married, and had a fascination with the occult. The report was detailed and outlined specific reasoning behind each prediction.

The second report was by a Norman Netter: no qualifications were presented. I read through this profile with a feeling that I was reading a James Bond novel. It read more like a work of fiction as opposed to Geisel's scientific report. Netter didn't make predictions, he made declarations. His theory was that the killers were a small cell of foreign terrorists. He claimed that the CIA had evidence that Iran had trained selected individuals in the art of cultural terrorism. This new type of soldier would bring urban myth to life, and sow mistrust between the citizens and those who were supposed to protect them. This sheer nonsense went on for a good thirty pages but provided no supportive evidence linking the actual case to the wild theory. Apparently though, the Commissioner and the FBI liaison had bought into this theory hook, line, and sinker. Here again was evidence of Limbo's meddling, and now I could understand Frank Cooper's rage at what was happening.

There was another table stacked with more files. These turned out to be the tip reports. There were thousands of them, and the Commissioner had ordered each one to be investigated and reported on. The officers of Task Force Banshee were being buried in a mountain of paperwork that barely left time for any real investigation. The last file that I found of interest was a report from detective Kapudo stating that her Temple University contact had retranslated the message left at each crime scene; one word was changed from "spirit" to "banshee". Looking back through some additional memos, I found that the Commissioner had named the investigating team Task Force Banshee before Kapudo had made her report. Coincidence? Not likely.

A look at the clock showed me that it was nearly two o'clock. I had been at this for nearly four hours. Members of the task force would be gathering in preparation for the afternoon briefing soon, and chances were good that Limbo's agents would be present. I decided that I had learned all I could here. I was going to have to do the leg work myself. Not bothering with doors, I passed through the walls of the Roundhouse and exited into the sunlit afternoon of Philadelphia. Geisel's report offered me a starting point to begin my search and so I set off to invade the city's many hospitals and medical centers.

14

SEARCHING A CITY THE SIZE of Philadelphia for an individual you only saw briefly once in your life is akin to searching for the proverbial needle in a haystack. I didn't have a name, address, or any other personal information for that matter. All I had to go on was the predictions of a criminal profiler. That, at least, gave me a smaller sand box to search in though Philadelphia has at least a dozen hospitals of various sizes; a couple score if you factor in the medical centers. A number of these hospitals are big enough to qualify as small towns in rural America, and my only chance of finding my killer was to actually see him or spot a picture of him. All in all, it was a ridiculous exercise in futility, but lacking any other means of finding the Tormentor, what's a girl to do?

So I spent a week searching, starting at the Thomas Jefferson University hospital and then moving on to Mercy Philadelphia, Pennsylvania Hospital, St. Christopher's Children's Hospital, Methodist Hospital, and finally Presbyterian. I came up empty. Not a whiff. Discouraged, I returned to my haunt in Limbo to rest and regain power. It wasn't my first trip back to Limbo, I spent an hour each evening recharging, but it was my first time going back to my haunt for a full rest. While I could operate in the living world for days at a time if I was careful with power usage, being away from the energies that sustain me for too long is uncomfortable. The feeling is akin to being trapped under-ground: you might be able to live there if you had the supplies but you'd quickly miss the wind and sun.

I translated back into Limbo right outside Franklin Court. I took a quick look around to make sure no one was watching before I entered the haunt. I decided to sleep in the basement armory behind the protection of the celestial steel door. I awoke from my sleep some time later and quickly exited the house. I checked to make sure no patrols were about and, satisfied that I was unobserved, I translated back into the living world. I started my search at Hahnemann Hospital then went on to Temple University Hospital, followed by Nazareth Hospital, and then Albert Einstein Medical Center. Finally, luck was with me at Northeastern Hospital of Philadelphia.

I was in the human resources office trying to get a look at the personnel files when a young man in an attendant's uni-form marched into the room. The HR employee manning the front desk had been sitting quietly reading a magazine. She sighed, disgruntled at the interruption, and put the magazine down cover side up. It was an issue of Philadelphia Magazine, and there he was, his smiling face featured on the cover. The lead article headline read "Primal Cuts, Philadelphia's Last Slaughterhouse", in smaller letters under the headline the words "James Paul Saunders, entrepreneur and owner shares his secrets to success". I stared at the magazine, stunned. I could have looked for weeks, months, and not gotten a sniff of this guy. I shook myself into action. I quickly searched for an empty office that held a phone book. It didn't take much effort. Once inside, I made my hands corporeal and looked up the address to Primal Cuts. The slaughterhouse was located on Shervood Road in Overbrook Farms in the west of the city.

I left the hospital and headed for the nearest SEPTA station. Overbrook Farms was on the extreme western part of the city. Traveling by train was the fastest way across town, short of going by car of course. It was early afternoon when I arrived at the Overbrook station. The area was an affluent suburb of Philadelphia. The Italianate architecture of the houses was a feature of the historic neighborhood which was also dominated by woodlands. Morris Park occupied its boundary and marked the outer limits of the city itself.

Primal Cuts was located on the eves of Morris Park surrounded by heavy forest. The main building was surprisingly large. The front third of it resembled a grocery store while the back two thirds looked like a factory. There was a zigzagging corral that led from a pen to steel double doors in the side of the main building. A small parking lot was situated at the front of the building while an access lane provided cattle trucks access to the pens in the back. There were several outer buildings on the property, including a barn and several industrial sheds. A small herd of a dozen or so cattle was being herded towards the slaughterhouse as I arrived.

I studied the location for several minutes trying to decide what to do. It seemed likely that Limbo's agents would be watching this place. At the same time, it was unlikely that James Paul Saunders did his other work here. I decided to circle the property to see if I could find any clues. In the back, I found a fairly well used dirt road; it was masked by one of the sheds and the natural brush that grew around the property. Growing excited, I followed the road for nearly a mile before it emptied into a large open space containing an old farmhouse and a barn. A pack of dogs ran about in an enclosure. They were raising holy hell with their incessant barking and growling. As I approached them to get a look at what was agitating them, they suddenly became quiet. I saw that they were all sniffing the air as if they had caught a strange scent. Then one by one they began to howl. I froze in shock. Could they have sensed me? Had they somehow been trained to feel the presence of a ghost and give warning to their master if one was detected? I briefly considered taking action against the beasts to shut them up, but I have a soft spot for dogs. Besides there wasn't enough time to bother with them right now. I had to move quickly.

I searched the interior of the barn but found nothing of interest. Behind it though, I found a foot trail leading into the woods. I followed the faint trail for about two hundred yards where it came to an abrupt end in a hollow. The hollow was surrounded by pines and the ground was covered by a deadfall of leaves and brush. Suspicious I concentrated, pushing the sound of the howling dogs into the background. The woods were strangely quiet here. Then I heard it: a sound muffled by something. It sounded like the hoarse wailing of a girl.

An overwhelming sense of danger suddenly gripped me, and I instantly dropped to the ground and rolled to my left. I felt something pass over head. I instantly sprang to my feet and whirled around while simultaneously drawing my blades. A male darkling was standing over the place I'd just been in a moment ago, its arm was extended and it was holding a devil's iron slave collar ready for my neck. I summoned the wind to grant me speed, and in a mind bending surge I performed three strikes on the attacker. The first was an upward slash of my celestial steel katana that resulted in the darkling's arm being severed and sent flying across the hollow. The second was a thrust of the knife that caught the darkling full in the side at kidney level. The third and final blow was a reverse stroke from my katana that took the darkling's head off. As it crumpled to the ground, its body turned to mist and dissipated.

I glanced around and saw two other darklings approaching me. They moved cautiously and were both armed with devil's iron swords. They stopped about twenty feet away.

"The Master will be pleased with us for bringing you back

home," the one to the right of me said in a baritone voice. "Delilah is very angry with you. You've caused quite a bit of trouble."

Fear clawed at my stomach as I frantically looked around to see if there were others in the woods. I'd killed the first one so quickly that I hadn't had time to even consider what I was do- ing. Now though, I felt deeply exposed and outnumbered. The urge to run was almost overwhelming. Then I heard the hoarse screams of the captive girl.

"You can't take us both, girl," said the other darkling; this one had a nasal pitch to its voice. "Drop your weapon and come with us."

"I'm the girl that's gonna kick your ass!" I roared, suddenly filled with a white hot rage. There was a girl somewhere nearby that was suffering and these things were trying to prevent me from helping her.

The darkling on my right sensed the change in my mood and took a step towards me. I turned to face him and let my rage spew forth in an earsplitting scream. The sonic blast that my scream produced was shocking. Everything in a forty foot cone in front of me was affected, both the physical and ghostly. Trees shattered into splinters, rocks and underbrush were sent sailing through the air or simply crumbled into dust, and the darkling itself was pulverized, disintegrating into mist before it even knew what had happened.

I stared around me in shock at the destruction that I'd caused. The hollow was bare now. Most of the pines that had sheltered it were gone. The brush and debris that had covered it like a carpet had been blown away. In the center of the bowl, an iron door lay, now visible to anyone passing by.

"That's impossible," stammered the last of the darklings. It was staring at me in shock and what I guessed was fear. "You can't be a banshee. You're a poltergeist. Everyone knows that."

"Apparently, everyone's wrong," I said coldly. The mists of Limbo began to churn around the ghost as it prepared to flee back home to report what it had seen. I pushed my will forward and grasped the mists as if they were a physical force. They yielded to my mental touch, and I pushed them away from the darkling effectively shutting him out of Limbo. It stared at me with panic flooding into its eyes. I smiled cruelly and without warning I sprang forward. The wind leant me speed, and I sent its head flying with a single sweeping arc of my blue blade. I paused a moment staring blankly into space. How was I doing the things that I was doing? I shook my head and pushed the thought away. There was no way to answer that right now. The luminary on the ferry had told me to trust myself and that seemed to be the best thing to do right now.

The girl was still screaming. The sound was clearer now that the hollow had been cleared. I briefly considered going down to comfort her, to provide whatever assistance I could, but I decided that the best help I could provide was getting the police here as quick as possible. I couldn't let the Tormentor get away nor could I let this girl die, but being a ghost does limit me in the living world.

15

I RAN BACK TO THE FARMHOUSE YARD. The dogs continued to howl; I ignored them. My thoughts were a jumble as I tried to decide how best to get the PPD to investigate this place. On a whim, I decided to get a quick look inside the house. It was an old two story Dutch Colonial farmstead whose exterior had been well preserved and maintained. The interior had also been preserved, although modern conveniences such as plumbing and electricity had been added. The place was immaculately clean. The furnishings were mostly tasteful wood antiques. Somewhere upstairs, music was blaring. I found pictures of James and his beautiful wife on the mantel over the fireplace. I recalled from the magazine article that her name was Anne. There were apparently no children and no obvious clues as to what had caused James to become a monster. That didn't bother me however; I wasn't here to figure him out. I was here to stop him.

I went upstairs and found Anne Saunders in the bathroom. The years hadn't been kind to her. Her hair had turned grey prematurely, her movements were mechanical, and her stare was vacant. She stood in front of a mirror. Her lips moved as if she were talking to herself, but I couldn't hear anything over the din of the music that was blasting from a room nearby. I saw in her dull, expressionless eyes that she knew what her husband had become. She played the loud music to drown out the sounds of the barking dogs which in turn covered the screams of the tormented girls. For a moment, I felt pity for her. What must it be like to know that someone you love is a monster? Had James changed because of some tragedy, maybe the loss of a child, or had he been this way to start and she'd been blind to it? My thoughts went back to the tormented girls, and my practical Russian heritage pushed aside the pity I felt for Anne. Whatever tragedy had befallen her and her husband, the fact that she did nothing to stop what was going on now made me furious towards her. These young women were someone else's children. How could anyone stand by and let this happen? A part of me realized that she could just as easily be a prisoner, fearful for her own life, but my heart and mind were too angry to accept the weakness that this woman was exhibiting. She could have stopped this, maybe even before I was murdered, and instead she'd allowed herself to be broken. No, I couldn't pity her. I hated her.

Not knowing exactly what I was doing, I walked up to her and stepped into her body. One of the first lessons Delilah had taught me during my training was to avoid going through living people. The body's of living people are occupied by souls, and those souls fight back whenever another spirit tries to occupy the same space. Possessing a living person can only be done by wraiths according to Delilah; all other ghosts experience a violent and disorienting push back whenever they try to enter a space already occupied by another soul. Anne's soul didn't push back very hard, however, and I spent a little energy to maintain my place in her body. Our two spirits grappled for a short moment then, with a sudden surge of power, I thrust her soul from her body.

In that horrible moment I knew that I'd just murdered Anne Saunders. Did it matter that at the moment her soul was wrenched free I'd sensed her enormous relief at being liberated from a life of misery? She was now free of a life of fear and self loathing, and yet it wasn't up to me to decide who should live and who should die. This was the sort of thing that the agents of Limbo did that I wanted to fight against. In my anger at Anne's weakness, I'd allowed myself to become the very thing that I despised; Delilah would applaud my actions if she were here right now to witness them. My thoughts went back to the screaming girl locked away in some underground dungeon. My father had taught me that in war leaders are often forced to make decisions that are less than moral in order to achieve a goal that benefits the greater good. It was right that I felt ashamed about what I'd done to Anne, but if I could use her body to stop James and the Dark Master then the deed would have some practical validity beyond being just an evil act.

The sudden jolt of sensory data that suddenly hit me once I'd assumed control over Anne's body was overwhelming. The music was blaring, intruding on my thoughts. A pain in my lungs told me something was very wrong, and then I remembered to breathe. I gasped, sucking in air and promptly started coughing as I inhaled too much of the fumes from the cleaning agent Anne had been using. My body ached, my hands and knees were stiff, and I felt weak with hunger and exhaustion. This is what it must feel like to get old I thought, suddenly glad that I wouldn't have to worry about that. I realized, with surprise, that I already missed my ghost form. I was very vulnerable in this body.

Shaking my head clear of all the sensations, I forced myself to focus on the task at hand. Turn off the music then find the phone. The music was easy to deal with, but the phone proved to be non-existent. James probably had his own cell phone but didn't trust his wife with one. Great. I was going to have to go find one at a neighbor's or a nearby store. I searched for a set of car keys but once again came up empty handed. Perhaps I'd been too hard on Anne. She'd been a virtual prisoner in her own house. I was going to have to do this the old fashion way; with Anne's two feet.

Anne's body was in poor condition. Running through the woods was arduous and slow. I fell several times, adding new aches to the worn down body. I was terrified that Limbo's agents would find me. I left the sound of howling dogs behind, running through the shadowy woods for what seemed like hours. Just as I began to fear that I'd gotten turned around and lost, I emerged from the forest onto a paved street that I was certain was Sherwood. I ran Northeastward towards a station I'd passed on my way to Primal Cuts. I reached it quicker than I expected and ran inside, gasping for breath.

The attendant and customers looked at me with a mixture of concern and alarm. I imagined what they were seeing: an old woman, out of breath from running, bruised and battered with a look of desperation in her eyes.

"Can I help you?" asked the attendant. "Do you need me to call the police? Is someone chasing you?"

"No, it's ok," I gasped. "Can I use your phone please?"

"Um…sure. Has to be a local call though, ok?"

I nodded my agreement and took the proffered cordless phone.

I called the Roundhouse main line and asked to be transferred to detective Frank Cooper or Wendi Kapudo. I was put on hold for a couple of tense minutes after which a female voice answered.

"This is Wendi, how can I help you?"

I recognized the commissioner's secretary and immediately hung up. I didn't dare bring the cops into this without knowing whose orders they would be following. I was guessing that Limbo would already be working on its cleanup plan. I had to get detectives Cooper and Kapudo over here. Grasping for straws, I asked the cashier for a phone book and hurriedly looked up the number for Temple University's theology department. I dialed the listed number and asked for a transfer to Dr. Kapudo's office. Among the evidence I'd viewed at the Roundhouse earlier were translations of the Tormentor's writing provided by Dr. Kapudo of Temple University. I recalled the conversation that Frank and Wendi had about her dad during their investigation of my murder. I was desperately hoping that he'd be able to get a message to his daughter without raising suspicion. As the phone rang, I silently prayed that he would be there.

"Hello," answered a quiet, commanding voice.

"Dr. Kapudo?"

"Speaking, what can I do for you?"

"My name is Anne Saunders," I answered. "My husband is James Paul Saunders, owner of Primal Cuts. He's also the man who has been abducting young women and torturing them to death."

There was a sharp intake of breath followed by a long pause.

"This is not funny, young lady. It's not a matter to joke about," he finally answered angrily.

"I'm sorry Dr. Kapudo, but I've never been more serious," I replied. "I'm calling you because I was hoping you might be able to get through to detectives Frank Cooper and Wendi Kapudo without having to go through the Commissioner's office. I tried calling your daughter but was routed up the chain. I don't trust that chain."

Silence for a long moment.

"You're serious?" He asked incredulously.

"Very. Can you get to your daughter fast, outside of normal channels?"

"Yes," was the simple reply.

"Then tell them to go to Primal Cuts immediately. They should only call for backup when they get into the Overbrook area. They'll find a dirt access road behind the middle shed in the back of the slaughterhouse yard. It goes to an old farmhouse about a mile into the woods. He's got a dozen or so dogs in a pen. His lair is in the woods behind the barn. They'll find a path that goes a couple hundred yards to a hollow where an iron door leads into the dungeon. He's got a girl down there right now, so tell them to hurry."

"I will," Dr. Kapudo answered tightly. "Where will they find you?"

"I'll be at the Stuart's on Sherwood Road. Please hurry. I think he knows that I left."

"I'll pray for you. Thanks for your help," he hung up the phone.

I sighed and prayed that the old theologian would be able to get through to his daughter. I returned the phone to the attendant and asked for the bathroom key. Once inside, I locked the door and went into a stall. I took one final breath and cut the tether holding me to the body. I slid out of Anna's former shell and looked back at the now lifeless corpse. Anne Saunders had died almost an hour ago at the moment I'd expelled her soul and taken its place.

I left Anne's body locked in the bathroom and, passing through the station's walls, felt glad to be my ghostly self again. I headed back towards Primal Cuts to provide whatever assistance I could give to the police.

16

THE RETURN JOURNEY TO Saunders's farm was much swifter than the trip out. Aided by the wind and my ghostly form's ability to pass through trees and underbrush as if they weren't even there, it was a matter of two minutes rather than the half hour or so that it had taken in Anne's body. It was eerily quiet as I circled the property, sticking to the wood line for cover.

The dog's had stopped their howling and lay about their pen; they obviously remained alert however. I stayed as far away from them as I could manage as I made my way around to the back of the barn. Fortunately, they didn't notice me. Instead of following the trail directly to the hollow, I went deeper into the forest and came into it from the opposite direction of the path. I saw nothing. All was quiet except for the continued wailing of James's current victim. A quick look around the hollow showed it to be in the same condition as I'd left it in. There were no signs of anyone having come here since I'd left more than an hour ago.

I was about to descend into the earth to see what I could do for the tormented girl below when the sound of sirens caught my attention. I cursed and sped back towards the farmyard. The dogs were barking again, and I discovered that they'd been let loose. A glance up the access road towards Primal Cuts revealed two pick-up trucks blocking the way into the yard. Two police cruisers were approaching the vehicular barricade; they were closely followed by an unmarked car. I sped towards the scene, keeping to the tree line and watching for any signs of Limbo's agents.

The police pulled their vehicles to a stop and exited their cars with pistols drawn. The situation was very tense as detective Cooper slid out of his vehicle and took up a defensive position behind it.

"I gave orders for no fucking sirens! Why the hell did you turn them on?" he shouted furiously to one of the uniformed cops.

"Sorry sir, but we got orders in from HQ. A direct call sir; they told us to turn on the sirens."

"Son of a bitch," Frank swore. "What else did they order?"

"Just that we were to wait till the Commissioner arrived on scene before taking any action."

I saw James Paul Saunders crouching behind one of the trucks. A man in a tailored suit stood at his side, and several other rough looking men crouched nervously nearby. Emotions threaten to overwhelm me at the sight of my killer. Chief among them was rage. I so badly wanted to destroy him. That sonic power I'd used on the darklings in the hollow earlier would tear him and his friends up quite nicely I speculated. I'd already crossed the line today though; if I wasn't careful I'd become the very monster that I was fighting against and that Limbo wanted me to become. I had to leave this in the hands of the police.

"What can I do for you, officers?" the man in the tailored suit called out.

"Move those fucking trucks aside," Frank shouted back. "We're here to search the premises."

"Do you have a warrant detective Cooper?"

"Who the hell are you?" asked Cooper. "We have probable cause to search the premises."

"I'm Herald Ikes, Mr. Saunders's attorney," answered the lawyer. "What is the nature of this probable cause?"

Before Frank could answer two more cars came roaring up the access way: a BMW and a dark sedan. The suits that poured out of the BMW were led by the commissioner, while the suits that exited the sedan were clearly FBI.

"What the hell is going on here Cooper?" roared the Commissioner. "I didn't authorize any Task Force Banshee actions."

Detective Cooper threw up his hands in frustration as he turned to face the commissioner.

"Sir, we got a tip that James Paul Saunders is the serial murderer and that he has a girl on the property."

"It's impossible that you got a tip, all tips come to my office first and we didn't get any tips!" the commissioner shouted, his face growing redder and redder with each moment. "That is unless some of my men are working outside the chain of command. I would be surprised to hear of such a thing about Philadelphia's finest."

"Sir …"Frank began but was interrupted by the arrival of two new vehicles as they roared up the lane. The lead car was a Ford Focus driven by Wendi Kapudo. The second was a Channel 34 WCAU-TV news van. Wendi brought her car to a screeching halt and jumped out waving a folded sheet of paper over her head.

"I've got the warrant here," she shouted.

"What the hell is this?" roared the Commissioner. "I didn't authorize any of this. Cooper, Kapudo, I'm suspending both of you for insubordination pending an investigation into this matter."

"Sir," Frank answered angrily. "Would you like to explain to channel 34 news why you are failing to execute a duly authorized warrant of the court? There is probable cause to suspect that

James Paul Saunders is the Tormentor and that he has a living victim on his property right now."

The camera's turned their glaring lights on the Commissioner.

"Is this true Commissioner?" asked Danna Harris, veteran reporter for WCAU. "Our sources tell us that the tip came from Mr. Saunders's own wife, Anne Saunders. Is this true?"

"We're going to sue you for libel, detective Cooper!" shouted James Paul Saunders's attorney. "These allegations are false. Mr. Saunders is an upstanding citizen of this community."

"Anne Saunders," spluttered the Commissioner. "She's crazy. You can't believe anything she says."

There was a moment of stunned silence at the Commissioners outburst.

"Do you know Anne Saunders Commissioner?" asked Danna. She looked like a shark circling its prey. "How do you know the Saunders family? Are they campaign contributors?"

"We don't have fucking time for this shit," detective Cooper roared. "We've got a search warrant and by god we're going to fucking tear this place apart till we find that girl."

The attack came suddenly, without any warning. I felt them come in a wave of cold energy. A large pack of dogs glided through the forest on both sides of the lane. There was something different about them now; they felt evil. I glimpsed one as it sprang forward and saw that its eyes glowed red. I realized with horror that Limbo's agents had taken possession of the pack of dogs from Saunders's farm turning them into physical killing machines.

Without thinking about it, I sprang into action sending a blast of wind into a Rottweiler that had leaped for detective Kapudo's throat. The blast sent it careening through the air. Its flight ended with a sickening crunch of breaking bones as it struck a nearby tree. All around me there were shouts of terror and screams of pain as the dogs went for the police. The Commissioner ran for his car and the dogs ignored him. The FBI agents had their guns out and were shooting, but their shots only succeeded in slowing the beasts down. The WCAU camera man was down. A German Shepherd was on him, tearing at his throat. Danna Haris was backed against the news van, a yellow lab menacing her. A loud boom and the unfortunate dog's head exploded in a shower of bone and brain matter. I turned and saw Frank Cooper standing a few feet away. He turned from the dead lab and leveled his massive Desert Eagle fifty caliber pistol at a new target. I assisted in the kill by destroying the now freed darkling with a single stroke of my sword.

"Shoot them in the fucking head," bellowed Cooper over the din.

I accompanied him as he strode through the battlefield leaving headless dogs in his wake. I kept the possessed creatures off of him with wind blasts and finished off the darklings within them with my blades. Frank's Desert Eagle and my katana proved too much for Limbo's forces and we soon had the area cleared.

I surveyed the carnage around me and felt sorrow for all the dogs that had been killed. I'm a dog person. Just as heart wrenching were the deaths of two uniformed officers, along with an FBI agent, and the television camera man. Sirens were once again blaring in the distance.

"Wendi," detective Cooper broke the stunned silence that followed. "Take charge of things here. I'm gonna take Ted and Bill up to the place we were told about."

"Wait for backup Frank," Wendi pleaded. "It's too dangerous to go without as many men as we can get."

"I'll be fucking careful Wendi," said Frank with determination. "But Saunders has fled the scene. I'm not gonna give him a fucking chance to kill again. Come on boys."

17

I FOLLOWED FRANK COOPER and the two officers accompanying him around the barricade of vehicles and into the farmyard beyond. Frank went straight around the barn and quickly found the path behind it. I was glad to see that Dr. Kapudo had relayed all of my information accurately. The two cops accompanying us fanned out to the left and right of the trail, flanking detective Cooper. They all had their weapons drawn, carried barrel pointing down.

We found James Paul Saunders in the hollow. He was desperately trying to raise the iron door, but it appeared that my sonic blast of the area had damaged it, making it impossible for one man to open it.

"Hold it right fucking there, Saunders," Frank growled pointing his massive revolver at James's back. "You are under arrest. You have the right to remain silent. Anything you say can and will be used against you in a court of law. You have the right to an attorney. If you can't afford an attorney, one will be provided for you. Do you understand?"

Silence.

"Go fucking cuff him Ted."

Ted moved forward cautiously, his pistol pointed at Saunders.

"Put your hands up slowly," Ted ordered. James complied. His whole body shook as if he were laughing. "Now kneel down and place your hands behind your head."

Ted cuffed and then patted Saunders down, finding several small knives and other tools presumably of the butcher's trade. Ted then turned him around to face Frank.

"Put him over there and keep a close fucking eye on him. Bill and I will try to get that fucking door open."

James looked right past Frank, directly at me.

"I see you," he said with a chuckle. There was a mad gleam in his eyes. "The one that got away. The Master has promised that you'll be mine."

I went cold all over and looked around nervously.

"What the hell is he talking about? What's he looking at?" Bill asked also looking around with trepidation.

"He's a fucking lunatic. Who cares about what he's talking about?" Frank answered in exasperation. "He's just practicing his fucking insanity defense."

Frank and Bill moved over to the iron door and worked on trying to get it open. Ted had Saunders lying on his face, hands cuffed behind his back, a few feet away. Suddenly, Frank began to curse and redouble his efforts to get the door open but to no avail.

"Jesus, I fucking hear her down there!" Frank cried in desperation. "We're coming Katie! It's the police. We're here to help you. Just a few more minutes!"

He grabbed his radio and put it to his mouth. "Wendi, do you copy?"

"Copy Frank, what's your status?"

"We've got Saunders in custody. There's a girl here, but we can't get through the iron door. Get some cutting and digging tools up here quickly."

"Ten-four, backup's on the way. We'll have the tools there shortly."

"Faster than fucking shortly," Frank said in a haunted voice. "She's screaming."

"Understood," Wendi answered sympathetically.

True to her word, the hollow was filled with police within minutes. Tools didn't prove to be necessary as a half dozen officers forced the doors open. Their intense desire to rescue the girl trapped below imbued them with the combined strength to force the damaged doorway open.

Cooper led a team of officers into the cellar that now yawned darkly at the center of the hollow. Their weapons were drawn, flashlights piercing the blackness. It was only a few moments before the first cries of horror came up from the darkness accompanied by the sound of vomiting.

"Get him out of here," detective Cooper's voice was heard rising from the depths. "And get the paramedics down here now. It's ok honey. We're gonna help you."

The girl's hoarse screaming continued to vibrate throughout the vale.

Two officers emerged from the dungeon and promptly fell to their knees retching. A team of paramedics went down joined by some other officers including detective Kapudo. One of the paramedics and most of the uniformed officers retreated back to the surface looking ill. The looks of murderous rage the officers aimed at Saunders told the story. The killer was back on his feet, an officer on either side of him, and he returned their glares with a knowing smile that further enraged them and raised the tension in the hollow. I wanted to go down to see what I could do, but I didn't think Saunders was as secure as he appeared to be. I couldn't sense or see any other ghosts around, but Saunders' ability to see me made me uneasy. I didn't dare to let him out of my sight.

It was a good half hour before the paramedics emerged with a stretcher between them. Detectives Cooper and Kapudo followed in their wake. The figure on the stretcher was barely recognizable as a human being. Her ears, nose, and eyes had been mutilated so that pits were all that remained. One leg and one arm were gone. The fingers and toes of her remaining appendages had also been severed. I knew from my viewing of the police photos at the Roundhouse that Saunders severed the body parts starting from the smallest and going to the largest. The sight of his latest victim made me want to vomit, and I had to turn away. A low moan continued to rise from her though I was certain they'd sedated her. I felt sorry for the girl. She would be the only victim of the Tormentor to survive. It seemed to me that the rest of us had gotten the better deal. Living with fear and the weakness of a ruined mortal body seemed like a further torment. I had gotten the best deal of all though. I'd better make it count.

I looked at James Paul Saunders and felt satisfaction; at least I'd done some good here. As if sensing my proud scrutiny of him, he turned his head and stared at me. A wide smile spread across his face as our eyes locked.

"The hour of reckoning is at hand Veronika."

The moment he said my name, I sensed the presence of an entity of overwhelming evilness. I knew that it hadn't just appeared but had in fact been there for some time, watching and waiting for this moment. I don't know how it could have masked itself so completely from my senses, but seeing as how I can do the same with my mist cloak it shouldn't have come as a surprise that other powerful ghosts would have similar tricks up their sleeves. I tried to react, but I was fatigued. Most of my power had been drained when I'd possessed Anne and during the battle with the darkling dogs. Consequently, I moved too slowly to avoid the hand that yanked me by the hair and snapped a devil's iron collar around my neck. I tried to draw my blades, but the sudden agony produced by the collar drove me to my knees. Hands grabbed me from all around, pinning me to the ground. My blades were ripped away followed by all the other celestial steel jewelry and weapons that I wore. The darklings poured over me in rage, punching, kicking, and taunting me. None of it compared to the agony of the slave collar though.

They kept the agony going for what seemed like hours, until finally I was dragged to my feet. Delilah was standing in front of me; a smile playing across her hauntingly beautiful face.

"Do you remember what I promised you if you ran?" She purred.

I nodded, trying to clear my head. I was so tired, and everything hurt so much.

"Well, it's going to be even worse than I promised," She said icily.

"Pissed off eh?" I said trying to muster up some bravado. How had they hidden their presence from me so completely? "I messed up your plans. You must have been in the dog house for a while. They have you on a leash now I bet."

"You think this is funny," she growled. "Let's see if you're still laughing a few minutes from now."

Rough hands turned me around so that I was looking back into the hollow. The paramedics were loading the stretcher into the ambulance while forensic teams were going down into the dungeon of horrors. Saunders was still in the same place looking straight at me. His captors were ignoring him. A cloud of black mist flowed into the hollow. This was the utterly evil entity that I'd sensed. Its only feature was a pair of fiery, glowing eyes. It glared at me for a moment and then slammed into Officer Ted White.

"No!" I cried out, suddenly knowing what was about to happen.

Ted's soul was violently cast from his body, and the mists of Limbo gathered around it, holding it till the harvesters came to claim it. Ted's body, now possessed by what could only be a wraith, probably the very Master of shadow Philadelphia, drew the pistol from his holster and shot James Paul Saunders between the eyes at point blank range. The hollow exploded into chaos as officers dove for cover and drew their own weapons. Possessed Ted killed two cops before his colleagues were forced to kill him. James Paul Saunders had died instantly, a smile of victory plastered across his face.

A skeletal thing with glowing red eyes stood above Saunders's bloody corpse.

"Welcome home, Tormentor," Delilah said to it. "Our Master wishes you to know that you have performed a great service for him, and that your place in his realm is assured."

I stared in horror as a darkling brought a black robe to the new ghost. I was watching the birth of a reaper: the one they called the Tormentor. Had my desire for vengeance made things worse? Was I responsible for the creation of something more dangerous than a serial killer?

"We will bring you to a place where you can rest and gain strength," Delilah told the Tormentor. "When you are ready, you will be able to play with our Master's first gift to you."

Delilah waved a hand in my direction, and I was pushed forward by darklings to stand before the new reaper. Its glowing eyes fell on me. The gaze was hungry and filled me with dread.

"The one who got away is yours, as promised," Delilah said. "You are tired my lord. A servant will guide you to your new haunt where you can rest. Your gift will be delivered to you soon."

A darkling stepped beside the Tormentor and the mists of Limbo billowed around the two and they vanished from the living world.

Delilah turned back to me with satisfaction on her face. "But before you are given into his custody you are mine to punish, and I will make you pay for your betrayal."

The collar began to pulse once more and agony filled my whole being. The mists of Limbo descended on me and the claws of specters ripped into me as they pulled me into the world of ghosts. Delilah let them play with me and I soon lost consciousness.

18

I'M NOT SURE HOW LONG the torture lasted. It was at least a few weeks if not a few months. I was kept on the edge of consciousness for most of it, and though I often passed out from the sheer agony, I was never allowed to rest long enough to gain any strength. My tormentors didn't have to worry about me bleeding out or dying from the sheer shock caused by the intense pain they caused me. They were free to inflict whatever indignities and torments they could imagine without fear of losing me. Delilah oversaw the entire process.

I was held in a room made entirely of devil's iron and my captors used tools made of the malignant ore. At various times they kept me in an iron maiden for hours on end, the devil's iron pressing against my ghostly skin in a claustrophobia caus-ing grip that sent shivers of terror down my spine. I could think of no fate worse than being left inside that cold prison for all eternity. Being removed from the thing to undergo fresh new torments was almost a relief. Pain has a finite quality to it. If you endure it long enough you'll be surprised at your ability to block it out. It becomes a background noise. Not so with the iron maiden; its power is over the mind. Its torment consists of the primal fear of loneliness and loss of the most basic of freedoms: the ability to move. Add to that the fact that the horrendous thing was made entirely of devil's iron, its touch seemed to suck energy out of me and replace it with a filthy essence which surely came from the pit of hell itself. When I drifted into a near unconscious stupor, my mind was filled with nightmares. In these dreams I stalked the nights of Philadelphia kidnapping young boys and tormenting them for my own base pleasures. Wakefulness in the maiden was worse; I heard voices whispering to me telling me to let go, to give in to my dark passions. Sometimes I would feel hot and gnarled hands groping me; they tickled, fondled, caressed, pinched, and slapped me. And always there was the smell, as of rotting eggs. While in the maiden these horrors clawed at me every waking moment; I was in a constant war to maintain my sanity and to hold off soul numbing corruption.

My existence outside of the iron maiden was no less wretched. Delilah personally cut off my ears, nose, and plucked out my eyes one day before giving me over to the aptly named Freak. She sang *Mary Had A Little Lamb* and other nursery rhymes while doing it, giggling to herself at every moan and scream that escaped my lips. Being blinded was a whole new terror; was I ever going to see again? And Freak with his deformed and greasy body parts defiled me in ways that I could never have imagined all the while whispering to me about how much he liked my cherry. The humiliation was soul shattering. Thankfully, ghosts regenerate, and our bodies heal unusually fast, though in my case the iron maiden slowed down the healing process. Of course, the down side to this was that Delilah was able to inflict this torture on me several times during the weeks that I spent in her clutches. My eyes, ears, and nose eventually grew back, but the damage I suffered from Freak's attentions stained my very being to its core. I told myself that I was a ghost, that what was happening to me was practically just make believe, not real, but in the end rape of any kind is soul damaging.

The torture continued with Delilah inventing worse horrors than the ones that went before. She pealed the top layer of my ghostly skin off. Sometime after that, I was given over to a gang of darklings for their own amusement. They taunted me by leaving the door to the cell wide open and daring me to run for it. I was too weak physically and emotionally to try anything daring at this point. They laughed at me, beat me and had their filthy way with me. For a time, I wished for nothing more than to be really dead. I told myself that I was used up trash now unworthy of love; I gave up, but Delilah didn't. And so it went on and on until one day my self loathing gave way to burning hatred. I'm not sure what caused the change; I was only aware of a growing sense of heat from the pit of my stomach. It was like I was being remade into something new. I reached out for that ball of heat like a drowning person reaching for a lifeline. Hate is a negative emotion that is bad for the psyche, but when you have little else to live for, it is a powerful lifeline motivator. Hate is what allowed me to endure the torture, it is what allowed me to bide my time and plan for both my escape and eventual revenge.

I was once more being placed in the ghastly iron maiden after a long day of fresh torments. I was becoming numb to the attentions of the specters and darklings that Delilah directed at me. They were running out of fresh ideas and I was becoming desensitized to the pain they were inflicting. Only the collar really hurt anymore; I could even endure Freak's attentions by imagining what I'd do to him when I got free. I tried to behave as I had before, screaming and cringing, but I saw in Delilah's eyes that she knew the torments were having less affect on me now. She remained confident and pleased with herself though. Like a sated cat that has had its fill, she seemed eager to get on to other things. She stepped up to me after I'd been crammed into the tight confines of the iron maiden. Its shell closed and locked tight around me. She gazed into my eyes, which were the only visible parts of me.

"This is the last time that I will see you," she purred. "Tomorrow I return to my real work for the Master. You will remain here for all eternity, removed from this thing only when the Tormentor wishes to play with you. I'm sure he will come for you tomorrow. As a matter of fact, I'd like to thank you for assisting us in his creation."

I stared back at her defiantly for a moment then I let tears well up in my eyes. I pushed forward the terror, humiliation, and self loathing that had become my constant companions these past few weeks and let them show in my eyes. I had to make her believe that my defiance was just a facade, that she'd truly nearly broken me.

"Please," I croaked, "I'm … sorry. Please give me another chance."

"You have been the subject of much debate in the Masters council chamber. Most of the reapers want you destroyed outright." She cocked her head at me, a troubled look crossing her features. "If I didn't know better, I'd think they were afraid of you. If they could see you now, they'd see how pathetic you are and how foolish their fears are. You are lucky that the Master made a promise to the Tormentor. He has, however, been ordered to discover what you are. You are a mystery to us: something that should not be. I'd imagine that the Tormentor's methods will not be pleasant. He has a skill for torture never before seen in all of Limbo. I wish you all the suffering you deserve."

I shouted out to her in desperation as she turned away from me and headed for the door. She ignored my pitiable cries, opened the devil's iron door, shot me a disgusted look over her shoulder, and stepped beyond my view. The door clanged shut with a metallic boom of finality. I sighed in relief, letting the hatred flow back to the surface. Yes, I was filled with terror and self loathing but the hatred was king now. I began to concentrate, pushing my will inward towards the bits of celestial steel, the

Wolverine claws, that I'd hidden in my body back at Franklin's Court the day I'd set out to capture my killer what seemed ages ago now. My mind found the bits of celestial steel, and I bathed in the healing aura of its power. I'd feared that all of the devil's iron surrounding me would interfere with the metal's properties, but I guess that my affinity for it and its presence within my body was enough to overcome this. Slowly, the aches and pains slid from my body and power began to flow back into me. I'd resisted the urge to tap into the celestial steel earlier for fear that it would be discovered before I was ready, but now was likely my last chance to escape. I'd barely avoided discovery when Delilah had flayed me. I couldn't count on my luck with the Tormentor, not to mention that sticking around for his attentions was not an option if there was any chance of pulling off an escape now. I was relying on the fact that I'd shown no ability to escape and on my acting skills, hence the pleading cries. I soaked in the steels energy for several hours, but I dared not take the time I needed to fully recharge. I only needed enough power to aid in my escape.

I reluctantly withdrew from the healing trance and took a deep breath. I wasn't sure if my plan would work, and I knew that even if it did, I would have very little time to make my escape. There was no way to do this quietly, at least none that I knew of. The devil's iron around me prevented translation into the living world, and there wasn't enough celestial steel inside of me to cut through the iron maiden that held me captive. I was going to have to use the only weapon in my arsenal that was truly destructive. I wasn't sure if devil's iron could withstand the banshee's wail but I was about to find out.

I took a deep breath, gathered in my hate and let loose with a scream that made the room shiver. The front shell of the iron maiden was blown off and shattered into fragments before it could hit the opposite wall. I was elated as I stepped out of the ancient torture device; the destructive force of my screams pretty much confirmed that I had the powers of a banshee. My elation at having freed myself slipped, however, as I suddenly stumbled and nearly fell to the floor. A wave of dizziness and fatigue washed over me. The bits of celestial steel that I'd used to heal myself couldn't erase weeks of torture and the soul draining effects of the iron maiden. I was horribly weak. Frustration and anger threatened to overwhelm me, but I calmed myself and instinctively channeled that raw energy into fuel that could keep me going for a time. It was like a jolt of adrenalin. I immediately felt stronger and more sure of myself, but I knew that this wouldn't last long; I had to hurry.

As I prepared to leave I found that I was still naked; I'd been forced to be in this state throughout my captivity in order to degrade me. A single thought was all that was needed and I was once more clothed in jeans, a black tank, and black high top sneakers. I called on the celestial steel in my body and it sprang outward from my fingers in a display of six inch claws. I moved to the door and unleashed the banshee's wail once more, and the red iron portal flew outward in a destructive shower of shrapnel. Two specters responding to the commotion from my cell were caught in the blast. Both my shriek and the devil's iron shrapnel from the door shredded them into oblivion. The cool thing about the banshee scream is that it seems to use relatively small amounts of power considering its destructive force. This was probably because a large part of the power came from within instead of from Limbo's negative energies. Rage and hate were the fuel behind the might of the banshee scream; I had both in spades right now.

I had no idea where I was, though it seemed likely that they'd taken me back to the Walnut Street Prison. I took a left after exiting my cell and headed down an empty corridor that was lined with empty cells on either side. A sudden sharp pain around my neck reminded me that I'd made a terrible mistake. Fortunately the celestial steel that I was wielding lessened the collars effects. Gritting my teeth against the growing agony, I raised a single clawed hand and, with a savage gesture, severed the collar. It is extremely fortunate for me that the collars are rather delicate otherwise I would have needed a better cutting implement than long claws. The pain ended abruptly as the collar fell to the floor. I looked up to see a darkling standing at the end of the hall looking at me in consternation.

I called upon the wind for speed and before the darkling could raise its weapon, I was upon it. My blue steel claws flashed in an arc that caught it below the chin and sliced upward through the skull, splitting its head in half. The darkling tumbled to the ground, its head dangling in two pieces on either shoulder. Then it turned to mist and dissipated leaving me alone in the corridor.

I was standing at the intersection of two corridors. A deep booming alarm was just beginning to reverberate through the building. I heard the sound of growls and dog like barks as more specters appeared at the end of the hall that I was standing in. A look back the way I'd come showed me more coming from around another intersection just passed my blown out cell. I was effectively trapped. No way could I risk a full on battle here where the enemy had endless reinforcements at its disposal. The only thing to do now was to flee.

I took a deep breath and faced the nearest outer wall, focused my desperate emotions, and let loose with an earth shattering shriek. The outer wall was blown out in a violent surge of sonic force that left a ten foot hole gaping in the side of the Walnut Street Prison. The force of my rage shook the building and left me momentarily stunned as I stared into the daylight mists of shadow Philly. A quick glance towards the oncoming specters showed me that they had also been stunned by what they'd witnessed. They now moved towards me cautiously with the fear of my destructive power evident in their reluctant movements. A reaper appeared behind them and whatever fear they had of me vanished in the face of its rage. They sprang towards me with renewed vigor. I turned back towards the gaping hole in the building, and, calling forth the wind, I leaped into the air and flew from the grounds of the Walnut Street Prison.

I called upon all of my power reserves to give me extra speed, and I flew through the skies of Philadelphia at break neck speeds pursued by a half dozen darklings who'd apparently been stationed on the roof of the prison. I stayed at roof top level, swerving in and around buildings and making as many turns as I could to evade my pursuers. Unlike the living city, shadow Philly boasted only one skyscraper taller than City Hall, the infamous One Liberty.

Only one of the darkling hunters came close to catching me. It surprised me when I whipped around a corner. It was hovering in place waiting for me. As soon as I made the blind turn, its devil's iron blade was swinging at my head. It misjudged my speed however, and I was able to avoid a killing blow by angling my body in such a way that the attack fell on my left shoulder rather than severing my head. The pain from the blow was barely noticeable to me as such wounds had been a daily occurrence for me during the past few weeks. The darkling wasn't so lucky though. I shot straight upward about ten feet, somersaulted, and dived at the surprised darkling with my arms outstretched and claws fully extended. The impact barely slowed me as I pushed the impaled darkling several dozen feet before it dissipated into mist.

I was really beginning to feel fatigued as I sped through South Philadelphia and then banked back towards Center City. My pursuers were still on my heels. The massive statue of William Penn perched on the top of City Hall attracted my attention, and I flew straight for it. The darklings broke off the chase, instead fanning out in an arc around the landmark. They kept their distance from it. I landed on the statues brimmed hat and took a moment to catch my breath. Hey, even ghosts get winded, just not in the same way as the living.

I quickly took stock of my situation and found it to be grim indeed. I didn't have enough juice left for more than a short flight, and my options for evading the darkling flyers were practically nonexistent. I briefly considered using the mist cloak to try to get away, but I discarded this idea as it would result in me revealing an ability they certainly didn't know I had. I looked down at the statue below my feet and decided that entering City Hall below me would at least give me a place to rest. As if sensing my thoughts and gaining a measure of confidence from the fact that I hadn't been destroyed by the statue, the darklings began to move towards me. A soft rumble began to build from deep within the statue and the darklings paused in uncertainty. I smiled as I felt a sudden surge of raw power. Bolts of lightning suddenly began to lash out in a wild circle around the statue. I stared in awe as the bolts struck and obliterated every darkling in the vicinity. The attack lasted less than a minute and the rumbling within the statue subsided. I silently thanked old Ben for his wards and for attuning me to them though it still astounded me that he could have pulled off such a feat without meeting me. I could sense a lurking power just below the statue's surface, but exploring any further at this point didn't seem like a good idea. I was badly in need of rest, and I needed to disappear. Not wasting any further time, I wrapped myself in a mist cloak and flew the few blocks to my haunt at Franklin Court.

I landed on a nearby building overlooking my haunt and watched the house and street nearby for a dozen minutes. I saw patrols pass by on the nearby Market Street, but as usual Limbo's forces avoid places associated with Franklin. Finally satisfied that my haunt was unwatched, I used the last of my strength to approach the house. Once inside I searched the whole building checking for any signs that an intruder had visited. Everything seemed undisturbed, and I proceeded to the armory where I collapsed into a bed of celestial steel and fell into an immediate and deep sleep.

19

I AWOKE SLOWLY. My thoughts were in a jumble, but my body felt better. My power levels were fully restored. I guessed that a few days had passed since my escape, but I had no real way of confirming this short of asking someone. Part of me just wanted to stay right here where it was safe. I stared at the ceiling and wished that I could go back to sleep. Eternal oblivion seemed preferable to a life of fear and torment. Freak's crazed features haunted me, and I couldn't shake the feel of uncleanness that seemed to soak deep into my soul.

Thoughts of the other banshees still held at the Walnut Street Prison began to intrude upon my self absorption. What horrors were they undergoing still? And the shades, what about them? The luminary bound to the ferry was also a victim. How could I lay here doing nothing? I was but one victim of thousands. The difference between me and them was that I was free. I had to use that freedom and my extraordinary power to help the others achieve liberty. I couldn't allow vengeance to cloud my judgment anymore. My real enemy wasn't the Tormentor or the

Master, it was the system. The system is what allowed monsters like Delilah and the Tormentor to do what they did. The system is what allowed slavery and turned evil into a virtue. It was the system that had to be dismantled.

Alone in my haunt, I was assailed by a deep depression that threatened to keep me immobilized in fear and self loathing. I knew that dad would be disappointed in me for being so weak. How could I face the world after letting myself be violated? A part of me knew that this line of thought was ridiculous; what had been done to me wasn't my fault, but my emotions were so raw that blaming myself for everything seemed like the only way to make sense of the utter loneliness that filled me. I had no one to talk too; no one to hold me; no one to tell me it would be alright. So I wept and wrapped myself in a blanket of celestial steel that I'd fashioned from the raw ore that lay about me, and I tried to hide from the world, from everything. Eventually though, the celestial steel's healing power began to work on my soul. It was a subtle change: a sense of peace and warm comfort allowed me to fall into a dreamless slumber. When I awoke again, it was like I'd been washed clean, and a strange new warmth filled the place near where my heart was. Weeping was replaced by quiet humming and then song. I bathed in the celestial steel, and it not only healed my ghostly body but also my soul. What had happened to me wasn't gone or forgotten, but I no longer loathed myself. I'd faced ultimate evil, and it had tried to break me; it had failed. At times white hot hatred tried to overcome me, but the new warmth near my heart reminded me to not give into my darker passions. I quashed this feeling as best as I could. Delilah wanted me to be a monster. Letting hatred consume me was a sure fire way of giving her complete victory over me. At the end of the day, it was the celestial steel that brought the healing power of song back into my soul, and song is what I used to combat depression and other negative emotions that tried to keep me still and inactive.

When I rose from my days long repose, I rose as something new. I was still Veronika Kane, but I was forged in the fires of suffering and that changed me forever. I now knew down deep that being a ghost didn't protect me from unimaginable torment. Though I no longer had a physical body, I could still be tortured. No matter how powerful I am I can still be defeated. My enemies aren't merely individuals, they are a part of an entire system that relies on evil and enjoys causing pain. There are thousands of victims of this system waiting for someone to set them free. I can't fight the system alone, but I don't have too. I just have to get things started. Every victim is a potential ally, and a potential soldier in the fight against the system.

I began to shape raw celestial ore as I pondered my situation. I hadn't been an artist or particularly skilled in any crafts while living, but shaping the celestial steel felt so natural to me. All I had to do was think about what I wanted it to look like and the metal flowed into that shape. The more detailed I was in my imaginings the more detailed the finished product would be.

There was nothing that said I had to stay in Philadelphia. Perhaps there was a place out there where good ghosts ruled. If I could find that place then perhaps I could get them to help me fight the forces of evil in Philadelphia thereby liberating the shades and banshees. This, however, felt like a copout to me. Such a city might not even exist, and there was no guarantee that I'd be able to find it let alone persuade the inhabitants to risk their own safety for strangers.

I finished shaping an axe and laid it aside and prepared to shape more steel only to find that there was none left. I stared around me in wonder at the scores of weapons that I'd made without really thinking about it. There were swords, daggers, axes, maces, spears, and even bows with hundreds of arrows. The basement of my haunt was now truly an armory. I had also fashioned dozens of mail shirts and a few suits of plate armor. One small pile, set aside from the rest, contained a fine katana, several knives, various articles of jewelry, and a fine suit of mesh armor. I equipped myself in the gear from this pile and instantly felt more in control.

I still wasn't sure about how I should proceed. The task ahead of me was daunting and I just wasn't feeling confident. I translated into the living world from my basement haunt. Although devil's iron inhibited translation between the worlds, celestial steel didn't have the same effect on me. I found myself in the Franklin Court Museum. The attraction was closed, and the basement was deserted and dark. Its layout was strangely different from the one in Limbo as some rooms seemed to be missing. I made my way through the collected relics of Franklin's long life and finally emerged into the early twilight. Though rush hour had passed some hours ago, the streets were quite active. I quickly determined that it was a Friday evening. Many of the citizens of the city were getting ready to party the night away.

I headed West. The glorious red of the sunset was a spectacular background to the glittering lights of the city of brotherly love. I wasn't sure exactly where I was going at first, but I soon found myself on Sansom Street in the Powelton Park neighborhood of University City. I passed the White Dog Cafe and finally came to a stop in front of University Dojo. The lights were still on inside, and the parking lot was filled with cars of all makes and models. I had been coming to this building almost every day since my kindergarten days. This was the place where my father had trained me to fight in the arts of Kendo, the way of the sword, and Jiu Jitsu: close personal combat martial arts. Years of hard work and dedication had resulted in me nearly mastering both combat styles. It was ironic that these combat skills had served me better in death than they had in life.

I hadn't come here to contemplate my training though. I'd come here to find courage. My dad had always been a bastion of strength for me: kind but disciplined, expecting my full effort and teaching that failure was a part of learning. You could only truly fail if you gave up, and you couldn't truly learn without failure my dad had taught me. Standing outside my dad's dojo,

I once again found my courage. Just being near him gave me strength. My capture was a failure that I must come to grips with and learn from. No matter how powerful and skilled I might be, I'm not invincible. Limbo's dark forces are cunning and numerous, but I had shown on several occasions that they could be defeated. The very fact that I stood here now, having escaped shadow Philly's mighty Walnut Street Prison, was a testament to this fact. Failure is a fact of life and, in my case, unlife. It will happen again. The only thing I can do is learn from it and move on. The emotional scars that I now bore were a reminder that I was no longer a little girl in training. They reminded me of the fact that I was a warrior fighting for more than just survival; I was fighting to change things for the good.

I desperately wanted to step into the dojo, to get a glimpse of my dad once more, but I resisted the urge. No good could come from such an indulgence. Torturing myself with something that I could never have was foolish: another lesson from my dad. Most importantly, I had to avoid the temptation of watching over my loved ones, to protect them, and ultimately interfere in the course of their lives as the evil ghosts of Limbo did. The ghost world must be pulled away from such actions. There was plenty for us to do without messing with people's God given free will. There were supernatural monsters preying on humanity; that was where we should focus our efforts.

For now though, I needed to return to Limbo so that I could begin work on the problem of starting a ghostly revolution. I needed to deal with the Tormentor and free my sister banshees.

20

I TRANSLATED BACK INTO LIMBO and immediately donned the mist cloak that afforded me the best protection that I knew of against limbo's agents. If they couldn't detect me, they couldn't catch me. Sansom Street was quite different in limbo compared to the living world. My dad's dojo and the White Dog Cafe didn't exist here. Instead, the street was dominated by an old Union hospital that had been torn down long ages ago in living Philadelphia. The place was dark and foreboding. I could easily imagine that some powerful ghost made the place its haunt. I left Powelton Park as quickly as possible and began my long reconnaissance of the city.

My problem now was that I needed a plan. The banshees were all held at the heart of the Walnut Street Prison; getting to them was going to be exceedingly difficult. I also had no idea just how broken they would be and how I was going to help them overcome their psychopathic rage. Controlled and focused rage had its uses. I'd demonstrated this on several occasions, but I couldn't risk unleashing crazed women with the power of mass destruction in their screams without coming up with a way to first heal their minds. The problem of the banshees was going to have to wait until an appropriate solution presented itself. I did not want to cause them or others more harm by not being prepared.

The problem of the Tormentor was also going to have to wait. He was a reaper with darklings and specters at his beck and call, not to mention his own considerable power. I dared not go after a captain of Limbo in his own fortress without an army at my back; such an action would be fool hardy and would likely result in my destruction.

I was left with starting a revolution as the best course of action. A revolution would be a game changer. It could change many factors including forcing the reapers to fight on grounds not of their choosing. A successful revolution would mean that I wasn't fighting alone, and that allies could bolster my plans and add to knowledge that I was sorely lacking. A successful revolution was also the only way to overthrow the system. In the living world, Philadelphia had played a key role in the American Revolution, perhaps it could do the same in Limbo. The odds of success weren't good though. For one thing I'm no Washington, and for another, it seemed like slave shades would be even less apt at being soldiers than the rough colonials had been. It had to be tried though; success was only possible if the effort was made. I couldn't let my own fears hold me back. I had to put my best foot forward and hope for the best. The question is, how do you start a revolution?

My knowledge of history wasn't going to help me much since all the revolutions I'd studied were carried out and led by a group of conspirators. I wasn't aware of any case where a lone person started a revolution over night, yet this was exactly what I needed to do. There weren't any bars or other social gathering places in shadow Philly where I could go to gather information or spread rumors of rebellion; at least not any where I'd be welcome. Only darklings frequented such places, and while I'm certain that it's in their nature to rebel, I'm equally certain that their world view would result in a worsening of the situation not to mention they'd probably sell me out before anything got started. Fundamental change was necessary particularly in how ghosts were interacting with the living world. I needed ghosts who weren't entrenched in the current hierarchy, ghosts who would be open to a new way of doing things.

The shades were my best option. They were slaves: a weak labor force that was controlled and abused by the darker beings of Limbo. Freeing the shades would give me a ready source of hopefully willing revolutionaries. The question was how was I going to free them and keep them alive long enough to turn them into a true threat to Limbo's Masters? Shades are the weakest ghosts in Limbo. Most have been slaves for generations. They naturally fear their powerful masters, and most of them probably have little or no training in combat. A small force of specters could decimate an army of shades ten times their size. The shades might even break before the specters had a chance to close with them. How could I overcome such challenges?

I spent a week crisscrossing the metropolis, lurking in alleys and rooftops watching and learning all that I could about how the shades were used. I kept the mist cloak about me and found it easy to avoid the patrols and search parties that were frantically seeking me. My escape was widely known, and I detected hints of fear and respect among some darklings. The specters had positively come to fear me. They called me 'the Mistress of Banshees'. Unfortunately, they took their fear out on the shades in their charge.

My growing reputation had an impact on the shades as well. Many of them seemed to resent me especially as the ill treatment directed at them grew proportionally to the amount of frustration I was causing Philly's Dark Master. Some small number of them, however, seemed to take solace in their Master's apparent fallibility, and they appeared to silently cheer me on.

At night after long hours of reconnoitering the city, I spent hours practicing with my blades and with my new found powers. The banshee scream was far too conspicuous a talent for me to practice; I didn't want to attract attention to myself after all. My skill with the mist cloak, however, led me to experiment with the mists of Limbo, and I soon discovered that I could do many things with the fog; I could essentially shape it like I did celestial steel. I found that I could create tools out of the mists, and, if I put extra power into it, I could make those tools become physical like celestial steel and devil's iron. My days were thus spent in sneaking about the city, and my nights were consumed by training and sleep. I barely noticed the passage of time.

I soon discovered an interesting fact: most of the city's shades were vanishing. Every week, a sizable number of shades were shipped out on the Northbound Philadelphia and Reading train. The Southbound train returned a few days later with a load of celestial steel and a new gang of specters but no shades. Where were all of those shades being taken to and why weren't they being brought back? The genesis of a plan began to slowly form in my mind as I kept the Reading Train Terminal under surveillance for an extra week. The guard on the train was relatively light, consisting of a dozen or so specters. The real danger however came from the Conductor, the reaper assigned to the train. Although attacking a train felt overly brazen to me, I also saw it as the best opportunity to free a large number of shades while simultaneously denying the enemy the advantages of home field. If all went well, I might even be able to free one of the luminaries and recruit it to the cause. Also, wherever the train was bound for, there would be a lot more shades there. Perhaps we could capture the location and use it as a base to train from and defend ourselves. Of course, the down side was that I had no clue what was at the end of the tracks. It would be a blind jump. The other challenge was that I was going to have to fight a reaper.

The decision made, I headed back home to get some rest and pack up as many weapons as I could carry. It seemed likely that the train was bound for a mine where celestial steel was the primary ore excavated, but it wouldn't hurt to arm some of the shades on the train as soon as I defeated their captors. I had three days to prepare before the week's most heavily loaded train headed north.

21

THE JOURNEY NORTH from the safety of my haunt was slow and filled with tension. I couldn't afford to be spotted, yet the route I chose was heavily inhabited by the city's darkling population. After clearing Center City, I entered North Philly carefully picking my way through until I reached Germantown Avenue. North Philadelphia is the most violent and chaotic part of the living city, and it soon became apparent to me what the cause might be. Darklings were everywhere here: hanging out on street corners, going in and out of dilapidated tenements on nefarious business, or going to rest in their haunts. The sheer number of them, a few thousand I guessed, was far more than what was common in any other part of the city save Center City, which was where the bureaucratic heart of the metropolis was located.

Avoiding the loitering gangs of darklings didn't prove too difficult. I intended to make my move to get on the train at Chestnut Hill in the Northwest of the city. Reconnaissance of the city over the past few weeks had shown me that most of the outlying neighborhoods were either uninhabited or so lightly populated that avoiding detection should be quite simple. I'd pondered the idea of assaulting the train somewhere beyond the city's boundaries, but a vague warning from Delilah during my earlier trainings had given me pause.

"Are there other cities?" I'd asked. "Of ghosts, I mean."

"Yes, but getting to them can be difficult, and you can not be certain of the reception you will receive. Every city has its own Master and its own rules. Strangers are often shunned; the communities prefer to trust only ghosts harvested within their own territories."

"So how hard can it be to get to a place like Harrisburg or some other nearby town?"

"Travel between cities is too hazardous. Only the rails afford a safe means of travel through the wilds. Most cities, however, cut the rails well outside their boundaries as a strategic defense."

"But we have trains coming directly into the city here," I'd stated in confusion. "Where do they go?"

"That is none of your affair," she'd answered in an icy tone that she often employed when I was asking questions about sensitive matters.

"What about walking or flying?" I'd continued stubbornly. "Can't a ghost get to a nearby town that way?"

Delilah had stopped in her tracks, grabbed me by the elbow, and whirled me around to face her. "You must never go beyond the borders of the city. The lands and small towns beyond lie in darkness and oblivion lurks in every shadow. If you want to survive, stay within the city."

"But …" I tried to protest, but she'd stridden away and thereafter refused to answer any more questions about the lands beyond the city's borders.

I'd always found it strange that a darkling such as Delilah should have a fear of the darkness that supposedly lay beyond the city's border. I was intensely curious especially given the fact that most things that discomforted Delilah had the opposite effect on me. Although I'd given serious consideration to making my attack on the train from outside the city, in the end I decided to go with Chestnut Hill purely because of the uncertainty of what I might encounter beyond the borders. I knew that I shouldn't assume that everything that Delilah feared would be good for me. In fact, the opposite was true. Though Delilah was my enemy, I didn't consider her a fool; anything she feared needed to be respected.

The ghettos of North Philadelphia finally gave way to old abandoned factories: a testament to America's industrial meltdown. The nation's thirst for cheap goods and its beliefs in open markets had combined to leave many of its rustbelt cities industrial wastelands. This part of Germantown Avenue was a shining example of the folly of such policies. I had to fly over the Schuylkill before the last of the depressingly empty factories finally gave way to the historic Germantown district itself. This neighborhood had been the site of the city's only Revolutionary War battlefield in which American forces had lost the battle but had given the Redcoats a good bloodying. Germantown had also been a hot bed of the abolitionist movement during the Civil War era. The famed Underground Railroad had a stop here. The area was also known for its unusually high number of churches.

Next, I passed through the suburb of Mount Airy: the final neighborhood before Chestnut Hill. I passed by the colorful Victorian and colonial revival houses with little interest. I was eager to get to my destination; the train would be coming soon. A nervous energy filled me, and I found that my normal interest in architecture and historical landmarks was replaced with mental planning for the coming action. The key to this whole operation was surprise. If I could eliminate most of the specters on the train before the Conductor became aware of me, I'd have a fighting chance. I considered attacking the reaper first, but I wasn't confident that I'd get close enough to him to deliver a killing blow before he became aware of me. I expected the fight with the reaper to be somewhat drawn out and my worst nightmare was having to fight it and all of its minions at once. The specters somewhat feared me already. If I could kill a majority of them in some spectacular fashion then maybe the rest would hold back while the Conductor and I battled it out.

I paused, suddenly feeling a tremor in the earth around me. I was no longer among the buildings of Mount Airy. Instead, the partially wooded Cresheim Valley that bordered Chestnut Hill and Mount Airy lay quietly around me. The area was a part of Fairmount Park in modern times, but in Limbo the old railroad still passed through on its way North. It was the steel road that was the source of my distraction now. I looked back the way I'd come and saw the train cresting the hill as it prepared to speed past me. I smiled. This was as good a place to board a train as any.

I watched the train approach. It was a thing of beauty; it glided across the celestial steel rails, its cars trailing in celestial blue behind the engine. The engine was long and sleek. A stylized gray skull with long black hair and glowing red eyes was emblazoned upon both sides of it. The name of the train, "Black Maria", was scrawled in red script below the skull symbols. I wondered briefly if the skull symbol was a representation of a reaper, one named Black Maria perhaps? I banished the thought from my mind. Now was not the time for such contemplation. I needed to focus on the task at hand.

As I'd hoped, the train traveling North this day was quite long with a total of fifteen boxcars following in the wake of the powerful engine. Most of these were the large box like freight carts that you often see in movies. Thirteen of these, I knew, would be full of shades packed in like sardines. The final two were passenger carts: one located in the middle and the other at the end of the train. These would contain a half dozen or so specters each.

I let the engine and most of the cars pass me by before I leapt into the air calling on the wind to give me flight. I timed it just right and landed on the roof of the final cart. I didn't dismiss the wind but rather redirected it into a shield around me that provided cover from the buffeting of the gusting winds caused by the speeding train.

I chose the last cart because I fully expected the Conductor to become aware of me relatively soon after destroying the first group of specters. It was my hope that being as far away from the reaper as possible would give me just enough time to wipe out one full group of specters before he and the second group could respond. Tactically speaking, it also protected me from being assailed from two directions.

I crouched low on the roof of the speeding boxcar and waited a few minutes. The affluent neighborhood of Chestnut Hill sped by, and we passed into the outer boundaries of Philadelphia. All remained quiet on the train; apparently my presence hadn't been detected yet. It was time to change that.

I used my index finger to trace a circle around me, willing the celestial steel of the boxcars roof to thin out so that the circular plate that I now stood on could barely hold my weight. I then drew my katana, and with a mental thrust willed the celestial steel to give way to my weight. Instantly the roof dropped below me and I fell into the passenger car below. Before the circular plate that I rode down on could hit the floor, I forced it to break apart into a thousand shards sending celestial steel shrapnel in all directions. The specters that occupied the cart barely had time to register the fact that I'd invaded their domain before three of them were shredded to bits by the deadly spray of celestial steel shrapnel. A fourth perished before any of the remaining survivors could howl in fear. My katana flashed through the air catching it in the upper torso and passed completely through it.

I landed on my feet and raised my empty left hand towards the fifth specter. It was fumbling around trying to get its claws on a collar controller. The wall behind it seemed to melt and then formed into a giant hand that grabbed the specter from

behind and pushed it down into a gaping hole that had suddenly opened in the floor at its feet. I ducked and rolled as the
last of the specters swung a brutal looking devil's iron axe at my
head. I avoided a second strike before the axe was ripped from
the specters clawed hands by another animated celestial steel
arm that sprang forth from the nearby wall. The specter that
had been pushed through the hole in the floor was screaming as
its body was dragged thousands of feet along the celestial steel
tracks before it evaporated into black mist. The last specter was
destroyed a few moments later. It howled in fear and pain as one
steel hand held it while several others pummeled it. After the
final specter had been destroyed, I willed the celestial steel arms
to return to their normal state, and I silently thanked God for
giving me control over the beautiful metal.

I didn't waste time savoring the victory. There were more
specters and a reaper to deal with. I'd improved my odds of
victory, but the battle was far from over. I willed the shards of
metal scattered about the cabin to reform into the disc that I'd
ridden down on and they did as directed. I called the wind to
me and I rode the disc back up to the roof where it remolded
itself with the train. A glance down the length of the speeding
train showed a dark figure moving rapidly towards me. Its dark
cloak flapped in the wind, and it bore a devil's iron sword in one
hand. Its skeletal head was uncovered; the glow from its hellish
eyes and the aura of its sword combined to make it appear as
though its head had been dipped in blood. It moved with grace,
leaping from boxcar to boxcar with complete ease. It moved at
an incredible speed.

I leaped forward to meet the Conductor, calling on the wind
to grant me super human speed. Our swords met two cars down
from the one I'd started from. The force of that initial clash
nearly sent me flying off the side of the train. The reaper didn't
seem fazed by the shock of the contact and, without missing a
beat, it pivoted in mid stride and sent its blade whipping low
towards my knees. I leaped over the blade and counterattacked

with a clumsy blow aimed at its shoulder. The Conductor smiled as it parried the attack.

"This time you will die, girl," it said as it sent a blow towards my stomach. I regained my momentum and diverted my blade to make the necessary parry while preparing to deliver a counterstroke of my own. Too late I saw that the blow was meant as a feint; before I could parry its blow, the reaper suddenly changed the direction of the attack, bringing the blade up in a sweeping arc that avoided my parry and slashed into my exposed flank. The celestial steel chain mesh that I was wearing saved me. The Conductor's blade cut through the protective links of the armor, but its momentum was slowed enough so that I was able to pivot aside before it could sink too deeply into me. I was left with a wound that might have been serious if I'd been a living person, but my ghostly body was mostly unimpressed. Don't get me wrong, it stung like hell, but the pain was manageable.

I somersaulted away from the Conductor putting some distance between us and giving myself a moment to regain my composure. While skill is one of the most important ingredients to victory in combat, it isn't the only factor. One's state of mind is critical to concentration and combat reflexes. An opponent who is afraid of another will be slowed by that fear, both in movement speed and movement planning. Battle is swift. Each move is directed by the mind, seeing the opponent's intent, and seeking his vulnerabilities. The Conductor had me at a disadvantage for a moment. It surprised me with its skill and sheer speed. Here was an opponent who was offering me a true challenge one-on-one. It was clearly stronger and faster than me. It had clearly won the first round, but instead of pressing its advantage, it stalked towards me cautiously. This confused me for a moment. Why was it being cautious?

As it approached me, I allowed myself to start breathing heavily as if I were winded or panicked. I also slouched a little. The Conductor stopped about ten feet away from me and leered at me. I tensed my muscles, preparing to spring into action. Once more the reaper surprised me when its empty hand shot up and it uttered a single unintelligible word. A bolt of dark energy shot from its palm coming straight for me. A moment of true panic almost overwhelmed me when instinct took over and I called my mist shield around me. Instead of using it as a cloak to hide me though, I willed it to harden into a thick shield. The mist shield coalesced around me, and when the dark energy struck the shield, it was dispersed and absorbed by the shield.

It was the Conductor's turn to be surprised. I took the opportunity to spring forward and attack. I called on the celestial steel below the reapers feet to grab it; to do whatever it needed to do to hamper the reapers movement. Arms and spikes flowed into existence. They grabbed and stabbed at the reaper, but it dodged here and there with amazing agility and was still able to parry a flurry of blows that I sent towards it. The momentum had shifted in my favor though, and the Conductor was now on the defensive. It howled its frustration, summoning the specters from the middle boxcar. I briefly considered blasting the reaper with my banshee scream but discarded this idea as it seemed too dangerous. I had no way of controlling the collateral damage that the power unleashed; it would probably destroy the reaper but it was just as likely to destroy the speeding train as well.

The Conductor was beginning to find a rhythm to the celestial steel arms that were attacking it. Its own attacks against me were once more becoming a real threat. I sensed the specters getting closer. I knew that soon I would be overrun. Inspiration born of desperation came upon me, and, remembering my earlier training, I shoved my mist shield away from me and towards the reaper. It tried to avoid the mist shield, but the shroud simply stretched and grew bigger until it had completely enveloped the reaper. I then willed the mists to become sticky, like tar. Instantly the Conductor's movements slowed; the downside was that my own attacks were stymied by the gelatinous shield as well. I willed a hole to open beneath the reaper's feet and the celestial steel complied. The Conductor tried to dance aside, but the gooey mists enveloping it slowed it too much and it screamed as it fell through the gap in the train's roof. Before it could plunge all the way through, I willed the celestial steel to close back up. The reaper howled in agony as the roof snapped back into place like the closing of a massive jaw. For a short moment, the Conductor was held in place protected by the shield that I'd placed around it. I banished the shield and took the reaper's head off with a single, vicious stroke of my katana. The Conductor's body remained entombed in the roof of the train, its lower half no doubt causing the shades below a great deal of consternation.

I turned to face the specters that had suddenly come to a halt one car away. It was plain that they were terrified of me; I felt no pity for the creatures.

"Get off of my train," I growled at them.

The specters bounced about in agitation for a moment until one of them had the courage to address me.

"No jump from train, furies eat us. We serve you."

"What will happen to you out there is less certain than what will happen to you when I set foot on your boxcar. Get off of my train, now!"

I began to move towards them, my pace measured and menacing. The specters cringed away from me, their gazes sliding between me, the headless reaper, and the dark countryside speeding by us. As I prepared to leap to the car they occupied, the specters made their choice and with howls of fear they leaped from the train, leaving me in sole possession of the Black Maria. I strode towards the engine. There would be a bound luminary there. For some reason they were the only creatures in Limbo that could propel the few vehicles that existed in the ghost realm. It would be the first slave that I set free.

22

A CIRCULAR PORTAL OPENED in the engine's roof in response to my mental command. I dropped into the compartment below, and the roof flowed back into its normal shape. I found myself in a chamber whose walls and floor were plated in devil's iron. In the center of the cabin was a celestial steel control wheel. A beautiful white angelic being was bound to it by devil's iron wire. The luminary gazed at me with curiosity showing in its large golden eyes.

"I'm Veronika Kane. I'm here to rescue you."

"What makes you think I need rescuing Veronika Kane?" it asked in a melodious voice. "This is my penance for having failed my God in life. I must endure this purgatory until I have fully paid the debt."

"What are you talking about? This isn't Purgatory, it's Limbo. Besides, how do you know God didn't send me?"

"Did He?"

"I've got no freaking idea," I answered in exasperation. "It's not like He talks to me or something. All I know is that I didn't do anything bad enough in life to deserve being enslaved and tortured for the rest of my unlife. I bet you haven't done anything to deserve this treatment either, right?

"I do not think so, but who am I to presume upon the wisdom of the Lord?"

"You really don't think that these things work for God do you?" I asked incredulously. "Even if you were bad in life, do you really think He would have you tortured and enslaved like this?"

The luminary just stared at me with a quizzical expression on its angelic face.

"Even if we are in hell or Purgatory," I continued. "Aren't we supposed to fight evil if we can? The masters of this place use their power to bring pain and chaos both to this place and the living world, I would think that the only way for us to gain redemption is to appose evil in all its forms, right?"

The luminary nodded slowly.

"Evil is evil. It doesn't matter where we find it, we must always stand against it." I pressed. "Just because we are dead doesn't mean we have to let evil dominate us. In fact, things are a little more obvious here than in the living world, the evil things here actually look like monsters. Letting them prey on the weak and unsuspecting is wrong, and you know that. Come on! You're a being of light! You've got to help me protect them."

"How do you know these things Veronika Kane? How do I know you're not a servant of the Conductor sent to tempt me?"

"I killed the Conductor. I can show you what remains of its body if you don't believe me. As for how I know what I know, well, I was trained to be a member of a sowing team. I've learned first hand how evil the Master and his minions are. I betrayed them and foiled one of their plots in the living world. I helped the living police capture a serial killer that turned out to be a pawn of the Master. For this I was captured and tortured. I escaped, and now I'm seeking allies to help me bring those evil bastards down."

The luminary stared at me in wonder for a full minute before replying.

"Out of the mouth of babes comes great wisdom, and apparently greater courage," he muttered under his breath. "I am Jonus. Pleased to meet you Veronika Kane."

"My pleasure Jonus," I said gliding over to him and beginning to cut away his bindings with my celestial steel knife. I smiled at him and flipped my hair back. "And thanks for recognizing my babe status, though you must come from a far more paternalistic era than mine to assume that women can't be wise or courageous."

Jonus stared at me in confusion. "I'm afraid I don't understand what you mean. Of course there is wisdom in many women just as the same is true with men."

"You aren't getting off that easy buster. I heard what you said. You can't deny that you expressed surprise that wisdom and courage could come from a babe like me."

"Please take no offense. I was simply speaking metaphorically about your obvious youth, not about your gender or status. It's a piece of wisdom from the scriptures that teaches us to listen to the young, for at times they have true pearls of wisdom to share with us."

"Oops," I sighed in embarrassment. Of course he wasn't talking about my looks. What the hell does that sort of thing matter to a ghost anyway? "Never mind. Let's get on with business. Can you bring the train to a stop?"

"So, you killed a reaper?" Jonus asked incredulously.

"Yea, and with far more difficulty than I'd care to admit, but it's completely destroyed. The specters are also all gone. Now can you stop this train?"

"Yes, but that would be dangerous. The furies would certainly come for us."

"That's the second time I've heard mention of furies. What are they?"

"They are the spirits of animals that have died violently," Jonus answered soberly. "They hunt in large packs and are extremely vicious towards human ghosts. The city ghosts hunt them for sport and enslave them. They are used in the making of gargoyles."

"Gargoyles?"

"Yes, gargoyles are statues who've had a fury bound inside of them. Once a fury has been tethered to the statue it becomes an animated creature. Gargoyles exist in Limbo and the living world at the same time."

I shuddered, recalling my experience at Fitler Square where I'd been attacked by five animated statues.

"Are demons ever used in the making of gargoyles instead of furies?" I asked.

Jonus stared at me his expression unreadable. "Why do you ask?"

"Because I fought some in Fitler Square."

"What makes you think they were demons rather than furies?"

"Because after I kicked the crap out of a couple of them, a fiery being came out of one of the statues and fought me with a flaming sword. What's with all of these questions? Were they gargoyles or not?"

Jonus gaped at me for a moment. He kind of looked paler to me, but that was ridiculous since he was largely a being of light anyways.

"Not gargoyles," he finally answered. "Golems. You're lucky to be alive. There's almost nothing worse than golems."

"What else is new," I answered flippantly, though internally I was shaking with terror at the memory. Neither gargoyles nor golems had been covered in my trainings with Delilah. I wondered what else she'd left out. "It seems like something is always trying to kill or capture me. Being a ghost babe isn't at all like the brochures said it would be."

"This is no laughing matter," Jonus said seriously. "You are attracting the attention of things that are way beyond you."

"I'm dead and I'm pissed off about it," I answered angrily. "I'll be damned if I'm gonna let these assholes push me around. I will not be a darkling or a slave, so the only alternative is to fight.

Are you with me or would you prefer to go hide somewhere? You don't have to tell me that the bad guys are scary. I already know that."

"You shame me," Jonus answered quietly. "I am with you."

"Good, now where is this train headed?"

"Normally it goes to the Devil's Forge in a place called Centralia."

Centralia was a name I recognized. It was a small coal mining town in North-Eastern Pennsylvania. It had become a modern day ghost town due to a mine fire that had broken out in 1962. The fire continues to rage in the mines below the town to this very day. It didn't surprise me that something called the Devil's Forge would be located in such a place. I wondered if the ghosts had had anything to do with the original catastrophe. It seemed very likely. I pondered the situation for a moment then made my decision.

"Bring the train to a stop a few miles outside of Centralia. We'll go in on foot."

"What do you mean we'll go in on foot? That place is full of specters not to mention Black Maria spends a great deal of time there."

"Black Maria?" I asked.

"The name on this engine denotes who it belongs to. Black Maria is an exceptionally dangerous reaper. Rumor claims that even the Master wraiths of the local cities fear her. She is the only known reaper that can shape devil's iron with a single thought. She is also said to be a spirit shaper, though I'm not sure what that means."

This sounded like a creature that would be best to avoid. The spirit shaping thing sounded particularly ominous. If she could do with spirits and devil's iron what I could do with celestial steel then she was exceptionally dangerous indeed.

"If we scout the forge out first, is there any way we can determine if she is present or not?"

"Yes. She travels in a black covered wagon pulled by large

mutated furies. Also, there will be many more specters present. Her elite specters are bigger than the normal kind, and they have devil's iron spikes all over their bodies."

The description of Black Maria's furies and specters confirmed my worries about her power to spirit shape. She would be too formidable to take on. Yet, I knew that something important was going on at the Devil's Forge. I needed to know what it was.

"How many specters guard the place when she's not there?" I asked.

"I'd say between twenty and thirty, no more than that."

"Ok, bring the train to a stop outside the town, far enough away that they won't see or hear us. Since you know the area, you'll go scout it out. We just need to know if Black Maria is there. I'll arm the shades with celestial steel weapons while you're scouting. If Black Maria isn't there we'll take the place and see what we see."

"I will do what you ask," Jonus said without a hint of nervousness, as if I'd asked him to go on a stroll in the park rather than to infiltrate an enemy town with a deadly reaper in it. "But you should be aware that there are no celestial steel weapons on this train. The only weapons are the devil's iron weapons of the specters and what the Conductor carried."

"I know that, but the whole bloody train is made of celestial steel, so it isn't a problem."

"We'll be in Centralia in a few hours. There's not enough time to forge celestial steel even if you had the equipment, and cannibalizing the train would take days."

"Who said anything about forging?" I asked. I waved my hand at the roof and the circular portal opened once more. I leaped through it, landed on the roof and bent over poking my head back into the cabin below. "Didn't I mention that I'm a celestial steel shaper? We'll all be armed to the teeth when we enter the Devil's Forge. Make sure you stop us well outside the town. I'm going to free the shades."

23

I JUMPED OVER TO THE BOXCAR immediately behind the engine. The roof opened up for me, and I dropped into the packed cabin below. The shades scrambled away from my falling form, giving me a small space to land. The pitiful creatures shied away from me, pressing themselves against the walls of the train in an effort to get as far away from me as possible.

"Who wants to be free?" I asked trying to give them my warmest smile. They all stared at me dully. Their black eyes remained expressionless as they watched me.

"Who's tired of being the specters bitch?" I asked raising my voice and adding a little contempt to it. This seemed to get through to a few of them, as shuffling feet indicated growing agitation. Still, none of them answered me. I sighed heavily.

"Look, I know what you're thinking. I'm not a darkling spy working for the Conductor. I'm Veronika Kane, the girl that put the whole city of Philly in a tizzy. I'm the one they've been looking for. I'm here to rescue all of you. I killed the Conductor and his specters."

"Being all tough is easy when you ain't the one wearing the collar," one of the shades replied in a surprisingly deep voice.

"I was a shade when I first came to Limbo. I was forced to wear the collar. I didn't like it, so I took it off."

"So now you're here to taunt us?" another shade replied bitterly.

"No, I already told you I'm here to set you free."

"Go away girl, you're only going to bring us more trouble," a shade with a shrill voice answered.

"I don't want to bring you more trouble," I told them earnestly. "But I can't stand by and let the Master enslave and torture ghosts anymore. If you are weaker or if you disobey his orders, you are punished. We might all be ghosts now, but we were all once Americans. We were born free, we died free, and we should demand freedom even in this ungodly place."

The boxcar was silent, and I could tell that I'd hit a nerve. Even in death most of these ghosts could still think of themselves as Americans, and liberty is almost a religious word to a US citizen.

"I'm here to help you," I told them in a quiet and respectful tone. "I'm also here to ask for your help. Our great city of Philadelphia is the city in which the Declaration of Independence was written and proclaimed to the entire world. We need to send a message to all of Limbo that Americans will not be slaves in life or in death. Join with me and together we will raise the flag of revolution so that liberty can be restored to our city."

The boxcar exploded in a din of voices. It was the most animation I'd ever seen from shades.

"Freedom!."

"Liberty!"

"USA!, USA! USA!"

The chanting went on for a good five minutes before one of the shades was able to make himself heard over the crowd.

"How can we fight against them? We are the weakest ghosts in Limbo!"

The shouts died down slowly as the question sunk in and the reality of the situation became evident. My heart thudded in my chest as my mind whirled, trying to grasp for the words that would make a difference. I'm not a public speaker, I'm a fighter. And no, my heart wasn't literally beating a mile a minute, but it sure felt like it.

"All of you have taken American history," I told them slowly. "You know that the men and women who fought against the mightiest empire during the American Revolution were farmers, craftsmen, and merchants. They were outgunned, out trained, and out numbered, but they prevailed because they believed in what they were fighting for: Freedom! This will not be easy, but it is necessary if we are to achieve liberty. We can win if we remember what we are fighting for."

There was silence in the car once more.

"I will fight," said the deep voiced shade that had first spoken up. He stepped out from the crowd. He was bigger than most of his companions. "My name's Bret. I'll join you if you'll have me ma'am."

Tears welled up in my eyes as I stepped forward and cut the collar from Bret's neck with my knife. There was an audible gasp of surprise from the onlookers and I saw that the mist surrounding Bret was dissipating revealing a tall, well muscled man with brown skin, black hair, black eyes, and a smile that could light up a room. He looked around trying to see what had caused the others to react so strongly. When he saw them all staring at him, he looked down and saw the transformation. He stared at himself for a moment, and then, without warning, he grabbed me in his massive arms and whirled me about in a dance all the while laughing.

"Thank you, thank you, thank you," he said over and over again.

"It wasn't me," I said when he finally put me down. "It was in your hands all along. You believed in yourself and made a choice. I just cut the collar."

This turn of events made it a much easier decision for most of the other shades in the boxcar. If liberty itself hadn't been enough of a reason for some to join, the hope of becoming something more than a shade convinced the holdouts to give it a try. Soon, all twenty six of the shades were freed from their collars, and all were shedding their grayness. I made Bret a captain of the unit and left him in charge of organizing his troops. I left them with a few weapons made from the roof of the train but explained that I couldn't take the time right now to arm them all as I needed to free the shades in the other cars before we got to our destination.

A little over an hour later, the train began to slow down. By that time, I'd finished with the final boxcar. After my success in the first passenger wagon, I'd expected things to go smoothly. I was sorely disappointed. The terror of generations of slavery wasn't an easy thing to overcome. My patriotic message worked well with ghosts who'd died within the last decade, but the longer a slave had been collared, the harder it was to convince them. I found it necessary to fetch Bret and a few others from the first car to help prove to the terrified shades aboard other cars that overcoming their slave status was as possible as transforming from a shade to a regular ghost was. Like on the first car, once a shade had made its mind up to join us and been transformed into a semblance of its old self, most of the others joined as well. Only in the boxcar on which I'd fought and killed the Conductor did persuading the shades prove relatively simple. Having witnessed some of the events of that battle, especially its conclusion, these shades were eager to join. Still, in the end, around fifteen percent of the shades refused to join us. They were simply too afraid.

After leaving each car with its own armed captain, I returned to Jonus in the engine. By this time, the train was crawling along at around ten miles per hour.

"How did it go?" he asked before I had even landed on the train's deck.

"Pretty well. Thirty one of them refused to join us, but that leaves us with two hundred and eleven of them," I answered with satisfaction. "The best part is that once they'd made up their minds to join us, they shed their shrouds and became something new."

Jonus nodded, not seeming to be surprised by this.

"It is as I've suspected. Who you serve here matters to such a degree that our very appearances are affected by it."

"Maybe you're right Jonus, but personally I think shades are simply baby ghosts. You become a grown up ghost when you accept yourself, the fact that you're dead, and consciously take responsibility for yourself. Shades are shrouded because they haven't become what their meant to be yet, their power is limited for the same reason."

Jonus was quiet a moment, seeming to contemplate the issue, or maybe he was just concentrating on his work with the train. We had slowed even further, almost crawling along now. He had his white glowing hand on the celestial steel wheel.

"You are a curious ghost Veronika. You are supposed to be a poltergeist, but I've heard the reapers discussing your banshee abilities as well as other powers that should be outside of your purview. All the ghosts I've ever seen, no matter how powerful, have an insubstantial or other worldly quality to them, but not you. You look like a living person. All the color and energy of life still surrounds you. I think that perhaps you are meant to not only fight here in Limbo but also in the living world as well."

"I don't want to interfere with the lives of living people," I said startled by the change in topics. "We don't have the right to mess with people's lives. That's part of what this fight is about."

"I agree, but in order to preserve man's free will someone has to fight on their behalf. Ghosts are not the only beings that can take man's will from him. Vampires, evil wizards, demons, and the fey are but some of the beings that prey upon living people. The wizards have long been the guardians of the living world, but time, the power of unbelief, and supernatural enemies have combined to weaken their order. There are just too few wizards left to adequately protect humanity from the numerous supernatural threats they face. It's possible that you are meant to be a new breed of guardian."

I shook my head in denial.

"The last time I tried to fill that role, I forced a woman out of her own body. I stole her life and free will so that I could get vengeance on my murderer. The end result was the creation of a new reaper, and the death of several cops, and probably the ruination of several of their careers."

Jonus stared at me in what I took to be disgust.

"I have heard the reapers talk about what you did in the living world. They were quite angry with you. Apparently the Master had wanted at least a score of banshees before he began his planned invasion of Pittsburgh, but your interference has left him with only nine banshees. The invasion will now be far more difficult. You saved the lives of at least eleven more girls. That is the result of your actions. As for what you did to this woman, it is clear that your conscience troubles you. If you did wrong, ask for forgiveness and find another way next time. But at the same time, remember that you may have to make difficult choices that have no happy or easy ends. Sometimes you have to sacrifice the lives of the few to save the lives of the many. Such is the burden of leadership."

I stared at Jonus in consternation.

"Do the reapers always talk so openly in front of you? Why does the Master want Pittsburgh, and when is this invasion supposed to begin?"

"This engine was one of the reapers favored meeting places. The Conductor himself was one of the most respected of their number, and his council was often sought by his colleagues. They spoke openly in front of me. Their arrogance would not allow them to contemplate the idea that I could ever escape from them. After all, there's never been a revolt in Limbo's history. As for why Pittsburgh, taking that city would give the Master dominance over the Celestial Fields: a series of mines that includes the Devil's Forge at Centralia. The Master has been plotting against Black Maria for ages. The two have skirmished on many occasions. Although Philadelphia has a clear advantage in numbers, Black Maria has always had more powerful ghosts on her side. The banshees are supposed to change that advantage."

"So when is the invasion planned for?" I asked excitedly. This sounded like a great opportunity to maybe take Philadelphia from the Master while the bulk of his forces were engaged elsewhere.

"We're here," Jonus announced bringing the train to a complete stop. "I don't know exactly, but soon. They planned to move while Black Maria was touring the Celestial Fields. Your interference with the Tormentor has moved their timetable up, I think."

I wanted to discuss this further with him and perhaps come up with a plan, but there was no time now. The newly freed former shades would need me, and the Devil's Forge was something I needed to investigate.

"If Philadelphia relies on its numerical advantage over Pittsburgh, why would they send so many shades out here every week? Most of them never return."

"It's the currency that Black Maria demands for providing specters and celestial steel. Shades do not participate in warfare. They are generally too weak to be of much use on the battlefield, but they are quite valuable as a labor force. Philadelphia's advantage is in its sheer number of darklings. Even with her superior numbers in specters, Black Maria can only field a force half the size as Philadelphia's."

"Are you saying that specters only come from Black Maria? They aren't harvested in Philly?"

"Yes. The secret of where they come from is tightly guarded in Pittsburgh. A covert war to uncover this secret has been waged for ages. Black Maria has sold the secret to a few other cities across Limbo. This loose alliance is known as the Styx Cartel.

The group seems to primarily be interested in the stockpiling of wealth."

"Hmm … I wish there was more time to discuss this," I said in frustration. "But we've got to get going. The shades will be getting anxious, and I need you to get a look at Centralia."

We disembarked from the engine and immediately set about opening the other boxcars. A steady stream of former shades disgorged onto the tall grass of the field the train had come to rest in. We were in a shallow valley between two grassy hills. There were trees of various types scattered about the surrounding countryside. The terrain to the North became more rugged with low hanging mountains in the far distance. To the South, the grassy hills gave way to farm country interspersed by small tangled forests.

The former shades milled about uncertainly as I approached the last of the boxcars and began to take it apart and shape the celestial steel into fine swords. As I worked, I ordered the captains to form up their units into a line opposite the car they'd ridden in. Each unit was given a number starting at the first boxcar after the engine. This one would now be unit one, commanded by Captain Bret. I finished making light mesh armor for Jonus, and directed him to take a sword and the armor.

After Jonus was fully equipped, I asked him to stand before me. I called the mist cloak to me. Once I was fully covered and judged that the cloak was having the proper affect by the gasps of surprise from the onlookers, I transferred the cloak to Jonus. I had to ask a nearby former shade if he could see Jonus, for even though the cloak clearly enveloped the luminary, I could still see him. The former shade, however, couldn't. I nodded in satisfaction.

"I have no idea how long it will hold itself around you, so be as quick as you can. Avoid contact with powerful ghosts. While my experience is that most darklings and specters can't see through the cloak, I can't guarantee that reapers won't be able to see through it."

Jonus nodded and immediately set off at a jog heading north. He vanished from sight after cresting a hill. As I set about making swords for our small army, my mind turned back to the intelligence that Jonus had provided. The former shades talked quietly amongst themselves, and I soon realized that the primary discussion had become what to call themselves now that they weren't shades. Ghost society had always consisted of four social groups; the ruling wraiths and reapers, the darkling nobles, the brutish specters, and the slave shades. Everything else was outside society and not worthy of consideration. Now a new kind of ghost had been introduced. The most popular name so far was 'common ghosts' while others were 'the chosen', 'the elect', 'the lost', and 'Veronika's Children'. This last one sent a shudder through me, and I suddenly turned to the small army.

"How about 'the Redeemed'?" I asked. "By making the choice to fight, you have reclaimed your birthright as free souls."

The mass of former shades stared at me silently for a moment and then one in the fifth unit spoke up.

"I like 'Free Souls' myself. 'The Redeemed' sounds a little too churchy."

Many of the former shades nodded in agreement, but most kept silent, feet shifting nervously as they waited to see how I would react to having my idea challenged. I smiled broadly and nodded in support of the suggestion.

"I like it," I declared, and the free souls cheered.

It took nearly three hours for me to shape weapons and armor for the entire company. When I finished, three boxcars had been reduced to slag. The shades that had refused to join us huddled together in the first boxcar to afraid to leave the protection of the train. I briefly considered forcing them to come with us but discarded the idea almost immediately; they would be to much of a liability. Neither could I spare anyone to guard them. Someone would come looking for the train eventually and they'd be found. If we succeeded in our revolution though, they'd eventually be given another opportunity to join the free souls. I turned my attention upon the impressive sight that the army of free souls made. Their blue steel armor shone like stars on a blanket of night. Jonus had returned an hour ago to report that all seemed normal in Centralia. Black Maria wasn't present. With that knowledge, I led the small army towards the burning town of Centralia and the secrets of the Devil's Forge.

24

"Why is there so little mist out here compared to Philadelphia?" I asked Jonus. We were marching up the side of a steep hill at the front of our small army.

"I don't know for certain, but I think the mists represent a weakening of the spiritual walls that separate Limbo from the living world. Anytime someone translates between this world and the living world, the mists swirl about them before they step through. I'm not sure whether the mists are required for translation or if they are a result of the translation. Whichever it is, the mists are most pervasive in the cities because that is where most of the translations take place."

I nodded and wondered a little nervously if Jonus's theory meant that it might be more difficult or even impossible to translate out here where there was almost no mist at all. It was disquieting to think that in an emergency, escape to the living world might not be an option.

"I have noticed something peculiar however," Jonus said interrupting my thoughts. He was looking at me with a curious look on his features.

"What?"

"The mists appear to follow you. It's hard to tell, but I think they may even be coming from you."

I gaped at him for a moment and looked around. I felt the presence of the familiar mists. They felt like an old security blanket, comforting and warm. Indeed there was mist nearby, and as we continued to move it did seem to move with us. A hundred paces beyond our moving group there was no mist at all. Perhaps my practicing with it, and my reliance upon it had created some kind of bond between us. I shrugged and turned back to Jonus.

"What do you suppose that means?"

"I don't know," Jonus answered ruefully. "But as we have already discussed, you are something special. You appear to have the ability to shape the mists to your desire. I have never heard of such a power, but what you did with that mist cloak bears this out."

The sky was rapidly growing darker as night approached. Soon it would be nearly pitch black out here away from the lights and glowing mists of the city. Darkness isn't a hindrance to ghosts, however, as our eyes automatically adjust to whatever the lighting situation is. The troops were getting restless, and the captains were having a harder and harder time keeping them in any semblance of a formation. Though we'd made plain the importance of silence while we marched, the free souls carried on conversations and even called out to mates in other units. Though the troops were restless their morale was high, so I couldn't bring myself to reprimand them. Unfortunately, an undisciplined army can lead to big problems as I was soon to discover.

"Can you hide the whole army as you did with me? We would gain an insurmountable advantage," Jonus asked.

I shook my head negatively. "Even if I could, it would use up far more power than I'm willing to burn this early in the operation. I need to hold back as much of my strength as possible in case of unexpected difficulties."

Jonus nodded unhappily and said nothing more. We approached the summit of the hill, and I raised a hand signaling the army to hold their current position. Jonus and I cautiously went up ahead to get a look at the valley Jonus called the Devil's Gorge. I did put a cloak around the two of us in order to provide additional concealment from anything that might be watching the heights.

A hellish red glow illuminated the valley, but thick billowing smoke obscured the gorge's lower reaches. Steep hills surrounded the deep valley on Southern, Eastern, and Western sides. To the North, a mountain loomed darkly, its shadow writhing in the undulating smoke below it, giving the gorge a feel of crawling horror. The celestial steel railroad tracks defied the obscuring smoke and blazed a visible trail through the heart of the valley. The air was hot and oppressive. Everything was still. There was no movement, and no sign of habitation other than the shadowed forms of buildings.

After assuring myself that there was nothing more to see from this vantage point, I released the mist cloak and waved the small force of free souls onward. As we descended into the Devil's Gorge, the temperature increased dramatically. We began to encounter areas where the ground was so hot that it actually bubbled. Presently, we came to a road that paralleled the tracks that came in from the South. We turned onto it, heading North towards the great mountain. We could only see a few feet in front of us; the smoke obscured everything but the tracks. As with the railroad, the armor and weapons bourn by the free souls defiantly resisted the efforts of the smoke to hide them from sight.

Dark shapes loomed out of the smoky landscape soon resolving themselves into a railroad station and warehouse. A pair of specters were approaching us from the station apparently drawn by the strange sight of the glowing blue brilliance of our celestial steel which pierced the normally shrouded gorge. They stopped in surprise when they saw us more clearly. They glanced at each other in confusion, and then lifted devil's iron collar rods and pointed them towards us.

Behind me, a roar of anger sprang forth from the free souls, and my army dissolved into a mob of charging, vengeful ghosts. The mob went around me as I stood frozen in shock; all semblance of discipline among the troops had vanished in an instant. Only Jonus maintained self control. The two specters were cut down before they could bring their talons to bear. A milling mass of free souls hacked at them violently even after they'd fallen and dissipated. More specters disgorged from the station and warehouse drawn by the angry shouts of the free souls. These also were overwhelmed and destroyed, although a few of them managed to injure some of their assailants.

"Let's go," I said to Jonus as I recovered from my surprise.

It was clear to me that we would not regain control of the raging ghosts for a while. They had split into roving bands and gone off in several different directions hunting for more enemies to vent their hatred on. I should have anticipated such a possibility. The free souls weren't soldiers accustomed to discipline. None of them probably realized the incredible danger that they'd put us in. If Black Maria's forces could get themselves organized, they'd destroy us without a single thought. God forbid if Black Maria herself showed up. We wouldn't even be able to retreat. We'd be scattered and hunted down to the last ghost. I needed to find Black Maria's local leader before it could get things organized.

"Where are the leaders likely to be?" I asked Jonus.

"The Bull's Head Tavern," he replied instantly and took the lead at a run. "This way."

We ran down the broken street passing a few old houses, a factory, a general store, and some other nondescript buildings. All of the structures were being invaded by bands of free souls intent on finding every specter that they could. The sounds of battle could be heard here and there as we ran for the town's center. A group of two and three story buildings were clustered around a square in the town's center, and a pitched battle was in full swing as we arrived.

A band of free souls was fighting desperately. A horde of specters and darklings attacked them from all sides. As we approached, a second unit of free souls joined the fray. The closer we got to the battle, the more dire the situation grew. In the span of a heartbeat I saw two free souls get cut down by a huge specter that was covered in red iron spikes. The creature was twice as large as any other specter that I'd ever seen. Its claws were as long and thick as a pair of short swords, and it used them to devastating effect. Even celestial steel armor was no match for those brutal talons. They cut a swath through the outmatched free souls. I wanted to challenge that beast of a specter, but I saw at least a dozen more of the large mutant specters pouring out of the Bull's Head Tavern. I had a sinking feeling that if I didn't deal with them immediately, all would be lost.

"Help them," I ordered Jonus, pointing towards the now terrified free souls fighting in the square. Without waiting to see if he was following my instructions, I ran for the oncoming gang of oversized specters and yelled a challenge to them.

"Over here you motherless sons of bitches!"

The creatures glanced towards me, and a darkling male standing on the porch of the Bull's Head Tavern pointed at me, communicating a silent command to the specters. In unison, the creatures turned, howled, and charged towards me. I stopped and smiled at the oncoming band. When they were a mere eight feet away, I unleashed my banshee wail upon them.

My scream reverberated throughout the valley followed shortly thereafter by the dismayed cries of ghosts on both sides of the battle. I had timed my wail perfectly, catching the entire group of super specters in the sonic blast. All of them were ripped to shreds; their incredible size and toughness was no match for the banshee wail. The Bull's Head Tavern sustained damage from the blast. One of the porch's support beams had splintered and the entire building drooped to one side as if drunk. The black clad darkling who had obviously been in command of the specters, lay sprawled on the porch. I called on the wind, and before he could react, I was standing over him my katana leveled at his throat.

"Where is Black Maria?" I demanded.

The darkling had cold, black eyes that stared back at me with malice. I was surprised to note that he was unafraid. "She'll be here soon. I'll be glad to present you to her."

He wiggled his fingers, and a black ball of dark energy leapt towards me. I jumped back and called on the mist cloak to protect me. The black ball of energy struck the shield and dissipated harmlessly. The darkling was on his feet now, a devil's iron sword in hand.

"What the hell are you? Who sent you?" the darkling asked angrily.

"I'm Veronika Kane. Who are you?"

"I'm Mordred. Who sent you?"

"Mordred?" I laughed. "Did your mother give you that name or did you change it after you became a ghost. I bet your real name is Sue or something like that. I work for King Arthur if you really must know."

He growled angrily and launched a vicious series of strikes at my head. I parried the blows easily and delivered a probing stroke of my own. Mordred deflected the blow nonchalantly, a sneer appearing on his face. He counterattacked with a swift strike that would have disemboweled me if it had landed, but I sidestepped the attack and riposted with a weak swing that the darkling easily parried. After another minute of back and forth action, I became certain that Mordred was only an adequate swordsman: one who relied heavily on intimidation rather than skill. Such bullying tactics were often effective until you encountered a true swordsman; then you were screwed.

Mordred was screwed, and I set about making sure that he was fully aware of it. I could have ended it within seconds. I should have done so. Jonus and the free souls needed my help, but rage coursed through my ghostly veins. Mordred became a personification of Freak in my mind, and I wanted to make him suffer. I launched a full scale attack against the darkling; my blade danced in and out, expertly avoiding his attempts to parry. Each strike scored a hit, bringing a gasp of pain and surprise to his lips. At first, Mordred's face was pinched with fury. He redoubled his efforts to strike me, calling on all of his supernatural speed, but it was to no avail. Not one of his attacks came close to striking me. I toyed with him until I finally saw the light of realization enter his eyes. My father would have been very disappointed with me if he'd been present at this moment. It was contrary to everything he'd taught me. Toying around with an obviously weaker opponent was very dishonorable. Looking at this darkling though, I could only see those who had tortured and raped me. Mordred bore the brunt of my rage at those who had hurt me.

In a final act of desperation, Mordred raised his empty left hand plainly intending to blast me with another bolt of dark energy, but before he could do so, my blade flashed out and severed it. He howled in agony as tendrils of mist rose from the stump of his arm. He tried to flee from me, but I kicked him behind the knee, sending him sprawling to the ground. I stood over him as he tried to rise.

"Please … don't kill me. I'll do whatever you want," he begged, his dark eyes full of fear.

"All that I want from you is for you to die," I answered coldly. I punctuated the statement by decapitating him with an arching swing of my katana.

I turned to the square and saw that the free souls had regained control of the situation with at least half of our total force having converged onto the scene. What the free souls lacked in skill and experience they made up with overwhelming numbers. Jonus was still locked in combat with the mutant specter. He'd suffered several wounds, but he'd given more than he'd received. My practiced eye judged that he would soon defeat the specter, and though there was still a chance that the battle could turn against him, I didn't want to interfere. Jonus had to establish himself as a warrior in his own right. I instead moved into the more contested parts of the fray, lending leadership and morale to the fighting groups of free souls.

Jonus finally defeated the specter after blasting it with a blue bolt of energy somewhat akin to the black bolt of energy used against me by Mordred and the Conductor. The bolt struck the specter square in the torso, and it let out a bellow of agony as it ignited into blue flames. The demise of the leading specter was so demoralizing for the rest of the enemy forces that they attempted to surrender or flee, but the free souls gave no quarter; they destroyed them all, their celestial blades rising and falling in a tide of death. I let them finish killing off the last of the specters then shouted for quiet.

"You are all damned lucky to be alive," I said angrily. "If Jonus and I hadn't come here when we did, you all would have been destroyed. You aren't a mob. If you want to enjoy your freedom for any length of time you're going to have to start thinking and behaving like soldiers."

Many in the mass hung their heads in shame while a sizable portion of them looked on with respectful defiance.

"Get back into your units," I ordered and waited for the company of grumbling ghosts to reform into their ragtag formations. "First, Second, and Fourth units are to search the town, destroy any remaining enemies, and get control of any straggling free souls that haven't rejoined their units. Once the town is searched you are to secure the train station. If you see any signs of an incoming train or large body of ghosts moving down the road, you are to fall back to this square and send word to me. Captain Bret will command this force. Now move out."

Captain Bret saluted me and yelled out orders and the three units moved out with as much precision as could be expected from former slaves.

"Units Three and Six will maintain defensive position in this square. Captain Stevens will command overall. Units five, seven, and eight will come with me and Jonus to the Devil's Forge. Let's move out."

Cops and robbers weren't the only shows that I'd watched with my dad. War movies had been among our favorites. Movies are a far cry from the real thing, I knew, but it did help to be able to fake it. Dad often said that appearances could trump fact under the right circumstances. I might have no military experience, but if I acted like I knew what I was doing people would follow me as long as I continued to produce victories.

I would have liked to spend more time getting my troops properly set up before heading out, but a sense of urgency coursed through every fiber of my being. There was something I needed to discover about the mines. I led the small force that I'd selected Northward. Jonus walked at my side. The smoke and heat grew more oppressive the closer we drew to the mountain. The road we traveled upon changed abruptly, its stony surface gave way to a blue paving that could only be celestial steel. I marveled at this waste of the valuable material till I saw that the earth on either side of the road was actually bubbling. Gaseous clouds emitted a foul stench that rose into the air, and dramatically obscured visibility everywhere except for along the road.

Tongues of flame began to erupt in various places on either side of us. The free souls accompanying me began to mutter nervously in response. Ahead, the road became a bridge crossing over a river of molten lava. Beyond that, the mountain rose, looming above us like a jagged tooth. The mouth of a cave could be seen yawning blackly from the cliff face. We approached cautiously, the landscape around us now completely in flames except for the road. We were only a hundred feet from the cave's entrance when the darkness of the cave itself seemed to move, causing us all to come to an involuntary stop. The moving shadows resolved itself into an enormous black hound. The beast had red eyes and gleaming white teeth. It was the size of a small pony: a war mastiff of truly terrifying proportions. It wore a devil's iron collar and a celestial steel chain trailed behind it, vanishing into the shadows of the cave.

"Stay here," I ordered Jonus and the free souls that followed us. I sheathed my katana and moved forward slowly, holding my hand out towards the beast. It growled at me menacingly, its hackles rising. Unperturbed by its threats, I continued to advance, hand outstretched in a gesture of friendliness. I saw its muscles tense up in preparation for an attack. I avoided meeting its baleful gaze, knowing that meeting its stare would only be interpreted as a challenge. It suddenly lunged at me, moving a heartbeat to slow to catch my extended arm. I had been anticipating such an attack from the hound and easily evaded it. While its jaws snapped shut on empty air, I called on the wind and with blinding speed somersaulted onto the beast's back.

I slid into a riding position, one arm grasping its collar, while I reached out for the celestial steel chain that bound it with my other hand. It let out a howl of rage and tried to dislodge me by shaking itself violently. When this failed, it tried bucking me off. Once I got a hold of the chain, I snapped it apart with a simple thought. Now free, the hound gave up on the bucking and instead tried to bite me by craning its neck around. I avoided its jaws and launched my own attack, swiftly wrapping the chain around its muzzle. I then willed the celestial steel chain to change its shape into a tight muzzle. The beast frantically tried to crush me by rolling over onto its back, but I leapt clear of it before it could dislodge me.

The beast came to its feet quickly. It tried to dislodge the muzzle with a brush of its enormous foreleg with no success. I stood before the thing, meeting its angry gaze. I raised my hand toward it and willed the mists that accompanied me to envelop the beast and prevent it from moving. The mists coalesced around the hound and thickened until the beast could no longer move. I strode forward and crouched so that I was looking directly into its eyes. I stared into those red eyes for a long minute, doing my best to communicate to it that I was the master; it would obey me for now on. I didn't want to kill the beast. I'd seen enough dogs die recently, but I wasn't at all certain that the thing was tamable. After another minute, I let the mist cloud return to its incorporeal form. The hound scrambled away from the mist but made no threatening moves towards me.

"Come here boy," I told it. The beast moved slowly towards me, its head down and tail between its legs. "It's ok boy. I'll get that muzzle and wretched collar off of you."

The hound wagged its tail hopefully and sat on its haunches a few feet away from me. I leaned over and touched the muzzle, willing it to flow into my hand. I then drew my knife and brought it to the beast's neck. We stared at each other for a moment. I could see it struggling with its instinct to defend itself against the danger of the drawn knife at its throat. It remained passive, and I used the celestial steel knife to cut the devil's iron collar from around its neck. I then shaped the muzzle into a blue collar and placed it around the hound's neck.

The hound rose slowly and shook itself. It studied me for a moment, then it sat back on its haunches waiting for my command.

"Good boy," I told the hound, patting it on the head.

It yawned and looked at me expectantly. It sniffed at the collar for a moment before it turned its attention to my hand. Jonus approached tentatively. The beast growled softly, but I quieted him with a shushing sound.

"Is this wise Veronika?" Jonus asked nervously. "This is one of Black Maria's shadow hounds. It has eaten many shades. It's exceedingly vicious."

The free souls muttered angrily and a few of them took a few uncertain steps towards the dark hound.

"I know what I'm doing," I answered, scratching the creature behind its ears. It watched the free souls and Jonus with suspicion, and I saw that it understood their unfriendly attitudes towards it. I needed to give it a name quickly and then get on with the mission. "This is Thor. He's my friend."

Some of the free souls complained bitterly at this pronounce-ment, but now that the beast had a name most of the tension in the free souls evaporated. There's power in names. Jonus still clearly harbored reservations, but he kept them to himself. For his part, Thor seemed pleased with his new name and changed circumstances.

"Fifth unit, hold the bridge and the entrance to this cave. Seventh and Eighth units are with me." Without further delay, I stepped into the dark mine entrance. Thor padded quietly at my side with Jonus close behind.

25

THE MINE SHAFT WAS WIDE ENOUGH to accommodate a large truck which allowed my troops to follow in their normal ranks. We moved through pitched darkness until we reached a large cavern nearly a quarter mile down from the entrance. The chamber seemed to be a storage and loading facility. Numerous crates were stacked haphazardly here and there around the area. Three smaller tunnels exited the cavern going off in different directions. A quick search of the crates revealed that they were full of raw celestial steel ore. After we'd searched the room thoroughly, I turned to Thor.

"Do you know the way to the Devil's Forge?"

Thor answered with a half growl and reluctantly padded towards the middle tunnel. I followed him with Jonus at my back. The free souls took up the rear in tighter ranks now. The passage descended sharply and the air became incredibly warm. The passageway curved sharply several times and the darkness gradually gave way to an orange glow coming from below.

The shaft flattened out after descending for about a half mile. It ended in a colossal chamber that dwarfed the one above. The source of the orange glow was revealed to be a gargantuan furnace that climbed nearly a hundred feet upward to the cavern's vaulted ceiling. Tongues of red, yellow, white, and blue flames billowed upwards into the caverns heights and produced a hellish heat. A half dozen tunnels led from this main hall providing access to other parts of the complex. The enormous room was strewn with the implements of forging: anvils, quenching buckets, hammers, tongs, and other implements that I didn't recognize. The roaring of the forge fire was nearly as loud as the sound made by a train. It was punctuated by the sound of a hammer pounding on an anvil. Over all of this din, there was a high pitched sound that frayed on my nerves.

The cavern was devoid of other ghosts except for one which was a creature of enormous size both in height and mass. It was working at the anvil and didn't seem to be aware of us. It wore only a loincloth. Its skin was translucent revealing its skeletal frame beneath. Then it suddenly hit me; I was gazing upon the form of the largest reaper that I'd ever seen or even imagined in my worst nightmares. It was nearly ten feet tall and had the mass of a bodybuilder. Its bones were actually shaped like muscles would be after years of weight lifting, going as far as to ripple with every swing of its mighty arm.

The high pitched sound seemed to emanate from the anvil on which the reaper was working. I moved closer in order to get a better look and saw with horror that the object being pounded was, in fact, a shade. Anger flared up inside of me, but it was tempered by terror. The Conductor had been surprisingly difficult to defeat, and this reaper made the Conductor look like a wimp. Sometimes when I'm determined to fight but so scared that I want to pee myself, I let my witty tongue loose so as to trick everyone into thinking that I'm really not afraid.

"You must be the Forge-Master," I said sarcastically. The reaper whirled around to face me, its speed impressive for a creature so large. In one hand it held a devil's iron hammer nearly as big as I am while the other hand clutched a wriggling ghost that had been shaped into a disc. "I destroyed the Conductor today, and Mordred was a loser, so I think sending you into that forge would constitute a hat-trick."

The Forge-Master stared at me with its hateful glowing eyes for a long second. I felt the free souls behind me fall back in terror, and even Jonus clutched at my arm in warning. I wanted desperately to turn and run from that horrible gaze, but I knew that doing so would mean the end of me and my revolution.

"I will forge you into a fine trinket for my mistress," the reaper boomed, raising its massive hammer in a threatening gesture.

"Ah, you're the Jeweler, not the Forge-Master. Here I was worried that this might be a tough fight," I said mockingly. The wittier my tongue, the more terrified and fucked I know I am.

I decided quickly that coming to blows with this creature on even terms would prove disastrous. To that end, I called on the mists with the intent of enveloping the reaper in the gelatinous shield that I'd used to great effect on the Conductor. For the first time since coming to Limbo, the mists didn't respond to my call. A quick glance around showed me that there was no mist at all in the cavern. I realized belatedly that the Devil's Forge itself was probably responsible for this. Heart in my throat, I dodged the Forge-Master's sudden attack, dancing aside from a mighty blow of its hammer. The reaper moved with bewildering speed for a creature of its size. It was upon me before I could recover from the realization that I'd have to fight without one of my most important tools. I called upon the wind to lend me more speed and was relieved to find that this power was unaffected by the forge.

The first part of the battle consisted of the reaper chasing me around the huge hall, its hammer rising and falling. I made damned sure to evade each swing since parrying wasn't even an option considering the reaper's vast strength. I scored an occasional hit upon it whenever I had a moment to counterattack.

My hits only produced minimal damage and the reaper was neither slowed nor weakened.

After dancing about the room to no affect, the Forge-Master changed its tactics suddenly charging directly into the ranks of the watching free souls. It destroyed two of the unfortunate ghosts before I could react. The others scattered, and it shrieked in triumph. The shriek was answered by hooting calls and a moment later specters began to pour into the vast hall.

"Hold for your lives!" I shouted, charging the Forge-Master with a desperate fury. "Jonus, rally them! Thor, to me!"

The battle was close and hard now. Both sides were aware that no quarter would be given. I took to the air to harry the reaper from above. This tactic had an enormous impact as my slashing strikes threatened the brutish reaper's head and could not be easily ignored. The aerial assault had the added benefit of weakening the skeletal ghost's attacks as it was forced to flail its hammer about ineffectually rather than using the downward crushing strokes that it was obviously accustomed to. While I attacked from above, Thor struck from below. His huge teeth tore chunks from the Forge-Master with each darting attack. The hound's teeth seemed to cause the reaper more pain than did my katana at times. All about me the battle was fierce and hard fought, but after the initial scattering and surprise entry of the specters, Jonus rallied the free souls. They fought with grim determination, making a good accounting of themselves.

The Forge-Master changed its tactics again. It suddenly dropped its hammer and, with lightning speed that belied its bulky size, it snatched the darting Thor up by the throat. With no effort, the reaper lifted him up to use against me as a shield. I pulled back from my own assault and the crafty brute hurled the hound at me. I barely had time to drop my katana before Thor could be impaled upon it. The careening hound struck me square in the chest and we plummeted to ground in a tangle of limbs. I was able to use the wind to cushion our fall, but that was the least of the dangers we now faced. Thor's full weight pinned me to the floor, his legs were splayed to either side of me. The Forge-Master had already retrieved its hammer and was striding towards us. Its hammer rose in a terrible arc that would certainly shatter both of us in a single fell stroke.

Thor was trying to regain his footing, but I knew that there wasn't enough time. I grabbed his head with one arm and pulled it to my chest. Thankfully he didn't resist. I craned my neck up as far as I could to get a look at the oncoming reaper.

"Keep still!" I whispered to Thor.

I watched transfixed as the devil's iron hammer descended towards us. It was like watching a slow motion replay of an NFL football game except this would be the final play for me if that hammer hit the mark. When it was only a few feet above us and the reaper was clearly in view beyond it, I let loose with my banshee wail.

This was something that I'd wanted to avoid down here in the mine complex. The collateral damage that the wail usually produced could bring the whole mountain down on our heads, but I had no other alternative. I didn't want to give this creature the opportunity to follow through on its threat to make me into jewelry. The sonic blast of my wail produced its typical results, shattering the oncoming hammer into shards. The Forge-Master's body was sent sailing through the air until it struck the far wall and shattered into millions of pieces.

Normally after I gave voice to my banshee wail, a stunned silence followed, but down here in the mines, the wail was repeated over and over again as it echoed through the miles of tunnels that made up the complex. The mountain above shuddered and everyone held their breath against the certainty that the walls would collapse. After another few moments of tense waiting for the proverbial pin to fall, the reverberations finally subsided and audible sighs could be heard around the room. I wanted to laugh. Ghosts don't need to breath, yet when it came right down to it, we fell into the habits of our past lives. A deep stillness settled over the mine complex. Only the Devil's Forge seemed unimpressed with recent events and continued its crackling roar.

The free souls were the first to recover. Seeing the reaper destroyed leant them a new found courage. They fell upon the remaining specters with vicious determination. The specters, for their part, attempted to flee, but they were outnumbered and terrified by the destruction of the Forge-Master. The free souls massacred the specters. None escaped. Thor continued to lay on me. He was panting heavily, still stunned. I gently got myself out from under him and massaged his head until he regained his composure. I retrieved my katana and waited for a report on our losses. Jonus dealt with the troops and after a few moments reported that a dozen free souls had been destroyed in the battle, one of which had been caught in my scream. I noted with sadness that the remaining free souls now regarded me with fear, flinching visibly whenever my gaze fell on them. My heart ached at the thought that I'd destroyed one of my own.

"I feared that we were finished when that brute attacked our line and then all those specters poured into the room," Jonus said shaking his head in astonishment. "I have never been part of such a combat. It is the kind of event that bards sing about. Well done Veronika. You saved us all."

"I screwed up bad Jonus," I said wanting to sit down and cry. "If you hadn't been here to lead the free souls, we'd have been toast. I put us in horrible jeopardy and killed some of my own troops."

"You are being too hard on yourself Veronika," Jonus answered with compassion in his voice. "You had little choice. If you'd fallen the rest of us would have followed soon after. You made the right choice."

I didn't want to agree with him. It hurt too much to realize what I'd done, but the alternative was to quit. I'd decided to lead this fight. I couldn't back out when things got tough or unpleasant. I had to do whatever it took to ensure victory, no matter the cost. Liberty and victory is what the free souls were expecting me to provide. Now I knew what the burden of leadership was all about. The free souls were my responsibility, I gave them the hope that allowed them to throw off their chains. I couldn't let them down. I sighed and looked around the cavern noticing for the first time that there were several celestial steel cages lined up in a row at the base of the Devil's Forge. Most of the prisoners in the cages were shades though a few were furies. All of the captives except a beautiful white owl seemed completely oblivious to their surroundings. Many of them were curled up into fetal positions. The owl stared at me; its large yellow eyes projected an air of calm and timeless wisdom.

"Jonus, leave a couple of free souls with me and take the rest with you down the tunnel that the specters came from," I commanded looking back at the luminary. "Send someone back for me if you run into trouble."

Jonus nodded and began giving orders. The free souls obeyed without question. I was gratified to see that Jonus had earned their respect. The few free souls left with me shuffled their feet nervously and looked back the way their companions had gone with longing. Thor padded over to my side and whined, shaking his head several times and prodding at my hand with his nose.

"I'm sorry Thor; you'll get your hearing back soon," I said rubbing below his ears. "I didn't have any choice. He would have smashed us both if I hadn't let loose with that scream."

Thor looked up at me and barked sharply. He bumped his bulk into my legs almost knocking me over. I got the message and laughed. He wasn't afraid of me and agreed with my actions.

I walked over to one of the cages that contained a shade and pulled the bars apart. The celestial steel yielded to my wishes. I waited for a moment, but the shade didn't react in any way. Perplexed, I stepped away from the cage and beckoned one of my free souls over to me.

"See if you can coax him out," I said pointing to the open cage. I moved to the next one and opened it as I'd done with the first. A minute later, the cages of all of the shades were open, but the free souls couldn't get any responses out of the shades even when they forcefully pulled them out. The same proved true with all of the furies except the owl.

I finally stood before the owl's cage which was the last one in the row. I was mystified by the near vegetative state of the prisoners. A message arrived from Jonus reporting that he'd discovered hundreds of shade prisoners below, and all of them seemed coherent. He was in the process of freeing them and trying to recruit them to the free soul cause. There were also a large number of furies being held in captivity as well, but we weren't going to free them yet as they presented a security risk to our forces. I shaped the bars of the owl's cage into a doorway that the creature could easily navigate through.

"Thank you," it said.

I jumped back in surprise and quickly looked around to see if anyone was playing a joke on me. The nearest free souls were gaping at the owl in astonishment as well. I looked back at the owl and squinted at it.

"You can talk?"

"Oh my, I can see that you're a bright one," it answered sarcastically. "Of course I can talk. Not all beasts are dumb."

Thor growled at the bird disapprovingly and it fluttered its wings nervously for a moment.

"Don't be so touchy," it snapped at the hound. "And yes I did see what she did to the reaper. Most impressive. She doesn't have the aura of a banshee, though I'll admit that I've never seen anything with an aura like hers."

The owl had its head tilted and it studied me thoughtfully, its unblinking eyes weighing me.

"What's wrong with the other prisoners?" I asked it.

"They have been put through the forge I'm afraid. There's nothing you can do for them."

"What do you mean? What has happened to them?"

"This is the Devil's Forge," the owl explained in exasperation as if speaking to a child. "Rumors say that these fires come from hell itself. The creature Black Maria uses her art of soul shaping here, creating specters and other things. Specters are created by combining several shade souls with some furies. The more you add, the bigger the specter. The forge is used to make the soul more malleable, and it erases the intellect of the creature going through it. The Forge-Master then beats the poor souls into a shape that Black Maria prefers to start with."

I stared at the owl in horror.

"Let me get this straight," I said. "You're saying that specters are created by fusing the souls of shades and furies together. Furthermore the forge alters the way souls think, basically turning them into a blank slate that can then be reprogrammed. Is that right?"

"That is a fairly accurate understanding, though you must understand that the forge itself taints the souls that pass through it. So most of the subjects thoughts are erased, but the ones that remain are corrupt and evil. It isn't as if you can take them and retrain them to be as they were before the forging. They are tainted and evil after going through the forge fires."

"What about you? You seem to have gone through it ok."

"Didn't you hear a word I said?" the owl said in consternation. "No one goes through it unchanged. Logic would then dictate that I haven't been through the forge yet, wouldn't you think?"

"I've got to destroy this monstrous thing," I declared angrily. The hellish device made my ghostly skin crawl. This thing is what allowed specters to be made. It was a malevolent tool that had to be destroyed. Looking at the gargantuan forge, I noticed for the first time that it was made entirely of devil's iron.

"You can't destroy this, it's indestructible," cooed the owl indignantly.

"How do you know it's indestructible?" I asked.

"Everyone knows that artifacts are indestructible."

"Well, I mean to try," I said and turned to the free souls under my charge. "Send word to Jonus to get this place evacuated now. Get everyone up top and across the bridge."

The free souls leapt into action, and soon they were pouring back into the cavern and heading up the tunnel we'd come down from.

"Are you a wizard by any chance?" the owl interrupted my contemplations of the forge.

"No," I answered turning back to it with interest once more. "Do you have a name? Why is it that you can talk while none of the other furies seem able to?"

"Of course I have a name," the owl answered. "I'm Sebastian, and I was a wizard's familiar in life. That's why I can talk."

"A familiar, what's that?"

"It's a wizard's companion," Sebastian answered gruffly. "Don't you know anything about wizards? Familiars help them with spells, and we collect things and spy for them."

"Well, Sebastian, I'm glad to make your acquaintance," I said earnestly. "Will the furies held below listen to you?"

"Probably," Sebastian answered. "You just need to know how to talk to them."

"Good. Would you go down and guide them out of here please?"

"But I want to stay with you," he said petulantly. "You are the most interesting thing I've encountered in all my long years in Limbo."

"Thanks for the complement Sebastian, but I need you to do this for me. You can return to me after you've gotten the furies safely out of here. Keep them away from my free souls. I don't want there to be fighting between us. I'm sure a familiar as resourceful as yourself can think of a way to do this. Find me when you're done if you wish."

Sebastian grumbled a little but finally agreed. As he flew off he sent a final hoot towards Thor who barked back a response. The evacuation continued, and I took some time to consult with a free soul who'd been an engineer in life. I needed to strike the most vulnerable point of the forge if I was going to have a chance of destroying it. When I explained to the engineer,

Andrew Milner, what I intended to do, he looked terrified. He told me that my plan might work but that it would most likely result in me being buried under the mountain. I reminded him that I was a ghost and not really worried about being trapped and it was unlikely that a cave in would cause my final death. All of the celestial steel veins in the mountain didn't pose a threat to me like it did with other ghosts since the metal would just part for me rather than crushing and trapping me beneath it. I just had to make sure that the devil's iron of the forge didn't topple on top of me. Andrew studied the forge for some time and provided me with advice on how to accomplish my goal.

It took nearly an hour to complete the evacuation and as the last of the prisoners and free soul units retreated from the mine. Word arrived from town that a train was approaching Centralia. I sent word to Jonus to pull everyone back into the village square and hold it as best he could. I would be there shortly I hoped.

I stared intently at the forge for a few minutes gathering up all my strength and rage into one burning spot in the pit of my stomach. The prisoners who'd been put through the forge lay at my feet. The fact that I couldn't save them made my ectoplasmic blood boil. When the rage reached a level that I could no longer contain, I let loose with the banshee wail. The cavern walls trembled as my scream reverberated throughout the complex. When the rumbling subsided, I saw that my attack on the forge had only produced a small crack. I gathered my will again and let forth my wail upon the forge once more. This time however, I didn't pause for breath but screamed again, and again, and again. The entire mountain was shaking and the walls and ceilings began to crumble. Still I continued my sonic assault, aiming each blast at a structural point of weakness as advised by the engineer; the crack on the forge grew larger, spreading across the surface of the artifact.

On the eighth blast, the flames of the forge erupted outwards, and I was forced to leap away in order to avoid the corrupting flames. A demonic being wielding a fiery sword emerged from the forge's fire and immediately sprang at me. I dodged the hell-ish being and continued the steady stream of wails against the forge.

"Noooo …!" the demon shrieked, but it was too late. With a thunderous crash, the Devil's Forge shattered, as if it were made of glass. The flames and the demon were instantly snuffed out. The mountain was falling all around me. I called the wind and flew with all haste for the mine entrance.

I was battered and fatigued by the time I made it to the sur-face, but I was alive, at least as alive as any ghost can claim to be. I was certain that I'd just destroyed one of Hell's greatest tools. Fatigue was a small price to pay. The mountain continued to shudder as the mine complex collapsed. Thor was waiting for me at the cave entrance and grimly herded me across the rocking celestial bridge and away from the mountain. A small group of free souls awaited me there.

"Jonus sends word ma'am," one of ghosts said. "Black Maria has arrived."

The feeling of elation at my victory over the Devil's Forge vanished. I was exhausted, near spent from the day's multiple combats and now perhaps one of Limbo's deadliest creatures had arrived to take her vengeance on me. With a sigh I drew my katana and started running towards the village square.

"Come on," I called. "We can rest when we're dead."

26

THE TOWN SQUARE WAS IN CHAOS. A pack of massive hounds that were exact clones of Thor had charged the front ranks of the free soul army while mutant specters followed in their wake. One side of the free soul line was bulging back, threatening to break under pressure from a pack of black hounds led by a particularly large mutant specter. Jonus had rallied the center, his celestial blade dancing in deadly arcs that left hounds and specters howling in pain and fury. The right flank was holding under Captain Bret's command. The free souls there fought in disciplined ranks that prevented the enemy from overwhelming them with their sheer numerical advantage. There was no sign of Black Maria yet, but I knew that she would make an appearance soon at a time and place of her choosing.

I could not afford to hold myself back as Black Maria did. The left flank was buckling; if it collapsed the entire free soul army would be in danger of being completely enveloped and destroyed. I charged into the fray, once more calling on the wind to lend me speed and power as I leaped over the milling ranks of my own troops. I sailed through the air and struck the lead specter feet first. Though it was much larger than me, my wind enhanced speed granted me force far beyond what my size would normally warrant. It grunted in surprise as the impact flung it back several yards and it was knocked prone. I landed gracefully astride its torso, and before it could react, I swung my katana in a flashing arc that removed its head. My feet hit the ground as the specter's body dissipated into mist.

I dodged the crushing jaws of a lunging hound and severed both its back legs as its momentum carried it past me. Two free souls finished the beast off with hacking blades. A ragged cheer went up as I slew two more hounds with serpent-like strikes that caught one beast in the eye and the other in the throat as it opened its jaws to howl in rage. Though a part of me cringed at committing such violence against the dog-like creatures, the aura of palpable evil that surged from the beasts assuaged my conscience. Beside me, Thor fought with a devastating blood thirstiness that left another half dozen hounds and specters destroyed or badly mangled. The line behind us solidified and the attackers all along our front fell back in confusion.

I saw that this momentary respite would not last long. More specters were arriving every second; a horde of the massive beasts soon outnumbered us five to one. Looking over my force, I saw that we'd sustained heavy losses. Though the ghosts from the Devil's Forge complex were more numerous than our original band, they were new to the cause and few were armed. The new free souls were also far more likely to cower before the oncoming specters. Not having been bloodied in a victorious fight as the original force had been, they tended to fall back onto old survival skills. The chief among these reactions was to cower before the specters. It was clear to me that victory wasn't possible here. We were going to have to retreat.

I signaled to Jonus to join me for a quick conference.

"I want you to take the new arrivals and find us an escape route out of this valley," I told him when he'd reached me. "We can't win here. They've brought too many and most of our force isn't properly equipped. We'll have to try to retreat."

"That is one of the most difficult and dangerous maneuvers in warfare," he said unhappily.

"I know," I answered, fighting against the exhaustion that threatened to overwhelm me. My stomach was tied up in nervous knots. "But we've got no other choice. Get moving, they'll be coming soon."

Black Maria's forces were indeed massing, clearly intending to hit us with such overwhelming force that we'd crumble like an egg being smashed by a sledge hammer. I sent word through the ranks that they were to fall back to the center of the square. The specter army took the retreat as a sign that our army was disintegrating. They howled with blood lust and came rushing forward in a massive wave. The remaining forces at my back retreated in perfect order and reformed at the center of the square. I stood alone with Thor at my side as the specters pressed forward with glee.

One of the specter captains recognized the danger that his force was in but was unable to pull them up on time. When the front ranks of the enemy army were within ten feet of me, I unleashed the banshee wail. I was tired, and reaching into myself for the surge of rage required to power the banshee yell was difficult until I let the memory of Freak raping me slide across my memory. The scream of hate that I unleashed obliterated the front dozen rows of the specters and hounds in a single moment. The following half dozen ranks were thrown back into their oncoming fellows. The whole mass was thrown into such disarray that vicious battles broke out within their own ranks. Tears flowed down my face as I stood facing my enemies, fatigue and soul deep pain robbed me of any elation at the havoc that I'd wrought among them. Arms embraced me, and I was lifted off my feet and carried to the front lines of the free souls. I let myself rest in the strong arms that held me for a moment. I felt strangely safe and warm for the first time in months. I looked up and saw Captain Bret looking down at me with compassion. I nodded my thanks to him and reluctantly motioned for him to put me down. The free souls were gazing at me with a mixture of awe and confusion; they didn't understand what had caused me to break down. Fortunately, the confusion in the enemy ranks was far greater than my own mental collapse. I had to get a grip on myself before I got myself and everyone else killed.

It took a few minutes for the remaining captains of Black Maria's army to bring a semblance of order back into their ranks. By this time several hundred more specters and hounds had been destroyed by their own companions as those in the front ranks tried to escape from the battle line while those in the back ranks pushed them forward in an attempt to prevent becoming part of the front line themselves. The specters that were being pushed back attacked their own forces in a panicked attempt to get away, many were trampled and killed in the confusion that followed. Meanwhile, I'd ordered my own troops back step-by-step to the very edge of the square. When word arrived from Jonus that a route of evacuation had been secured, I immediately ordered the retreat to begin. The trick to an ordered withdrawal is to maintain a strong defensive line so as to blunt the harrying force's ability to do much damage to the retreating troops. Captain Bret's company had proven itself the most skilled and disciplined unit of the army, so I chose them as the defensive line that would cover the retreat of the rest of the army. Though the enemy horde had been brought under control, the captains were unable to force their troops forward while I stood in their path. The terror that my wail instilled in them was palpable, so despite pleas for me to join the retreat I stayed with Captain Bret and his troops in the rearguard.

A high piercing shriek broke through the din of the stalemated battlefield. The enemy horde went still and silent, an air of anticipation apparent in their suddenly confident stances. A movement from the back ranks caught my eye and a wide avenue opened down the center of the horde. A dark figure strode down that lane; its movements were unnaturally graceful. The figure was clearly female. Long flowing black hair dangled over a bleach white skull, and misshapen breasts could clearly be identified through its tight black leather clothing. Unlike any reaper I'd ever seen though, her eye sockets were shrouded in a miasma of dark shadow rather than the glowing amber light that normally shone from other reapers. The dark miasma of Black Maria's eyes also hung about her like a cloak. She was armed with a sword that was sheathed at her left hip.

I signaled the troops behind me to speed up the retreat. I had a sinking feeling that avoiding a full out battle with this creature was my best course of action. The aura of evil that hung around her was unmistakable.

"So you are the creature that has troubled those fools in Philadelphia for so many weeks," Black Maria stated as she reached the front ranks of her army. Her melodic voice carried as if amplified by an advanced digital sound system. "You have now cost me a great deal. Do you have any idea how much trouble we go through to gather up the furies? The shades are only sent to us in dribbles. It will take months to get things back to normal."

"Oh, I'm guessing that the Forge-Master and the Devil's Forge itself will be even harder to replace. What a shame," I retorted, proving once again how my mouth gets away from me when I'm scared shitless. "I'm all too glad to be a pain in the ass to anyone who keeps slaves."

Black Maria was silent for a moment, her dark eyes boring into me.

"You lie; the Devil's Forge cannot be destroyed."

"Everyone always says that. Haven't you ever heard of the Titanic? Anything can be destroyed, either through bad luck or God's will. In the case of the forge, it was a whole lot of screaming that did it. My mom always said that I had a voice that could crack Mount Rushmore. I guess she was right."

Black Maria cocked her head and said in a low voice. "They are attempting to retreat through the Western pass. Take half the force around through the South gap and cut them off before they can complete the retreat. I will deal with these insignificant flies myself."

It wasn't clear to me who she'd directed the command to, but without any confusion the horde split in two, one of the halves marching back the way they'd come. The force had barely moved a thousand yards when it was suddenly attacked by a host of howling furies. I saw Sebastian flying at their head and quietly blessed the owl for his timely intervention.

"Retreat!" I yelled knowing that the furies were here only to help us escape. They could not turn the tide in our favor, but they did move much more swiftly than the free souls. They would provide a distraction, and then get away when it was time. The troops behind me retreated in good order. Bret's unit was always covering the rear against attack.

Black Maria sprang at me. She moved faster than lightning. She drew her blade which was made of a black metal flecked with crimson. I barely managed to parry the deadly stroke that she sent towards my head. As I dodged a second blow, her free hand lashed out and caught my shoulder. Immediately I was struck by a powerful will that commanded my body to contort in on itself. As her blade moved towards me in a lethal counterstrike, I felt my will collapsing against the dominating presence in my mind. Thor struck her from the flank, and her hand was wrenched from my shoulder. The mind bending presence instantly vanished. I ducked the now clumsy strike at my head and desperately called on the mists for aid. The mist responded. A roiling cloud seemed to explode from my body and enveloped Black Maria. The mists were almost instantly pushed back by the black miasma that surrounded the reaper. The two forces rose above our heads and locked into a battle of their own.

Black Maria grabbed Thor by the back of the neck and shook him violently as if he were a rag doll, then hurled him into a nearby building. I sent a series of swift strikes against her, but she parried these with ease and delivered her own blazing attacks which I found much more difficult to evade. The battle around us raged. The furies had caught the dark army by surprise and had savaged it badly, but the specters had regrouped and were exacting revenge on the wild beasts who were not particularly well suited for fighting against formations in close combat. They had done their part however, for most of the free souls had made their escape. Only a small force was now holding back the horde while Black Maria and I dueled in their midst.

Black Maria tried several times to get a hand on me again, but I stayed vigilant against such attacks and managed to evade them. Thor returned to the battle limping but still proved invaluable as he provided distractions at important moments of the fight. The mist and the dark miasma continue to battle overhead. It appeared that they were evenly matched. Eventually though, Black Maria got below my guard and scored a hit against me. Her evil blade plunged deeply into my side. The pain was excruciating, and I dropped my katana with a groan. The free souls around me cried out in fear and charged the reaper. As soon as the blade had penetrated into my body, the powerful presence of Black Maria's mind once again invaded my body, and her will crushed down upon me. I felt her malevolent power and knew that she intended to shape me into a creature of hideous evil that would be the crown jewels of her dark empire.

Fear and loathing overtook me, and I let loose with a roar of denial that seemed to shake the very foundations of Limbo itself. The banshee wail struck Black Maria full on at point blank range and sent her hurtling through the air to crash in a heap nearly a hundred feet away from me. Hundreds of specters and hounds were once again destroyed in the wake of my cry, but amazingly Black Maria was still moving, albeit slowly. This was the first time that anything had withstood the direct blast of a banshee wail and not been utterly destroyed. The fact that Black Maria had taken the best I had to offer and was still moving scared the crap out of me. A group of free souls rushed to my side and the black blade was pulled out of me, triggering a bought of agony that left me weeping and gasping for air that I of course didn't really need. All the strength had gone from my limbs and I felt myself falling into torpor. The free souls lifted me onto Thor's back and we retreated as best as we could.

The furies had been routed and were in full retreat by now. Instead of an ordered evacuation however, they fled pell-mell in all directions. The band that covered me was forced to send Thor ahead, against my protest. Before losing consciousness I saw them fighting valiantly against overwhelming odds, knowing that they would all parish. Captain Brett led the first unit that covered our final retreat. Their sacrifice and the aid of the furies made it possible for more than four hundred free souls to escape Centralia into the dark wilderness between the cities.

27

WHEN I AWOKE, IT WAS LIGHT OUT and the odd swaying of Thor's gait made me feel dizzy. I suddenly realized that I'd never really seen the sky in Limbo before; Philadelphia was always shrouded in mists. I must still be in the wilderness between the cities where violent death touches the living world less frequently than it does the large metropolitan areas. I felt mostly rested though not completely. This was surprising considering how long I must have been out for. It had been full night when I'd confronted Black Maria.

A flapping of wings and the sudden appearance of a white owl with glowing yellow eyes gazing down at me unblinkingly startled me to full wakefulness. I sat up quickly. The owl hooted in displeasure dodging aside and flying about my head before alighting on Thor's head facing towards me and giving me a disapproving stare. Thor growled and shook his massive head, sending the owl back aloft. A hearty laugh from nearby led me to look around. I was riding astride Thor while all about us marched an army of free souls. We were moving through a wide valley with the empty abyss of a river on our left flank. I saw that small groups of free souls had been detailed to scout ahead while others fanned out in skirmish lines. All of these scouts wore the celestial steel chain of our original train veterans. The majority of the free souls that marched behind me were not armed and were probably prisoners rescued from Centralia. Walking on my right and the source of the laughter was Jonus. I was astonished to see two luminaries I'd never met before walking at his side.

"What's so funny?" I asked irritably. "And what happened? Who are your friends?"

"Thor and Sebastian are funny," Jonus chuckled again. The owl gave him an indignant hoot and landed on the luminary's head for good measure. Jonus took this in stride and continued to smile. Sebastian, for his part, ignored everyone around him and instead began to preen himself.

"I don't see what's so funny. Do we know if Black Maria's forces are following us? And what about Captain Bret and his troops?"

"Black Maria's forces aren't following us at the moment," Jonus answered all traces of mirth vanishing. "Sebastian has flown back along our trail several times and spotted no sign of pursuit. Captain Bret and the free souls of his company fought so doggedly that they forced Black Maria forces to cut them down to the last man. Their sacrifice allowed us to escape."

I closed my eyes fighting against the tears that threatened to reveal my weakness. Memories of the first time I'd met Bret, the first of the shades to transform into a free soul; he'd grabbed me in a bear hug and twirled me about in a dance of joy. It had been his warm arms and compassion that had comforted me during the battle with Black Maria's forces when the dark memory of my time in the Walnut Street Prison had nearly overwhelmed me. Now he was gone and grief threatened to break my heart.

"Black Maria sent the train back to Pittsburgh for more reinforcements," Sebastian continued unaware of my personal struggle. "She is very angry with you. You destroyed her forge and you killed half her army. She won't rest until she has her vengeance."

"Well she'll have to take a number and get in line," I retorted bitterly. "Keep making the flights if you would, and thanks for bringing those furies into the battle. It really saved our asses."

Sebastian hooted his pleasure, and I smiled briefly before turning back to Jonus.

"Where are we headed?"

"I thought it best to head back South," he answered. "I know where the Master keeps a storage depot outside the city. There will be plenty of celestial steel there for us to fully equip everyone."

I nodded, pleased with his initiative and wisdom. Philadelphia was where I wanted to go.

"Who are your companions?" I asked again.

"These are Barnabas and Rachel," he said by way of introduction. "They were prisoners in the mines."

I greeted both of them. Barnabas was a few inches taller and broader than Jonus, though he wasn't as handsome. His features were too square for my tastes. Rachel, on the other hand, was stunningly beautiful, having long flowing hair, piercing blue eyes, and a lithe, curvaceous figure. Like all luminaries, they were both bathed in a white glowing aura that highlighted their beauty and strained the eyes if you gazed at them for too long.

"We were shackled to the drilling machine that they use to extract celestial ore from the mountain. Jonus found us and cut us free," Rachel volunteered. "I understand that we have you to thank for our rescue."

"The only thanks I need is for you to join our cause. We took some heavy losses, having a couple more luminaries on our side will boost morale," I replied my heart aching for Bret.

"You're a brash lass if I've ever seen one," Barnabas replied in a booming voice. "What you did in the Devil's Forge shows that you've got more than balls, you've got power and luck. I'll join anyone with the balls, luck, and power enough to take on the likes of Black Maria."

"As will I," Rachel said looking askance at Barnabas. "Though I'm sure there's a less crude way to say we'll join."

I immediately liked Barnabas. He was the first luminary to make me feel comfortable. Jonus made me feel like I was a little girl in catechism again; I didn't know how to talk or act around him, and Rachel gave off the same vibe. I hopped off of Thor, patted him on the head for thanks, and joined the luminaries as we marched South.

"What can you tell me about Black Maria, and what she was doing at Centralia?" I asked Rachel.

"She is a Shadow-Reaper: a rare and deadly creature that can challenge a wraith. It is truly amazing that you were able to stand against her as long as you did and then to actually have pushed her back." She shook her head in amazement. "You are truly a unique banshee."

"She kicked my ass," I said with a snort. "If Thor hadn't been at my side I would have been toast. Nothing has ever withstood the banshee wail. She is one bad ass bitch. I hope there aren't any of these shadow-reapers in Philadelphia."

"Philadelphia is ruled by a wraith. The Master would not tolerate a creature that could potentially challenge him," Jonus answered.

"Do all shadow-reapers have the ability to soul shape?" I asked with a shudder as I recalled Black Maria's dominant will crushing my own.

"Oh heavens no," answered Rachel. "That is a gift unique to her, thank the Lord for that. But every shadow-reaper does have a power that is unique to it, as do wraiths."

"So is it true that the Devil's Forge was being used to meld shades and furies into a combined beast that we call a specter?"

"Yes, though Black Maria was able to make far more than just specters," Rachel said. "The prepared souls that eventually become gargoyles also come from her diabolical forge. The cities trade their shades in return for specters, gargoyle templates, and celestial steel. Some of the richer cities even purchase Golem templates which also come from the forge. She, of course, keeps the most powerful creations for herself."

"Aye, that black twat has the power to discover all of a ghosts potential powers with a simple touch. She keeps the most powerful shades for herself so that her specters are more powerful than the normal ones that she sells," Barnabas explained.

"Are you saying that the shades have untapped powers that only Black Maria can discover?"

"Aye, I believe that's what I said lass."

"I've already been testing the free souls," Jonus chimed in. "I believe that your theory about the shades being simply undeveloped, children as it were, may be correct. The free souls are exhibiting powers that they did not possess during their first testing. Their powers mirror those of the darklings."

This news was stunning and a potential game changer. The shades were the most numerous of Limbo's ghosts. If they could be shown that they just needed to grow up, to take responsibility and accept who they were, then they could unlock their full potential. They weren't lesser beings at all. They were just scared and confused. If they could grow up they could literally change the face of Limbo. The fact that most ghosts remain as shades in spite of being offered clear advantages if they would only embrace their darker natures gave me real hope that most ghosts were like most people: confused and unsure about themselves, but certainly not evil by nature. Given the choice, I guessed that fighting for freedom would motivate them to grow up. Despite our loss in Centralia, I realized that we had gained far more in our war effort. We had clearly cut down on the supply of specters as well as unlocked the ghostly potential of all shades.

"So if Black Maria is able to shape souls herself, what does she need the Devil's Forge for?" I asked.

"That monstrous artifact is what completely corrupted the

souls that were heated in its flames," Rachel answered, visibly shuddering at the thought of the thing. "It burns away all the good within a soul and leaves only the evil. That is why specters are such good soldiers. They are mindlessly evil."

"Aye. The blasted device severs the soul's connection to the living world forever. That's why the bloody specters can't translate into the living world," Barnabas added.

These explanations made sense in light of what I'd seen in the forge chamber and my own personal experiences with specters. The loss of such a relic of power was going to be felt in Limbo for some time to come. We may have been driven from the battlefield, but the damage we'd caused, the secrets we uncovered, and the souls we freed, were going to change the face of the war.

"The forge at Centralia was not the only artifact of its kind in Limbo," Jonus said breaking into my thoughts. "There are three more that I know of in the area corresponding to North America, and who knows how many others scattered about in the far reaches of Limbo."

"Aye, that's true," Barnabas agreed. "The loss of the Centralia forge will put the local cities in turmoil. The economic system will go into depression, and only the richest cities will even be able to contemplate importing specters from abroad. I believe the nearest bloody forge is up in Nova Scotia."

"Pittsburgh, under Black Maria, must be the strongest city in our area, right?" I asked.

"In every way except one," Rachel answered. "Philadelphia has the greatest number of banshees of any city that I've ever heard of."

"Aye. Toronto is spoken of in awe when it comes to banshees and they only have three compared to Philly's six," said Barnabas.

"Nine," I corrected. Barnabas and Rachel stared at me in shock for a moment.

"Bloody hell, it's a wonder that Philly hasn't conquered the whole blasted world," Barnabas said shaking his head.

"Not if we rescue them first," I said quietly. The others stared at me in stunned silence for a few moments.

"Are you bloody mad lass?" Barnabas spluttered. "Because the banshees bloody are. How the bloody hell would we control them?"

"And even if we could control them, they are under the tightest security there is. The Master would likely turn them on us before we got to them," Jonus objected.

"We aren't going to control them," I said. "We will set them free of both their chains and their madness. We'll offer them freedom just as we've done for the shades."

"But how?" asked all three luminaries simultaneously.

"Leave that to me," I answered. "I know a thing or two about banshees from personal experience. As for the security, it's definitely a problem. It's gonna take a full assault on the Walnut Street Prison."

The luminaries gaped at me in shock. Their objections were loud and vociferous but I ignored them and picked up the pace, forcing them to run after me.

"Your objections are noted, but we must do this for two important reasons," I answered them when I'd finally gotten them to stop giving me reasons why it couldn't be done.

"First, as long as the Master has the ability to use the banshees against us and anyone else for that matter, he threatens our entire revolution. Second and just as important, they are my sisters, and I will not abandon them to madness and miss use."

I could see that they still wanted to argue with me, but my determination silenced them. They were all obviously troubled by what I guessed they thought were reckless emotional reasons on my part. I couldn't deny the emotional ties I felt with the Tormentor's victims. I was damned if after all they'd suffered that it should continue for all eternity. Nor could I let the Master achieve his goal of Limbo wide dominance through them. I'd found freedom and even happiness in pursuing a goal that was bigger than me. I wanted that for the banshees as well.

"We'll need to find out how many of the free souls can fly. I'll take volunteers for the assault from among them. I want to begin this operation as soon as we possibly can, hopefully before word of Centralia reaches the city."

28

WE REACHED THE DEPOT AS darkness settled over Limbo. The land we traveled through was devoid of any signs of civilization. There were no towns or hamlets, just primordial forests and lonely grasslands. We saw only two old farmhouses, and both appeared abandoned and felt creepy. Jonus explained that these structures were used as way stations by gargoyle teams sent out to hunt for furies.

The depot was an old gunpowder factory located a half dozen miles outside of Philadelphia along the railroad tracks. The structure was old and sprawling having seen heavy use during the Civil War. The complex also included a four story structure which had been a union hospital and later an asylum. I was relatively certain that neither structure remained standing in modern times in the living world. The region around the depot was heavily forested and hilly, affording us the ability to approach unobserved. I placed a mist cloak around Jonus and sent him to get a closer look around the facility.

The free souls were in very high spirits having learned that their transformation had likely unlocked their full potential, meaning that most of them would no longer be the weak anisi. The free souls were far more used to loss than I was, so they didn't appear to be phased very much by the destruction of an entire unit from their own ranks. They were mostly elated to have escaped. Fear of the future still gnawed at them, but hope was an over riding force that kept them together and kept them going forward into peril. They had marched all day while trying out new powers. I sent the luminaries among them to retest and help guide them with their new abilities. I also walked among the troops, encouraging them in any way that I could. It was Sebastian however, who proved the most useful in this endeavor. He was able to sense what a free soul's gifts were and, through much coaxing, he helped them unlock their full potential. The owl seemed to know how each power worked and how to coach each soul in its use. So, by the time that we reached the depot, all of the free souls in our army had been retested and had a passing familiarity with their new abilities. Of the four hundred and three free souls in the army now, there were no longer any anisi, though half the force was classified as apparitions while the rest were phantoms and a small number of poltergeists. Among the entire host we were able to identify forty seven free souls, all three luminaries, and myself, as having strength enough to fly for more than an hour at a time without rest.

"There is a far larger presence here than there should be," Jonus reported upon his return nearly a half hour after he'd departed on his scouting run. "They have nearly fifty specters in the depot itself and more than a hundred darklings are swarming over the asylum. The good news is that they have about two hundred shades locked up on the ground floor of the factory where the specters are located."

"Did you see any celestial steel?" I asked nervously. There was little reason to go after this depot if there wasn't any of the precious metal that we so desperately needed. The two hundred potential free souls did make it necessary that we try though, steel or no.

"Yes. There are scores of crates with raw ore piled in a corner of the factory," Jonus answered. "They are planning to use it to extend the railway towards Pittsburgh. It seems that the invasion plan is moving forward."

"In that case, we'd better hurry."

Fifty specters and a hundred darklings would be a big problem for us. Though I had over four hundred free souls with me, only a hundred and sixty four of them were properly equipped with weapons and armor. Nearly half our veterans with their celestial steel weapons had fallen in the Battle of Centralia. Our forces would have the element of surprise on our side, but aside from that the enemy's combat experience would make up the difference of our somewhat larger numbers.

"Alright, Jonus you'll take the flyers to the roof of the asylum and begin your assault on the top floor," I said grimly. "Kill all darklings and specters you come across. Hit them hard and fast. Give them no quarter. Clear each floor before you move down."

"Rachel," I continued. "You'll take the remainder of the armed free souls save for half a dozen or so who'll be held in reserve. Your force will assault the ground floor of the asylum and work its way upward until you meet up with Jonus. Both of you will await my signal before beginning the assault."

"Barnabas, you'll stay back with the reserves and those that don't have weapons or armor. Make sure they stay out of trouble. Set a watch along the railroad."

I turned to my two animal companions. "Sebastian, you'll be messenger between the combat units. Start with Jonus if you will. Thor you stay with Barnabas. Make sure nothing escapes." Thor whined unhappily but padded over to the large luminary and sat on his haunches, waiting. Sebastian flapped his wings vigorously, bobbing up and down in apparent assent.

"What about the bloody specters?" asked Barnabas, not looking pleased with his assignment. It suddenly struck me that here

I was giving orders to beings who were much older than me both in terms of how many years they'd lived as living people and as ghosts in Limbo. They all dwarfed me in experience and knowledge, yet here I was giving orders to them. None of them seemed troubled by this however, and I could see that even though Barnabas didn't like his orders he didn't question them or me. I wavered for a moment. I shouldn't be giving them orders, but then the reminder of Franklin's message gave me resolve to press on. For whatever reason, I was the one who'd been chosen. I was the one who got this started; this was my vision. I had to lead it for now.

"I'll deal with the specters myself," I said. "Begin your assault when I give the signal. You'll know it when you hear it. Now, let's get moving."

The luminaries left me and began assembling their units. All of the flyers had already been armed earlier in the day as it was determined that they were the most versatile troops we had and could be used tactically in many important ways. After I was sure that everything was moving along as ordered, I shrouded myself in the mist cloak and headed for the factory.

The brick building loomed over the countryside. The thick pines that were so common to the region grew right up to it. A dirt track led from the building's large cargo doors down to the railroad platform barely visible at the bottom of the hill. The structure was three stories in height. Its dark windows stared vacantly like the empty eye sockets of a skull.

I phased through the brick facade of the factory's ground floor. I emerged into what appeared to be a storage closet full of crates that were made of celestial steel. An inspection of the crates revealed them to be full of raw celestial ore.

I stuck my head through the storage closet's door and looked into the very large main chamber beyond. The room was lit by devil's iron globes which gave the whole room, with its twenty foot ceiling, an ambiance of hellish menace. A staircase against the Western wall disappeared into the shadows above leading to what I guessed would be the third floor. In the Southeast corner, I could see more celestial steel crates piled in neat stacks. They gave off their own faint blue glow which banished the hellish light of the devil's iron globes from their immediate vicinity. A large mass of shades were huddled near the celestial steel crates. They instinctively leaned towards the softer blue light of the steel. All of the shades wore the awful red collars of their station. Specters wandered the whole room. Unlike the shades, they shied away from the area touched by celestial light.

I withdrew my head from the storeroom door and waited patiently for Sebastian to bring me word that everyone was in position. I was extremely nervous, not for myself but for the free souls who were putting their trust in me. I didn't want to disappoint them and more importantly I didn't want to get them killed though that was totally unrealistic. I was feeling quite healthy, yesterdays ordeal wiped away in a single night of rest. Mentally though I could sense the madness lurking below the surface. It lurked near the place in my gut where the banshee wail was fueled, yet it was separate. Now that I was examining it, I saw that it was now a permanent part of me. The madness, hatred, rage, and aggression had become an almost tangible part of my being, they were separate but somehow linked together. It was something that I could tap at will in order to unleash devastating power. I had to learn to control it though or it could prove as great a threat to me as it was to my enemies; this I'd learned yesterday when I'd broken down.

The owl suddenly appeared without warning pulling me out of my revelry with a start. Sebastian signaled that all was ready. I nodded my understanding, and the familiar went back the way it had come, passing through the back wall and returning to Jonus's unit. I stepped through the storage room door into the cavernous room beyond and moved into a position that put the greatest mass of specters in the area of effect of my banshee wail. The specters were milling about restlessly. Their pent up aggression seemed to overwhelm any desire or need for sleep.

I unleashed my destructive scream, trying to control the flow of my rage in order to lessen the collateral damage to the building. I was successful. The building didn't collapse although it did shudder a bit. The specters in the blast area didn't fare as well as the brick wall however. They were shredded into bits of mist in an instant. A good twenty of them were destroyed by the scream, and the others shrank back from me in terror.

I called the wind to me and, with supernatural speed, I was among the remaining specters. My katana and knife were dancing in deadly arcs and rapid thrusts that left my enemies howling in agony or, in most cases, destroyed. At the same time, I called on the mists to form a translation portal and then sent it whirling into the black beasts. The mists began to churn and twist forming into a miniature vortex that moved from specter to specter swallowing them whole. The creatures howled in terror and tried to flee, but between my speed enhanced combat skill, and the translation vortex, not a single specter made it out.

I turned my attention to the shades who were cowering in such a tight mass that the entire group took on the appearance of a fallen cloud. I approached them carefully, but they fell back from me in fear.

"It's ok. I'm here to rescue you," I told the terrified shades. "I've got friends who are dealing with the darklings in the next building. Stay here until we've secured the area. I'll send someone in to give you more information."

A hooting call alerted me to Sebastian's arrival. He phased through a nearby wall and glided over to a stack of crates and landed. Cries of alarm rose from many of the shades as the mass of them shied away even further.

"Jonus has cleared the upper floor. Currently he is locked in heavy combat on the third floor," the owl said without preamble. "Rachel's force hasn't been able to enter the building. They've got the first floor reinforced with celestial steel mesh."

"Damn it," I swore. I should have thought of that possibility. Now Jonus's force was in danger of being overwhelmed. "Go to Barnabas and tell him the factory is clear. Have him send some of the unarmed free souls here to help keep this lot out of trouble. Maybe they can start doing the recruitment work. After that, get word to Jonus that I'll be coming up with Rachel and her team. Tell him to hold his position. We'll smash the darklings between us."

"As you command," Sebastian answered cheerfully and flew off. I gave the terrified shades one last look. I didn't want to leave them unattended, but I couldn't afford to delay any further. I called the wind and the building blurred past me as I sped towards the asylum. In less than half a minute, I was standing besides Rachel who was directing an assault on the front door. She blinked in surprise at my sudden appearance.

"They've got this floor lined with celestial steel mesh," she reported unhappily. "I'm sorry but we haven't been able to break through."

"Not your fault Rachel. I should have anticipated this. Gather your company and form them up behind me." I whistled loudly as I walked towards the west side of the building. There were no doors or windows on this side. I reached my hand through the building and found the celestial steel mesh. I smiled and looked behind me to assure myself that Rachel and her troops were waiting. A blur of movement alerted me that Thor had arrived in response to my call. I patted him on the head, pleased that he'd understood the purpose of the whistle.

"On my mark, charge in and kill every darkling you can find. We need to get to the third floor as quick as possible."

Rachel and her grim company nodded, eager for the action they'd thus far been denied. The sound of battle from the upper floors was muffled, but we all knew that our forces were heavily outnumbered and would likely be desperate for our assistance by now. I pushed my will down through the hand that still grasped the celestial steel mesh inside the building, and ordered it to shatter like glass into millions of shards. The steel suddenly shattered, and before the shards could hit the ground I willed them to shoot outward spraying the entire room beyond with deadly shrapnel. There was no hesitation. The steel did as directed; the sound carried clearly through the walls.

"Now!" I yelled and pushed myself forward into the chaos inside the asylum. The room was in shambles. Large shards of blue steel protruded from the walls and furnishings. The deadly spray had taken out a half dozen darklings; a few still thrashed on the floor their ghostly bodies riddled with hundreds of blue steel shards of all sizes and shapes. Their companions had fared more poorly by comparison. Clouds of dissipating mists were the only evidence remaining of their prior existence.

Thor had lunged into the room ahead of me and was locked in combat in the hallway beyond. I sprang over the debris and joined Thor who was keeping three darklings at bay. I swung my katana high at one of the male darklings while Thor attacked his mid section. I parried a vicious thrust from the lone female darkling who was wielding a devil's iron sword with my knife. I ducked under an arcing blade delivered by the third darkling and sent him sprawling with a powerful kick to the chest. The first darkling chose to parry my blade, and Thor tore into his stomach. The darkling tried to stab Thor with a downward stroke of his blade, but my own counter stroke took his hand off at the wrist. I parried another attack from the female darkling, and before she could react, I flung my knife catching her in the throat. Rachel joined the fray, falling upon the darkling that I'd knocked down with the kick. Her troops were bunched up in the doorway behind her. Thor, meanwhile, leaped onto his assailant driving him to the ground. He tore the darklings throat out with one powerful snap of his jaws. The female darkling I faced stared dumbly at the knife that protruded from her throat. Before she could recover from her surprise, I stabbed her in the face with my Katana, and she quickly dissipated into mist. I caught my knife before it could hit the ground.

Thor and I pushed forward working in tandem to swiftly cut down any darklings that got in our way. Rachel and her free soul company cleaned out the rooms behind us making sure that any lurkers could not wreak havoc on us from behind. In this way we gained the stairs in a matter of minutes and began our ascent. We had a short but vicious battle on the landing of the second floor, but the combination of my high speed strikes and Thor's powerful jaws were just too much for darklings who were not accustomed to violent opposition. I sent Rachel and her unit in to clear out the rest of the second floor while Thor and I held the stairwell against any counter attacks that might come from the third floor.

The sound of battle was loud here on the second floor landing. It carried down from the third floor. I wanted badly to rush up and assist them, but discipline told me that I must hold this landing until Rachel had secured the floor otherwise I could expose her to attack from an area that she thought to be secure. Two full minutes passed, though it felt like an hour, before I saw Rachel and her team return from their sweep of the floor. The second floor had been empty after all; it seemed that the enemy had concentrated on the third floor.

Thor and I led the way up to the next level. The darklings here were massed and waiting for us. A volley of black energy bolts darted down towards us. I barely had time to cover both Thor and I in a mist shield. The bolts were consumed by the shield, but they kept on coming and I felt the shield shudder under the stress. Rachel poked her head out from behind me and sent a brilliant ball of blue fire into the mass of darklings. The ball struck home, and a darkling burst into blue crystal snowflakes that showered the landing. The darklings recoiled in shock, and before they could regain their composure, Thor and I launched ourselves upon them with ferocity. I shoved the shield from us, willing it to take on the oozing gelatinous form I'd used against the Conductor. It caught a full half dozen of the darklings in its sticky grasp.

After Rachel's intervention, the fight on the landing was short and one-sided. Half of the darklings were dramatically slowed by my gelatinous shield and were unable to put up much of a fight. Rachel blasted two more darklings with her blue fire. The rest tried to flee but were cut down by eager free souls wielding their blades with enough skill to get the job done. From there, we slammed into the back ranks of the forces opposing Jonus. It took nearly an hour to finally clear the darklings from the building. The final score of enemy souls proved to be highly skilled and very powerful in their own right. We lost nearly forty free souls during the battle. In the final moments of the fight, some daring darklings tried to escape via flight. A mad chase ensued which ended in a stomach churning aerial combat with me and all three luminaries throwing ourselves at the darklings who were every bit as skilled as we were.

The toll was heavy on the free souls, and no one that participated in the battle came away uninjured. By the time the engagement was finished however, nearly one hundred and eighty more free souls had been added to our ranks. I immediately set about shaping the celestial steel we recovered into weapons and armor. The army now numbered over five hundred souls and it took me several hours to shape weapons for all who needed them. I spent a couple more hours shaping the remaining steel into spare weapons to be given out to future recruits.

After exhausting myself on this work on top of the exertions from the battle and the wounds I'd taken, I finally allowed myself to collapse into a dreamless slumber. When a ghost is wounded, she bleeds like when she lived. Rather than blood, she bleeds out the power that sustains her. Wounds on a ghost heal very quickly but bleeding out just a little bit of power in this way is far more draining than using it up through normal ghostly activities. A ghost that looses all of its power dissipates into a cloud of mist to never awaken again. Normally I need less rest than the average ghost, but I was finding that getting wounded changed that equation. Losing power because of injury dramatically increased the amount of time that I needed to rest. So it wasn't to surprising when I woke again that I found that an entire day had gone by. While I slept, Jonus and the other luminaries had reorganized the army into four companies; a company for each of them and for myself to command. Each company was further broken down into platoons and squads each of which was led by an officer with some kind of military experience. These officers were drilling the troops hard as I surveyed the entire force. My company was the smallest of the four and was entirely made up of flyers: the army's new special forces unit. The atmosphere around the camp had changed noticeably. The free souls were actually behaving like soldiers. I realized that the battle for the depot had been our first true victory; We'd defeated the enemy utterly and we controlled the battleground.

I was introduced to the lieutenant of my company: a tall, skinny man named Donald Quinn. He was an Iraq war veteran who'd been murdered during a convenience store robbery while on leave in Philly. Indeed most of the men and women of my unit turned out to have some experience in combat, a large number having served in the military or on the PPD. I was amazed to meet a grizzled veteran of the force who'd been Frank Cooper's mentor when the detective had first joined the PPD.

"That kid was tough ma'am," former detective Aeron Bird told me when I asked him if he'd known Frank Cooper or Wendi Kapudo. "He was a good kid too. Right from the start he crusaded for one thing or another. I warned him that he should slow down, but he was always butting heads with the brass. He hated bureaucracy, especially when it got in the way of saving lives. I wonder how things turned out for him."

"I saw him recently," I told the wistful detective. "He was investigating my case. His crusading helped put an end to the Tormentor's reign of terror on the city."

"Really?" Bird brightened at this news. "I always knew that kid would do something special. He was a good, smart kid; foul mouth though."

I nodded with a pang of guilt. Last time I'd seen Frank was on the day James Paul Saunders had been taken into custody, but things had gone to shit when Delilah and her people interfered. I'd been captured and had completely forgotten to check up on the two detectives. I had a bad feeling that the powers that be in Limbo and in the living world had made the two pay for having the audacity to save a life and interfere with the plans of the Dark Master. The only thing I could do about that now was to make sure that Limbo couldn't or wouldn't interfere in peoples' lives in the future. For that to happen, Philadelphia would have to be liberated.

Several other former PPD officers had known my father and trained under him at his dojo. One of them had even sparred against me, though I didn't remember the man myself. It felt weird to be so young and in command of all of these experienced men and women, but none of them had balked at the strange situation. When I asked a former Navy Seal if he thought it might make more sense for someone like himself to be in command rather than me, he shook his head vigorously.

"Fuck no Miss. Yesterday I was a slave cowering from those black hearted specters and their masters. Then you showed up and blasted them with a scream and cut the rest of them down with a sword that moved faster than what I could see. You created a tornado that you commanded and it ate the rest of them devils up. I've since learned that I can be free, that I can fly, and that I can kick some ass again. But I ain't got nothin' on you. You're a bad ass ghost bitch that I'm glad to follow. Just point me at what needs killin' and I'm your man."

I stared at the man in consternation. His fellows looked at him askance; they seemed to worry that I might blast him and those around him into oblivion.

"What Jack means ma'am, is that this ain't Kansas anymore," a former marine chimed into the nervous silence. "Things work different here. If we want to stay free, we need to fight for it and we need leaders who are both smart enough and tough enough to lead us to victory. Everyone agrees that you've killed reapers, escaped from Walnut Street Prison, and figured out how to transform us from shades to what we are now. I'm more than happy to serve and follow your commands ma'am, and so are the rest of these louts."

The entire group murmured their agreement and I thanked them for their support. I spent time meeting each person in the unit and then moved to the other companies to spend some time with everyone that I could talk to in the short time before dawn. At first light, the entire army was assembled and I stood before it with my three captains at my back. My stomach roiled with nervousness, all I wanted to do was turn around and lead the army towards our next destination. But a quiet voice inside of me urged me to speak to the army and put into words my vision; to tell them why they should risk all. It was imperative that if I fell in battle along the way that the vision not die with me. And so I pushed aside my fears and began to speak in a ringing voice that carried across the small valley.

"My fellow free souls, there are difficult and dangerous times ahead of us. But even more despair and danger has been left behind. We have all faced death and we all know that there is life beyond that which we experienced in our corporeal lives. When we arrived here we were given two choices, serve the will of evil or be enslaved by it. We have since learned that there is a third choice. To live free. This choice, however, requires us to fight that which would enslave us, not just for our own sakes but for everyone's sake. The forces of evil that rule this land not only enslave us, but they cause chaos and death in the living world. We must fight for our freedom and we must fight to oppose evil. We must fight to set our brothers and sisters free, and we must fight to protect humanity from the deprivations of evil in the living world. The fight will be hard and long. Many of us will parish in this endeavor. Fear and loneliness will be our companions. Let no ghost fool himself that this will be easy. We will have victories and suffer terrible defeats, but we must always endure, and always fight until freedom has been won."

I paused as a great cheer went up from the free souls.

"Today we begin the first step in this war. Today we begin the fight to liberate our city of Philadelphia from its evil masters and restore it to its glory as the City of Brotherly Love! Are you with me?"

A great roar went up from the army and saluting the troops, I turned to lead them on the march home.

29

WHILE WE MARCHED, I HELD a quiet conference with my captains. Taking the city of Philadelphia was going to present some problems other than the obvious one: defeating its armies. The biggest challenge was going to be the Schuylkill River which completely split West Philly from the rest of the city. While taking Center City was the most important objective, the Western part of the metropolis was where the greatest number of shades were held. If we focused on the West however, the Schuylkill line could be fortified against us. If that happened, the crossing would result in terrible losses for us.

After several hours of debate, we decided that we had to launch the attack from the Eastern bank of the river. Our initial invasion would be two pronged. My special forces unit would attack the Walnut Street Prison and free the banshee's while Jonus and Barnabas's units attacked Gray's Ferry. Rachel's company would wait in reserve taking up a position on the Benjamin Franklin Parkway. Once my unit rescued the banshee's, we'd clean out Washington Square and then march to Rittenhouse Square to do the same there. Holding Gray's Ferry would be pivotal as it would give us access to the ferry barge though the Ferryman would have to be dealt with. I had great confidence in the abilities of Jonus and Barnabas, but I wished I didn't have to send them up against a reaper. There was nothing I could do about it other than give them advice based on my own experience fighting the Conductor. I was likely going to have to deal with my own reaper, the Warden, and maybe even the Tormentor as part of my mission. We were all going to have to face great peril in this undertaking.

We decided that Phoenixville would be the best place for a crossing of the Schuylkill. The town was another of Philadelphia's outposts, and there was a chance we could even take a barge there if we were lucky. According to Rachel, who'd been enslaved on a barge before being sold to Black Maria, Phoenixville was an advanced trade post where the allies of Philadelphia came to make bargains with the city's rulers. Apparently the Master was paranoid about having any outsiders in his city, so business with foreigners was conducted well outside the city limits.

The plans having been settled, we turned the army Eastward and continued the march through the wastelands. We saw bands of furies watching us from afar, but clearly none of them wanted to tangle with a force of our size. A sudden thought occurred to me, and I turned to Sebastian who was riding shotgun on my shoulder.

"Do you think you could rally an army of those furies again? They would be a great help with the invasion."

"Of course not," Sebastian answered derisively. "The furies would not come within a mile of a great city like Philadelphia. Doing so would result in their destruction or enslavement."

"But if they help us, they won't have to be so afraid of Philadelphia anymore. We'll make sure they can come and go as they like as long as they don't cause trouble," I argued.

"Promises won't mean anything to them," Sebastian said. "As long as the furies are preyed upon by the current masters of the city, they will not risk such a venture."

I sighed disappointedly. I suppose I couldn't blame them. Being forced into a statue for all eternity wouldn't be a pleasant threat to face. Recalling my own experience with the iron maiden, I would do anything to avoid such a fate myself. The thought brought back the simmering fear that had lain dormant ever since my escape from the Walnut Street Prison; could I truly go back to the place that held such awful memories for me? Maybe Jonus could take my place and I'd go to Gray's Ferry instead. I let a trickle of the roiling anger that was a constant furnace of burning energy at the core of my being now well up and consume the fear. I was getting much better at controlling the rage. Practice makes perfect. The banshees were my responsibility. I had to go to the prison because if anyone had a chance to get through to those tortured souls it was me.

It was near dark by the time we reached the Phoenixville area. Jonus went ahead, wearing the cloak of mist, to get a look at the town. The army rested in a shallow valley between steep hills, but Jonus wasn't long in returning.

"There is a ferry at dock. There is also a great deal of activity in the town."

The others were nervous about this information and counseled caution. Though I respected their advice, I knew that if this town could stand against us, slow us down, or even turn us back, then we had no business contemplating an assault on Philadelphia. The army had marched all day and knew that an important objective lay just over the hill; if we turned aside or delayed our attack, their morale would take a hit. We had to be bold and decisive if victory was to be achieved. Yet nervous tension caused me to pause before giving the order; what if they were right? A wrong order here could be disastrous; wouldn't it be wise to follow the advice of my captains? Play it safe an inner voice whispered. The roiling energy at my core screamed at me to act. After a moment of indecision I chose action over caution.

"I'm sorry, but we can't afford to be cautious at this point. It won't be long before the Master learns of our actions in Centralia and the depot. Once he does, he'll be waiting for us. Phoenixville has the ferry that we need for our invasion and we're going to take it. The fact that the town is occupied by unknown forces is dangerous, but if we can't take it, then we certainly won't be able to take Philly. This is a test of our readiness."

The three luminaries stared at me unhappily for a moment then one by one nodded their agreement.

"My unit will take and hold the docks as well as the ferry," I said. "Rachel will accompany us. Once we've secured the docks and ferry, she'll pilot the barge back to the Western bank to pick up the rest of the army. Once the crossing has been accomplished, Barnabas's company will take and hold the Northern end of the town. Rachel, you'll hold your troops in reserve on the ferry while Jonus will take and hold the Southern end of town. My unit will overfly the city making sure no one escapes."

Without waiting for possible objections to my plan, I strode over to Lieutenant Quinn and gave him orders to get the aerial corps ready for imminent action. I stood quietly while he went about organizing the troops into the formations he thought would be most appropriate to the mission. The detachment had practiced aerial maneuvers throughout the day as we traveled to Phoenixville, and I'd been impressed with Quinn's tactical skills. Barnabas had also spent time with the company teaching them how to fling blue bolts of energy. Only half of the unit had the strength to cast the blue bolts and most of them could only throw one of them without risking serious power drain. Quinn had divided Banshee Company, the voted upon name chosen by the units members, into smaller squads that could effectively work independently of each other as well as in their normal formations; it gave the unit more tactical flexibility. Quinn assigned two squads the task of taking and holding the ferry while the remaining squads of the formation would secure a beachhead on the docks. Orders were given that none but myself or one of the luminaries were to engage any reapers that might be present.

I stroked Thor's shaggy head nervously as I contemplated the road ahead.

"Stay with Jonus," I told Thor when Quinn informed me that Banshee Company was ready. I nodded to the lieutenant and called the wind to me and took to the sky.

I rose above the tree line and the hills until I could see the black ribbon that marked the Schuylkill and the faintly illuminated town on its far shore. I launched myself at full speed towards the ferry which hovered quietly at dockside. Banshee Company flew in my wake; they were flying in a spear formation with me as its tip.

As I rapidly approached the ferry, I saw that there were only a half dozen specters aboard and a luminary was lashed to its control wheel. I overshot the ferry leaving it to the squads Quinn had assigned to the task. I slammed into a specter standing guard at the ramp leading down from the docks. I impaled the ghost on my katana; the momentum of my diving attack drove the blade clean through its back and out the other side. The specter dissolved into mist, and I landed roughly. I rolled with the fall and narrowly avoiding a specter's claws as it struck at me. I jumped to my feet prepared to take on the dozen specters on duty here.

Banshee Company robbed me of the chance of more mayhem however. The squads swept in right behind me, and they engaged the remaining specters immediately. Flying free souls struck the dock guards like an avalanche, sweeping the enemy from the boardwalk and ferry in less than a minute. A cry of alarm was going up in the town as I saw Rachel take command of the ferry.

Our assault was so sudden and ferocious that it took almost five minutes before the enemy could mount a counter attack. By that time the ferry had almost reached the opposite shore. I wanted so badly to press the attack, but our job right now was to hold the docks so that the army had a safe place to land. Specters and darklings were pouring out of nearby buildings, and my incorporeal heart skipped a beat when I finally got my first glimpse of a reaper. A few groups of specters charged our newly formed line before any semblance of order could be established among their ranks. These were met with swift and decisive blows that resulted in most of the attackers being annihilated. Once on the field, the reaper exerted its will and forced its troops into orderly formations. There were more than a hundred specters and a dozen darklings facing us.

The ferry had reached the other shore and was filling quickly with free souls by the time the reaper moved against my out-numbered Banshee Company. The darklings opened up with a volley of black bolts which I countered by calling upon the mists of Limbo. The mists erupted from the ground in geysers that struck the bolts and swallowed them completely. I staggered as a wave of exhaustion hit me. I steadied myself as the mists continued to pour from the ground forming a wall before us. An internal survey of my power reserves revealed that I'd just used half of it with one action, and using so much at once was extremely taxing. When the reaper ordered the specters forward, they balked at first, and then charged as the reaper used its abil-ity to control them to force them forward. They broke off at the last second before reaching the mist wall I'd created. They split into two groups, each going to either side along the wall. This divided them and slowed their assault. The specters that broke off to the left emerged from around the wall much closer to our line than did those that went right. Seeing the affect the mist was having on the specters, I willed a portion of the mist wall to shift so that the wall was now in an L shape. The new configura-tion effectively blocked the farthest group of specters from us because the bottom of the L was anchored against the river; If they wanted to reach the battle line without encountering a wall of mist, they'd have to go all the way back around following the first group's route. Manipulating the mist that I'd already created was easy and far less of a drain on my power compared to creating or pulling the stuff from god knows where.

It was several minutes before the reaper noticed what was happening and called for a withdrawal. Quinn, however, had seen the opportunity for what it was and instead of holding the line ordered a full assault. The free souls opened up with a wave of blue bolts of their own that decimated the oncoming specters and left them reeling. The charge that followed from Banshee Company sent the specters fleeing into the mists and the entire attacking force broke.

A glance towards the river showed me that the ferry was now on its way back ladened with the entire army. A terrible roar brought my attention back to the battle field just in time to see three huge, misshapen creatures fly through the mist wall. One of the newcomers plummeted towards the troops of Banshee Company while the other two sped over us heading towards the oncoming barge. Three huge gaps were torn in the mist wall by their passage and the reaper's remaining forces resumed their stalled assault. I wanted to go to the aid of the ferry, but I had to trust that three luminaries could handle the threat posed by the two newcomers. My unit only had me, and it was my responsibility to help them. I sprang forward to meet the charging specters and darklings using my speed to keep me apart from my own troops. When I was just within two sword lengths of the enemy's front line I let loose with a wail that shredded their charging ranks, leaving the reaper, who'd stayed in the rear, with only a token force.

The newcomer, a huge stone monster, had raked my line with green flames that engulfed half a dozen free souls and sent them up like roman candles. They screamed horribly as they were burned away. The discipline of the unit held as Quinn shouted out orders and half the squads turned to fight the threat; the other half held their ground against the reaper. I was faced with an agonizing decision as the reaper approached our line: fight it or go after the thing that I guessed must be a gargoyle. As dangerous as reapers were they could at least be defeated with celestial steel weapons. The gargoyle on the other hand presented too many unknowns. Although I was certain that I was going to lose far more men to the reaper than I wanted to, I was equally certain that they could take it down. The gargoyle on the other hand was an unknown threat that had killed six of my people already. I made my decision and launched myself towards the gargoyle yelling at Quinn as I did.

"I've got this thing. Concentrate all forces on the reaper. Kill it if you can!"

I slammed into the gargoyle and would have bounced off if I hadn't grabbed on at the last moment. It was huge, maybe eight feet tall. Its body was vaguely human shaped with two legs, two arms, and a head on its bulky shoulders. I struck it at shoulder level and it didn't even notice me. It was busy swinging its massive clawed hands at free souls who were dodging in and out, trying to hurt it with their celestial steel blades. Rage welled up in me as I prepared to unleash the banshee wail upon it. The gargoyle, somehow sensing the danger, turned its head around to look at me. Our eyes met and a jolt of static power echoed through both of us. I stared into the gargoyles eyes mesmerized by the cool power that flowed between us. The new power settled somewhere close to my heart rather than in my gut where my rage resided. This power was clean, compassion was its fuel and it opened up the gargoyle before me, revealing to me its entire being.

This gargoyle had been a pit bull once, and had lived in a happy home with a family that had loved it and that it had loved in return. I saw the images of its happy life flash before me in rapid scenes. Then the night came in which it was stolen from its home. The men who abducted it were cruel; they beat and starved it and then forced it to fight other dogs for its food and for fleeting affection. It had been a good fighter but eventually it died a vicious death. It had barely remembered its former life by that time. In Limbo, it had roamed freely for what seemed like forever until the day that the man ghosts had come to its pack. Baron, his name suddenly came to me, hadn't been afraid. He was a great hunter and knew all the lands around. The human ghosts turned out to be crafty and stronger than he'd expected; they'd killed some of his pack but most, including himself, were captured. The men ghosts then did the worst thing to him: they trapped him in a stone body and took his will away. They made him do bad things and he didn't even get love for it. He was so lonely and angry. He would gladly kill every human ghost his masters would let him kill.

I saw all of this in a flash of memory and the anger within me was pushed back down into my gut as overwhelming sorrow and compassion for this poor creature that wanted only to be loved settled over me. I understood that I must destroy this beast or it would destroy my people, but try as I might, I couldn't bring the anger back up. Instead my compassion grew. Compelled by those who'd created him, the gargoyle opened its maw to blast me with a jet of green flame.

The swelling compassion in my heart for this creature suddenly burst from me in a torrent. The sound that escaped my lips wasn't a wail, it was a melody. I found myself singing "Tears In Heaven" by Eric Clapton. The power that had lain dormant near my heart since its awakening after my captivity rode upon my voice, amplifying it and sending a cool wind over the gargoyle. The gargoyle's mouth snapped shut and the look in its eyes changed; it cocked its head at me and let out a quiet whine. I sang louder as I reached the chorus and the power pushed outward from me, rushing over free souls, darkling, and specter alike. The power was like a cool summer breeze that brings comfort and peace. The effect on the combatants was nearly instantaneous and utterly shocking. The darklings and specters stopped fighting and stared at me in mesmerized fascination. The free souls on the other hand seemed buoyed by the song. They remained vigilant but didn't attack enemies under the mesmerization. The din of battle gave way to the power of my siren song.

I was suddenly distracted by a great cry that went up from the ferry. I turned to see what was happening, though I didn't stop singing. The two gargoyles that had gone for the ferry had caught the barge and were threatening to dump my entire army into the endless void of the river. In a panic, I rose upon the wind and swiftly flew to a point half way between the docks and the barge; my voice rose in a crescendo as I once more reached the chorus. The moment at which my voice reached the ferry was plain to see as the gargoyles suddenly froze in mid motion and the cries of terrified free souls died out. I silently willed the gargoyles to drag the barge to the shore and they both raised their voices in a momentary howl of sorrow and then they began hauling the ferry to shore.

I turned my attention back to Phoenixville and saw that the reaper was countering me with its own power, bringing its forces back under its control. I was pleased to note, however, that Baron ignored the reaper's mind control. He continued to watch me instead. I let the final chorus come to an end and silence descended on the town.

The reaper saw that there was no longer any chance of victory and was trying to pull off an orderly retreat. Baron roared in sudden rage and leaped into the midst of the fleeing specters, cutting them down with fiery breath and frenzied claws. The army was now disembarking from the ferry and Banshee Company leaped forward to assist Baron. Once the barge was secure, the other two gargoyles joined the battle, and I watched in satisfaction as the three beasts took a measure of vengeance on the reaper, tearing it to pieces before it could escape.

Rachel's company remained to hold the docks while each of the other units dispersed into the town, attending to their assigned tasks. The three gargoyles stayed at my side and whined at me, begging me to sing to them some more. Both Thor and Sebastian had rejoined me. While Quinn took Banshee Company aloft to patrol the skies of the town, I stayed on the dock and sang to the gargoyles, finding pleasure in having a power that brought comfort rather than destruction. I was elated by the turn of events and also quite exhausted. I'd always enjoyed singing; classic rock of the nineteen-eighties was my favorite. So I sat quietly singing ballads from Journey, Def Leopard, Poison, and Meat Loaf. The battle for Phoenixville was all but over. All that remained was to search the entire town; hunting for hiding stragglers, and searching for celestial steel ore and shades. This work could be done without me, though my menagerie and I were ready to fight at an instants notice if needed.

Reports reached me of a few minor street skirmishes that were over practically before they started. The free souls went door to door, flushing out every concealed darkling they could find. A veritable treasure trove of devil's iron was recovered as well as a mountain of raw celestial steel ore. Most importantly, a little over a hundred shades were freed; most of them became free souls without much cajoling. I ordered that the devil's iron be dumped into the river which caused some consternation among the troops. A stern glare silenced the objectors. It frankly surprised me how quickly some ghosts were willing to overlook the evil nature of the devil's iron favoring instead to only consider its value.

Most interesting of all the finds in Phoenixville was a report from Barnabas claiming that a delegation from Newark, led by a reaper and consisting of a half dozen darklings and a score of specters, had waved a flag of truce and were demanding safe passage home. Intrigued by this development, I followed the messenger to an old brick mansion built in the federal style. Its three stories loomed over the smaller, more modern structures in the neighborhood. The Newark delegation waited just outside the old carriage house located at the front of the property. The estate was surrounded by free souls who waited impatiently. They were clearly in no mood to give quarter. Barnabas stood alone a dozen paces from the reaper who stood a few feet apart from its own retainers.

"What's this Barnabas?" I asked when I reached him. Thor padded along at my side and the three gargoyles followed in our wake. Sebastian rode upon Baron's head. All three constructs growled menacingly upon seeing the reaper. I raised a hand to forestall them.

"They put up a bloody flag of truce and claimed diplomatic immunity," Barnabas answered, deep voice betraying no emotion.

"You lead these abominations?" The reaper croaked in its grating voice. I met its glowing eyes and noticed that the bones that made up its body were red as though it had bathed in blood. The thought made me shudder internally and its glowing red eyes seemed to grow more intense. "Give me the shades and the iron I paid for and we will leave."

"And if I don't?"

"There is no reason for my city to involve itself in the affairs of another unless that city provokes us. You don't want to do that. Give me what is mine and I will go."

I stared at it for a moment and then I smiled.

"I'm sorry. We threw the devil's iron into the river. That stuff is foul and shouldn't be left around. You can send a bill to the Master if you'd like. I'll even carry it for you."

"You impudent shadeling, I'll make you scream for centuries," It said, voice rasping with anger. It took a step towards me but stopped when loud growls rose up from Thor and the gargoyles. The entire army was prepared to leap forward and the reaper saw that it had no chance of carrying out its threat here. "Give me the shades and order these tainted souls out of my way."

"You aren't in any position to give orders," I said in a bored voice. "In case you're blind or just stupid, we just sent a reaper and more than a hundred specters and darklings into oblivion. Why shouldn't we do the same to you?"

The reaper stood silent for a moment. I could see the wheels turning in its bony head. It wasn't sure what to make of the situation, but it clearly didn't fully grasp the danger that it was in.

"As I said a few minutes ago, there is no reason why my city should be brought into this business. If you have a quarrel with the Master of Philadelphia, take it up with him. The laws of Limbo demand that you let us go. Any complaints that we have with what has happened here will be forwarded to the Master and he can deal with you himself."

I laughed at this: a quick hard, mirthless laugh.

"Do you think we care about the laws of Limbo?" I asked with scorn. "We don't. We plan to rewrite those laws in fact. No, I'm afraid that you know too much. It will be best if your city doesn't know what happened to you. I'm sure delegations have been lost to the furies before. Traveling the wilds is quite dangerous you know."

The reaper knew I had just pronounced its death sentence. It lunged at me in the hope of at least taking me down with it. I was faster however, having already been building up the rage within me. I let loose with the banshee wail when it was still ten feet away. The scream caught the reaper and its entire delegation along with the carriage house and shredded them all. Silence followed and then was broken by the plaintiff whine of Baron who was miffed at having nothing to kill.

"I know," I said soothingly, walking over to the massive stone gargoyle and rubbing its round belly. "I'm sorry that I made such a horrible noise. I can really be a bitch sometimes."

I turned away from the destruction that I'd wrought and went back to the docks. There I found Rachel and a new luminary named Gideon handling the logistics of loading the new celestial ore onto the ferry and organizing the new recruits into our existing ranks. Our losses were relatively light. My own unit had suffered the greatest casualties: eight flyers, most of them killed in Baron's initial attack. The new recruits put the army at over six hundred. Six new flyers replaced the ones we'd lost, bringing Banshee Company to near full strength. Once the barge was loaded and the town fully secured, I ordered the army to gather on the docks. We observed a moment of silence for our fallen comrades, and I made use of my newly discovered talent by memorializing our fallen to the haunting "Candle in the Wind" by Elton John. We then took six hours to rest and then the army boarded the ferry. It was a tight fit but we were able to get everyone aboard with a little room to spare. The three gargoyles also came, apparently having adopted me as their sister. It was decided that Baron would be made part of Banshee Company while Max and Miya would go with Jonus and Barnabas respectively.

Gideon took the control wheel of the ferry and we launched away from the shoreline of Phoenixville. The barge hovered over the abyss that was the Schuylkill and Gideon pointed the bow towards Philadelphia. We were finally on the last leg of our journey to liberate our fair city.

30

THE CRUISE DOWN RIVER TOOK three hours. During a good portion of that time, I shaped the celestial ore we'd recovered in Phoenixville into weapons and armor for Gideon and the new recruits. We rounded a bend in the Schuylkill and the city finally came into view; clouds of billowing mist marked its location. We soon plunged into that mist, and, within minutes, buildings and paved roads became visible on either side of us. I held a quick conference with Jonus and the other luminaries to go over any last minute details. Rachel offered up a prayer to the All Mighty for our safety and success. I tend to hold to the tenant that God helps those who help themselves, but I didn't object to the prayer as I knew it gave comfort to the others. After this, I rejoined the troops of Banshee Company and we began our preparations to disembark.

When the ferry reached the point where the Wissahickon Creek met with the Schuylkill River, I gave the signal. I called the wind to me and launched myself aloft then sped towards the Eastern bank. Sebastian and Baron flew just behind me while the rest of the company followed a little further back.

I'd chosen this launching point because it led into the most densely wooded area of Fairmount Park. I flew low, staying just a few feet above the tree line. Once I was deep enough into the park and away from the river, I turned us due South making straight for the museum district. Luck was with us for I saw no signs of the enemy. We passed over the Philadelphia Museum of Art and there we turned onto the Benjamin Franklin Parkway following it Southeastward. As we approached the Vine Street Expressway, I brought us down lower till I was flying only a foot above the pavement of the street. It was tense passing under the ordinarily busy thoroughfare but all seemed quiet. I was aware that the second landing would take place in just a few minutes with Rachel leading her force onto the Vine street bridge and then Eastward until they reached the off ramp leading to the Parkway. There they would have to hold the Expressway against any enemy forces that tried to move Westward.

We made our first landing on the grounds of the Free Library of Philadelphia right off of Logan Circle. The imposing and dark edifice of Eastern State Penitentiary made its menacing presence felt throughout the district though it lay some distance to the North of our current position. Most of the museum district had been touched by Benjamin Franklin in some way, however, and the evil ghosts of Philly avoided it like the plague. The fear that Franklin's haunts imposed on Limbo's ghosts was warranted; many of these locations were heavily warded and had proven deadly to unwary souls. I intended to use these landmarks as staging areas for resting and regrouping our troops. The wards were meant to protect secrets hidden within these places and should pose no threat to our troops as long as we didn't try to access these structures; at least that was my hope.

A quick headcount was made, and once we were sure everyone was accounted for we sprang back aloft and continued Southward until we reached Market Street. Here we encountered our first specters. Two of Quinn's squads took these out before they could escape or raise the alarm. We encountered a much larger force at Chestnut Street, but, rather than get into a pitched battle, we simply sped over them continuing our journey to the Walnut Street Prison. The large company of darklings and specters watched us pass over head but none cried out. Though we were a strange sight, who in Limbo could have imagined that the city was under invasion from a force of former shades? These darklings and specters apparently assumed we were some new kind of force going about our business for the Master.

Instead of taking Walnut Street directly, I decided to go up and over the buildings turning Eastward and paralleling Walnut Street. The East-West arteries here in the center of the city seemed choked with traffic heading West towards the rail and barge lines at Gray's Ferry. It seemed prudent to avoid notice as much as possible. The darklings and specters might be fooled by what we were, but if a reaper caught sight of us it would know that we were enemies and the jig would be up. Not to mention that there were more than a few darklings and specters who could recognize me on sight. In this way we approached Washington Square, finding it a beehive of activity. Fighting units arrived and departed every few minutes taking up supplies that lay in great heaps around the plaza. We ignored this, shooting straight overhead, garnering stares of surprise as we made for the roof of the Walnut Street Prison. I signaled Quinn to join me as I landed on the rooftop. I had chosen a spot overlooking the inner courtyard where the isolation block and testing yard were located. The cries of the imprisoned banshees could be heard clearly up here. I was allowing a trickle of rage to flow to the surface of my being from its molten core in my gut in order to stave off the horror and anxiety that the very sight of this building caused me.

"I want four squads holding the gate," I ordered Quinn as he landed beside me. "Leave three squads up here in reserve, two squads can go into the prison to free whatever prisoners they can find, and I'll take the remaining three squads into the courtyard. Baron can handle the job of one squad. Right boy?"

The gargoyle barked in agreement and would have jumped straight down into the courtyard below if I hadn't held him back.

"Whoa boy, just a minute," I said with a smile and turned back to Quinn. "I want you to take charge of the gate. Hold it until I'm ready. Sebastian will stay up here and be our eyes and ears."

"Whatever you say mistress." The owl flapped its wings in ascent.

"Alright, let's do this."

I flew straight down into the courtyard and landed a few feet from the celestial steel door that barred entrance into the solitary confinement block. The door was thick but posed no difficulty for me as my control over the blue metal was complete. I willed the metal to part so that I and one of my companions, a free soul named Jully Sandborn, could walk through. The metal melted away revealing a layer of devil's iron imbedded in the middle of the thick door. Behind us, Baron and the other free soul squads assigned to the courtyard were locked in battle with the specters that patrolled the yard.

I had expected a higher level of security for this part of the prison. After all, it did house the Master's greatest treasure. The added security of the devil's iron gave me the opportunity to test the flexibility of the banshee wail. I gestured to Jully to step back, and I gathered the rage necessary to power the sonic blast of the wail. I kept the rage under tight, focused control rather than letting it surge through me as I normal did. I gathered it into a tight ball of energy and then released it in a single shout that was focused tightly on a single point of the doorway before me. The door was blown apart, but, rather than spraying the entire area beyond with deadly shrapnel, the debris was flung in a tight mass that was far less destructive to the entirety of the space beyond. As I led Jully into the cell block, the sounds of battle behind me subsided as my forces quickly cleared the area of enemy forces.

It grew suddenly quieter as Jully and I entered the cell block.

The banshees moaned quietly instead of their usual hysterical crying and screaming. My heart pounded as I found myself so close to the women who'd become such a part of me since the day that I'd read their files at PPD headquarters. Could I truly help them? They'd all suffered so much more than I had and I was nearly broken myself; what could I do for them? The cool power of compassion stirred within my chest, and I suddenly knew what I had to do. Two specters interrupted my thoughts as they rushed out of a room at the end of the corridor and charged us. I directed another controlled burst of rage into a scream that obliterated both of them instantly with limited collateral damage to the surrounding building. The hallway was lined with celestial steel doorways: one at the end of the corridor was ajar. With trepidation, I approached the first door on my right, and, hearing soft cries coming from within, I willed the steel to part for me and it did so.

The room beyond was small and empty except for an iron maiden made of the hateful red devil's iron. I could see nothing of the girl held within except her eyes. I couldn't use the banshee wail on the terrible device. Even a controlled burst would likely destroy the ghost within. I pushed the anger that roiled within me down deep and tapped into the cool power at my heart and then I began to sing "I'll Stand by You". The refreshing power of the siren song swept out from me with dramatic results; the moaning cries subsided and the eyes that looked at me through the iron maiden were suddenly lucid. Indeed, the entire cell block had grown still, encouraging me to sing louder so that everyone in the block could hear me clearly. I belted out the lyrics of the Pretenders ballad with all of the enthusiasm and skill that I could muster.

An idea struck me as I finished the second verse. I called the mists to me and sent it flowing into the iron maiden. The girl within was clearly afraid of what was happening, but my reassuring voice and words kept her calm. I continued to sing. At the same time I willed the mist to fill every crack and joint in the torture device, and then I had the mist solidify into a shield and had it push outward. The iron maiden groaned in protest for a moment and then exploded in a spray of shards. Fortunately, Jully and I were forewarned by the iron maidens groans and we'd taken shelter in the corridor. I rushed back into the room and immediately recognized the woman that was left standing in its center as Melanie Baker. I recalled that her file had said that she'd been twenty three years old and a mom when she'd been murdered. She was wearing a chain mesh of devil's iron that covered her from head to foot. I guessed the purpose of this suit was to prevent her from being able to use her powers effectively.

Jully and I rushed to her side and helped her get out of the hateful suit. I continued to sing while we worked, "I'll be There for You" by Jon Bon Jovi followed "I'll Stand by You". Jully helped the now freed banshee put on several celestial steel rings and bracelets which she produced from a steel mesh bag that I'd given to her while preparing for the mission on the ferry. Jully explained to Melanie that the jewelry would help her heal and keep her mind clear. I was far more worried about the state of their minds than of their bodies, but the jewelry seemed to have the desired effect. Melanie was clearly confused by the sudden turn of events, but her mental fortitude impressed me; she decided quite quickly that she was going to put her faith in us and follow our lead. Once in the hallway Melanie showed her true colors when she held back from bolting for the open door to freedom; she instead looked at the other cell doors and looked back at me with a question in her eyes. I nodded to her in agreement.

At this point, aware that this whole effort was taking a great deal of time, I went up and down the row of doors and opened each of them. We got a surprise in the final cell across from the one that the specters had emerged from; a luminary was chained within.

"I am Enoch," the luminary told us as we set about to free

him. Once freed, he showed me how the maidens were opened with a key used in several places. Under his direction, I shaped several keys from the celestial steel of a cell door. We worked quickly in pairs: Melanie with me, and Jully and Enoch together. We used the keys to free the banshees one by one. We had four of them freed when the Warden arrived. The sound of battle was heavy once again in the courtyard. Baron was bellowing in rage and battle lust. Sebastian had just arrived to inform me that the front gates were holding, but that the roof squads had been swept away by the arrival of the Warden and a powerful contingent of darklings. The Warden arrived a few seconds after I'd received the report. It stood in the doorway surveying the scene while several darklings waited at its back.

"Enoch, Jully free the others," I ordered moving towards the Warden. "Sisters, follow me."

"You have troubled us for the last time," rasped the Warden as he waited for my approach. "The order has been given to execute you. No quarter will be given."

Instead of my usual wiseass remarks, I screamed. The short, focused burst of anger hit the Warden full on. It should have torn him to pieces, but he stood unaffected and laughed.

"I am protected from your screams by a hell shard," the Warden mocked me. "So you see, your one little toy is useless now."

I called upon the mists and sent them towards the reaper, but the cloud fell apart as soon as it came within three feet of the Warden. It laughed again. The reaper took a step in my direction, and I felt the banshees behind me grow terrified and desperate. My own anxiety level was growing, but I hadn't used up all my tricks yet.

"Steady ladies. He's dead, he just doesn't know it yet," I said and the Warden laughed once again. "I've had it with your stupid laugh. Let's see if you find this funny."

The shards of celestial steel littering the hallway suddenly began flying towards the reaper in a deadly spray that struck it.

The Warden snarled in rage and tried to evade the shrapnel as best it could, but I'd made a veritable cloud of it. Celestial steel is like poison to reapers. He launched himself at me, a red blade of devil's iron appearing in his hand. The celestial steel of a door he was passing suddenly reached out and grabbed his legs with steel fists. The door across the way had formed itself into spears and started stabbing at him. He tried to defend himself, but the building was layered in celestial steel. This was my domain now.

"How does it feel to know that you will be annihilated by your own security measures?" I asked cold rage bubbled within me. I wanted to hurt the Warden. I wanted to give him just a small piece of what he'd been giving others for who knows how long. More and more of the steel in the structure was rooting itself up and attacking the reaper. The front part of the hallway was filled with a deadly hale of blue steel of all shapes and sizes. They were flying about and stabbing at the now fallen reaper. The Warden had its head shielded with its arms and was coiled in a ball that didn't offer much protection.

"Let me live and I will serve you," The Warden croaked desperately. I was surprised to hear such an offer, but I didn't trust any darklings, let alone a reaper. One of the truly liberating aspects of Limbo is that the dividing line between good and evil is so much clearer than in real life. A reaper was a being born of evil; it could not be converted to good. Therefore it must be destroyed.

"No thanks. We have a policy of discriminating against reapers in my army. Sorry, have a nice day."

A few minutes later, the Warden collapsed in on itself and dissolved into oblivion. The darklings that had watched from the doorway turned and fled. After another three minutes we had all of the banshees freed and properly attired with celestial steel jewelry, mesh armor, and weapons that had been made from the steel that had destroyed the Warden. This bit of justice satisfied my sisters greatly. The courtyard was now back under our control, and Baron had retaken the rooftop. Sebastian reported that the front gate was still being held, but that they were being pressed hard and wouldn't hold for too much longer. The banshees themselves were in remarkably good shape and spirits considering their ordeal. They seemed to view me with a mixture of awe, fear, and gratitude.

"Who are you?" the youngest of the banshees, fifteen year old Amber Morgan asked as we exited the isolation block.

"My name is Veronika Kane. I was murdered by the same guy who tortured and killed you all. I'm leading a rebellion against those who did this to us, and I was hoping that you'd help me. You are all banshees; the rage that boils in the pits of your stomachs can be used to destroy your enemies. The ones that did this to you, to us, they had a hand in your murders and mine. We can't let this go on. Other people are in danger, and I can't let them be harmed like we were. I can't do this alone though. Will you lend me your strength and help me make this world a better place?"

Despite being confused and terrified, Angela, Amber, Catherine, Danielle, Melanie, Melisa, Susan, Sonya, and Bridget all nodded and as a group the banshees marched out of captivity and forward to war

31

OUR LOSSES WERE FAR HIGHER than I'd expected them to be. Three squads from the roof and one squad each from the courtyard and gate were destroyed. That amounted to more than thirty free souls in all. We hadn't anticipated that half of the city's army would be converging on Washington Square. As far as I could tell, every unit in the city was passing through the square to pick up its share of supplies. The entire city was clearly mobilizing for war; our timing couldn't have been worse.

I sent the remaining squads from the courtyard to join Baron on the rooftop. Enoch, myself, and the banshees headed for the front gates. We didn't encounter any resistance in the halls leading to the main entrance of the facility and so found ourselves arriving behind Quinn's beleaguered force within a few minutes of leaving the inner courtyard. The gates had been blasted to smithereens allowing those of us in the prison's entryway a full view of the square beyond. It was full of specters, darklings, and even a few reapers. There were thousands of them and Quinn had held them at bay with twenty four free souls. I was in awe of this feat. The free souls were being attacked by a massive press of specters and under fire from the darklings who hurled black bolts of energy every chance they got. I could see that the line was near exhaustion. They would not be able to hold much longer.

"Sebastian, tell Quinn that when I give the signal his men are to drop to the ground and roll backwards."

"Yes mistress. I will go at once," the owl said.

I gathered the banshees around me and gave them quick instructions. Then we formed a line behind our fighting free souls. Fear and adrenalin raced through my ghostly veins as I sized up the banshees. All of their features were pinched with fear but also determination. I smiled my encouragement at them and turned back to the battle playing out before us. If anything went wrong in the next few seconds we could all be dead again or even worse: taken prisoner. Once we were ready and I saw Quinn keeping an anxious eye towards me, I gave the signal. Quinn roared a command and the free souls dropped to the ground as one and began rolling backwards. I stepped forward, hopping over two rolling soldiers. The banshees to either side of me did likewise. The enemy let out a great clamor when they saw the entire line collapse, and they surged forward in mass only to find themselves confronted by a line of beautiful women. The entire horde paused in confusion; it was the last thing they ever did.

I raised my hand and let it fall as I let loose with a torrent of rage that came out in a wave of sonic energy. All nine of the other banshees let their wails loose simultaneously, and Washington Square was nearly purged of every ghost in its confines. It was as if a nuclear bomb had gone off in the square. Thousands upon thousands of ghosts were obliterated. Buildings all around the square collapsed into heaps of rubble. Even ghosts who had been flying above the square were not immune to that terrible blast. The shock wave sent them tumbling end over end to crash into buildings, or they simply plummeted to the ground.

No one said anything or moved for nearly two minutes after

the blast. Part of it was that everyone was deafened, but more telling was the shock that everyone felt at the level of destruction. Even I, who had the most experience with the destructive power of the banshee wail, was quite unprepared for the sheer scale of destruction that a squad of banshees could produce. No wonder the Master had put so much effort into acquiring so many banshees. With them he could wipe out whole armies. It really was quite frightening to have so much power.

"Well," I said breaking the silence, my voice cracking a little betraying the shock that I still felt. "I didn't quite expect that … but well done. That's a few thousand of them that won't be killing our people."

Many of the banshees looked mortified at the damage they'd wrought. My words hit home and most of them nodded in agreement, though a few still looked uncomfortable.

"Sebastian, get down here," I shouted to the sky above me. A few seconds later, the owl flapped its way to my side, hovering a few feet away.

"Here I am mistress. How can I serve?"

"Would you stop that mistress crap? I was never anyone's mistress, certainly not yours," I said in exasperation. "Go to Jonus and report what has happened here. Get a report from him and a report from Rachel, then come find me."

"I live to serve my lady," Sebastian said with a mock bow and winged away before I could rebuke him. I sighed heavily as I heard snickering coming from some of the banshees.

"He's very cute," Danielle Stanton observed with a smile. "Can I have one too?"

"He's not a pet," I informed her. "No one owns him. He just follows me around, annoying me with titles from the middle-ages. He is quite handy to have around though."

"Is the war over now?" asked Sonya Taylor. "What do we do now? We are dead right? These last few months haven't just been a terrible nightmare that I'm gonna be waking up from, are they?"

"I'm afraid not," I answered sadly. "There is still fighting to be done. And yes, we are all dead. There is a lot of evil in this ghost world called Limbo. The Master of Philadelphia enjoys destroying the lives of living people. He was responsible for what happened to you … and to me. That's why I'm here. I don't want lives to ever again be destroyed by ghosts. I want to free the souls that haven't yet been corrupted and I want to help protect the living from other monsters that do exist. I hope that you will help me put an end to the Master and his servants once and for all."

There was silence for a few moments. The women before me either studied me or their surroundings as they considered my words.

"These seem like worthy goals to me," Melanie Baker finally said in a quavering voice. She was the oldest of the Tormentor's victims and her eyes glistened with unshed tears. "I left two children behind. I don't want them to be prey for any kind of monsters. I agree that we should not interfere with their lives, but we can protect them from unnatural monsters that should not be. Will you teach us to do the things that you can do and how to live in this place?"

"Yes, I will teach you all that I know," I said as I moved to embrace the heart broken banshee, offering her what little comfort that I could. "You are all my sisters, and sisters have to stick together."

"I've always wanted sisters," interjected the petit Amber Morgan. She had shoulder length curly brown hair and beautiful green eyes that were far to grown up for her age. She was the youngest of us, only fifteen. I recalled that her file had suggested that she'd lived a quiet sheltered life until becoming the fourth of the Tormentor's victims. The thought made me want to go after him now. I'd hoped he would be present at the prison but no such luck. I guessed that he would be holed up at the Eastern State Penitentiary. Catherine and Melanie both put their arms around the girl and we were all soon embroiled in a group hug.

A nervous clearing of the throat brought me out of my sister bonding moment with a start. There were things to do.

"What's up lieutenant Quinn? Do you have a report?" I asked while disentangling myself from the group. They mainly remained together, offering each other badly needed comfort. They did watch me carefully however.

"The prison is secure ma'am," Quinn reported stiffly. "We've freed more than a hundred shades. Most of them were awaiting testing. Aerial scouts report the area clear of enemy forces for up to five blocks in all directions."

"Thanks, lieutenant. Have the shades been assembled for the recruitment speech?"

"Yes, Ma'am. In the courtyard. I assigned Jully to do the honors."

"Excellent choice," I said. "I will be taking my sisters to observe." Quinn saluted and I beckoned the banshees to follow me which they did reluctantly, not wanting to go anywhere near the place of their long captivity.

On the way, I explained to them the social structure of Limbo. They had received no training or testing. They were simply kept in isolation until today. They were universally appalled by the plight of the shades, so by the time we reached the courtyard they barely even noticed their old prison but instead were focused on the shades.

Jully was already in the process of giving her speech when we arrived. The parts that I heard amazed me; she had a gift for oratory. Shades were already beginning to shift into free souls even before she'd finished speaking. When it was all said and done the entire group had made the transformation. One hundred and twenty free souls were added to our crusade. I immediately began to shape weapons for them from the materials left in the prison, of which there was no lack. All of my sisters tried to manipulate and shape the steel themselves, but none of them proved to have that gift.

At one point during my work, Jully approached to give her report.

"You did a fantastic job Jully. You have a gift for speaking."

"Yes Ma'am," she answered shyly. "I grew up in a political family. My father is a Republican Congressman, and my older brother is a councilman."

"They taught you well, and you learned even better," I said with a smile. "I could use someone like you as a personal assistant, an aide de camp if you will. Perhaps you would be interested in such a position?"

"I would be honored ma'am," she answered earnestly.

"Well before you do agree to anything, I want you to consider two things," I said. "First, being around me is dangerous. Someone is always trying to kill me it seems. I'm not hiring you to be a body guard. You need to stay out of the way and run when things get too hairy. Do you understand?"

She nodded unhappily.

"I'm not questioning your bravery or skill with weapons Jully. Don't worry, at my side you'll get more combat than you can stand. I just don't want you playing the hero and getting yourself annihilated because you tried to fight the Master or Black Maria."

Her eyes went wide at these suggestions and she shook her head negatively. "No ma'am, I won't play that kind of hero. I promise."

"Good," I said with a smile. "Along with your other duties, you will participate in combat training with me every morning. And the second condition is that you will call me Veronika, not ma'am."

"Yes ma'am ... I mean Veronika," she said with excitement.

"Very good Jully, welcome aboard." I held out my hand for her to shake but at the last second I decided to give her a hug instead.

Baron chose that moment to drop into the courtyard and almost got blasted for it. My sisters stared at the massive gargoyle in terror. I quickly told the banshees Baron's story, and by the time I was finished the girls had surrounded the huge gargoyle studying him with fascination. They all wanted to be tested for the Siren's Song ability right away and in the end it turned out that only Melanie and Amber possessed the gift.

Sebastian winged his way over the prison's rooftop and descended rapidly, coming to a hovering stop in front of me.

"Jonus has secured Gray's Ferry. There was a fierce battle. Jonus and Barnabas engaged the Ferryman. They defeated the reaper, but Barnabas was slain in the process." Sebastian paused to let this terrible news sink in. "The gargoyles made the difference. Jonus has freed more than a thousand shades and more than six hundred have already transformed. He wasn't able to equip them all, but the majority, at least, have a sword."

"What about Rachel?" I asked my heart sick with the news of Barnabas's final death. I'd expected losses, things were going rather better than I'd dared hope for, but losing Barnabas was a body blow.

"She and her force are in danger of being enveloped by an army of darklings coming from North side. Jonus is sending help, but your flyers would get there faster."

"Jully," I called to my aide. "Tell Lieutenant Quinn to gather up Banshee Company. We leave in three minutes."

I went to my sister banshees and gave them a crash course in flying. Those of them who still weren't sold on this whole ghost thing were sold on it the moment they took to the sky. This is where true freedom was experienced. I asked Enoch to lead the non-flying free souls to the Benjamin Franklin Parkway where they could join the rest of the army. Having given orders for the disposition of the new recruits, I led the banshees back to the front gate of the Walnut Street Prison where Banshee Company awaited us. I nodded to Quinn in silent salute and launched myself skyward. Jully came to my side while Baron and the Banshees followed on our heels. Banshee Company took up the rear guard position as we sped towards the Vine Street Expressway.

32

THE VINE STREET EXPRESSWAY came into sight about five minutes after we departed the Walnut Street Prison. It was a symbol of the modern age, a thoroughfare of asphalt and iron, an engineering feat that cut through the heart of the city. It wasn't a thing of beauty by any means. Few designs in the modern era have any aesthetic appeal. Instead it was built for pure convenience and utility. In Limbo, it rose above the surrounding neighborhoods as a monument of the military industrial complex that had come to characterize modern America.

Through the mists that shrouded the city, I could see that there was a milling mass of darklings moving West from the Chinatown exit. I changed my direction Westward towards the Benjamin Franklin Parkway exit ramp where Rachel's reserves would be located. A knot of around fifty darklings led by a reaper sprang into the air and made straight for us. I cursed softly under my breath. The force was larger than my own, and the delay of an aerial battle could have serious consequences for Rachel and her troops. Already the forces that had been left on the expressway were picking up speed, double timing it toward Rachel's position. The banshees were of limited use in aerial combat, posing just as much a threat to ally as to foe. The girls were just too inexperienced for this kind of action and few of them had any training at all in close combat which meant they would all be in horrible jeopardy. I made a quick decision and raised my hand signaling a halt. The company came to a hovering stop. Some of the banshees had difficulty with this maneuver and were forced to hold on to Baron in order to stay aloft.

"Quinn, you'll need to deal with those darklings on your own," I said pointing to the oncoming aerial force of darklings. "Baron you deal with the reaper if you please. I'll see you at the Parkway exit, now go!"

Quinn saluted and bellowed orders. At his command, the company wheeled around and sped towards the advancing darklings. Baron flew at their head with Quinn. A pang of guilt and worry stabbed at my stomach as I watched them go; had I just sent them to their deaths in order to protect the banshees? Melanie made as if to follow, but I shouted at her.

"Not you, Melanie. The others need us, follow me!"

I launched myself Westward once more not waiting to see the initial clash of the aerial combat. If I'd just sent them to their final deaths I had to make sure their sacrifice wasn't in vain. I angled downward toward the wide road that was Race Street and finally settled for flying ten feet above street level. In this way, I hoped to avoid any aerial scouts that the enemy might have aloft. I gestured to Jully to fly closer to me.

"I want you to fly ahead," I told my aide de camp, wishing that I didn't have to give her such a dangerous assignment so early in her service to me. "If the way stays clear by the time you reach the Parkway go to Rachel and tell her we're on our way. We'll need to spread my sisters out throughout the army. They'll need adequate protection."

"Understood." The girl nodded once and without a trace of fear sped off ahead of us. I was keeping us at a moderate speed not wanting to overdo it for the inexperienced banshees. I was very proud of the girls. So far they all seemed to understand the gravity of the situation, and although the temptation must have been strong to go off and explore this new wonderful ability of flight, they all remained attentive and serious. Even young Amber was proving to be mature past what her age would warrant. I'd been very worried that trying to integrate the banshees into our efforts would be like trying to herd a group of angry and lunatic cats around, but they were proving to be disciplined and supportive of each other in a way that I could hardly have hoped for. They truly viewed themselves as sisters. To them, I was like the older sister that could get them out of trouble and teach them a thing or two about the world. Having grown up as an only child this was both terrifying and exhilarating for me.

A warning shout and pointed finger from Bridget brought my attention to a large gothic style building on the South side of Race Street. Two large granite gargoyles were perched over the impressive Norman Porch and walkway leading into the building. Their eyes were glowing red and staring right at us. The stone around them seemed to flow and melt, and the now living stone gargoyles peeled themselves away from the edifice they had been built into.

"On the ground now!" I shouted as I dove, making a slick landing on the street below. The girls followed with varying degrees of success in their landings. Angela and Catherine both ended up on their backsides, not injured except for their pride, while Melanie and Bridget landed with grace as if they'd flown their entire lives.

"Angela and Catherine, come stand by me. You'll blast the creatures with your wail when I give the signal, ok?" The two banshees nodded, brushing themselves off in self conscious nervousness. "Melanie and Amber you stand behind us and sing *One of Us" by Joan Osborne* with me. We'll try to free them if we can. If it doesn't work, Angela and Catherine will blast them. Sonya, I want you next to Melanie. Danielle, you stand by

Amber. The two of you must guard your singing sisters. The rest of you take up the back ranks and keep an eye on the sky and behind us. If you see anything, let me know."

The gargoyles were shaking out their stone wings. They reminded me of the flying monkeys from The Wizard of Oz. Wings free of dust and cobwebs, the stone creatures sped toward us. I began to sing. Melanie and Amber joining in, though Amber only hummed, apparently unfamiliar with the song I'd chosen. The effect was immediate; the gargoyles broke off their swooping charge and slowed down to circle us. Both creatures keened: a mournful sound that was heartbreakingly beautiful. The lead gargoyle came down near Danielle who recoiled in fear and almost blasted it with a scream. I put a calming hand on her shoulder and gestured for her to move aside so that the gargoyle could reach Amber as it clearly desired. It stepped forward and brushed its stone head against the petite banshee, almost knocking her over. The girl had a look of astonished wonder on her face as she reached a tentative hand out to pet the beast's stony head. It let out a purring sound that caused Amber to giggle with pleasure.

The second gargoyle landed in front of me, but as it moved to greet me, I stepped aside and waved Melanie forward and she did so. The gargoyle looked at me with longing for a moment, and then it sniffed at Melanie. It greeted her with a rumbling purr of its own. I sighed in relief. I had my own pets to worry about as it was, along with an entire army. I sure didn't need another.

The only warning we had was the gargoyles suddenly going rigid and growling angrily. Both beasts suddenly leaped into the air and intercepted the reaper that was dropping like a stone from above us. The gargoyles hammered into it ten feet above our heads and drove it sideways. Their jaws and claws tore at the skeletal ghost. I looked around quickly and spotted a group of darklings coming from a nearby alley. They were flying low and heading straight for us. I pointed them out to Angela and

Catherine. I put a supportive hand on each of their shoulders. They were both tense with nervous anticipation and would have released their wails too soon if I hadn't been there to calm them. As the hit squad approached, they began to fan out so that they wouldn't present a single large target for our sonic attacks. I squeezed Angela's and Catherine's shoulder giving them the signal to unleash their wails. They both let out powerful screams of intense rage that tore through the majority of the darkling ranks. The remaining darklings milled about in confusion for a moment before breaking off their assault and fleeing for their lives.

As the battle with the reaper continued, I noticed with some alarm that Amber had wandered too close to it. I called on the wind and just managed to save her life as the reaper also noticed the opportunity and left itself open to the gargoyles in order to take the offered gift. The devil's iron blade whipped towards Amber's head. Her battle awareness was so minimal that she barely registered the threat. My own katana slammed into the reaper's blade, knocking it aside mere inches from Amber's face. The gargoyles took advantage of the opening the reaper had left them, tearing into it with wild abandon. My counterstroke took the reapers legs off at the knees. Without waiting to see its end, I grabbed Amber's hand and led her away from the violent scene. The wonder that had been in her eyes a few minutes ago was replaced by horror. I sighed sadly. Such was life in Limbo.

We left the now silent street behind, continuing to fly low but at a greater speed than earlier; urgency spurred us now. The air of the city crackled with tension and I sensed that the outcome of the entire invasion would be decided in the next few minutes. The gargoyles followed behind, alert to any further threats. Luckily, the road ahead remained clear of enemies. Then as we approached Nineteenth Street we heard a roaring sound. We couldn't make out words at first, but as we moved on, the words became clear.

"MASTER! MASTER! MASTER! MASTER!" The chant rose in a crescendo that seemed to shake the entire city. They were calling the Master out, and if he came all might be lost. I decided at that moment to take the biggest risk I'd ever taken. I formed the banshees into a square and we rose together, up and up until we rose above the lip of the Vine Street Expressway and looked down upon a milling horde of specters and darklings. There were thousands of them; they almost completely enveloped a small force of a few hundred free souls, who were desperately fighting for their lives. Rachel had kept control of the Benjamin Franklin Parkway exit, and her force was withdrawing upon it inch by inch. Further West, I could see a slightly larger force of free souls trying to gain purchase on the expressway, but a larger force of specters was keeping them at bay. The three parts of my army were separated and in danger of being destroyed in sequence. If Rachel's company was overwhelmed the rest of us would soon follow.

My sisters and I continued to rise, and the enemy flyers began to turn to make their attack run upon us. One thing I hadn't really considered when planning the invasion of the city was just how much of an advantage the Master would have in aerial forces. This was clearly a major factor in our current predicament. I called the mists of Limbo to me, letting my instincts take control. I reached out with desperation, begging it all to come to me, and wonder of wonders, it did. Mists began to swirl around me and my sisters. More and more of it poured in, leaving the city naked as never before. The airborne darklings paused in their advance, unsure of what was happening as vapors of mists flew past them to join a massive cloud that surrounded me and my sisters. The reapers drove them onward and they came.

When the first ranks of darklings and reapers were within thirty feet of us, I released the mists willing them to become vortexes, and they did. Thousands of small tornadoes shot out of the ever smaller cloud of mist until it was completely gone.

The vortexes spread out across the city, and whatever soul they touched they tore apart into small pieces and scattered them into oblivion. The mini tornados passed through buildings without causing any damage, but no soul could withstand them. They passed over the entire city in every direction and then vanished from sight beyond the horizon. No living soul was left in the sky aside from me and the banshees. I desperately hoped that whatever aerial forces we'd had in the sky at the time had had the sense to land as soon as they'd seen the tornadoes approaching.

"What did you do?" asked Bridget in shock and awe. "How far will they go?"

"I don't know," I answered tiredly. I wished desperately that I could land and take a long nap. "We're not done yet. I need your help now. I'm too tired to do much more. Follow me."

I picked out a spot in the enemy's army that was made up entirely of specters. The battle had paused for a moment as everyone tried to come to grips with what they'd just witnessed. When the specters saw us approaching their position, they panicked and tried to flee: a fatal mistake. Their panic left a wide enough space in their ranks for me and the banshees to land. As soon as I touched down, I ordered the banshees to let loose their wails upon the enemy. We were in a rough square formation facing outward in all directions. Hundreds of enemy troops were instantly annihilated in a hundred foot radius around us when we let loose our raging screams.

Again there was a pause in the battle and then the flying free souls of Banshee Company were landing among us. My heart soared upon seeing Quinn, Baron, and the free souls of my company. Not only had they survived the aerial battle I'd sent them into, but they also managed to avoid being destroyed by the tornadoes I'd unleashed on the skies of the city. Without having to be directed, Quinn assigned free soul soldiers to each banshee for her protection, and, with a nod from me, we all began walking towards the remains of the enemy's army. That was all that they could take. The Master's grand army dissolved before us. They broke and fled before the wails of the banshees, scattering in every direction.

33

THE FREE SOUL ARMY WOULD HAVE pursued the broken army of darklings and specters, but I sent orders for the army to form up at Logan Square. The park at the square's center is dominated by the massive Swann Memorial Fountain. Its three sculptures of Native American river gods were a representation of Philadelphia's three primary waterways: the Delaware, the Schuylkill, and the Wissahickon. In the living world, the turtle and swan sculptures that also make up the fountain shoot jets of water into the sky, offering the neighborhood's children relief and fun in the summer. In Limbo, there is no water. Water is an element of life, so the fountain was empty except for its fine sculptures. The square is the heart of the Parkway and the magnificent edifices of The Free Library of Philadelphia, Moore College of Art and Design, The Franklin Institute, the Academy of Natural Science, and the Cathedral Basilica of Saints Peter and Paul surround it with majestic glory. The Square was a perfect location for our scattered forces to regroup in relative safety and from which to launch our final assault upon the Master's own stronghold of Eastern State Penitentiary.

"Why did you call us off?" asked a disgruntled Jonus when he arrived at the mustering ground. "We could have completely destroyed them. Now they'll be scattered throughout the city. It will be nearly impossible to find and dig them all out."

I was standing by the male Indian sculpture that represented the Delaware River. Rachel and Enoch were talking quietly a few feet away. Gideon and another luminary followed in Jonus's wake and, with a start, I realized that I recognized the new luminary. It was the one I'd seen several times on the ferry before my captivity. The same one whose face I'd seen sliced off by the Ferryman and the one who'd encouraged me to believe in myself.

"I'm sorry Jonus, but we've got bigger fish to fry," I told him. "The Master and his inner circle are still the most dangerous ghosts in Philly. I couldn't allow us to get scattered across the city and give them a chance to escape or strike back at us in some way we don't expect. We're going to Easter State Penitentiary to put an end to that monster. The others will be a pain in the ass to root out, but without a head to lead them, they'll be less likely to pose an organized threat."

The tension seemed to go out of Jonus and he regretfully nodded his understanding.

"You're right of course," he said bitterly. "I shouldn't have let emotion guide me. The loss of Barnabas, it just …"

"It's ok Jonus, I understand," I said putting my hand on the luminary's shoulder. "We are all sad about losing Barnabas and so many others, but we have no time to lick our wounds, nor can we let our emotions guide our actions. We have to maintain discipline and keep our objectives front and center. Now introduce me to your new companion. We've met several times and I'm eager for a proper introduction."

"Sometimes it is hard to believe that you are so young," he said with a shake of his head. "Veronika Kane, allow me to introduce you to Ezekiel. Ezekiel it is my honor to present Veronika Kane."

Ezekiel stepped forward with a broad smile on his angelic face, and he actually bowed to me.

"Welcome to the free soul cause Ezekiel," I said earnestly. "Without your encouragement those two times that we met on the ferry, I don't think that I'd be here today. You inspired me to believe in myself and to not fear adversity. I am so glad that Jonus was able to free you. Thanks for your courage."

"I am honored to stand with you," Ezekiel answered in a quiet voice. "I did nothing but obey the intuitions that God sent me. You are the one who has used your God given talents to help others. You could have risen far in the ranks of Limbo, perhaps even become one of its masters, but you chose the more difficult path, and now we have a chance to change Limbo for the good. I am pleased to help you in any way that I can."

"Thank you," I said gratified by his words. "Now let's get this show on the road."

After another ten minutes of consultations, orders were given and the army marched from Logan Square heading North towards the roiling darkness that enveloped Eastern State Penitentiary. We traveled on the Parkway for a short distance then turned onto Twenty-First Street. This route took us due North until we came to Fairmount Street. The impressive medieval structure that is Easter State Penitentiary stood silently and dark before us. The first penitentiary built in the world, Eastern served as a model for hundreds of prisons built around the world. The outer walls are thirty feet high and six feet thick built of Pennsylvania granite. Imposing towers stand watch at each of its corners. The front entrance is a massive gate built into a looming crenellated tower that leaves visitors feeling as if they'd somehow been transported to London or Paris instead of being in downtown Philly. There were no visible guards anywhere along the walls of the fortress nor did we see any watchers peaking through the windows and slits that pierced the wall at irregular intervals. The only proof that the Master was still holed up within was the presence of the black miasma that hung over the complex like a foul smog.

I signaled to the banshees who traveled together in a group

behind me. Danielle and Sonya stepped forward to stand at my side and the three of us turned to confront the massive gates of the penitentiary. They stood defiantly closed and seemingly impregnable. I nodded once more and the two ladies let forth their wails, and the gates of Eastern State shattered as if struck by a battering ram wielded by a titan. The first five rows of specters standing quietly behind the gates were destroyed instantly. The horde that remained roared with battle lust and charged forward. Bridget and Amber stepped forward to replace Danielle and Sonya. They met the enemy's charge with a duet of screams that devastated more of the Master's army. More continued to pour out of the fortress however. Christina and Melanie were next to unleash their fury upon our foes. An army of darklings suddenly burst through the doors and windows of surrounding buildings, falling upon my waiting troops without warning. The surprise attack was devastating; scores of free souls perished in the initial assault. The free souls, however, proved their metal. Instead of buckling under the pressure, they doggedly met the new threat and held together as a cohesive force.

The dark miasma over the prison began to surge forward, rolling over the penitentiary walls and into the street beyond. Shapes moved in that black mist, soon resolving themselves into scores of reapers. Jonus, Rachel, Gideon, Enoch, and Ezekiel gathered together in a line and raised their hands in unison. In a single voice they shouted "El Luminis" and bright beams of light sprang from their outstretched hands. Both the black miasma and the reapers gave way before the holy light cast by the luminaries. Baron and four other gargoyles took to the sky and charged the oncoming reapers. Bolts of light continued to push back the black cloud, and a reaper was instantly obliterated every time a luminary aimed a beam at one of them.

The lead reaper and a few of its companions managed to get clear of the deadly gauntlet of gargoyles and luminary light beams. They desperately charged straight for me and the other banshees. Apparently they hadn't expected the luminaries to be so effective against the dark miasma. Their strategy was collapsing and killing me was their last desperate chance to achieve victory. They didn't make it to us before Banshee Company sprang aloft, intercepting the reapers a mere twenty feet away from us. The company dissolved into squads, each one enveloping a reaper. A half dozen blue steel swords stabbed the skeletal ghosts making it impossible for them to adequately defend themselves. Quinn led two squads against the lead reaper who bellowed in fury and tried to push its way through to me but was unable to overcome the free soul assault. In the end, Quinn took the lead reapers head as it tried to shoot a bolt of black energy at me. I was relieved to be able to avoid battle. I was exhausted and I needed to conserve what power was left for the forthcoming battle with the Master.

I watched the raging battle around me and decided that it was time for me to go after the Master. I signaled Jonus who was still driving off the black miasma with the beams of light from his hand. He nodded to me and I turned to the blown in gates of the Eastern State Penitentiary knowing that Jonus would take charge of things in my absence. I left the banshees with Quinn and his souls and strode alone into my enemy's lair. Nervous energy coursed through me; I'd come further than I'd dared hope for. Everything came down to the next few minutes. The war would be won or lost here. I'd endured so much to arrive at this moment and time, and so many people were counting on me. The weight of it all should have crushed me, but a still calmness settled over me. Even the roiling rage at the core of my being was only a whisper. I strode forward confident in myself and those who still battled behind me.

After passing through the outer wall, I found myself in the outer courtyard of the facility; a parking area and loading zone were off to my right while exercise fields were located to my left. The prison itself was built in a hub-and-spoke style, consisting of an octagonal center atrium connected by seven corridors radiating outward like the spokes of a wheel. Each corridor was a cell block containing scores of single occupancy cells. I chose cell bloc seven. Its door opened easily when I pulled on the devil's iron handle revealing an empty corridor beyond. I moved forward cautiously, looking into every cell to make sure that they were empty before move further into the facility.

I finally stepped out of cell bloc seven into the central rotunda where the roiling mass of black cloud that was the Master awaited me. Red points of flame marked its eyes in the otherwise featureless being of dark power. The evilness that emanated from it filled me with dread, and I suddenly wondered what I was doing here by myself. A clanging of doors slamming shut all around me reinforced my growing fear; the plan wasn't going to work. What could I do against this thing? Would my banshee wail work against it? A low terrible laughter echoed through the floor and building as if the world itself were laughing at me, and maybe it was.

"Go on," said a horrible echoing voice that felt like ten thousand insects crawling upon my body. "Try your screams, your bewitching song, your sword, your mist magic, you may try what you like."

Not pausing to even think about it, I blasted the wraith with a concentrated blast of my wail. Very often when someone blathers that your power doesn't concern them, they are just bluffing. Not so with the Master. Though my wail blew apart one of the cell block doors and cracked the walls and floor nearby, the Master was completely unaffected. I began to sing "Blaze of glory" by Jon Bon Jovi. At the same time I launched myself at the wraith swinging my celestial steel katana in deadly arcs and thrusts. Neither my siren's song nor my katana had any effect on the Master in any way. He mocked me with his chilling laughter. I continued to sing the Hollywood cowboy battle hymn just so that I could hold on to some vestige of courage. My blade slashed and pierced. I struck at the eyes and every inch of the smoky being that I imagined might be vulnerable to the celestial steel, but to no avail. The mists were no help either; there wasn't enough of it around since my vortex gambit had pretty much left the city devoid of its foggy presence, and I was too tired to conjure up a worthwhile amount of it.

The Master chuckled deeply at my ineffectual attacks, and it suddenly lashed out with a black tendril that struck me across the face. The agony was like nothing I'd ever endured before. The shock alone caused me to drop my weapons and collapse to the ground. I writhed uncontrollably while it watched. When the pain began to subside and I started to rise to my feet, the Master struck me again, this time with two black tentacles. The affect was much the same but magnified by the second blow. My experience with being tortured had led me to believe that the body could only endure a certain threshold of pain. Once you reached that level, the mind stops registering additional pain. The Master showed me that I was wrong however. There was no safe threshold of pain for a ghost. If one had the knowledge and power to do so, one could increase pain to infinite levels.

"Who are you to have destroyed my servants and meddled with my plans?" The Master roared at me, anger making its voice quiver. A dozen more lashes struck me, increasing the pain levels I was suffering from exponentially. The collar hadn't caused half as much pain as this. "You are an insignificant worm that I will keep with me at all times for all eternity. I will make you beg for release into the pits of hell, but no such mercy will be granted to you. I will never tire of tormenting you. You will be an everlasting example of what happens to those who dare to defy me."

The roiling cloud that was the Master surged forward and enveloped me. The world went dark except for twin points of flaming eyes that burned my soul. The Master flowed into me and it felt as though I were being smothered by a billion crawling worms. I wanted to breathe, to cry out, but I couldn't. I was completely helpless against this terrible being of boundless power.

"Yes, I see that you are beginning to understand the breadth of your arrogance in thinking you could appose me," said the Master.

"You … Don't … Know … Everything," I managed to croak. Those were the four hardest words I'd ever spoken. I wanted to vomit, gag, and scream all at the same time. My eyes felt like they were on fire. My bones felt as though they'd been pounded into powder. My brain felt like it was slowly being devoured by maggots, and my mouth, lungs, throat, and stomach felt like they were filled with writhing worms. The torment was unbelievable, and for a moment I was really scared that I might truly go mad before I could utter another word.

No other words were necessary however. The four words I'd spoken were the signal that my allies had been waiting for, and multiple doors leading into the rotunda shattered before the screams of my sisters. Five glorious luminaries stepped from five different doorways surrounding the Master and me. I immediately felt the Master's fear and loathing for these soldiers of heaven. The Master's tentacles lashed out at the luminaries, but the black appendages all reared back in sudden agony before striking their targets. The luminaries were bathed in a holy aura that the wraith's dark form couldn't penetrate. As they had done in the street outside the penitentiary, the five luminaries raised their hands in unison and spoke the words of power "El Luminis" and a beam of pure light shot from each of their hands and struck the Master.

The Master screamed in agony, and in its moment of bewildered surprise I took the opportunity to roll away from its grasp. I sucked in air as if I'd been drowning. Bridget and Melanie ran to my side and pulled me to relative safety behind Jonus. The luminaries kept up a continuous barrage of light beams on the Master; its form seemed to shrink in on itself under the withering attack. It tried several more times to lash out at its attackers, but the holy aura that surrounded the luminaries kept it at bay.

"You are the arrogant one," I said shakily to the wraith as it continued to gyrate, trying to get away from the beams that were destroying it. "You assumed that I was like you and would demand the glory and honor of facing you myself," I snorted in derision. "My father would say I could be foolish sometimes, but I don't have stupid written on my forehead. I have my skills and talents, but they weren't what we needed for dealing with you. That's what God gave us luminaries for. I'm glad you were too arrogant to see through our ruse."

The Master's end came swiftly as the black cloud was burned away by the blazing beams of light that continued to scour it. The flaming eyes were burned away and then the black miasma that was its physical shape in Limbo collapsed into a mini vortex. My friends kept the light beams pointed into the vortex and after a few more minutes it too collapsed. Tiny wisps fell away and then there was nothing. All that was left of the Master was a black smear imbedded in the floor of the rotunda.

"Using yourself as bait was dangerous, even foolhardy," said Jonus, as he slumped tiredly against the rotunda wall. "It could have killed you or driven you insane before we could intervene."

"You aren't kidding," I shuddered at the very fresh memory of its horrific touch. "It was necessary though. I think he would have fled if I hadn't given him the opportunity to avenge himself on me. If I knew what I know now when we planned this out in Logan Square, I'm not sure I'd have had the courage to go through with it. He was so damned powerful."

Jonus nodded in agreement. Rachel came to stand over me; she held out a hand as if to help me rise. As soon as our hands met a jolt of power surged between us. I felt immediately invigorated. I wasn't anywhere near full power but I was in significantly better shape than I'd been in a few moments ago. Rachel on the other hand looked horribly fatigued.

"Veronika!" someone shouted before I could protest or even thank Rachel for her actions. "You have to see this."

Fear gripped my belly and I moved quickly towards where the female voice had called from: the corridor of cell bloc twelve. I saw Melanie standing half way down the otherwise empty hallway looking into one of the cells. I called the wind to lend me speed and was at the banshee's side in the next second.

She started at my sudden appearance at her side but recovered quickly and nodded towards the cell. I let my gaze fall upon the small chamber and saw immediately what had attracted Melanie's attention. The cell was empty except for a message scrawled in devil's iron upon the wall.

"I'll be waiting for you on the other side. Take your time. I just know that it's going to take some time for me to make that bitch cop scream properly."

34

"This is an obvious trap," Jonus said angrily. "He wants you to go after him. He's daring you to do so. We can't afford to lose you at this stage of the battle and he knows it."

"I'm not going to let him start up his reign of terror on the living world again," I replied. I was pacing nervously in the confines of the small cell where the Tormentor had left me his message. "I know he's baiting me, but I can't leave Wendi to fend for herself. I'm going after him. You don't need me for the mopping up stage. Jonus, you are in command. Melanie will lead the banshees."

"We're going with you," objected Bridget. "I want a piece of that asshole."

"I'm sorry ladies," I said turning to the banshees standing in the corridor. "You need proper training before you can operate in the living world. Your powers are far too dangerous to let you loose on the other side. You all have as much right to that beast as anyone does. I ask you to let me do it on your behalf. I promise he won't hurt another woman ever again."

"What training do you have that qualifies you to go rather than us?" Angela asked in challenge.

"There's no time for me to explain all of the training I've received in living world operations. All you need to know right now is that I was trained by Delilah and made part of her sowing team. I've operated in the living world. More importantly I know who his target is and I have an idea as to where she might be. You are needed here."

The girls still looked like they wanted to argue but Melanie spoke up.

"We've already screwed his plans up. He's got nothing left but to try to bait Veronika into a trap. She rescued us, set our minds free and has given us a chance to make something of ourselves here. I say we trust her and let her do what she thinks needs to be done. We can help the free souls and Jonus clean up here and make this into a proper home."

One by one each of the banshees nodded their agreement. I breathed a silent sigh of relief, and thanked God that Melanie had taken on the mantle of leadership among the banshees.

"But promise us that you will teach us how to safely operate in the living world when you get back," Bridget said clearly unhappy at the thought of being left behind.

"I promise to give you that training as soon as things are made safe on this side of Philly," I replied. "We will need some new protocols for how to operate on the other side first however. The ones I worked under won't be acceptable under the new regime."

Jonus had observed the exchange quietly and now looked frustrated instead of angry.

"At least take your guards with you," he said pleadingly.

"I don't have time to argue with you Jonus. You need every skilled fighter we have to finish things off. They would be of limited use to me in any case. Sebastian, can you operate in the living world?"

"Of course mistress," answered the owl who was perched on the open door to the cell.

"Good. I'll take Sebastian with me. He can come for help if it's needed."

Seeing that this was the best he was going to get out of me, Jonus nodded his unhappy ascent. We exited the cell and went out into the penitentiary exercise yard where a large part of the army waited to be deployed. Though a sense of urgency filled me, I couldn't just leave without giving the free souls an explanation for my departure; rumors could be very demoralizing to an army.

"My friends," I addressed the army. "What you have done today is nothing short of miraculous. Victory is near at hand but has not been totally achieved yet. There are still some hard fights ahead. Do not grow complacent. Liberty's enemies will counter attack, and indeed they already have. I have learned of a threat in the living world that I must attend to immediately. Jonus will command in my absence and the other banshees will continue to fight at your side. Though it pains me to leave you, please know that I am doing this to preserve what we are all fighting for. The living world must be protected from the vile depredations of Limbo's masters. We fight for a new order, an order that will end tyranny in Limbo forever. Know that while you fight here, I will be fighting for the same cause on the other side. May God bless you all and preserve your free souls for all eternity."

The army saluted me and I returned the gesture. I asked Thor to remain at Melanie's side till I returned. Finally, I gave instructions to Baron and the other gargoyles who followed me, and then I went back into the corridor of cell block twelve where Sebastian awaited me.

35

WE TRANSLATED INTO living Philadelphia and found ourselves surrounded by leering teenagers, most of whom were
peering into a nearby cell while a tour guide lectured on the
history of Eastern State Penitentiary. A sandy haired kid made a
morbid joke that caused most of the girls in the group to cringe
in revulsion. I suddenly understood why some ghosts enjoyed
the work assigned to phantoms. It certainly would be fun to
scare the crap out of the juvenile punk who liked to get under
the skin of his classmates.

We threaded our way through the mass of youths, apparently part of a local high school that had come to Eastern
State Penitentiary as part of their US History class. We finally
made our escape from the prison and onto Fairmount Avenue.
It was early afternoon and the sun was shining brightly. Both
pedestrian and vehicular traffic were steady at this hour. We
turned onto Fairmount Avenue heading Northeast until we
reached the Broad Street intersection. We then turned South
onto Broad, passing a major public transportation hub whose

massive complex included below ground subway terminals and regional train and bus facilities above ground. At Spring Garden Avenue, we turned East once more and then headed South again on Twelfth Street. By this time we were in the Callowhill neighborhood where Wendi Kapudo had resided the last time I'd seen her personal information at the Round House.

Callowhill had once been a thriving industrial sector in the city and the majority of its structures were old brownstone factories and warehouses usually four to six stories high. The neighborhood had suffered a population decline in the nineteen seventies and eighties, but in recent years the factories and warehouses had gone through internal renovations and now featured some of the most desirable residential lofts in the city. The strategy had paid off magnificently and now the area was known citywide as 'the loft district'. Wendi lived in one of these apartment buildings on Twelfth Street near the Vine Street Expressway and the Reading Viaduct.

The building was one of those numbers where you have to swipe a key card to get in: secure like a hotel. Sebastian and I ignored the security. I did note that there were cameras in the lobby, but an attendant wasn't part of the service here. We used the stairs to reach the third floor where Wendi's apartment was located. I began to experience a nervous tension in my belly as we reached the stairwell landing on the third floor. Sebastian didn't help those flutters when he suddenly stopped midflight after we passed through the stairwell doors. His wings flapped quicker, almost like a humming bird's wings, and he bobbed up and down: a gesture I'd come to recognize as nervousness.

"What is it?" I asked.

"Don't you smell that?"

"What? I don't smell anything."

"Concentrate. Think about your sense of smell. When it comes, try to enhance it."

I did as the owl instructed and was amazed at how quickly and easily the sense of smell came to me. The first thing I noticed was the scent of carpet shampoo and other cleaning agents recently used in the hallway. The place smelled fresh. I concentrated harder, focusing on scents that were overwhelmed by the chemicals. One odor suddenly came through to me and it overpowered all of the other aromas. It made me want to vomit. It was the smell of rot, of something so foul that I couldn't believe that I hadn't noticed it before. I closed myself off to that stench returning to my normal state of not really smelling anything at all.

"What is that?" I said breathing heavily and leaning against the wall. Such gestures weren't strictly necessary for ghosts, but our human habits don't go away easily and we tend to react to things just as we would have in life.

"My guess is that it's a ghoul," Sebastian answered. "A zombie wouldn't be so subtle. We'd smell it right over the chemicals."

"What the hell is a ghoul?"

"A ghoul is what a person becomes when their soul has been pushed out and replaced with a darkling," Sebastian said, turning his body towards me and staring into my eyes.

I stared back in horror at him; disgust rose from deep within me.

"I can see what you are thinking Mistress," he said breaking the silence. "Master Jonus told me what you did to the Tormentor's wife. Your actions in this situation did not result in the making of a ghoul. Wraiths are typically the only beings that I know of that can possess living beings and make use of their bodies without becoming slaves bound to the transformation. Apparently you have this ability as well. When a darkling possesses a living creature however, it becomes bound to that body until it is destroyed. All of the dark potential of the ghost is enhanced and any good, sane part of the living creature is wiped away. Ghouls are about as vile as you can get. They are very strong and fast and they are cannibals. Their existence is so wretched that no darkling would ever volunteer for such an assignment. They are almost always forced into this servitude. Hunger is what drives them, and they eventually become so uncontrollable that by the laws of Limbo they must be destroyed as soon as the purpose for which they were created has been achieved."

"Shit!" I breathed and pushed myself forward towards Wendi's Apartment. The door was ajar, clearly having been forced by something powerful and impatient. I passed through the door and found myself standing in a small hallway. There was a closet to my left and the wall on the right held a small shelf; a neat stack of mail rested upon it along with a set of keys. The short hall opened into a larger room. The ceiling rose twenty feet above my head here. Immediately to the left after passing through the entry hall, a staircase wound its way up to what I presumed would be the loft area. Straight ahead, three stairs led down into a recessed living room which was dominated by a sixty four inch LCD television and stylish black leather couch and loveseat. Immediately to the right of the entry hall, the room opened into a large dining room furnished with an elegant table, chairs, and china cabinet. A hardwood railing trailed along the border of the recessed living room and level dining area. Beyond the dining room a large arched doorway led into what I assumed must be the kitchen. The floors were of shining hardwood.

The television was on though no sound issued from it. There were dishes on the table, food only half consumed on them. There was no one in sight, though I could hear voices up stairs. I motioned Sebastian towards the kitchen, while I moved towards the stairs going up. The stairs rose in a half circle and deposited me on a wide hallway that overlooked the living and dining rooms on one side, and a wall with two doors on the other. The first room was the master bedroom which was beautifully furnished with cherry wood bed and dresser. The final room was an office with a large wrap around desk dominating the space; the walls were lined with book shelves filled to overflowing with books. The usual office equipment littered the desk including a computer. The voices I'd heard below came from a police scanner perched on the corner of the desk.

A commotion downstairs brought me back out into the

hallway where I could look down into the lower part of the apartment.

"Detective Kapudo!" called an anxious voice from outside the apartment door. "It's officer Kranz. We got a call that said you might be in trouble. Can we come in?"

Silence greeted the officers and I heard the door being pushed open. Looking down into the room below, I suddenly saw something that hadn't been visible to me from the entryway. On the far end of the dining table there was a clutter of smashed dishes and silverware lying strewn across the floor. There was also a small pool of something dark that I feared might be blood. Sebastian emerged from the kitchen area and, seeing where my attention was focused, flew over to the area to investigate. Two police officers dressed in their traditional blue uniforms had emerged from the entry hall and were giving the place a quick once over as I'd done myself. Both of them had drawn their pistols. The scene of broken crockery and congealing blood was hidden from their view by the dining room table.

"Wendi Kapudo!" called one of the officers once more. When there was no response he signaled his partner to investigate the upstairs while he went for the kitchen.

"It isn't her blood," called Sebastian after examining the scene for a moment. The cops remained oblivious to our presence of course and would not hear us unless we wanted to be heard. "I think its cow's blood."

An extremely small bit of tension went out of me upon hearing this. It was very likely that Wendi was still alive; she was, however, in extreme peril.

"Can you tell how long since they've been here?" I asked. Deciding to forego the stairs, I simply let gravity pull me through the floor and I sank towards the living room below. Of course, when I reached the living room I had to tether myself to the ground otherwise I'd just keep on sinking until I reached the first floor.

"No more than an hour," Sebastian replied with certainty.

By this time the officers had quickly but cautiously searched most of the apartment. It only took a minute before the officer on the bottom floor spotted the mess by the dining room table. He moved in to search the area and gave a cry when he ascertained that the pool of dark fluid on the ground was indeed blood. The second cop, having cleared the upstairs, quickly joined his partner and a call for back-up was made.

"There's nothing more to learn here," I told Sebastian. "Let's go."

"What's this?" one of the officers said as I reached the apartment door. I paused, waiting a moment to see what they'd found.

"Looks like a wallet," the other officer replied. "Here I've got gloves. I'll check it out."

My heart pounded in my ears as I waited with dread to hear what they'd discovered. I don't even have a heart anymore, but I can still feel it pounding at times like this. Amputee's often have the same experience of feeling pain or an itch from a limb that isn't even there anymore. The wait seemed like an eternity.

"Here's the license. It belongs to a Frank M. Cooper."

"Son of a bitch!" I swore. The Tormentor was clearly trying to kill two birds with one stone here. This was a complication I really didn't need at this moment.

"Hey, wasn't that the guy who got kicked off the force over that Tormentor serial killer fiasco?"

"Yea, that's the guy alright, and Kapudo was his partner."

"Do you suppose he had anything to do with her disappearance?"

"I don't know, but I think this makes him our lead suspect. He got kicked off the force while she got promoted. I'd call that a motive."

"Agreed, we'd better call this in."

I listened to the two officer's conversation, my mind racing. Rescuing Wendi was a top priority because she was the one in physical danger. However, now that Frank had been brought into this situation, it seemed only fair to let him help. He was a good man with a strong character and good to have in a fight. It figured that he would pay with his job for his heroic actions in the Tormentor case. No good deed goes unpunished is the motto of Limbo. Though I was a strong believer in ghosts staying out of the affairs of living people, except to protect them from supernatural threats, I felt that Frank's life had been irrevocably shattered by Limbo's interference. He deserved to know what he was up against. He had the right to know what he was fighting. I made up my mind.

"Sebastian, see if you can track the ghouls," I ordered. "Return to me as soon as you've found where they've taken Wendi. I'm going to help Frank."

"Is it wise to interfere with the affairs of mortals mistress?" Sebastian asked me.

"I'm not sure," I answered. "But I think he may be of use to us against the ghouls, and he deserves a chance to keep on fighting. I don't think we'll be able to protect humanity from all of the monsters out there. Some people are gonna need to join the fight. Frank is the kind of guy who could be good at monster hunting."

"I understand mistress. Be careful," and with that the owl flew off to follow the ghoul's fetid trail. I called on the wind and took to the air, flying through the building's outer wall and back into the Philly afternoon.

36

FRANK COOPER LIVED IN SOUTH PHILLY in a row house located on Fitzwater Street between Twenty Third and Twenty second Streets. The neighborhood was known as the Devil's Pocket because a priest had claimed that the community's kids were so bad that they would steel change from the devil's own pocket if they could. As I approached the neighborhood, I wondered if the sobriquet might not have a more sinister origin, perhaps one relating to the amount of supernatural activity within the vicinity. The area was primarily residential. Poorly maintained brick row houses were the dominate architectural feature here. On the West side of the Devil's Pocket near the Schuylkill river, the former US Naval hospital had been converted into condominiums now called Naval Square. Old dilapidated factories abandoned decades ago could also be found throughout the district, many having been converted into low rent apartment buildings.

I approached Frank's row house with trepidation. It would not be long before the cops came hunting for him. I was going to have to be very direct with him; there was no time to open his eyes to what the real world was like in a gentle manner. It was going to have to be a rush job, quick and hard. I hoped his psyche could handle it.

I passed through Frank's front door and found myself at the bottom of a staircase that went up. Immediately to my right was the living room fully furnished with an old sofa, two reclining chairs, and a battered end table with a lamp on it. There was a forty-two inch flat screen television in the corner; a John Wayne movie was on at the moment. Beyond the living room, I could see a small dining area and beyond that lay the kitchen through an arched doorway. Frank was lounging in one of the recliners in the living room. There were beer cans scattered across the floor and on the end table. It looked like he hadn't showered or shaved in weeks and beer had become his primary food source. He looked like hell.

I cursed my luck. Of course I would find him in a state of self destructive depression. I was very disappointed in the man. I'd expected much more from the former detective. I guess the job really had been his life. The whole situation just pissed me off to know end. I couldn't let the Tormentor get away with this.

"Frank!" I yelled at him, projecting my voice to carry into the living world. "Wake up."

Frank stirred and looked around blearily. "Who ...?" he muttered and then spotted the still half full can of beer he'd been drinking before passing out. He reached for the can and I hit it with a tightly focused burst of my banshee's wail before he could lay his hands on it. The can exploded in a shower of beer and aluminum particles. Frank gaped at the mess and rubbed at his eyes.

"Are you listening to me Frank? Wendi's in trouble," I said, trying to get through to him once more.

"Who's there?" he asked looking around. Unable to find anyone nearby, he focused on the television apparently deciding that his drunken state was responsible for the weird things going on around him. I walked over to the table and willed my hand to become solid enough so that I could pick up and manipulate the television's remote control. I raised the controller and waved it in Frank's face and hit the power button which turned the television off. I dropped the controller and it fell to the floor with a clatter.

"What the fuck," Frank swore, eyes darting around the room. He broke out into an immediate sweat and his temple throbbed visibly, but all in all he was keeping it together batter than I would have in his place. I'm pretty sure I'd have wet myself. "Who's there? Show yourself."

I saw that Frank was rapidly becoming sober; his survival instincts told him that he was in danger. I willed myself to become solid enough so that he could see me.

"Who the fuck are you? How the fuck did you get in here?" he asked gaping at me. His right hand moved down the right side of his recliner and came back up with his Desert Eagle monster pistol. He held it unsteadily but it seemed to comfort him.

"Don't be an ass," I told him. "You can't fire that thing in here. Even if you could kill me, you'd likely kill some of your neighbors as well."

"Who the fuck are you?" he demanded not seeming to care about my warning. His grip grew steadier, and that crusading flame of emotion returned to his eyes. "How the fuck did you get in here?"

"My name is Veronika Kane. I'm a ghost, so getting in here was easy," I replied.

"Well then, go fucking haunt someone else. I'm fucking busy," he retorted tiredly. Then surprise suddenly flooded across his features. "Wait … did you say Veronika Kane?"

"Yes I did," I answered. "I hope you haven't forgotten me after such a short time. I know it's a shock to be talking to a ghost, but we do exist you know."

"I know," Frank answered quietly. "It fucking feels like it did that day. You were there weren't you? You helped me with those crazed dogs. Why are you here? The bastard that killed you is dead. Why are you haunting me?"

"Yes," I agreed, this time I was the one surprised.

"We couldn't have made it without you," he nodded to himself. "The way the wind blew that day. You kept them off of my back. You fucking killed so many of them, and kept me from being overwhelmed."

"We don't have time for this Frank," I told him. "The Tormentor is a very powerful ghost now and he's come back for revenge. He's taken Wendi and plans to torture her to death. He also framed you for the kidnapping."

"What the fuck are you talking about?" Frank said. "How can he fucking frame me? Where's Wendi? How can a fucking ghost kidnap someone? This doesn't make sense."

"Turn on your police scanner," I commanded. He stared at me for a moment and I roared, "Do it!"

Frank jumped to his feet and went into the dining room where the scanner was located; he turned it on. Two minutes of listening to the police chatter confirmed everything I'd told him. He paced back and forth for a moment then turned back to me.

"How the fuck did they do this?"

"Where's your wallet?" I asked.

"Over here," he said walking over to a small shelf near the door. He stared at it for a moment then started looking around the room.

"You won't find it here Frank," I told him. "The police found it at Wendi's apartment near a pool of blood. The Tormentor came here and stole your wallet. Ghosts can pick up things and take them if they want. Look." I demonstrated by picking up the fallen controller and put it back on the table.

"Oh God," Frank moaned. "Was there a lot of blood? Is she dead?"

"It wasn't her blood, probably cow's blood," I told him. "He won't kill her yet. He'll want to make her suffer first, and she's part of a trap to catch me."

"Why does he want you?"

"Because I've been screwing up his plans ever since he killed me."

"So what do we fucking do? How do we get to her? Where is she?"

"First we need to get out of here before the cops get here to arrest you," I said. "Bring your gun with you. Let's get going."

"What the fuck is a gun going to do against a ghost?"

"Those dogs you fought at Primal Cuts were possessed by ghosts," I told him. "We call such creatures ghouls. The Tormentor has done the same to some people. Those people are now ghouls, and they are major bad asses. Very dangerous. Your gun will work against them, though I think I'll give you a little ghost mojo to make sure that it does."

Frank looked skeptical but nodded. He put on his shoulder rig, holstered the massive gun and retrieved two extra clips. He put on a jacket, grabbed his keys, and then led me out onto the street where his black nineteen eighty six Monte Carlo sports coupe awaited us.

"You still haven't told me how we're going to fucking find her," Frank said. He started the car and revved the engine a few times before pulling out into the street and heading east down Fitzwater.

"Head North towards Callowhill. I've got a friend tracking the ghouls," I said. "A more exact location should materialize soon. Now let me have your revolver and ammo clips."

"What the fuck for?"

"You really should try to quit swearing so much," I chided him. "I told you, I'm gonna give your big gun here some ghostly mojo."

"My momma never fucking got me to quit swearing even with all the bubbles she made me blow. That just made me fuck-ing swear more. I don't think a fucking ghost girl is going to succeed where my momma failed."

"Just pass the gun over," I sighed.

"You'd better not fuck up my baby," he said suspiciously. He handed it over, and I used the celestial steel jewelry that I wore to plate both the pistol and bullets with the blue ore. Delilah had told me that neither devil's iron nor celestial steel could exist in the living world. I once again found her knowledge to either be lacking or deliberately misleading. I was able to manipulate the steel on this side; it maintained the shape that I gave it wherever I was. In the end, Frank's Desert Eagle was now a blue black color and the bullets were much the same.

I was working on the ammo when Sebastian came flapping down through the cars roof and landed on the dashboard in front of me.

"I found them mistress," He said without preamble. "They are in an abandoned subway station on Spring Garden Street and Ridge Avenue."

I relayed the information to Frank and he sped up feeling a great sense of urgency. I ordered Sebastian to keep any police cruisers in our path or coming up from behind, off of us. We had a quick discussion about what measures he was allowed to use in order to fulfill his mission. I told him that he could not do anything that would cause harm; things like stalling out their cars was ok. I told him to be creative and he flew off. A number of the PPD's cars experienced engine trouble that afternoon.

"So are vampires and werewolves real too?" Frank asked in the tense silence that lay around us like a blanket as the Monte Carlo roared towards the abandoned subway station in north Philly.

"Yes."

"That fucking figures," He grunted sourly. He was silent for several minutes then asked. "Will what you did to my gun work against them too?"

"I think so," I replied.

"Good," he said. Another few moments of awkward silence followed. "If we save Wendi and live through this, will you help me fight them? I've seen a lot of unsolved cases in my career. I bet these fucking monsters have something to do with that."

"We'll talk about that when this business is done," I said. "I've got some things to do in Limbo first, then we'll talk. But yes,

I'll probably help you. It just has to be done carefully otherwise you'll just end up dead."

"That doesn't seem to be so bad."

"It could be worse. We're fighting a war to keep things decent. A few months back, you either became a slave for eternity or you became an evil bastard."

"What the fuck is Limbo anyway?"

"It's the place where ghosts live."

"Here we are," Frank said pulling his car off the road and into a parking garage a block from the closed off station.

"Let's do it," I said.

37

THE STATION AT SPRING GARDEN and Ridge Avenue had been abandoned since the early nineteen-nineties due to its poor condition and the elevated crime rate of the surrounding North Philadelphia neighborhood. It had once been a busy commuter stop on the Broad and Fairmount line but ridership had declined significantly by the nineteen-seventies and the station hadn't been considered worth maintaining. It had become just another cog in the urban blight that had settled over north Philly. The entrance into the underground station had been sealed off with corrugated steel and cement slabs. Now only passengers traveling between Fairmount station and Chinatown station got a glimpse of the abandoned station as their train passed through the dimly lit terminal. The neighborhood kids and hoodlums had still managed to get into the barricaded site somehow, and they'd turned it into a well known example of an underground urban graffiti museum.

When we arrived at the station entrance, there was a gaping hole where the steel plating and cement slabs had sealed off street side access. The corrugated steel and chunks of cement lay in a heap near the entrance. Cement stairs descended into the yawning darkness of the terminal below.

"Holy fuck," swore Frank. He was staring at the mangled remains of the steel plates. "How the hell did this happen."

"The ghouls did this," I said. "They have super human strength. Don't let any of them get a hold of you."

"You don't have to fucking tell me twice," he replied fervently. "How's this gonna go down? It won't be long till the PPD shows up. Someone will have called this in."

"Sebastian will stay up here and run interference just long enough for us to reach Wendi," I said. "I'll go down ahead of you. You follow about ten feet back. I'll let you know where the ghouls are and you can shoot them with your big honking gun."

"Who the fuck is Sebastian?" Frank asked looking around.

"He's my owl familiar," I answered and sighed when I saw the confusion and more questions behind his eyes. "We don't have time for explanations. He's a ghost friend that will keep curious people out of here. That's all you need to know right now."

"All right, this is your gig. We'll do it your way."

I nodded and waited for Sebastian to return to me. It wasn't long before he did, and I gave him instructions to keep the PPD and others from entering the abandoned station for about ten minutes. I took a moment to focus my sense of smell so that I could once again detect the foul odor of the ghouls, and then I headed down into the subway station. I was feeling tired despite the power that Rachel had given me but nervous anticipation was dominating all of my thoughts; in a few short minutes I'd be confronting the beast that had started all of this for me. There were twenty stairs and then a short landing followed by twenty more stairs before I reached the bottom. At this point, I found myself in a long hallway with ancient vending machines lining the wall on the right. The stench of rotting decay was strong here, but there were no ghouls in view. One fluorescent lamp illuminated the entire corridor from the half way point which meant most of the hall was in shadow. Instinct led me to look up, and in a darkened corner of the corridor's ceiling near the entryway where the stairs finally came to an end I spotted a ghoul.

The creature was crouched, its feet and hands seeming to stick to the ceiling. It hung upside down like a bat. Its eyes glowed a malevolent red and its gaze was directed straight at me, though it didn't seem inclined to strike. Its head was cocked, listening. I realized that it smelled the oncoming human. It was hideous to look at. The once human flesh had turned a dark gray. In many places its skin hung in strips, revealing the bone underneath. A thick black, putrid ooze seeped through all of its opened wounds. It was dressed in barely recognizable tattered clothing and a majority of the hair on its head had fallen out.

"There's one clinging to the ceiling on the right as you reach the bottom," I called to Frank. The ghoul hissed and tried to scuttle away to a new position but I called up the wind and directed the force at the ghoul. The creature was strong enough to push its way through the wind blast, but it was slowed. Frank Cooper reacted by leaping down the final few stairs with his Desert Eagle pointed upwards. As soon as he spotted the thing, he trained his revolver on it and pulled the trigger.

I have become quite accustomed to the impossibly loud screams of banshees over the past few months, but even I took notice of the roar that a fifty caliber gun makes. The shot caught the ghoul in the abdomen, and its entire stomach area was blown apart in a shower of black ichor. The ghoul let out a scream, more of rage than pain, and dropped to the ground crouching on all fours like an ape. Its malicious gaze was locked on Frank. It growled; its lips parted, revealing rotting teeth. It inhaled as if preparing to scream at the former detective. Instead of noise issuing from its mouth however, what came out was a jet of green vomit-like ooze that flew straight at Frank.

I hit the vomit stream with a blast of wind, pushing it away from Frank. The stuff slammed into the nearest vending machine instead. The old artifact began to smoke and dissolve as soon as the fluid made contact with it.

"Jesus Fucking Christ!" swore Frank, now terrified. "You didn't tell me these things could spit acid!"

"I didn't know either. Shoot it in the fucking head," I shouted back.

Before the ghoul could launch another acid stream at Frank, I struck it with a controlled blast of my banshee wail, sending it careening through the air to crash into another vending machine. The Coke machine exploded in a shower of plastic shards and the ghoul lay in its ruin, momentarily stunned. As it started to rise, Frank once again fired his Desert Eagle. His aim was true; the ghoul's head exploded in a shower of bone and black fluid.

"Holy mother of God!" Frank moaned, his weapon still pointing at the ghoul as he waiting for signs of any movement. "You said these things used to be fucking people?"

"I'm afraid so."

"Fuck!" he swallowed hard and finally lowered his arm. "We'd better get moving. They'll have heard us, and I don't want Wendi being touched by these things."

I turned away from the scene of carnage and headed down the corridor once more. I was amazed by Frank Cooper's bravery and strength of will; most people would have turned away at this point. The hallway emerged into a larger room containing a bank of ticket booths to the left and a large open space to the right. The entire room was painted brightly in a shining example of urban art, otherwise known as graffiti. Even the glass enclosures of the ticket booths were painted along with parts of the ceiling and floors. This was not the work of a few individuals over a small span of time but that of a great many individuals over a period of years, maybe even decades. The room was lit by two fluorescent lamps. There was just enough light in which to appreciate the fine street art. I fully expected this place to be opened as an art museum someday. The Philadelphia Graffiti

Museum had a nice ring to it. There were bathrooms located on the right side of the room and what probably was an office on the left side near the ticket counters.

The two ghouls waiting in ambush here didn't bother waiting for Frank to appear. They sprang from their hiding places behind the ticket counters, leaping through the painted glass in their excitement to get to me. The shattering glass was too good of a weapon not to use, and with barely a thought, I summoned up the wind and formed it into a vortex and released it on the hapless ghouls. They were both instantly caught in the funnel cloud as was most of the painted glass from the ticket stalls. The ghouls cried out in fear, pain, and frustration as they were picked up and buffeted by winds that could strip the paint off of a car. The tornado held them and they were sliced, diced, and pierced by shards of glass of various sizes and shapes that whipped around and through them.

"Holy shit," exclaimed Frank as he cautiously entered the room. "Are you doing that?"

I nodded.

"Remind me not to piss you off."

I sent more blasts of wind to shatter the remaining windows and corralled the new glass into the tornado. It wasn't long after that that I let the wind fall apart and the butchered remains of the ghouls fell to the floor like so much ground beef. Frank stared at the mess in fascinated horror.

"Why didn't you do that to the other one?" he asked. "You don't need me."

"It takes a lot of energy to do what I just did," I replied. "These guys just presented an opportunity that couldn't be passed up. And I do need you. You need to get past what you've lost and see that there are other ways to fight the good fight. I need a living person on this side that can help me protect the rest of humanity from these kinds of monsters. I trust you, and I believe that you are the right man for the job."

He stared at me for a moment then nodded.

"How you got yourself killed by James Paul Saunders, I'll never understand. You're smart, and from all the interviews I conducted, everyone agreed that you could kick the shit out of almost anyone."

"I made a mistake," I said sadly. "It got me killed. I've learned, however, that there are second chances even when you're dead. Even if you lose everything you thought was important to you, you can find meaning in other things and in other ways. You just have to stay true to yourself."

"I can do that," Frank replied. "I always thought that the boys in blue were the good guys; that they were the only fucking line between good and evil. But that isn't true. Politics and money govern the department just like everything else in this fucking country. But if you're offering me the chance to fight true evil, evil that most people can't even imagine, I'm fuckin' with you on this all the way."

He hefted his gun for emphasis and strode towards the stairs leading to the subway platform.

"Whoa, cowboy," I called after him. "Wait here while I check the bathrooms, office, and other nooks. I'd rather not have a ghoul sneak up on us if we can help it."

Frank stopped in his tracks, turning red, clearly embarrassed by his rashness. Once I was sure he was going to stay put, I called on the wind and sped my way through the bathrooms and office, phasing through walls and doors. The search only took a minute, and I returned to Frank confident that no threats remained on this floor.

"That is cool shit," he said when I reached him. "Passing through walls and shit. Can you fly?"

"Yes," I said "Let's go."

The rumbling of a passing train vibrated throughout the complex. The platform was darker than any other part of the station which was illuminated by only two fluorescent lamps at opposite ends of the massive terminal. The area was segmented by large pillars that left deep shadows throughout the entire room. Every surface here was also painted in colorful graffiti giving the dimly lit room a lurid appearance. There were benches scattered haphazardly around the room.

I found Wendi in a particularly dark part of the platform. She was moaning quietly as a ghoul tore at her clothing. The creature clearly wanted to rip into her flesh, but some compulsion was preventing it from doing so. Instead it carefully ripped clothing off of her. As far as I could tell, Kapudo wasn't bound nor were there any visible wounds on her.

"I knew you would come," said a crawling voice that echoed throughout the station. "And I see you've brought me another detective to play with."

"Show yourself Tormentor!" I shouted angrily. "You and I have unfinished business."

"We do indeed bitch!" the tall form of a reaper emerged from the shadows to stand a few feet away from Wendi. "You shouldn't have come. You've put yourself into my hands."

"What have you done to her?" I demanded.

"Nothing yet," said the Tormentor. "Ah, you mean why is she so compliant? Haven't you heard Veronika? I'm a Shadow Reaper. My special gift is to dominate the minds of lesser beings. I will torture this wretched girl and make her like it."

"Like fuck you will," said Frank Cooper stepping out from behind a pillar and raising his Desert Eagle to point straight at the Tormentor's head.

"Ah, if it isn't the drunken former detective," mocked the Tormentor turning his frightful gaze on Frank. "Welcome, now put the gun down."

Frank's temples began to pulse visibly with the effort of withstanding the dark reaper's will. He broke out into a cold sweat. Out of the corner of my eye, I saw a dozen or so darklings emerge through a doorway that was probably a bathroom. Two more ghouls emerged from the shadows and began to stalk towards Frank. I prepared to launch myself on the Tormentor, but he turned his baleful eyes on me and the weight of his mind hit me like a hellfire missile fired from an Apache helicopter. His mind was just as powerful as Black Maria's except he was using the power on me without even touching me. I struggled to move, to speak, to say anything but I could do nothing.

"My power over you is limited," the Tormentor all but purred. "I can't make you do things against your will like Black Maria can, but I can prevent you from moving. Take her weapons."

Two darklings rushed forward and pulled my Katana and knife from my hands and tossed them aside.

"I've invited some old friends of yours to join us Veronika."

Delilah emerged from the shadows, a wicked grin plastered on her beautiful face.

"Thank you my lord for inviting me," Delilah said with a bow to the Tormentor. She turned her cold stare on me and regarded me for a moment. "It's a good thing that you are so predictable Veronika, otherwise you would truly be a threat. I'm the one who provided the lord Tormentor with a means to trap you. I told him that your weakness was these humans. I'm glad you didn't disappoint me."

I wanted to scream, to charge and strangle this bitch who'd been such a thorn in my side. I wanted to rip her throat out with my teeth for what she'd done to me at the Walnut Street Prison, but the Tormentor's mind locked me down as thoroughly as the iron maiden had.

"Don't worry Veronika. I've brought an old friend to be your companion as we watch the lord Tormentor work on your human friends."

My heart skipped a beat when I saw a familiar shape glide out of the shadows. It was a form that haunted my waking dreams, a misshapen creature whose name matched his deeds. There was no one in the world that I wanted to kill more than Freak; there was no one in the world that I was more terrified to see at this moment than him.

"Hello my precious," Freak said in a gravely British accent.

"I've missed you this past month. It was unkind of you to leave without letting me know, love."

He sauntered up to me and ran his disgusting hands over my shoulder in a possessive fashion. I tried to cringe away from him, but even this involuntary movement was denied me. Inside I screamed and wept in horror.

"I told you my lord that she'd be happy to see our Freak," Delilah purred to the reaper who watched with gloating interest. "Do you smell the fear and revulsion coming off of her in waves? It's so delicious."

The Freak slid in behind me and pressed his body against me. He reached an arm around my neck and cupped one of my breasts in one mangled hand. He pushed aside my dark hair and ran his wet tongue across my neck like some beast tasting its dinner. His hand suddenly tore violently at my shirt, and without my mind to control it the fabric tore away revealing the tight fitting celestial steel mesh below it.

"What a bother," the Freak said in annoyance, but despite the discomfort that it clearly caused him, he slipped his scarred, mutilated hands under the armor so that he could hold my ghostly flesh in his hand. He kneaded my breast with his long fingers for a moment; my body's natural reaction to the stimulus added to the humiliation. The caressing fondle turned suddenly rough as the Freak began to twist my nipple in a painful pinch that would have made me cry out in shocked surprise if I'd been able to. "I'm going to punish you for leaving me, love. I'm going to show the lord Tormentor all of your secret passions; all of the things that we love to do together."

Freak's other hand had reached around my waist by this time, and as his long, disgusting fingers found there way between my legs. My mind nearly broke. I could not go through this again.

I was saved by Frank Cooper. The Tormentor had underestimated the former detective, and he'd focused most of his will on me leaving only a small portion of it on the weak humans. Frank is a stubborn bastard, and more importantly he's a genuine freaking hero. If you're going to do bad things to him and his friends, you'd better not give him time to fight back. He's got an amazing will.

"Get … the … fuck … out … of … my … head!" he suddenly roared, and with a force of will that made blood start to pour from his nose, he pulled the trigger of his trusty gun.

Frank's aim was impeccable as usual, and even the amazing speed of a reaper couldn't save the Tormentor from his fate. The celestial steel coated bullet struck him square between the eyes. The Tormentor staggered and sank to one knee; he stared at Frank in stunned disbelief. Everyone froze and waited with anticipation as the reaper shook himself and ponderously pushed himself back to his feet. The Tormentor locked his gaze with Frank once more. Freak continued his vile groping, but my mind barely registered the degradation now. I felt the Tormentor's hold on me weakening, and the enemy had no idea what I'd done to those bullets; my vengeance was at hand. I could hold on. There was a new hole in the Tormentor's skeletal head; this one burned with blue flame.

"I will make you scream for a thousand years," the Tormentor said with a malice that caused everyone to quail in fear and shy away from him. "And Wendi will suffer even more abominations for your impudence."

The blue glow coming from the hole in the Tormentor's head was spreading, but for a moment he seemed unaware of it. His minions however did notice, except for Freak who was having too much fun. The rest of them stared at the Tormentor in shock. Frank Cooper was nonplussed by everything going on around him. He simply turned his gun on the ghoul manhandling Wendi and blew its head off with a single shot.

"Noooo …"cried the Tormentor, suddenly aware of his impending demise. The hold on me suddenly vanished, and I smashed my elbow violently into Freaks unprotected face as he nibbled at my ear. His face exploded in a shower of ghostly goo. He tried to bear hug me, but I levered myself and flipped him over my back. Both of his arms were made momentarily useless as they were caught in my celestial steel clothing. It's generally a bad idea to have your hands in someone's pants when they decide to flip you. He'd barely hit the ground when I started stomping on his head. From there I put down the most vicious beat down that I'd ever handed out. Not even Mordred had suffered what I did to Freak. Meanwhile, Frank had splattered the heads of the two remaining ghouls with a double tap of his monster gun. He made it look so easy. The Tormentor's head was completely engulfed in blue flames by this time and he was desperately thrashing about trying to put them out. The darklings had translated back into Limbo, deciding that survival was the better part of valor. The rest of the Tormentor's body caught on fire and it screamed for several minutes before finally falling to the ground and dissipating into mist. I continued to beat Freak, caring about little else than making him pay for all the degradations he'd put me through. Frank finally came over and tried to put a calming hand on my shoulder. I shrugged him off but paused long enough to catch my breath, even ghosts get tired. Somehow Freak was still alive; he'd tried to escape by translating back to Limbo, but I'd prevented that with my own flagging power. I wasn't going to let him get away.

"He's fucking dog vomit Veronika," Frank said gruffly. "I'm guessing he's a ghost or something. No human could take that kind of beating. The PPD will be here shortly; finish him off or take him into custody or whatever you do over there in Limbo."

I wanted to keep beating Freak, but unfortunately Frank was right; time was short and I had other responsibilities. Besides, beating him wasn't going to heal what he'd done to me, but it sure felt good anyways. I brought myself under control with great effort of will and walked over to my discarded katana, picked it up and went back to stand over the Freak.

"What ..." it croaked up at me through a gash in its ruined face. It spoke volumes about the beating he'd taken that none of his wounds were regenerating. "Do you think I'll beg for mercy, love? You might kill me now, but I'll always live in your memory as the Freak who popped your cherry."

As Freak laughed maniacally, I chopped his head in two, not at the neck but at the nose.

Frank shook his head in disgust and ran over to Wendi and began helping the confused detective to her feet. I surveyed the carnage around us in stunned silence for a moment. It appeared that Delilah had made her escape.

"And you thought I didn't need you," I said dejectedly to Frank. "You saved my ass. I'll always be in your debt."

"I guess you were fucking right," he said with bemusement in his voice. He was offering his jacket to Kapudo who was mostly naked due to the ghoul's attentions. "I guess I have a knack for this monster killing business. Do you suppose you could get me some more of those ghost mojo rounds?"

"I'll see what I can do," I replied dryly. "But for now I need to return to Limbo. I left some unfinished business there. I'll look you up in a few days and we'll talk. Will you be ok with Wendi?"

"Who's that?" Kapudo asked, the shock was finally wearing off. "What are you doing here Frank? Some crazed homeless people kidnapped me from my apartment."

"I'll explain everything Wendi, but first you should take my gun," Frank replied. "The PPD will be down here soon, and I think it will be better if you have it rather than me."

I made a quick search of the premises to make sure that no other threats lurked. The sounds of many sirens could be heard in the now quiet station. I wanted to sit down and try to absorb what had just happened: my nemesis, the Tormentor had been destroyed. More importantly to my own sanity, I got to kick the snot out of the Freak, haunter of my dreams. I needed time to process this stuff, time to cry, time to heal, but there wasn't any time. I had responsibilities; the free souls were waiting for me. I sighed in resignation and flew up to the entrance arriving just as the first squad car squealed to a halt in front of the station.

"Alright," I told Sebastian as he landed on my outstretched hand. "Our work here is done for now. Let's go home."

38

WE TRANSLATED BACK INTO LIMBO emerging on Spring Garden Street near Ridge Avenue. The lack of mist was disorienting, but we knew we were back in Limbo for we found ourselves instantly set upon by a gang of enlarged specters with devil's iron spikes protruding from various parts of their bodies. I was taken totally by surprise and was almost destroyed in the initial onslaught. Sebastian saved me by hooting a warning and flying directly into the face of the lead specter. I barely had time to duck under a blow that would have taken my head off. Even so, I was struck in the shoulder and thigh by two different stabbing swords. I blasted the front ranks with my banshee scream and then leapt into the air to avoid the attacks of the specters on my flanks and rear. With a grunt of pain, I pulled the two blades from my body and immediately felt power bleed out from me. Fortunately the wounds closed up quickly before I could be drained completely.

"These look like Black Maria's goons," I yelled to Sebastian as we hovered over the milling gang of specters below us.

Fortunately, there were no darkling flyers with them. I wanted to blast the rest of the group into oblivion, but I knew that I was nearing the limit of my power for the day. I would need to rest soon. "Come on. Let's find Jonus and find out what's going on."

We flew towards Eastern State Penitentiary: the last place we'd seen Jonus. Soon, however, we came across more of the enhanced specters. There were war bands of maybe a hundred super specters, some of which were led by reapers. Realizing that this must be a full scale invasion by Pittsburgh, I turned towards the Benjamin Franklin Parkway knowing that that was where the free soul army was to rally in case of an emergency.

As we approached the Parkway, I saw that I'd been correct. The free souls had mustered at Logan Square and were completely surrounded by a milling army of specters, reapers, hounds, and darklings. My heart sank to see so few of my army. Only half of it seemed to be present in the square while Black Maria's forces outnumbered them twenty to one. I fervently hoped that the rest of my people had simply been cut off and forced to take shelter elsewhere.

Black Maria's forces were staying back a respectable distance from the free souls, likely in respect of the banshees that could pulverize their lines. The air was thick with darkling flyers, giving Black Maria total air superiority. As soon as I was spotted, a group of them rushed towards me. Instead of turning to flee, I flew straight for them. The lead darkling recognized me and tried to signal his group to break off, but it was too late. I blasted twelve darklings out of the sky and sped onwards towards my enveloped troops. More darklings came for me going for my flanks and attacking from below and above, but all of them avoiding a direct engagement. I twisted, flew in zigzags, sped up and suddenly put on the brakes, whatever maneuvers I could manage to evade my attackers. I took several more wounds. All were superficial, but they also added to my overall fatigue. A particularly cunning and swift party of darklings almost took me out in the end, but Lieutenant Quinn and Banshee Company took to the air and slammed into the darkling squad, scattering them and saving my butt. They escorting me safely to our lines where I landed gratefully among the free souls. Quinn took me immediately to Jonus who was grimly watching the enemy mass for another assault.

"What's going on Jonus? How did this happen?" I asked.

He looked at me tiredly. "They came about an hour after you left. We were conducting clean up operations and were scattered throughout the city. They appeared in small war bands at first, and then the main body arrived. I kept the banshee's with me and took up a reserve position here in the square. I sent Rachel out to free more shades. Enoch, Gideon, and Ezekiel led fresher troops on clean up missions throughout the city. Ezekiel made it back here before the main wave arrived, but we watched helplessly while Enoch and his brave souls were cut down to the last. We haven't heard or seen anything of Rachel or Gideon. The banshee's have kept the army at bay, but they are tiring. Amber and Susan have already fallen into unconsciousness due to fatigue. Black Maria has been harrying us with forces large enough to pose a threat but has avoiding the use of her main army. She is forcing us to tire out the banshees. She's fighting a battle of attrition and we're losing."

The despair in Jonus's voice and eyes made my heart sink. We were all tired and on the verge of exhaustion. We'd won an impossible victory against the Master, and now, without anytime to even savor that victory, we were looking at complete destruction at the hands of Black Maria. I thought about Frank Cooper and Wendi Kapudo and the million plus living people of Philadelphia who were counting on us to make a real change here in Limbo. Ninety-nine point nine percent of those people didn't know anything about Limbo, but if they did, most of them would be praying for our success. We couldn't let them down. I felt certain that Black Maria would be a worse villain than the Master if she gained control of the city. I couldn't allow that to happen.

I looked around me hoping to gain some inspiration. The free souls looked determined to fight to the end, but despair was clearly creeping in. They were beginning to believe that Logan Square was the place where they'd be making their final stand. The hordes of the enemy were waiting with impatient anticipation. All around us were some of the most magnificent and historical buildings in all of the city. Within some of them, Benjamin Franklin had hidden secrets. Could any of them offer help to us here, I wondered.

My eyes brushed over these great symbols of past glory to the Philadelphia skyline beyond. It was strange to be able to look at the skyline. Always before the mists had obscured it from my view. As I'd noticed on many occasions, the city looked quite different in Limbo than it did in the living world. The older buildings tend to dominate in Limbo, giving way to new structures only grudgingly. Delilah had explained to me that things only really took hold in Limbo when enough of its inhabitants had forced a change through their memories. The more ghosts that believed that a certain building or bridge should exist, the more likely that it would become true. New buildings were not built by hands in Limbo, they were built by the memories of the ghosts who lived here. Change was slow to come because the memories of ghosts warred against each other. New ghosts might believe that a certain department store should exist on a certain block, but the memories of older ghosts said otherwise. Only when there are more ghosts that remember the store than ghosts who don't will that store finally become reality in Limbo.

This fact was readily apparent as I gazed at the skyline and could see only one skyscraper towering over the cityscape. One Liberty Place was probably the most memorable skyscraper in Philadelphia for it was the first to have surpassed the height of the William Penn statue perched atop City Hall. One Liberty Place was unique enough of a skyscraper with its pointed spire that it had become part of Limbo relatively soon after its actual completion date in the living world. A sudden thought hit me like a ton of bricks as I stared at Philly's two tallest structures. I recalled the gentleman's agreement that had purportedly required that no structure be built taller than William Penn on City Hall. The legend behind this agreement spoke of a curse if it should be broken. No one knew who the agreement had been between and why it should have been made in the first place, but ever since it had been broken in 1987 when One Liberty Place was completed, everything that went wrong in the city was blamed on the curse.

I suddenly wondered if the agreement had something to do with the supernatural world and whether its breaking had somehow given evil beings free reign in the city. I recalled the bottled up power I'd sensed coursing through City Hall while I rested on Penn's hat during my escape from the Walnut Street Prison. I was suddenly very certain that our only hope lay atop City Hall.

"Get everyone ready to move Jonus. We're leaving." I didn't even wait for his response but went looking for Melanie and Baron to give them their instructions. Ezekiel came to me while I gave orders, and like Rachel had done before, he gave me a little of his power with a simple touch. I smiled my thanks to him knowing that he'd sacrificed much of his remaining power to keep me going. By this time most of us were running close to empty. I felt guilty about accepting the power from the exhausted luminary, but I knew that our survival and freedom would depend on me in the next few minutes. No pressure or anything.

Five minutes later I gave the order and the free souls charged forward heading down 19th Street. I led the charge with Bridget at my side. We blasted a hole through the ranks of our surprised enemy with our banshee battle cries. Jonus assisted with his celestial bolts of blue flame while the two banshees positioned on each flank and three positioned at the rear kept the enemy from mounting an effective counter attack. Baron and the other gargoyles took to the sky along with a few flyers that could be spared from banshee guard duty and kept the darkling flyers at bay. Once we were completely through the enemy line, we half ran down 19th Street with the enemy in dogged pursuit.

At Market Street we encountered an enemy war band, but the swiftness of our attack and march down 19th street hadn't given them any time to prepare for our sudden assault. Bridget and I made quick work of the specters and the army continued onward, turning East on Market. Up ahead, One Liberty Place loomed over us. I brought the army to a halt one block away from the imposing skyscraper and turned to Jonus.

"You must hold here," I told him. "I'm leaving you two banshees. The rest are coming with me. When One Liberty Place collapses, get the army moving towards Penn Square. We make our stand there."

Jonus gaped at me, not sure where to begin with the questions. I sent a signal to Melanie and the preselected banshees came forward with their bodyguards and our group sprang forward sprinting towards the offending skyscraper. Behind us, Danielle and Sonya were letting their shrieks fly as they attempted to hold the enemy at bay. Some flyers tried to impede our progress, but we blasted them out of existence without slowing down.

When we reached One Liberty Place, we broke up into three groups and took to the sky. Each group went to a different corner of the structure. We flew up to the five hundred feet mark, or there about, and then we all started screaming for all that we were worth. One Liberty Place shook at the first blast, windows shattering all the way down the sides of the structure. Our screams continued unabated and great chunks of the edifice began to fall as the walls directly impacted were blown in, leaving no support for the upper levels. Darkling flyers attempted to get at us, but our guards screened us and kept the darklings at bay. The battle that was being waged in the streets a block away remained Black Maria's priority however. She couldn't know that what we were doing could lead to her defeat. After two minutes of sonic detonations, the building began to truly implode. At the moment that One Liberty Place fell to below the height of William Penn on City Hall, I felt a surge of power and an electric thrumming pulse passed through me. The power vibrated throughout the whole city.

"Get the others and get back to the army," I told Bridget who was partnered with me. "Tell Jonus to get moving to Penn's Square. I'll be waiting for you there."

I turned and sped towards the thirty seven foot statue of William Penn perched upon the roof of the gleaming tower that is City Hall. I wasn't sure what to do once I got there, but I intuitively knew that the statue held the key to our survival. I landed on Penn's wide brimmed hat and surveyed my surroundings. I saw the army of free souls fighting desperately as they withdrew down Market Street and were just now arriving at the ruins of One Liberty Place. Only a quarter of the structure remained standing, its memorable spire having been replaced by jagged fingers of varying lengths. A glance Eastward on Market showed me another force of specters and darklings converging on the heavily outnumbered free souls. At the rate Jonus's force was moving they would barely arrive at Penn's Square ahead of the force coming from the East. To make matters worse, I could see more war bands approaching from the North and South on Sixteenth and Seventeenth Streets and probably along other side streets that I couldn't see from my current vantage point. The air was boiling with masses of darkling flyers. It was clear that Black Maria intended to crush us here and now, banshees notwithstanding. Despite the hope that had blossomed in me for a short period of time, seeing the total might of Black Maria's army brought black despair rolling back into the pit of my stomach.

Anger swelled within me. It started in the place where my banshee wail comes from: a place that is deeper than my stomach or throat. It starts in the soul and rises like a hurricane. The anger pulsed in me and blended into the same rhythm that pulsed through City Hall. I let go, giving myself over to the pulsing power within me, and instead of shrieking, I sank down into the statue of William Penn. To my astonishment, just below the surface of the statue's brass skin, I encountered celestial steel. As usual, the steel parted for me and I passed through several feet of the holy ore until suddenly I entered an empty place within the head, and without thought or plan, I tethered myself to the great simulacrum of Philadelphia's founder.

39

INSTANTLY EVERYTHING CHANGED. I was no longer Veronika Kane the banshee. I was now the Guardian. I felt so alive and powerful. I looked down at myself and saw that I was encased in armor. I wondered why this should be. My skin was made of blue steel, the hardest substance in the dead lands. I tried to think but I couldn't remember. Who am I? Who is Veronika Kane?

I suddenly became aware of the screams of thousands of angry beings. I looked around and saw a battle taking place on the streets below me. The abominations of Tartarus and the pits below it walked on my streets. They made war on the Chosen. I stared in surprise and confusion. When had the Chosen come to my city? They must have awakened me, for I sensed that they were in great danger. They stood on the brink of complete annihilation. I concentrated, and I became aware of everything that was happening in the city. I am the city and the city is me. The abominations crawled all over me. They were an insect infestation that needed to be purged from my body. I saw that the other guardians yet slumbered. I could and would not allow the Chosen to be destroyed.

I, Veronika Kane, tried to assert control over the Guardian, but the spirit of the city overwhelmed me. Not yet, a voice in my head screamed. The Chosen must be saved, you must let go. I shook my head; no time for contemplation. The question of who I was must wait. I shook my body violently, and my skin bulged outward like corded muscles. The restraining weight of the brass armor crumbled away revealing my celestial steel carapace to the world of the dead. The battle below me paused as all eyes look up and stared at me in wonder and fear. I opened my mouth and screamed. A part of me didn't want to, fearing the destruction that would follow, but my voice did not destroy. It awakened the sleepers. I felt the others stir, and I urged them to rouse quickly to defend the Chosen.

The battle resumed, both sides fighting with urgent desperation knowing that something important had happened. The Chosen were going to die. It was time to join the fight. I raise my hand and found that I was holding a scroll. I am momentarily confused. How can I fight with this? Then I sense Veronika Kane welling up inside of me and she shows me how to shape my skin as desired. Who is Veronika Kane? Who am I? There is no time. The Chosen are dying. I do as Veronika Kane has shown me, and I am surprised to see the scroll and other parts of my skin flow, molding themselves into a large sword of oriental style and a large knife in the other hand. The knowledge of battle has always been within me, but I sense that I now know more. How can celestial steel flow as if it were liquid and shape itself into what I desire? How can I awaken all the gargoyles in the city and sense what they, the Chosen, and the abominations are doing, all at the same time? This last question comes from the voice in my head, the one called Veronika Kane. Too many questions and no time. We must fight.

I leap into the air ready to drop into the street below, but Veronika Kane once again intrudes on my thoughts and shows me how to fly. I try what she says and I soar high into the sky and look down upon my city. I dive towards the battlefield below and laugh with pleasure as I swing my sword while passing over a great mass of abominations. My sword cuts through scores of them, sending them back to the pit of hell where they belong. I see other guardians joining the fight. There are nearly a hundred of them in the central tower of the city alone; none as large as me of course, but their numbers give aid and comfort to the Chosen. All across the city the guardians now engage in battle with the abominations, and the fear they cause in the black hearts of the invaders is palpable. The Chosen cheer and fight with renewed determination. All over the city they emerge from hiding to join the fray.

Veronika Kane urges me to fight the flying abominations and I do so. Her will is strong and her grasp of tactics is sound. I sense that she is surrendering herself to me and that I must do the same for her. Together we blaze a trail of glory through the skies of the great city. Below, I watch as the three guardians of the waterways cross a chasm that is but the shadow of a river and then engage an army of thousands of abominations. A small group of Chosen are there too led by a female who throws bolts of celestial flame. I feel Veronika Kane's elation at seeing these Chosen; she feared them destroyed. I suddenly realize that Veronika Kane must herself be one of the Chosen: perhaps their leader.

I look around. The skies are clear now. I drop down to the ground to assist the river guardians and the one Veronika Kane knows as Rachel. The battle is short. The abominations flee before my wrath. I am suddenly aware of a new threat. A new presence has entered the outskirts of the city. I once more take to the sky and fly North. We fly to the boundaries of the city. The further away I get from the city's heart, the weaker I grow. And then I see them. Thousands of nature spirits flow into the city in waves. I watch in astonishment as they attack all abominations they encounter. I have never seen or heard of such a thing, but

Veronika Kane has, and I recall the images from a past battle in which the Chosen once again faced annihilation. The nature spirits had given them aid, saving them from certain doom at the cost of many of their own. I am impressed that the nature spirits would take such risks for the Chosen, and here they came once more.

As I watch the nature spirits, I notice an abomination within their ranks: one that they do not attack. I swoop down to destroy the offending creature, but Veronika Kane stops me with a desperate scream that rings throughout my being. I stop, puzzled by Veronika Kane's sudden anguish. A name intrudes into my thoughts: Thor. I look around to see if the legendary god of thunder is approaching. I do not recall one of the guardians being made in Thor's image, not here anyway, but I do not know all of the guardians. There are many of them who bare the likeness and names of the ancient gods. I look back at the abomination and realize that Veronika Kane has herself named the creature. I study the abomination for a few minutes and perceive that there is something strange about it. The corruption of Tartarus is missing and it wears a celestial steel collar. How could such a thing be, I wondered. Creatures of Tartarus are supposed to be beyond salvation. I suddenly remembered the old prophesies; the laws of the dead would change forever once the Awakening happened. The final war is nigh I thought. My great city was blessed indeed to be the City of the Chosen.

I feel myself tiring. The power that fuels me and the other guardians isn't infinite. Already I feel many of the others returning to their resting places. I to must return to the great tower soon. Veronika Kane urges me to make another sweep of the city and we do so. The fighting is all but finished now. The nature spirits have taken up the hunt for the weary Chosen; they harry the routed abominations to the city's boundary and beyond. My heart leaps with joy to see so many Chosen alive, but I sense Veronika Kane's sorrow at the losses they have suffered.

I want to stay awake and observe the Chosen, but I know that if I am ever to be of use to them again, I have to sleep so that the power that fuels me can recharge. I am blessed to have had a Chosen within my being. I have to be satisfied with this experience for now. I approach my resting place, land and prepare to rest once more. Veronika Kane thanks me and once I am sure that all the other guardians have fallen back into slumber, I do the same.

Epilogue

THE BATTLE OF PHILADELPHIA was over and the free souls were in command of the city. It took days to hunt down all of the specters and reapers who, after finding their escape from the city blocked by the army of furies, had taken refuge in various locations throughout the city. Digging them out had been hard work, and they'd fought with the desperation of cornered animals. Though we were able to find and destroy most of the darklings that had likewise gone to ground they proved to be far more skilled at staying hidden. Philadelphia is a large city and chances were better than good that individual darklings managed to evade our sweeps. There would continue to be haunted locations in the city for the foreseeable future.

Our losses were terrible. Both Enoch and Ezekiel had been lost and nearly half of the free souls we arrived with had perished. Ezekiel's death was the one that haunted me the most; he'd been the symbol of hope for me from the first day I'd arrived in Limbo. By the time we freed all of the shades and recruited them into the ranks of the free souls, the city's population reached some two thousand ghosts including a Luminary named Daniel who'd been enslaved on the Delaware ferry.

Black Maria had fared far worse. She herself escaped the city with a small retinue, but the rest of her army was completely annihilated. Of Delilah's fate none knew, but I had the uneasy feeling that she'd escaped and would attempt to menace me again in the future. Black Maria's forces had been joined by troops from Newark. As far as we could tell, none of those forces made it out. Both Black Maria and the Master of Newark were immediately confronted by shade rebellions in their own cities, and though both regimes survived by cracking down on their populations with an iron fist, we benefited by gaining nearly three thousand new free soul refugees from those cities. Indeed for the first time in Shadow Philly's history our population grew daily not from deaths in the living world, but instead from refugee ghosts from all over the region. The word about the true nature of shades and their potential to be free souls was spreading throughout Limbo, and the only safe place for them was in Philadelphia. In a few places however, the revolutionary free souls proved too strong to be simply crushed in a single battle, and war raged in those cities. Houston was one such example where free souls and luminaries proved strong enough to truly challenge the status quo.

The furies had come to our aid because Thor had gone out to them, and from what I could glean from Sebastian, the shadow hound had gained an audience with their king. When the king of the furies refused to get involved in the affairs of the two legs, Thor had challenged him to a duel and ultimately defeated him thereby himself becoming king of the furies. I lost a companion in Thor, but Shadow Philadelphia had gained a valuable ally. Once the battle and clean up action was done, the furies returned to the darklands beyond the borders of the city, Thor at their head.

After the Battle of Living Statues, as the final battle for Philadelphia would later become known, Jonus and I breached the wards of City Hall and entered the tower to investigate the strange power that permeated the building. In the basement of the great tower we found a deep cavern with a lake of liquid celestial ore. The source of the emanations of power was a massive blue green stone rising out of the center of the lake. Although we wanted to investigate further the wards were pushing back at us, and rather than jeopardize their integrity we decided to withdraw. The excursion had shown us that the fuel that powered the city's defenses were half depleted. Who had created the defenses in the first place was a mystery, though I strongly suspected that Benjamin Franklin had played a role in its development. The fact that such a defense system had been created at all bespoke of the power of prophesy.

We found it necessary to mount an invasion of Canton, New Jersey immediately across the Delaware from Philly because it was too much of a threat to our stability. The city's proximity and the fact that many specters and darklings had fled there made it vital to our security that we clear and hold it as an outer defense post. The campaign lasted for two weeks and was led by Jonus. He proved himself once more to be an able strategist and commander, fulfilling his objectives with minimal loss of souls on our side.

Meanwhile, a government was being formed in the city. The free souls tried to draft me as their new governor, but I refused the post. I informed them that I had started and led the revolution because no one else was willing or able to do so, but now there were plenty of talented souls that were far more qualified than myself to lead. Rachel was then elected to the post of Governor and soon after an election resulted in the seating of the first Free Soul Assembly. The Assembly was tasked with drafting laws while the governor enforced them. The new powers that be in Shadow Philadelphia next tried to draft me into the army, offering me the position of High Marshal. I once more refused them advising instead that Jonus be appointed to the position. I, of course, relayed my intentions to be part of the city's defense and would indeed serve in the army if we should face invasion once again, but I really felt that I needed to be involved in protecting humanity from supernatural threats of all kinds.

In their third bill, the Assembly created the Ghost Watch, an agency tasked with enforcing law and order in Shadow Philadelphia and likewise in the living world. The Ghost Watch would further have the task of protecting mankind from all supernatural beings and would be the lead agency in diplomatic activities with organized preternatural beings who inhabited the living world. I was asked to advise in the development of bill number four which codified the laws that governed the activities of ghosts in the living world. This having been accomplished and the bill passed, Governor Rachel nominated me to be the Ghost Watch's first Captain. This post I gladly accepted and my nomination was unanimously approved by the Assembly.

It was a time of uncertainty and great hope. My heart was filled with pride and satisfaction to see the free souls coming together with such order and harmony. The Assembly met daily in Independence Hall while Governor Rachel took up residence at Old City Hall adjacent to Independence Hall. I chose the Pennsylvania Hospital, the nation's first hospital established by none other than Benjamin Franklin, as the headquarters of the Ghost Watch. I know, it's a strange choice, but I have my reasons.

The banshee's took on varying roles throughout the city. The Assembly passed a law requiring all banshee's to have a personal guard of no less than twenty souls. The proponents of the act argued that we were far too important a resource to have picked off by assassins. Though I and the other banshees tried to protest, the bill was passed unanimously and signed by the governor. As promised, I spent several hours each day training my sisters in the art of personal combat and in safe interaction with the living world. Melanie and Danielle joined the Ghost Watch, while Angela, Catherine, and Melisa joined the army. Amber remained a private citizen, opening a music salon. The salon became known as the Siren's Den and was the hottest spot in Shadow Philly. Every ghost in the city came to be soothed by Amber's siren voice. Susan O'Connell and Sonya Taylor were elected to the Assembly. Bridget became the commander of Governor Rachel's personal guard. My former aid Jully became the Speaker of the Assembly while Lieutenant Quinn was named Marshal of special forces. Sebastian remained my ever faithful companion as did Baron. And I also fulfilled my promise to Frank Cooper, teaching him what I knew about the supernatural world. He was the Ghost Watch's first non ghost employee. He opened Cooper Investigations, providing investigative services for the unexplained and weird.

The battle for Philadelphia was over but the war was just beginning. This was only the opening salvo in the Ghost Wars. The powers that be throughout Limbo and those from the Pitt would eventually seek to destroy us. In the meantime, we had a peace to secure. More importantly to me, I had the task of protecting humanity from the monsters they either didn't believe in or barely understood. I felt confident in our future. Surely the hardest days were behind us, right?

The End of *Wail of the Banshees*. Veronika's story doesn't end here though, stay tuned for *Death Toll*, book two in *The Ghost War Saga*. A beta sample chapter of *Death Toll* is available in the following chapters.

About the Author

Robert Poulin was born and raised in the New England state of Connecticut. After spending his late teenage years in Boca Raton Florida, Robert moved to upstate New York where he lived with his uncle Wilbrod Poulin and attended the State University of New York at Plattsburgh. After earning a Bachelor's in Political Science and a Master's in Teaching, Robert went back to Florida where he taught Social Studies for a few years. After returning to Northern New York, Robert took a job with the North Country Center for Independence: a disability rights and advocacy organizations. Robert has worked for NCCI for thirteen years and is now the Executive Director. *Wail of the Banshees* is Robert's first novel; he has been a huge fan of fantasy and science fiction since second grade when he discovered *The Hobbit*. Urban fantasy in particular has become Robert's favored genre in the past decade. Robert has been legally blind since infancy, but thanks to a mom that encouraged independence, hard work, and a healthy dose of dreaming, the disability has mostly just been an inconvenience. Robert is currently in the editorial process with his second novel, *Death Toll,* and is writing *Echoes of Madness* the third novel in the Veronika Kane saga.

About the Editor

Jaimee Finnegan grew up in Keeseville, NY. She was first introduced to the beauty of the novel in her youth by her 4th grade teacher who instilled a love of reading in her. Since then, she always dreamed of working with literature. Whether it was writing or reading she always found herself drawn to the written word. Jaimee went on to attend SUNY Plattsburgh and graduated with a Bachelor's degree in English Literature. She enjoys editing any sort of piece that comes her way whether it is from old college friends or new friends that she meets along the way. This will be the first published piece that she has edited. Jaimee still lives locally in Keeseville, NY happily surrounded by her supportive friends and family.

About the Cover Artist

Hannah Carr has always had a love of books and has even bound a few of her own, but this is the first time she has designed a book cover. Most of her commissions have been tattoo designs and paintings, so working on a piece to be mass produced while still maintaining an intimate, hand crafted feeling was a new kind of challenge for her. Hannah received her Bachelor of Fine Arts in Metalsmithing and Jewelry Making from Maine College of Art. She is currently living and working in Cadyville, New York.

Note: The following is a sample chapter from *Death Toll the exciting sequel to Wail of the Banshees*. This version is the beta version and hasn't gone through the professional editing process yet.

Chapter Eight

I LED THE STALWART GROUP through the maze of halls until we reached the downward staircase where I'd taken out the two guard zombies. I signaled the group to wait while I scouted out the room below. I untethered myself so that I wouldn't be visible, at least not to most beings. The stairs ended in a large, dark room with two open doors leading into corridors. One of the hallways was lit providing the dim light in the landing room. The room was devoid of furnishings, and the walls were painted in lurid scenes of alien vistas populated by monstrous beings that defied description.

I was momentarily mesmerized by the alien landscapes depicted in the murals; they looked so real that I imagined that I could step into them and find myself in those very worlds. The thought of going there and being in the presence of those terrible beings sent a shiver through me. When one of the creatures suddenly moved I saw that it was actually not part of the painting at all, but instead, it inhabited the very same room that I myself stood in. It was froglike covered in lidless eyes with writhing tentacles swarming from its crouching body. It was the size of a pony, and its hundreds of eyes glowed. Each eye glowed a different color. There were more colors and shades than the human mind could conceive of. The thing had no aura that I could discern, and I felt my mind wanting to crawl away; to hide where the monster couldn't find me. I shook off the madness, and turning from it, I went to peer down the lit corridor to see what else I could spy out.

I gasped as a searing pain suddenly shot through my left shoulder and across my chest. I looked down at myself and found a tentacle with serrated bone protruding from its scaly skin latched onto me. I tried to pull free from it, but its grip was like a vice, and I felt myself being pulled backwards. I maneuvered myself around so that I could see the thing that was attacking me. I watched in horror as dozens of the things eyes split and a huge mouth gaped open. It let out a screeching sound that paralyzed me. A monstrous tongue covered in dripping, thorny protrusions lashed out and struck me across the face. The agony that the attack provoked was so intense that I found myself swooning. I wanted to let forth my banshee scream but I couldn't. I felt my mind going numb and insanity threatened to overwhelm me as I was inexorably pulled towards that alien maw.

A shout and a blinding light suddenly cleared my head of the growing darkness, and the horror stopped dragging me towards it though the tentacle continued to hold me. Nathaniel Carter stood at the foot of the stairs; a glorious golden light shown around him bathing the room in warm light. The creature hissed at him clearly uncomfortable with the light.

"What the Fuck is that?" cried Frank in a tremulous voice.

"It's the face of chaos and madness," answered the wizard. "It has a hold on Veronika. Shoot it in the eyes!"

I saw that both Frank and Brianna had accompanied the wizard. Both stood a couple of stairs above him and aimed their pistols at the hideous chaos monster. A pair of the beast's eyes exploded as the detective and the shifter opened fire. Rage at my own folly suddenly filled me, and I tethered myself and willed my blade to take on physical form. I sent the blue Katana into a wide arc that struck the tentacle that held me and instantly severed it.

The chaos monster let out a scream that filled my head with a momentary feeling of crawling things all over me. Just as quickly as the feeling came it was banished by the comforting golden light that filled the room. I stared at Nathaniel Carter in awe as I realized that it was his power that was pushing back the drowning madness that the chaos beast invoked with its cries. It was amazingly fortuitous that we'd been waylaid by him this night. Without the wizard we may very well have perished down here.

The creature's tongue lashed out at me again, but I sliced a good foot off of it with a defensive stroke. I considered charging it but didn't want to get in the way of Frank and Brianna's withering fire, so I stayed back and played defense.

A tentacle lashed out and struck Nathaniel in the forehead. He staggered and blood poured from the wound, but he didn't lose his hold on the light ward that he was protecting us with. More tentacles began to whirl about and Frank, Brianna, and Nathaniel were struck multiple times. Their firing faltered. Madness hammered at all of us for a second as Nathaniel's ward slipped. The wizard got control of his spell through sheer force of will, and drove the madness back once more as the ward shone brighter than ever. Regaining my own composure, I called the wind to me, and in less time than it takes a person to blink, I was standing before Nathaniel, my back to him and my sword raised to defend. I howled my defiance at the chaos beast and met every tentacle that it thrust at my friends with my celestial steel katana. The thing roared in its own mad rage as all of its attempts to get through my guard met with a steel curtain that left its appendages shortened. Frank and Brianna resumed their deadly assault on the creature giving it an entirely new reason to scream.

"Hold your fire!" I yelled when most of the creatures eyes facing us had been obliterated and the thing was a mass of gory meat that madly flung too-short tentacles in all directions. Trusting that they would do what I asked, I leaped forward my speed enhanced body moving faster than what a normal human eye could track. I followed Franks last bullet as it slammed into a glowing purple eye. My sword slid into the gaping wound as I drove my blade in up to my elbow. The chaos beast only had a half second to shutter as I twisted the katana and sliced upwards. A quarter of the beast's grotesque body rolled away leaving a gory trail across the floor. I didn't pause to see if the thing was dead; I swung again and again until I felt a firm hand grasp my uninjured shoulder. I paused, startled, looked at the hand, and followed it up until I stared into Nathaniel Carter's stormy grey eyes.

"That's enough, Veronika," he said gently. "It's quite dead."

"Jesus Christ!" exclaimed Frank. "You're one crazy bitch Veronika! You chopped it into salsa."

I stared at Carter seeing the blood pour from a deep gash on his forehead and cheek. Looking down, I saw blood soaking through his shirt and jeans in at least a half dozen places.

"We need to get you to a doctor," I said huskily, my eyes once more drawn to his. A strange feeling settled over me, one I had thought lost forever. Come on, I'm a ghost. I can't fall in love, can I? Besides, this guy was old enough to be my dad. "Thanks for coming when you did, that thing really surprised me."

"I'll be fine," he said. "We don't have time for doctors right now. Whatever called this thing up is still around here. We can't let it go causing this kind of mischief can we?"

"No," I agreed, staring at the hand that still held my shoulder.

"How can you touch me? I'm barely tethered. Your hand should pass right through me."

Carter withdrew his hand with an embarrassed expression on his face.

"I'm a wizard," he answered with a gleam in his stormy eyes. He was a bloody mess, but I suddenly found this mysterious stranger to be the most beautiful man I'd ever met.

I took stock of my surroundings noting that both Brianna and Frank were also bleeding from open wounds but both seemed determined and eager to continue. Of the beast there was nothing left but small chunks of meat strewn about the room, black ichor splattered the walls, and I was drenched in the gore. I shuddered at my own murderous ferocity and untethered long enough to let the gore slough off of me. Re-tethering myself I led my friends into the lit corridor.